THE KNOT GARDEN

Also by Gabriel King

The Wild Road
The Golden Cat

The Knot Garden

Gabriel King

Century · London

Published by Century in 2000

1 3 5 7 9 10 8 6 4 2

Copyright © Gabriel King 2000

Gabriel King has asserted the right under the Copyright, Designs and
Patents Act, 1988 to be identified as the author of this work

First published in the United Kingdom in 2000 by Century
Random House Group Limited
20 Vauxhall Bridge Road, London SW1V 2SA

Random House Australia (Pty) Limited
20 Alfred Street, Milsons Point, Sydney,
New South Wales 2061, Australia

Random House New Zealand Limited
18 Poland Road, Glenfield
Auckland 10, New Zealand

Random House (Pty) Limited
Endulini, 5a Jubilee Road, Parktown 2193, South Africa

Random House Group Limited Reg. No. 954009

A CIP catalogue record for this book is available
from the British Library

Papers used by Random House
are natural, recyclable products made from wood grown in
sustainable forests. The manufacturing processes conform to
the environmental regulations of the country of origin

ISBN 0 7126 8078 0 (Hardback)
ISBN 0 7126 8083 7 (Paperback)

Typeset by SX Composing DTP, Rayleigh, Essex
Printed and bound in Great Britain by
Biddles Ltd, Guildford and King's Lynn

For the cats, and those who save them.

Acknowledgements

Thanks to Cath for Hackney and light ale, and Jamie for the country lore; to Sara and Alex for Agas and cottages, and to Sarah, whose garden quickly became Anna's. Thanks must also go to Jonathan Lloyd for his encouragement, and to Kate Parkin and Kate Elton, for their patience and enthusiasm; and to all at Century and Arrow.

Prologue

THE DAY before he died, my grandfather told me how he had been taken by his own grandfather up to the big house to witness an instance of magic. At the time, neither of them had any true understanding that this was what they had seen: rather, it seemed to them no more than one of the bizarre and pointless activities that people often indulge in, and I cannot boast that I would have been any more perceptive myself; indeed, experience has rather taught me otherwise. But I have learned a great deal since the days of my headstrong and wilful early youth, more than it is comfortable to know. In particular, I have learned that while the ways of the wild world may appear awesome and strange, the ways of people – with their compulsions, their terrors and their passions – are stranger and wilder by far.

It was dawn, my grandfather told me, when they made their way into the garden. The light of the new day was shifting through indigo to the soft grey of a woodpigeon's wing, before emerging at last as an ominous red. Shreds of mist clung to the ornamental magnolias and the single huge cherry tree, its limbs loaded with blossom as if after heavy snowfall, then drifted off across the wide lawns to disappear between brooding yew hedges, so dark in that light as to appear black, and pillared gateposts of soft yellow stone.

Nothing stirred.

It was the sharp complaint of a robin, perched upon the crumbing orchard wall, chest fluffed out against the cold, which broke the serenity, disturbed by the appearance of the predators. The two cats paid it little attention: instead, they stalked across the lawn, dark patches marking their progress through the silvered grass as the hoar-frost turned to dew. At a low, manicured evergreen hedge they stopped and peered through a gap.

The old cat – a tortoiseshell – held his tail stiff and horizontal.

The unseasonable weather had left its mark on every leaf and stem, the silver tracery of frost etching its own subtle complications into the man-made intrications of foliage. Great whorls and chains of greenery wreathed across a perfect square, crossing and recrossing one another with obsessive intent, as delicate as embroidery upon the earth. From corner to corner the chains ran in unbroken lines of rue and hyssop, germander and myrtle, traced by pathways of red dust.

But the older cat's attention was held not by these curious designs, but by a figure emerging from the house beyond.

Tall and spare, its long bones clad only in scanty flesh, it made its way across the glistening flagstones of the patio and headed for the knot garden, its naked skin puckered and goose-marked by the cold.

The tortoiseshell's tail twitched once, twice in agitation. Keeping well below the level of the herb-hedge, shoulders jutting, he slunk around the corner, beckoned for my grandfather to follow him, and disappeared stealthily into the shrubs abutting the orchard wall. The robin chirruped derisively at its enemies' retreat, then itself took flight for the safer perch of a tall cedar.

From their respective vantage points cats and bird watched the naked figure enter the knot garden.

Once inside, the figure hesitated for a second, as if gathering itself, then began to pace back and forth over the low hedges, its movements as formalised and deliberate as any dancer's. It turned stiffly here and made a high step there, legs thin and pale and luminous in the extraordinary light, sometimes following the planted pattern, sometimes deviating from it as if to create a counterpoint. Strange sounds – neither strictly speech nor song – spilled from its mouth. The red dust coated its bare feet.

Throughout this odd activity it carried an object clutched to its chest. A vase? A bottle? An urn?

Breakfast?

Cats and bird stared.

Reaching at last the centre of the little maze, the human seemed to have completed its private dance. Facing east with the sun in its eyes, it laid the object upon the ground. The harsh red light did neither subject any favours. Released from the shielding hands, the object was apparently revealed to be a very ordinary-looking little pot, bulbous and opaque, its glassy surface scratched and pitted from years of use. Its owner, too, appeared to have seen better days. When it crouched it did so in such a manner as to suggest many aches and pains, and the skin was stretched tight everywhere upon its gaunt frame, as if there was not quite enough of it to go around. Even so, a wealth of wrinkles fanned out across faded cheeks; deeply scored lines ringed the neck and ran down into a withered, hairless chest. Its hands were claws as it fiddled with the stopper.

After a few moments of undignified wrestling, its elbows sticking out like a chicken's wings, the stopper flew out and landed at its feet. Thick and viscous, the liquid inside appeared reluctant to relinquish its hold on the pot. The figure straightened awkwardly, shook the vessel fretfully once, twice, three times and at last a grudging quantity spilled out into its hand. With what might seem an undue haste, the human immediately began to rub this stuff into the skin of its face. Then it captured more of the fluid and worked it into neck and shoulders. It massaged it into wasted arms and flanks. Chest and abdomen received their attentions. The human rubbed the skin of its long legs. Bending, it dusted its feet, then worked the liquid into those as well.

Dawn colours burned and flowed: rose-pink, rich amber, silvery-gold.

The robin was vastly intrigued. Into the air it rose, made a circle over the knot garden and peered down.

Below it, the figure rose, suddenly all lithe grace, made a final, hieratic gesture to the rising sun, then upended the pot. Three or four drops fell to the earth and were instantly absorbed. The human scooped up the discarded stopper with energetic impatience and inserted it firmly back into the pot's fat little neck. The movement made its biceps contract and swell. Smooth skin glistened. Then it turned and walked back towards the house.

The robin, bold as only a robin can be, launched itself from the cedar and landed without a moment's hesitation upon the spot the human had just vacated. It scratched at the ground, dipped its beak once or twice, then took off again, disappointed that the pot had contained no food.

As it flew back across the knot garden, towards the comfort of its roost on the orchard wall, its breast feathers caught the sun, so that they gleamed as vermilion as blood, bright with unwonted vitality.

The cats watched the bird go, eyes blankly reflective, unsure of what they had witnessed. Then, out of the shrubs my grandfather emerged, ears wary. He wandered the edge of the knot garden, sniffing cautiously. At the place where the human had entered he stopped and sniffed puzzledly. The tortoiseshell, meanwhile, began to trace a path to the centre of the maze. At last, reaching the scratches in the dust the bird had made, he bent his nose to the ground. His muzzle wrinkled. He pawed at the red earth, sniffed. According to my grandfather, he stayed there for several minutes, pawing and sniffing, the very picture of bewilderment.

Over on the orchard wall, the robin cocked its head, fascinated by the cats' odd behaviour. At last, the old tortoiseshell turned and followed one of the diagonal pathways out of the square, until it reached the young cat on the further side of the square. Here, separated from the knot garden proper by a foot or so of trimmed grass, someone had planted a complicated border of evergreen box. It was more overgrown then the rest, its pattern obscured. The old cat shouldered its way into a gap in the planting and sat there, as still as a garden ornament.

Cats, even those as erudite as my great-great-grandfather and his protégé, cannot read words when they are written on the page, or planted in the ground. But they can feel their meaning when they find them in human dreams; they can hear the sound of them in people's minds.

I know now that the planting made along the top of the knot garden spelled out the words *Tempus fugit*.

Time flies.

Just like birds.

My grandfather swore that robin was still alive, and that it would outlive us all.

4

One

A NNA STARED out of the kitchen window.

As soon as the weather's better, she thought, I'll do something about the garden.

Fine rain mizzled the old glass. It fell across a pocket-handkerchief lawn, softening the bare outlines of the roses in the surrounding beds, the dwarf apple trees and straggling lavender bushes – leggy and woody and comfortably past their best – which in the summer would hum with black and gold bees. Anna looked forward to that. She looked forward to foxgloves and monbretia. She liked the garden shed, with its lapped, peeling white boards and dim quartered window. Thanks to the efforts of some former owner she had inherited a proper cottage garden, intimate and pretty; even now it was in good heart, despite the long winter.

Past the shed, though, where a vine-trellis made a sort of tousled archway, the garden changed character, becoming a square of flat, rather bleak grass, separated by a few strands of raw new wire from the three-acre pasture beyond. Though in the recent past someone had tried out a hedge of copper beech it had not thrived, and nothing else grew there. Even the weather seemed different at that end. It was always windier there. The rain swept across it like rain across a council estate in Hackney.

Anna thought: I wish I knew more about fruit trees.

Almost simultaneously, staring through the arch, she thought: It's really two gardens.

As if this idea had liberated something there, a ripple seemed to go across the view; and Anna witnessed an event so odd that afterwards she was unable to describe it properly to herself, let alone anyone else.

She saw a fox talking to a cat.

It had been raining since she woke up, on the last Sunday of the wettest April in living memory. She had been thinking about making more coffee, or putting on her Barbour and braving the damp lanes; she had been thinking about starting a cassoulet for supper. She had been thinking about Max Wishart – a beautiful man, and, if the truth were told, a complete sod – and how she would always blame herself for what had happened between them. She had been thinking: Why did I really come here? Now she found herself unable to think at all.

A few stray gleams of sun illuminated the bleak end of the garden. The fox and the cat stood nose to nose in this anxious light, absolutely motionless as if whatever was happening between them was more important than cover or shelter. They're touching, Anna told herself. They're sniffing each other! Can that happen?

The fox was the exact colour of the copper beech leaves, with a splash of cream at the throat and down into the rough fur of his chest. A patch of greyed fur ran along one flank. His yellow eyes glittered with intelligence. He must have slipped into the garden under the lowest strand of wire. He was the most elegant animal Anna had ever seen. Shining in the rainy light, he looked, she thought, less like a fox than an advertising picture of one – sharp, brilliantly clear, somehow more than himself.

The cat was a shabbier proposition, its tabby coat matted, its white socks dull and uncared-for. It held itself awkwardly and seemed reluctant to move. Every so often a shiver passed along its spine and it swayed where it stood. After thirty seconds or so, it turned its head away from the fox and took a step or two towards the pasture. Instantly, the fox swivelled on his haunches, and, head low, teeth bared, urged the cat back towards the house. His eyes gleamed. Was he amused? The cat hissed and spat, dabbed out in an uncertain way with one front paw, then sat down suddenly and stared at its tormentor. To set against the fox's energy and intelligence, Anna sensed, the cat had only endurance – the quiet acceptance of its own condition, its own needs. Would that be enough? She had no idea what she meant by thinking these things.

'They're animals!' she told herself aloud, as if to correct some other assumption.

Their fur was sodden, they were only animals; but she was afraid to make the tiniest movement in case they saw her and were frightened away. Rain pattered against the kitchen window. The wind agitated the lavender bushes. Beads of water trembled and fell. Then a further ripple seemed to spread across the scene at the end of the garden, and at this the fox raised his head to sniff the damp air, gave the tabby what could only be described as a look of warning, and made off across the pasture without glancing back.

Anna thought: He brought her here and now he has abandoned her. Then she thought:

How can I possibly know that?

The tabby stared after the fox for a moment or two, then got to its feet and stood swaying, head down in the wind and rain, blinking numbly at the grass in front of it. It looked towards the house then away again, as if trying to make up its mind what to do next. Anna, as if released from a spell, ran out of the kitchen to find her shoes. She saw now that the cat was ill. She kept as quiet as she could, so as not to alarm it. But inside herself she was already calling:

Wait! Oh wait! I'll help!

Her shoes were at the bottom of the stairs by the front door. She was putting them on when the telephone rang. Without thinking, she picked it up.

'Damn!' she said. 'Hello?'

It sounded like a long-distance call. There was a silence that reached away from her like an empty arena, a space in which things might happen. Remote ticking noises. Something that might have been breathing. Then a voice said:

'Anna Prescott?'

'It is,' she was forced to admit. 'But look, I wonder if you'd mind ringing back. There's—'

'Anna Prescott?'

It was a woman's voice.

Anna thought: If I ask who she is I'll have to talk.

'Could you ring back?' she said. 'There's a cat in my garden.'
Silence.

'I'm sorry,' said Anna, 'I'll have to ring off now.'

'A cat?' said the voice.

'I'm really sorry,' Anna said. 'I've got to rush.' She was already putting the phone down as she added:

'If you could just call me later . . .'

By the time she got into the garden, it was empty. She stood at the wire fence with folded arms, a tall, dark-haired woman in her mid-thirties, wearing a man's fleece jacket (it had belonged to Max), and stared out across the empty field. There was no sign of either animal, though she could just make out the track the fox had left, meandering through the wet grass towards the far edge of the pasture where it fetched up in a tangle of bramble and a sketchy line of hawthorn branches. A chilly wind blew rain into her face, though the sun was now visible on and off as a pale disc through a thinning in the clouds. The beech leaves rustled. Back in the cottage, the phone was ringing again.

'Oh go away,' she said. And then, 'Damn. Damn. Damn.'

Turning reluctantly from the field, she noticed her own footprints, so much less elegant than the fox's, on the rain-silvered lawn. Wondering if it was too early to cut the grass, she saw how winter had taken its toll: the leaves of the espaliered quince on the south-facing wall were already sugary and grey with greenfly, the vine-trellis needed support, the garden shed needed paint.

The shed!

Bad weather had warped the door open two or three inches and wedged it there. Anna levered at it until it creaked and gave, then went in as cautiously as she could.

'Hello?' she said. 'I won't hurt you.'

Inside there was a smell of damp canvas and weedkiller. A greyish light fell through the cobwebbed window on to a lawn-mower, two or three deckchairs, and a bicycle which had seen better days. The shelves were littered with objects – rusty clippers and secateurs, some peanut-butter jars filled with nails of different sizes, those tins and packets of garden chemicals you use once and then leave to harden invincibly over the years until you have to buy them again. Every surface, every object, had collected a thin film of dust Anna couldn't see but which she could feel when she rubbed her fingertips together. (It was grittier than house-dust, and clung less to your finger-ends.) There was a pile of dry sacks in a corner. On it, regarding her with a kind of dull anxiety, lay the tabby.

'I won't hurt you.'

The animal got slowly to its feet, its green eyes fixed on hers. When she picked it up, it bowed at once to the inevitable. It seemed stunned. It purred in its pain and confusion. It was warm and so frail she could feel every bone. It was just a lot of heat and bones in her hands.

'There,' whispered Anna. 'There you are.'

She was thinking: They always know when a human being is their last chance.

At first the tabby seemed to have no will of its own. Wherever she put it, it stayed. At the same time it would not rest or relax. It crouched awkwardly on the kitchen table, caught halfway between standing and sitting, while Anna found a cardboard box. Occasionally, it turned its head to one side, as if listening. It peered over the edge of the table at the quarry-tiled floor, and a shiver went through its hindquarters as if perhaps it meant to jump down. The moment passed; it stared ahead again. This uncertainty was transmitted to Anna, who, after lining the box with newspapers and lifting the cat carefully into it, could think of nothing to do but boil the kettle, with some idea that she might need hot water. She turned the central heating as high as it would go (for some reason she had been unable to understand when it was explained to her, the oil-fired Aga remained unconnected to this system, and therefore could be used only for cooking), and placed the box near the kitchen radiator.

'There,' she said. 'You've been in the wars, but you'll be safe here.'

The tabby blinked up at her. She could see now exactly how ill-cared-for it was. Its fur was matted and spiky, falling out in patches to reveal, under greyish skin, ribs as thin as a fish's. It smelled. It was starving. It was female.

It was pregnant.

'Oh you poor thing,' Anna said.

She took down a little blue-and-white saucer – orphaned from a set which had come to her on her grandmother's death and one of the few possessions she had felt it worthwhile to bring with her from London – and poured milk into it. The cat lapped at the milk for a moment, licked one of its paws in a disconnected way, then fell asleep. Reassured, Anna crept off to make herself a cup of tea and consult the list of useful telephone numbers her predecessors had left pinned to the kitchen wall above the Aga. Heat and steam had curled the card like a dead leaf; most of the numbers, having been written in pencil, were faded and illegible: but she found 'Vet', followed by something in brackets she couldn't read. When she rang the number there was no answer, so she consulted the card again. This time she was able to decipher the appended instruction: 'Not Sundays'. She was on her own.

Anna, who had – to balance a cheerful faith in her practicality – only the vaguest idea of what might be useful in the circumstances, went round the cottage gathering up cotton wool, antiseptic and an armful of old towels, just in case.

'Kittens!' she thought.

She went back to the kitchen and had a peep inside the box. The milk remained, but the tabby had vanished.

At the turn of the century, the ground floor of Pond Cottage had consisted of a single room barely bigger than its own fireplace, with a low oak-beamed ceiling, walls of bare local stone, and a scullery at the back. In the thirties someone had plastered the walls, extended the scullery into the garden and added mains drainage. After this, the pace of improvement had slowed; but by 1975, when the rush to the country began in earnest, successive owners had added a lean-to 'breakfast' room and a garage. Further extension gave rise to a proper kitchen, while internal remodelling discovered space for the microscopic study and, upstairs alongside the second bedroom, a bathroom which would have delighted a doll.

The result was higgledy-piggledy, rather poorly lit and sometimes hard to keep clean. Anna had to watch her head on the beams. But the core of the house had a satisfying sense of history.

On winter afternoons, with the firelight flickering off the leaded-light windows and ducks quarrelling sleepily on the village pond across the road, it was all you could ask from a cottage in the country. And if nothing else, Anna reflected, its size made it easy to search.

'Puss?' she called. 'Come on, puss!'

While she was out of the kitchen, the cat had found its way quietly upstairs, levered open the door of the tiny eye-level airing cupboard next to the bathroom and settled itself on the top shelf along her warm, clean, sweet-smelling pillowcases. They stared at one another.

'Oh dear,' said Anna. 'Are you sure that's where you want to have them?'

The cat purred.

Anna went downstairs, thinking: Cassoulet! We can both eat that! She looked at her watch. 'I've still got time to get the beans on,' she said aloud.

Two

ALL CATS reminded her of her old cat Barnaby, who had shared her life for fourteen happy years. Barnaby had worked his way up from the smuggled, illegal existence of a kitten in a university hall of residence to part-ownership of a garden in one of the leafier parts of West London, developing from a ball of marmalade fluff – pampered half to death by young women rich with suppressed maternal hormones – into a cat of considerable dignity. Along the way, he had survived some bizarre flat-shares – left to himself all day with the smells of spilt face-powder and ten-minute pasta, content to play with the strap of a bra drying on a hall radiator or blink patiently down at the dogs in the street, the very picture of a metropolitan cat. Barnaby had loved prawns, cream and people, perhaps not in that exact order, and in later years the fruit of these affections was a girth to match his fine, broad English head. 'Tommed-off,' was how Max Wishart had described it when he and Barnaby were first introduced: 'And hasn't he such a nice, round, tommed-off head!'

They were friends immediately. When you thought of Barnaby, you couldn't help but think of Max too. Max Wishart had all his twenty-eight years stored in his amused green eyes. His talents were various: he had made a successful career as a violinist specialising in Early Music, but he loved to cook, too – anything French, as he said, anything with shellfish. Relaxed, happy, made for pleasure, Max had wandered into Anna's life with a sense that he might leave at any time – as if his attention was already distracted. In the end he had stayed long enough for her to forget that, so that when he wandered out again, with a bemused look at her pain and an almost cheerful, 'But you didn't seem to need me,' she thought she would die of it. Barnaby, she allowed herself to believe, had died of it: wandering into the street one sunny afternoon a month or two after Max left, straight under the wheels of someone's BMW. However hard she tried to be sensible – after all, cats are run over all the time in busy London streets – she couldn't help thinking that Barnaby's attention had been fatally distracted.

In her best memory of Max and Barnaby, they were sitting, the pair of them, reflected in the polished floor of the music room of her house in Barnes, lost in amiable contemplation of the Baroque. The morning sunlight streamed in around them. Eventually Max put down his bow and sighed regretfully, 'Well I'll never be the fiddler of my generation, then. Let's go and find some fish,' after which they strolled into the kitchen, the cat looking up at the musician, and ate fried whitebait together.

'You two!' she complained.

'Ah but you love us,' Max said. 'You love our pretty ways.'

In this memory there was a bouillabaisse on the stove for later, salty and garlicky and full of the things all three of them liked to eat. Hake for Anna, moules for Max, unpeeled prawns for Barnaby. In all her best memories of Max Wishart, he was stroking her cat behind the chin, the tips of his fingers eliciting a purr so magistral she could feel it resonating in her own chest. I'm a cat too, she wanted to say. Stroke me.

Anna thought about these things. She gave the cat a small portion of cassoulet, ate a larger portion herself, drank a glass of red wine and went to bed. 'How could you, Max,' she asked the bedroom wallpaper, 'when he loved you so? He was such a survivor until you came. If you couldn't stay for me, you might have stayed for him.'

Later, still unable to sleep, she looked in on the airing cupboard, just to be sure. It was dark, she couldn't see anything. There was a smell of linen, and cutting across that the smell of the sick cat. Cheap-rate electricity ticked away in the silence at the back of the shelves, heating the water for tomorrow.

'Hello,' she whispered. 'Has anything happened yet?' Green eyes opened suddenly, lambent with some emotion she couldn't put a name to, and stared out at her.

Nothing had happened yet.

Anna went back to bed. When sleep came at last, it was a turbulent dark stream, out of which slowly coalesced shapes she did not recognise. The woman in the dream was Anna, but not Anna. A telephone rang, but when this woman picked it up no one was at the other end. She put down the handset as if burnt, but the telephone continued to ring helplessly: and, ringing, seemed to float away into the distance. In another act of the same dream, Anna found herself back at university. She recognised everything, everyone. The difference was that she wasn't old enough to be there. She was a girl – a bad little girl – and Barnaby had got himself locked in a storage cupboard, high up in the narrow communal kitchen with its clever hospital-coloured fitments from the 1930s. Who could she turn to for help? After all, she had no right to be there. When she managed to climb up to the cupboard and open it at last, the cat wasn't Barnaby at all. It wasn't even a cat.

Anna woke, happy to be herself again, to another cold morning. The Aga was reluctant, the kettle slow to boil. The radio yielded only Saint-Saëns' 'Symphony with Organ', and then, when she changed the station, a man's voice which said: 'I think the real problem here is agriculture itself.' At that moment the milkman delivered the milk. Anna went to the door in her dressing gown; stood for a moment on the doorstep with the milk bottles in her hand. The front garden path – worn old brick in a herringbone pattern – looked spongy and waterlogged. The clouds were grey and low over what she could see of the village of Ashmore, and a wet mist clung to the earth the other side of the pond.

'Brr,' said Anna.

She had closed the door and was turning towards the kitchen when she heard the faintest of noises from upstairs.

'Oh no!' she said.

She called: 'I'm coming, I'm coming!'

In the airing cupboard, which was full of a thick, pungent smell at once coppery and animal, a disaster was in the making. When her eyes adjusted to the gloom, she saw that three kittens had arrived. Two of them, though they looked bedraggled and hardly the size of mice, were moving about quite strongly, making small piping cries. The third, Anna thought, had only just been born. Its mother, licking and tugging with a kind of distracted, undependable energy, was still trying to help it out of its birth sac. Every so often she abandoned this task to sniff nervously at the still-unsevered umbilical cord, or stare up at Anna in a puzzled way, as if she wasn't sure why these things had happened to her. She was exhausted. There were too many things to do. Her fur looked damp, her eyes milky with stress. As Anna watched, she made one more attempt to free the youngest kitten, then gave up. The other two pulled themselves towards her, mewling, and nuzzled at her swollen nipples. She fell back heavily and shut her eyes.

'Don't sleep yet,' urged Anna, staring helplessly at the unbroken cord, the kitten trapped in its cloudy grey membrane. 'Please. We have to do something about this.'

No response.

She fled down to the study, where she found *Everything You Need to Know About Your Cat or Kitten*, purchased when Barnaby was tiny enough to hold in the palm of one hand. Barnaby, blessed with the constitution of a donkey and the digestion of a dustbin, had repaid this forethought by never being ill in his life, leaving the book to gather dust on a succession of home-made shelves from Kilburn to Barnes and thence to Ashmore, its unconsulted pages yellowing steadily with age. Anna recalled clearly the bookshop in which she had bought it. For a second she felt the whole weight of the fifteen years that had passed since then. 'My life's going by,' she told herself with surprise.

The book had a rather old-fashioned tone, firm without being entirely reassuring. 'If a queen fails to rupture the birth sac, you must do it yourself. The umbilical cord should never be severed too cleanly. Use your thumbnail to make a ragged cut. Always be calm.'

'Easy enough for you to say,' said Anna, staring nervously into the airing cupboard then back down at *Everything You Need to Know About Your Cat or Kitten*. She was used to step-by-step photographs.

'Don't wait too long,' the book advised.

Anna gritted her teeth, picked up the odd little bundle in its translucent membrane, and did what was necessary. The third kitten breathed in suddenly, mewing at the wash of air against its face, and, drawing up its back legs, began to wriggle. Anna felt elated. Relief washed over her. 'You're alive!' she said. She stripped off the rest of the membrane, blotted the kitten with a bit of old towel, and, ignoring the advice of the book, tied off the umbilicus and cut it neatly with a pair of sterilised scissors. The kitten squeaked. 'Yes,' said Anna, holding it up and staring into its tiny blind face. 'Yes, you're here!' She placed it carefully against its mother's side. The tabby opened her eyes and purred suddenly.

'Your turn now,' Anna told her.

☯

Darkness and warmth: then a rush of air, chill against a skin still slick from my recent journey. The touch of something vast and alien. I recall that much; yet how could I have known more? Blind as a stone, I was, and not much more aware. And though the images that came rushing up to meet me as I came into myself might be evidence of the nine lives we are said to possess, I cannot say for sure whether they came from an earlier existence, or whether I was being welcomed into a shared dream of life.

For certainly, life had started to pour itself into me: like light or water, it has a way of seeping through the tightest cracks in the world, and I was hungry for it.

☯

The tabby drank milk. The kittens suckled busily. Anna ate some toast. After breakfast she moved her new dependants out of the airing cupboard. 'You live here,' she explained, introducing them to the cardboard box by the kitchen radiator. 'This is where you live.' The tabby, who seemed rather tired now, eyed Anna dubiously; while her family burrowed about in the newspaper, bumping into one another. 'You see?' said Anna. 'You like it.' She dumped the soiled linen in the Hotpoint, made herself a second cup of tea, and, finding that the morning post had arrived, took it with her into the study to open.

There was a Visa bill, an offer from BT, and a change-of-address card from her old friend Ruth Canning, who, as part of an unlikely but long-running love affair with the Borough of

Hackney, had been moving happily around the same four or five cheerfully shabby streets since she first arrived in London at the age of eighteen. (Almost as an afterthought, she had collected three rowdy children and a man called Sam who seemed to work in solid state electronics, although he would shyly reveal, when you knew him well enough, that his real love was Queen's Park Rangers football club.) Ruth was a financial journalist, whose days were spent tracking the scandals, the insider deals, the international economic pressures that lie behind the stockmarket headlines. *Call us*, she had scribbled across the printed part of the card. *Or we'll send you the kids. This is not an empty threat.* Anna laughed. She owed Ruth and Sam a visit; she owed them a lot more than that.

She propped the card up on her desk where she could see it, then switched on the computer and sat down in front of it with a sigh. In the year before she left London, her last year with TransCorp Bank, Anna had discovered a talent for internet stock-trading. Soon she had found herself managing several share portfolios as well as her own: day-trading for fun had turned naturally into a new career. It was hard but exciting work, using many of the skills – and all the financial intuition – she had developed at TransCorp. She liked the freedom of it, the edge of risk.

All morning, as she worked on the strings of figures that filled the screen, Anna could hear the kittens rustling tentatively about in their new home. It was hard to keep her hands off them. They were stone blind. They smelled of milk. One of them, she thought, was going to be marmalade in colour, just like Barnaby. The tabby comforted and encouraged them with drowsy little maternal chirrups. Anna felt comforted and encouraged too.

Lunch was soup. Leafing through *Everything You Need to Know About Your Cat or Kitten* while she ate, Anna wondered if the tabby was less recovered than she should be. She had a look in the box. 'Didn't you want your food, then?' On an impulse, she dialled the vet's number. Nothing, not even a ringing tone. When she looked out of the kitchen window it was raining again.

At five o'clock, work being over for the day, she put on her Barbour and wellington boots and announced to the inhabitants of the box:

'I always have a walk about now.'

The kittens ignored her. They were fast asleep in a pile, stunned by the maternal heartbeat. The tabby, who still hadn't eaten anything, struggled up and rubbed her head against Anna's hand. The effort seemed to exhaust her, and she fell down again immediately. This woke the kittens, who milled about piping for a moment or two before they fell down too. Anna stroked the tabby's head.

'I worry about you,' she said.

Two hundred yards from the front gate, a green lane gave access to woods. Anna crossed the stream and climbed up briskly between the trees until, a little out of breath, she came to the summit of a ridge from which she could see the village spread out below.

Ashmore had evolved, like Pond Cottage, by addition. From a core of wood-framed dwellings tucked under the breast of the downs, later structures trailed away south and west. There was a bit of an old castle on a knoll, quite a nice church with a sixteenth-century lych gate, and – rather a long way from the modern centre of the village, with its three pubs and single tiny, all-purpose shop – a manor house you could buy a booklet about. Though the effect was marred here and there by a 1970s porch extension or a row of bungalows with imitation stone fascias, it was still possible to find buildings which retained their original 'cat slide' thatched roofs and pocket-handkerchief orchards. Ashmore was protected from a more general development by its inaccessibility. To the south, the bed of an old railway ran along-side one of James Brindley's first canals. The canal still hosted a seasonal traffic of peeling houseboats and shabbily converted barges, but no train had pulled into Ashmore station since the branch line cuts of 1965. And while there were plenty of lanes here on the north side, the steep swell of the downs cut them off from the area's only major road, giving the village a picturesquely secret air. At this time of day its honey-coloured local stone and attractively spalled brickwork seemed to glow in the late sun. Everything had an ambered quality, as if it had been preserved in light. Anna could hear a dog barking. She could see smoke rising from a chimney.

How perfect! she thought. And at the same time: How extraordinarily familiar, as if I've been here a thousand times before.

Behind her, the downland rolled away. If she liked, she could follow its sandy wooded ridges for miles. Instead, she looked at her watch and descended again, aiming this time for the Green Man, her favourite of the Ashmore pubs. The footpath dropped quite steeply at first, then levelled out and ran along the top edge of the churchyard, a muddy slot recording, in the medium of wellington boots and Labrador paws, the quiet traffic of village life. By the time she got there, the woods had begun to fill with evening, so she cut down through the churchyard, where thick yellow sunshine still cast the shadows of branches on the ivy-covered knapped-flint walls, and the church lay like an empty ship anchored on a quiet green swell. There were graves everywhere, long, eroded wafers of Horsham slab interspersed with stubby new granite plaques as polished as the front of a high-street bank.

The oldest stones – among them two extraordinary Saxon coffin-lids unearthed from the vestry floor during restoration in 1854 – were clustered beneath the massive graveyard yew, quite close to the church, on and around the site of a long-demolished Norman transept. The westering sunlight cut into this ancient corner, failing to warm it. Pausing at the lych gate, Anna turned back and caught sight of a figure beneath the yew.

'Hello,' she called, beginning to open the gate. 'What a lovely evening it's going to be!'

No reply.

Anna stood with her hand on the bleached grey wood of the latch. She felt slightly foolish. The air was clear. There was nothing wrong with her eyes. Not twenty yards away, the silent figure was caught as if in a photograph, its face turned to hers; yet she couldn't quite decide what she was seeing. At first she had assumed it was a woman in early middle age, of healthy appearance and well dressed, stooping over one of the older graves with what looked like a pruning knife in one hand: now she wasn't so sure. The figure was taller than it had seemed. She had an idea it was old. Dressed in brown. It had definitely been cutting something. Suddenly it seemed to draw itself up and walk

19

off behind the church, with a gait somehow stiff and graceful at the same time.

Disconcerted, Anna made her way to the Green Man.

'I've just seen something in the graveyard,' she told Alice the barmaid. 'A ghost or something.'

Alice, who was all of eighteen years old, laughed grimly. 'That's just the beginning,' she said. 'Later you claim to have been taken away and impregnated by space aliens. After that they send you on holiday for your own good.' She pumped beer into two glasses, a pint for Anna and a half for herself, and eyed it critically. 'I like these old light ales,' she said. 'Not too much of a head, and a nice flowery taste.'

'There was someone there,' insisted Anna.

'There often is someone in a graveyard,' Alice reminded her. 'People go to put chrysanths on their mum and dad.'

'I suppose so,' Anna said. 'I suppose that's what it might have been doing.'

'Make up your mind,' recommended Alice.

'Pardon?'

'Either you saw a ghost or you didn't.'

'I wonder if it's ever that easy.'

The two women contemplated this idea in silence. Anna drank some of her beer. After a moment she began to tell Alice about her adventures with the kittens. 'I would never have believed how tiring it was,' she said. 'I'm going to keep them. I couldn't let them go after all that.'

'They're a lot of work, cats,' was Alice's opinion.

'Good company, though,' Anna said.

Alice narrowed her eyes. 'You want to get out more, you do,' she said, with the air of someone who had been waiting for the opportunity to deliver this advice, 'instead of mooning about in that cottage all day. That's just the way women used to end up.'

Alice, you felt, would never end up doing anything unless it was by choice. She wore leather trousers with cropped skinnyrib tops in the colours of Liquorice Allsorts, and had her hair done in a peroxided brush cut. She drove a motorcycle round the country lanes. Her father owned the Green Man, and other pubs between Ashmore and Drychester, but no pub could contain Alice. She was off to Cambridge in the autumn, on an arts scholarship, and after that, she had decided, London or New York. (The local boys were visibly relieved to learn this. She was a weight off their minds, a disaster averted, an itch they would otherwise have spent their lives trying to scratch. Alice hadn't noticed.)

'Seeing ghosts,' she said, and shook her head pityingly. 'Keeping cats.' After a moment's thought she decided: 'It's Quiz Night tomorrow. You could come to that.'

Anna shivered. 'I'd rather be impregnated by aliens,' she said.

'You don't have to do the football questions.'

'Perhaps I'll just stay out of the graveyard,' Anna said, finishing her drink and heading for the door. 'Perhaps that would be best.'

Alice laughed. 'Take care of yourself,' she commanded.

Three

IT WAS almost dark when Anna got back to the cottage. The moment she entered the kitchen she knew something was wrong. The box by the radiator smelled sour and damp. Inside, the kittens nuzzled at their mother; she lay unresponsive, her eyes almost closed. She hadn't even tried her food. She felt hot and dry to the touch. Anna sterilised the bathroom thermometer, raised the tabby's tail and took her temperature. The tabby opened her eyes and gave Anna a wounded look. 'I know,' Anna said. 'I know it's undignified. I'm sorry. Shh. Shh.'

'If the queen refuses to eat,' recommended *Everything You Need to Know About Your Cat or Kitten*, 'offer her a little Brand's Essence.'

'What is that?' Anna asked the kitchen angrily. '"Brand's Essence"! I don't even know what it is!'

She tried the vet again.

Nothing.

All night, the tabby lay panting. She seemed to lose weight by the hour. She refused water, or, if she drank it, threw it back up again immediately. The more listless she became, the more the kittens demanded from her, until she hissed and turned her back on them. Anna was upset.

'No,' she said. 'No, you mustn't.'

Two o'clock in the morning, then three: unable to contemplate sleep, Anna poured a measure of Jameson's into a cup of tea. She tried to read a book. She dragged an armchair into the kitchen, wrapped herself in the quilt from her bed, and sat dozing by the radiator. She was visited from time to time by dreams chaotic and formless, as full of mewling noises as the cardboard box. 'Hush,' she heard herself say absently, not quite sure whether she was awake or asleep—

'Hush.'

Just before dawn, the tabby seemed to improve. She encouraged the kittens to suckle, then did her best to clean them up, nuzzling and pushing and licking at them one by one. She raised her head and allowed Anna to stroke it. She set up a curious, fluttering purr. Two minutes later she was dead. Anna looked dully into the box. Horror, pity, anxiety: she didn't know which to feel first. She hardly knew what to feel. The kittens, failing to understand what had happened, were burrowing determinedly about again, their squinched-up eyes giving them the look of little old men.

'You funny things,' she said absently. 'What am I going to do with you now?' Then she took the cooling tabby up in her arms and went into the garden.

It was raining gently, a fine grey rain in the faint grey light of a new day. Beads of water hung on every branch, every blade of grass. The air was still and expectant. Barefoot and dressed in her old towelling robe, Anna carried the frail bundle of bones and fur across the lawn, under the vine trellis and up to the wire fence at the end of the garden, where they could both look out at the pasture stretching away, full of spiderwebs silvered with rain, to the distant line of the hedge. 'That's where you came from,' she said. 'Over there.' A thrush began to sing. Anna hugged the cat. 'I hope I was a help,' she said. And promised:

'I'll look after them.'

How much do I remember of this drama, or the drama of my other lives? I could feel them tickling at my skull, but already they were beginning to haze away. Time blurs and swirls as ivy grows around an oak, obscuring the original shape, only to create another; adding detail where before there was none; hiding the whorls and knots and the ancient storm damage beneath a chaos of tendrils.

But one thing I remember clearly is this:

I dreamed. All creatures dream, great and small: I know that now.

In my dream, I was a fleck of life fixed to the very centre of the world by one fragile link. Everything in me and around me pulsed in time with the beat of this link. I had no idea what it was: only that if I were to let go, even for a moment, something truly terrible would happen, for the world beyond was a limitless void, waiting to swallow me up. I floated in my dreams, clamped relentlessly to this lifeline for unknowable moments. Then something happened. The lifeline began to shrink in my mouth. With a perception born of pure panic, I felt it pucker and recede. I scrabbled after it with my mouth, my paws. In a moment, it was gone!

And then I was falling.

Down and down into endless black space, my little torso twisting in panic, limbs swivelling, toes spreading, braced for a terrible landing . . .

And when I woke up, my mother was dead.

Was it a premonition? The embodiment of my greatest fear? Or my body's way of making sense of an inexplicable tragedy? I cannot tell you for sure. All I know is that whenever I think of my mother even now, all I remember is the sensation of falling.

☯

By late morning, she was frantic.

The tabby had been buried quietly at the end of the garden, the kittens transferred to Anna's study, so she could keep an eye on them while she worked. On the advice of the book, she had wrapped a hot water bottle in a towel and placed it in the box with them. It was a pitiful substitute for the love and care they had lost. 'The tick of a clock,' the book added, 'may also help, by simulating the heartbeat of the missing mother.'

'Only a man would think that,' said Anna. 'Anyway, clocks don't tick any more.'

She resented *Everything You Need to Know About Your Cat or Kitten*. Nevertheless, she followed its instructions as carefully as she could, diluting warm goat's milk in water for two-hourly feeds, which she tried to get the kittens to take from a plastic eye-dropper. Their blind ancient faces yearned towards the smell of milk, then turned away again in disappointment. 'Just try,' she wheedled. 'Please?' But they only squirmed in her hands –

energetically at first, then less so as their last good meal wore off – and whimpered for their mother. Despite his undignified entry into the world it was the marmalade tom, runt of the litter, who did best. He found the dropper more often than his larger, more active sisters; he took a little milk each time before turning away.

Just after midday, Anna went to the village shop to buy baby formula, in case they could be persuaded to try that instead. While she was out, one of the females, whose temperature had been on the high side for an hour, went into convulsions and died. Anna stared helplessly into the box, her eyes stinging with tears. She picked the little thing up in her hand. She could see that it was going to be a tabby, perhaps with one white sock. 'Keep a close eye on your kittens,' the book warned. 'Or you may lose them.'

'They won't eat!' Anna raged. 'What can I do if they won't eat?'

Two o'clock in the afternoon found her exhausted at her desk, nails still dark with earth from burying the kitten next to its dead mother, trying to drink a cup of tea. Propped up by the computer screen, Ruth Canning's card with its scrawled injunction, *Call us, or we'll send you the kids*, made her smile again. She missed Ruth. They had arrived at university together; survived in their third year the emotional bumps and bruises of a shared flat. For years after that they had borrowed each other's clothes and – until Max – approved each other's choice of men. 'I've got a family of my own now,' she told the card softly. She picked it up, turned it over, tapped its edge against her thumbnail. These actions liberated a curious half-memory – Ruth, in some noisy pub or other, some evening not too long ago, turning away from the bar to shout: 'I do their accounts.'

Anna frowned and drank her tea. She couldn't recall the occasion, only how Ruth had laughed and added, 'Touchingly primitive by your standards I expect, but the fact is that most of the old dears have forgotten how to add up.'

'Old dears?' Anna asked herself.

What old dears?'

'AWC,' she remembered. 'Of course!' And she picked up the phone.

'Ruth,' she said. 'Is that you, Ruth? It's Anna. I got your card. Listen—'

'Anna! You're coming to see us!'

'Well,' said Anna, 'I—'

'You're not coming to see us,' interrupted her friend. 'Fair enough. I warned you. They've got streaming colds, all they ever talk about is PlayStation, and they're on the first train down to you.'

Anna laughed. 'No, listen—' she said.

'Too late! Too late now!'

'I am coming to see you. Soon. But I've got a problem I need your help with.'

'Ho,' said Ruth. 'I don't sense anything new on the negotiating table here. I don't sense an offer. I ought to warn you that it's not only PlayStation, it's whine whine whine all day about the violent games their friends are allowed to have—'

'Ruth,' said Anna, 'shut up. Do you still work for AWC?'

'For who?'

'Animal Welfare Coalition. The charity. You know. You did their accounts.'

'Good grief,' said Ruth. 'That was a few years ago.'

'Oh, don't say that. I've got kittens here, and I need help. Ruth, you'd love them. They're only a day old. They're so sweet, and their mother died, and they aren't doing well, and the local vet is too bone-idle to answer his phone—'

'Anna—'

'—and I don't know what Brand's Essence is. Do you?'

'Anna, hang on and I'll—'

'I mean, have you ever heard of bloody Brand's Essence?'

Ruth laughed. 'No,' she admitted. 'But I can find you someone who has. I put all the AWC stuff on the computer somewhere, in case I ever needed it again. Just hang on.'

Anna heard the light clatter of a keyboard, then some cheerful swearing.

'OK,' said Ruth.

'What?'

'Entire list of field workers by area.'

'Brilliant!'

'Don't get your hopes up,' warned Ruth. 'That means about fourteen old ladies scattered across the British Isles. And two of them have certainly passed on since the list was last updated.' The keyboard clacked again. 'We were never a big organisation. Let's see . . . Well, I can't quite believe that. Ashmore. You're in luck.'

'There's someone here?'

'Yep. Got a pen? It's a woman called Stella Herringe – fine old name, that. I've heard it before, but I can't think where.'

'Do hurry,' said Anna.

'Anna, are you all right?'

Anna laughed. 'Of course I am,' she said. Suddenly she confessed. 'I miss you, Ruth. How are you, really?'

'I'm fine.'

'And Sam?'

'Sam's fine. It's you we worry about, Anna.'

'Don't be daft.'

'I don't like to think of you stuck out there on your own.'

It was an old complaint. Ruth couldn't imagine how human life sustained itself without air smelling of Jamaican food and burnt diesel. But there was more. She meant: you were always so brave before. She meant: why did you allow yourself to run away from the things you loved? She meant: why did you take Max Wishart so to heart?

'I'm not stuck, Ruth,' Anna said. 'I just wanted a change.'

The two remaining kittens chose that moment to emerge from a dull sleep, calling fractiously for something only their mother could supply. 'Hush now,' Anna told them absently. She put her hand into the box. They laid their heads against its warmth and tried to forget themselves again. 'After Max, I felt . . . well, what I felt doesn't matter now. Look, give me this Herringe person's phone number. I must—'

'I know: you've got to go. Just remember we're here.'

'I will.'

Anna wrote down the number. 'Ruth?' she said.

'Yes?'

'One of them looks exactly like Barnaby.'

Ruth sighed. 'Come and see us soon, Anna.'

'I will. And Ruth?'

'What?'

'Thanks.'

After what seemed a long time, she was diverted, with a lot of busy clicking and banging, to Stella Herringe's old-fashioned answering machine. 'There's no one here,' said the indistinct voice on the audiotape. 'Leave a message, or call back at a better time.' As soon as Anna opened her mouth, the machine began to switch itself off again. 'Hello?' she said. 'Hello?' And then desperately, 'My name is Anna Prescott, I'm at Ashmore 732521, and I have a problem with some kittens—' In the end she wasn't sure she had managed to leave a message at all; but a moment or two after she closed the connection, her phone began to ring. At the other end, someone said:

'Yes? Who is this?'

Anna, for some reason imagining that Ruth had called back on a bad line, answered: 'It's Anna.'

'Anna who?'

'Ah,' said Anna: 'you're Stella Herringe, aren't you? I left a message on your answer machine—'

'I'm aware of that, dear.'

'I wasn't sure it was recording.'

There was no reply to this.

'Sorry,' Anna said. 'You must think I'm a complete fool.' No reply to this, either. 'I'm so sorry to bother you, but—'

'These kittens. Are they female?'

Anna was puzzled. 'Well, one of them is,' she said. 'The other female died. I don't quite—'

'And is it in good heart?'

'They're just not eating,' said Anna. 'That's the problem.'

'Have you tried a little Brand's Essence?'

'I'm afraid I don't know what that is.'

'Hm. Look, this is rather a challenge for someone who's never done it before.'

'I'm sure they'd be fine,' said Anna. 'If I could get them to eat.'

'To be honest, you've done marvellously well to keep them alive at all. Do you know what I think? I think you've done all you can do by yourself. Hand-rearing's a bit of an art. Why don't you bring them over to Nonesuch and let me try? Do you know Nonesuch? It's the Tudor building on the left at the end of Allbright Lane.'

Anna couldn't picture Allbright Lane. She tried to remember the village as it looked from up on the downs: nothing came to mind. Who was Stella Herringe? Anna couldn't picture her, either – though now she remembered, from her walks in the church-yard, that Herringe was a notable local name. Relieved to share the problem but not quite ready to have it taken away in this manner, she found herself saying cautiously:

'It's very good of you to offer—'

'That's what we're here for.'

'—and I'm so glad to have someone to talk to. I've been ringing and ringing the local vet, but he doesn't answer.'

There was a dry laugh at the other end. 'Andy Corcoran drank himself to death two years ago. You won't find a vet closer than Drychester now.'

'Oh.'

'You'd be better bringing them to me.'

'Well,' Anna began, 'what I really wanted was advice—'

There was a silence.

'That is my advice, dear,' said Stella Herringe.

The silence drew out.

Into it, Stella Herringe said cheerfully: 'They'll be quite safe with me, and I'll soon be able to give you an idea if they're worth continuing with. Bring them over. Or if you haven't any transport I can get someone to collect them. Now, let's see: where are you?'

Where was she indeed? Outside, grey cumulus clouds lowered over the downs. The wind flung a handful of hail against the windows. Anna could see it bouncing and leaping like a lot of white insects on the hard earth between the rose bushes. Chilled without knowing why, the kittens mewed and clung to one another in their box. Her heart went out to them. It would be such a relief to have them properly looked after. But I promised their mother, Anna thought. She brought them to me. It was me she trusted. I can't go back on that.

'Are you there?' said the voice on the phone.

'I think I'll keep them for now,' said Anna.

'Do remember that they're little live things,' said Stella Herringe, 'and not just a problem to solve.' Her voice, coming and going on the undependable connection, had a strange effect, pleasant enough, often rather reassuring, but at the same time clipped and practical. It was the voice of a woman who, after years of work on behalf of others, has grown used to having her good sense recognised. 'Whatever you do, don't let stubbornness get in the way.'

Anna could make nothing of this. 'Well, I think I'll have another try,' she said.

'Suit yourself.'

There was a clatter at the other end. Stella Herringe had rung off.

Anna stared out at the weather. For the rest of the afternoon she battled with the kittens, wondering every so often why Stella Herringe had made her feel so nervous. People who pride themselves on their practicality often seem rather too interested in taking charge. I shouldn't have let that rub me up the wrong way, Anna admitted, but really I don't think her manner bothered me as much as . . . well, what? In the end, she thought, the phone call itself was what remained puzzling. How had Stella Herringe managed to ring back so quickly? Had she been monitoring Anna's call all along? Anna thought she had. It was hard to get rid of an image of this bossy old lady leaning over her ancient answerphone, quietly listening to someone else's struggles on the tinny loudspeaker and doing nothing to help. It made Anna shiver with embarrassment. To take her mind off it, she told the kittens sternly:

'Now. We're going to try formula this time, and you are jolly well going to eat some. See? You like it! Oh dear.'

By late afternoon the battle was lost. The kittens had ceased to respond to the eye-dropper. Their cries diminished and then died away altogether. Anna switched off the computer, moved the cardboard box into the kitchen and tried everything, from cold chicken stock to Marmite in warm water. Nothing raised their heads. Little faces set grimly, they curled up tight into one another and every so often a single shiver went through them, as if they were one organism. They had decided not to accept the world. They were prepared to wait it out, in mourning for the one thing they could never have again. Anna gave them her hand to cuddle against, and waited for them to die. Then she lost her temper with herself and tried goat's milk again. She renewed their hot water bottle. At five o'clock, she picked up the phone for the first time, putting it down immediately. Over the next ten minutes, she picked it up and put it down four times. She stared out of the kitchen window at the damp, hard earth around the rose bushes, wiped her eyes impatiently and asked herself, 'What does it matter if I liked her or not? I just don't know enough to help them. I have to admit it.' She dialled the number quickly, so there wouldn't be an opportunity to change her mind. Every time she looked at the kittens she started to cry again.

'Oh dear,' she told them. 'This is no good.' Then: 'You'll be better off with her and I suppose I'll never see you again.'

But things didn't work out that way. At Stella Herringe's house, the machine was switched off and no one was answering the phone. It had been ringing emptily for some minutes when Anna looked out of the kitchen window and thought she saw two animals running down the garden towards her in the rain and failing light.

Four

OUTLINES BLURRED and indistinct, they seemed to ripple under the natural divider of the vine-trellis, and then they were among the rose bushes right under the window, and quickly out of sight. Anna stood up and craned her neck to see better. Nothing. How odd, she thought. For a moment she had gained the distinct impression that they were *decreasing in size* as they ran. She put down the phone and without thinking went to the back door. The latch rattled, cold air spilled round her feet. The empty garden awaited her, its softened perspectives greying away into haze and distance. Lights were coming on at the far edge of the pasture.

'Hello?' she said.

Nothing. Her voice sounded thin in the silence. She was turning to go back inside when something caused her to look down. There on the doorstep sat two ordinary domestic cats.

One of them was a scruffy old thing, with eyes on the orange side of yellow and a thick tortoiseshell coat blanched by the evening light. He was rather larger than you would expect of an entire tomcat, but properly short-coupled, compact, broad of head. He had been in the wars all his life, by the look of him, and possibly not just with members of his own species (though the scars of such honest social encounters had left the skin around his eyes spectacular with hard dark tissue), for some brief engagement with an object even more durable than himself had pushed in the left side of his face. The muscles of the damaged cheek, contracted permanently by trauma, dragged back his lip to reveal two sharp snaggle-teeth. In the shifty evening light, his face had a lopsidedness at the same time engaging and roguish.

His companion, a female cat younger than him – though not by much – and white all over except for a circular black patch the size of a penny on one thin haunch, stood up and stretched as Anna appeared, revealing a curiously elongated back. Her blue eyes had a marked bulge. When she arched her spine and rubbed her head against Anna's ankles, she resembled nothing so much as a cat from a sixteenth-century woodblock illustration. Her manner was anxious, and she matched the old tomcat's serviceable, independent air with a clear need to please.

'Well, you're a pair,' said Anna. 'And no mistake. What are you doing here?'

She bent down and extended her hand to the tom, who gazed calmly at her for a moment then fluffed up his fur and spat. Anna backed away in surprise. 'You old devil!' she said, making ineffectual shooing motions. 'I was only trying to be friends.' While her attention was occupied in this way, the female cat slipped past her and into the kitchen. 'Hey!' said Anna, turning just in time to see a white rump disappear neatly into the cardboard box of kittens: 'Come out of there!'

Too late.

The kittens mewed, then fell silent.

'Oh no,' said Anna. 'Oh dear.'

She fled across the kitchen, expecting the worst whatever that might be, afraid of so many things she couldn't articulate a single one of them. When she looked into the box, with its soiled newspaper and discarded eye-dropper, she was astonished.

The white cat lay on her side, the rather scraggy length of her belly displayed, to reveal rosy pink nipples among the thinning fur. The marmalade kitten had found her, and was already suckling greedily; as Anna watched, his sister struggled up next to him. The white cat looked at Anna – who said in surprise, 'But you're lactating!' – and purred suddenly. Soon, both kittens were settled, pulling with a kind of busy thoughtlessness at their new mother. The box was full of warmth and the smell of milk. It was a different place for them now. Anna said, 'Aren't they lovely?' and reached in to touch them. Immediately the white cat extended one front paw and struck out at the back of her hand. There was some force behind the blow, and though the cat's claws were retracted the warning was clear. 'You're right of course,' said Anna. 'I'm sorry.' Half amused, half rueful, she withdrew her hand. Well, she told herself, I wanted someone to look after them. But I never . . . What an extraordinary coincidence! This reminded her of the tortoiseshell tom, who, apparently unaffected by these events, had sat himself down on the sisal mat outside the door and begun washing diligently.

'Why don't you come in and take over my kitchen, too?' she invited him.

His dark yellow eyes glittered at her. He let her have the full benefit of them, holding her gaze in that way cats have when they want you to know that they are more intelligent than you; then he got deliberately to his feet and walked off into the darkness. The white cat's head appeared over the edge of the cardboard box and she stared after his retreating form. For a second it seemed she might follow him. Then the kittens mewled for attention, and she turned philosophically back to her task. Anna watched him cross the garden and disappear into the pasture beyond. The stars were out, night was in the apple trees. She shivered a little. Then she closed the door and laughed. 'Have it your own way,' she said. And, to the nursing queen, 'Is it warm enough in here? Would you like the radio? You know, I think I'll put the kettle on.'

She made a cup of tea and ate two slices of Marmite toast, cutting off the crusts as if she were spoiling a child. She was ravenous, but still a little too excited to settle. She tried to phone Ruth: Ruth was engaged. She looked round the kitchen. I'll boil an egg too, she thought. When she next looked into the box, the kittens had finished feeding. Their foster mother's purr rose rough and loving as she set about them with a determined pink tongue. They held their ground blindly against these attentions, like little swimmers breasting a wave, and slept the moment she stopped.

'At this age,' advised *Everything You Need to Know About Your Cat or Kitten*, 'a healthy kitten is either feeding or sleeping.'

'Well then,' said Anna smugly.

Later, she opened a can of meat-and-liver dinner and forked half of it into a bowl. At the sound of the can-opener, the white cat's head came up. She trembled. She jumped on to the side of the box. Balanced there for an instant, paws together in a neat row, she looked hungrily at the can in Anna's hand, then back at her charges.

'They'll be fine,' Anna reassured her.

She ate with a kind of refined greed, stopping every so often to stare at the food as if something about it had made her think, then setting to again with renewed energy.

'Where have you come from?' Anna asked her. 'What's your story? How did you end up at my door?' The white cat ate faster. 'You like that,' Anna said. 'Well, you can always have it. We should call the girl Vita – you know, "life"? As for her brother: to start with I thought he'd be Barnaby, after my old cat who was the same colour. But is that fair? He deserves a name of his own.'

She thought for a moment.

'Let's call him Orlando,' she suggested.

The white cat purred.

Next morning Anna found that while she slept something had got into the garden and dug up the dead tabby and her daughter, leaving behind on the bleak little lawn by the pasture fence a steep-sided hole and an extraordinary litter of loose chocolate-brown earth. There was a ferocity in the way the turf had been ripped up and flung about, a rage so pure it could never be described, only enacted. What had become of the pair was impossible to say. 'How cruel,' said Anna, blinking down into the empty grave. 'What a cruel thing to do.' It was eight o'clock in the morning. Two crows flapped lazily into the air from the pasture and hung there against a sky rinsed blue by early rain. She wiped her eyes.

Later, at the Green Man, she asked Alice: 'What sort of animal would dig up a dead cat?'

'Kids,' said Alice laconically. She noticed Anna's expression and said: 'It was a fox, I expect.'

Anna stared at her. 'Why do you say that?' she said, more loudly then she had intended. 'What makes you say that?'

'I think you'll find we always blame the fox,' said Alice, 'here in the country.' She made a vague gesture, and went down the bar to pull two halves of Guinness, taking an order for organic lasagne and chips while she waited for the glasses to fill. The Green Man was filling up, breathing on its customers the familiar comfortable breath of beer and food and cigarette smoke. 'Anyway, what else could it have been?' she continued when she could next spare the time, concluding less certainly: 'Foxes dig things up. Don't they?'

Anna shook her head. 'I don't see why it should have been a fox,' she said. 'It could have been a badger, a dog: anything.'

'I expect you saw a lot of badgers in Barnes,' said Alice demurely. She held a glass up to the light. 'What do I know?' she asked herself. 'I hate the country anyway.' She brightened up. 'There's a DJ on later at the Yelverton in Drychester. You should go along, do you good. Tell you what,' she suggested: 'I will if you will.'

Anna thought about it. 'I want to get an early night tonight.'

'It's ten past one in the afternoon,' Alice pointed out. 'Just listen to yourself.'

The kittens thrived. They ate, they slept, they squirmed about energetically. The white cat – whose regard, though critical, was not without pride – kept them clean and tidy. After about a week, they opened their eyes, and, astonished by the obvious possibilities, redoubled their efforts to walk like proper cats. When, with her own eye on the future, their foster-mother moved them out of the confines of the cardboard box and into the wider world, she chose for their next home the seat of Anna's favourite chair. 'I'll get you a nicer cushion for that,' Anna said. Dimly remembering the name of a wet-nurse in some old book, she had taken to calling the white cat 'Dellifer'. Dellifer padded about the cottage at night, putting her nose into things. She was easily persuaded to sit on Anna's knee, but she wouldn't leave the house. If Anna opened the back door, Dellifer would hurry across the kitchen, gather the kittens to her and begin grooming them fiercely. 'How funny you are!' Anna told her. Then, holding the door open for a moment more: 'Sure you won't go out? Oh well. You've got the Plastic Palace, I suppose.' The Plastic Palace, a space-age dirtbox, hooded, two-tone blue and equipped with filters, had come from the pet shop in Drychester. Dellifer, having accepted it with caution, introduced her charges to it as soon as they could walk. The kittens loved it. They went in one at a time and threw gravel about in an important way. The house was full of scratching and scratting noises at inappropriate times. 'Less of that, you two,' Anna would call. 'Or I'll send you to Hackney.' The kittens ignored her. They knew she was captivated. Anyway, it was more important to get control of their legs. They wobbled after Dellifer to the bottom of the stairs then, unable to follow her, gazed up in awe and sat down suddenly without meaning to. Soon, though, they had mastered the stairs, too, and discovered again the warm confines of the airing cupboard, where they clambered over clean linen and swung on towels, pulling loose threads out with their sharp little claws. They fell asleep there under the sheets, thinking they could not be seen. They ambushed one another from behind doors, behind the sofa, behind their foster-mother: ambush was a big joke to them. They reared up on their tiny hind legs and sparred with Anna's fingers. They were hungry from dawn to dusk. Their energy was phenomenal, but when they had spent it they fell asleep where they stood.

From the very outset, the old tortoiseshell tomcat kept his eye on them. Anna could never tell when he would appear on the back doorstep, calling out in a rusty voice until she opened the door. It was the only time he asked for anything – thereafter he barely acknowledged her, or even the nursing queen, but gave his full attention to the kittens, sniffing and licking and breathing on them as if they were his own. At first Anna was anxious. 'As all breeders are aware,' *Everything You Need to Know About Your Cat or Kitten* warned her, 'a loose tom will kill any or all the kittens in a litter.' But it soon became clear that whatever the old boy wanted it wasn't that. It wasn't food, either, though he sometimes persuaded himself to eat a morsel from Dellifer's bowl; neither was it Dellifer herself. She seemed unconcerned by these visits, though she hissed at him if he was too rough with her charges. This he took good-naturedly. He seemed simply to enjoy being with the kittens, though he gave less attention to Vita than to Orlando.

By then, Orlando was the perfect red tabby. His sparse fluffy fur shone exactly like sunshine through marmalade on a spring morning, and flames had kindled along his stubby little sides. His eyes were mischievous one moment, dreamy the next. His legs were unsteady, his paws huge and he was taller than he was long: but he was up for anything. He regarded the old tom with interest. What a smell! What scars! This new creature had appeared at just the right time in his life. He followed it about, jerkily imitating its walk. He buried his face in its thick coat and growled. He fixed it with a beady eye, and engaged it in play battle. Some quite hard blows were delivered during these bouts, but Orlando never seemed to mind.

Anna was less certain. Over the next few weeks she found the old cat's developing relationship with the kittens difficult to accept. She hated it when he was openly rough with them, because they were so puzzled. When placatory gestures failed, they didn't know what to do. Vita had some success at avoiding him; but with Orlando he persisted, chivvying him out of the airing cupboard or from under the TV where he liked to have his morning sleep. There was a great deal of hissing and spitting. Anna would come across the marmalade kitten backed into a corner, looking puzzled and hurt, its face turned away so as not to provoke the older cat. 'Come on. If you can't play nicely, shoo,' ordered Anna; but whenever she looked up from her work the tortoiseshell was there, sitting on a windowsill, waiting at the door in the late afternoon gloom, watching the kittens from across the room, with hard, intelligent eyes. Their foster-mother seemed less inclined to confront him, and their encounters became brief and predictable. The tom dropped his head and fluffed his fur. Dellifer edged away, looking comically anxious. 'Stop that, you old devil!' Anna ordered. 'Stop it!' He regarded her stonily, the fur on his back slowly settling itself. The message was clear. 'Right then,' she said: 'That's enough.' But when she stopped answering the door to him, he only got in through the kitchen window. She phoned Ruth Canning.

'What can I do?' she said.

'Close the window.'

'Ruth, you have no idea how hot that Aga gets.'

Ruth laughed. 'Have you thought of assertiveness training?' she said.

'Oh dear,' said Anna.

But it is in the nature of kittens to grow up. Soon, Dellifer had taken them out into the garden, where she marshalled their activities as if there were six or seven of them. At all times of day she could be seen walking in a no-nonsense way round the flowerbeds, her tail up like a flag, while Orlando and Vita dawdled along behind, investigating the things they found. They snapped at insects. They tried to eat snails and worms. They tried to eat bees. They fought with one another, tearing round the trunk of Anna's lilac or tumbling down the terraces of the little rockery. They struck gunfighter poses. They struck poses of death or glory. Dellifer continued their education. 'This,' Anna imagined her saying, 'is a flower. And this is a flower-pot.' She taught them to freeze and look hard at things. She taught them stalking. Bottoms stuck up in the air, they stalked anything that moved – leaves, paper, the wind in the grass. They stalked Anna's foot. In all seriousness they stalked the washing on the washing line.

'They're so satisfying to watch,' Anna told Ruth.

'Anna, you need a man.'

'Shut up, Ruth.'

Ruth was interested in Orlando's progress despite herself.

'What about the old cat then?' she said. 'The bane of your life?'

'He doesn't come into the house so much. I see him in the garden with them. God knows what he gets up to out there. Orlando seems fine.'

Soon Orlando was more than fine. He had filled out. His legs had grown longer and sturdier. He looked less like a kitten than a young cat. He stood up sniffing the air on the heights of the rockery in the morning light, every orange-gold hair glowing with life. 'You beautiful thing,' whispered Anna. Orlando loved his sister, despite their disagreements. He loved the outdoors. Anything else that went on in the garden went on out of sight. Anna a cat-flap put in, and fretted less because she saw less. She suspected that Orlando was now making excursions outside the garden.

'Soon you'll be a grown-up,' she told him.

She hugged him hard, and he gave her a puzzled stare.

She was happy. She had allowed the cottage to slow her to its own pace; she had allowed the quietness of her new life to seep into her. These mornings she often found herself swirling a cloth about aimlessly in the warm washing-up water, thinking about nothing much at all, while the kettle on the Aga filled the room with steam.

'The kittens make me feel as if I've arrived at last,' she told Ruth Canning on the phone one night. 'They make me feel as if I've caught up with myself.'

'That's very profound, Anna,' said Ruth.

Five

YOUR JOB, as a kitten, is to learn about the world as fast as you can. For me, it started with a small, warm cupboard at the top of the stairs. You would not have thought there was much to be learned in such a place, but I was to discover otherwise. In the depths of that cupboard was a whole living world.

High up against the ceiling, tiny creatures spun shining threads across dusty corners. Against the peeling paint of the old woodwork their babies lay in clusters, asleep. If you were a cat, even as tiny a cat as I was then, a cat who lay very still amongst the woman's clean bed-things, you could hear them breathe.

Down in the bottom of that cupboard was a colony of life. Hordes of tiny, armoured grey beasts raised families there; and great, spiky many-legged creatures hunted them amid the dust and fluff, and the softening wood of the old house.

I could hear feet scurrying. I could hear the shriek of the captured and the dying. And all the time, tiny flies, bored with their journeys across the lazy green pond I had seen outside, would come in through the slatted doors, wings iridescent in the late afternoon light. The flies made hardly any sound at all. To me, then, they were magical beings, barely visible to the naked eye, tiny, sparkling shards of life.

But I could hear their cries as they got caught in the shining webs; and when the many-legs despatched them with glee, the whispery paper-sound of jaws breaking through their crispy skins.

I watched them, too.

My whiskers twitched. My paws itched. Something about the pattern of hunter and hunted excited me; but I didn't know why.

My ears flexed to follow the progress of the flies, noted their flight-paths and their sudden ends; marked the frantic speed of escapees, the hunting-paths of the spiky ones, the intricately hidden nests. I was fascinated by it all. So much life: so much death. It seemed like a marvellous dance; a game, even. To me, then, everything was a game.

I played and fought with my sister and thought nothing of the scratches and bites we inflicted on one another. I wandered into the back garden, and from there into other gardens, where I sat and watched with interest how insects ate the plants, and birds ate the insects, and how, from time to time, a cat might catch and eat a bird. And I yearned for the day when I would be big and nimble enough to become a hunter too, and take my place in the game.

I cannot be proud of the fact that it would take me so very many lessons to learn the truth of the matter. That nothing, really, is a game.

My lessons were soon to start in earnest: and not just how to clean my paws, or behind my ears; or that biting my sister would get me cuffed about the head by Dellifer. I thought that I had tumbled through the dark spaces of my falling dream, only to land foursquare on to soft carpets, and that tuna fish, garden sunlight and gentle hands would be my lot.

But I had reckoned without the old cat.

Of all the things in my young life, he fascinated me most; his random appearances, his uncertain temper: 'mercurial', Dellifer called him. 'Your grandfather has a changeable nature, Orlando,' she would warn me. 'You watch yourself around him.' Which only beguiled me more.

'How did you get your name, Granfer?' I asked him one day as we sat in the garden. He had taken to chivvying me outside, no matter the weather, to teach me the names of the things that I saw there, the birds and insects, the plants and the trees, and I went willingly, flattered by his attentions, and the fact that he took no such interest in my sister.

The old cat blinked lazily and the sun struck off his yellow eyes, so that a flash of gold abruptly lit their opaque depths. I had a sudden vivid picture in my head of the tiny pond two gardens away, where ornamental fish swam through water hazy with sediment: a glimpse of gold disappearing tantalisingly into the dark and tangled weeds below.

If I was entirely truthful, I would admit to being a little afraid of my grandfather, afraid of the dark and tangled depths I sensed lurking all too close to the surface. Afraid too, of his sharp teeth and fast paws.

'When you get to my advanced age, laddie,' he said, 'you'll have had so many names you'll never be able to recall them all. Nor wish to, neither.'

I had no idea, then, what it was he meant by this. How could anyone have too many names? And what did a name matter anyway? It was just what everyone called you by, and not necessarily how you thought of yourself.

The old tortoiseshell rolled over so that the sun could warm the other side of his face, the side with the permanent snarl where the muscles had shortened and thickened. Two teeth, still sharp and white despite his years, snaggled out over the tight pinky-black lip. I was curious about the reason for my grandfather's alarming expression, but had been warned most explicitly by Dellifer not to raise such a personal subject. Left to ourselves Vita and I had devised many ingenious explanations of our own, and in truth, I did not want to know exactly how he had come by his spectacular injuries, for the truth would only spoil the glamour we saw in him.

'It's a wound he sustained fighting for the honour of a queen,' Vita had decided. 'He took on ten brutish tomcats intent on rape and fought them all off, one by one. They wounded him so terribly that the queen could not look upon him, and banished him from her sight for ever after, so the greatest wound he cannot show; for it is his broken heart.'

At this, I had merely snorted with derision. 'A romantic champion? Old Hawkweed? He hasn't got a heart.'

I preferred my own theory: that somewhere out in the wilds, patrolling in the bleak of night, my grandfather had encountered a monster, and had to fight for his life.

The wound was the clincher for me: it was a badge of honour; a visible manifestation of the old cat's soul: sort of twisted and hard, and at the same time deeply mysterious. I wanted to have a wound just like it. But somehow his name didn't seem to fit well with his exotic appearance.

'I mean,' I continued with foolish persistence: 'Hawkweed. It's well, proud, and at the same time . . .' I hesitated, as well I might, '. . . common.'

My grandfather fixed me with an unfathomable, unblinking stare so that I felt as uncomfortable as a fly in resin.

Then he heaved himself to his feet.

I got ready to run.

Hawkweed laughed, a brief and creaky sound, but a laugh, nonetheless. I had spent just enough time with my grandfather to recognise it as such. It didn't always augur well.

'Come with me, laddie,' he said.

He trotted briskly out of the meadow, up the dusty path that skirted the cottages, and I followed, at once curious and a little afraid. Then we were out in the open on the village's main road, the sun beating down on us with an almost physical force.

Out on the road! Dellifer had expressly forbidden such a thing, fencing it about with dire warnings of great, stinking beasts that roared along, looking for cats to maim and kill. Hawkweed's ears twitched and flexed as if checking for such dangers, then he ducked into a wide open space between houses. Here, though, upon the pebbly ground, a dozen great gleaming monsters sat silent in the sun, some of them ticking quietly to themselves, giving off an ominous, stinking heat, as if they were only resting and might spring out at us at any moment. Hawkweed skirted them swiftly and I followed in terror, running beneath tables of old silvered wood, emerging breathless beside a trellis wreathed with a dusty vine, and stone planters colonised by straggling forget-me-nots and ragged robin. In the wide brick building beyond, I could hear the dull hum of human voices and the clink of glass upon glass. We passed quickly by, slipping with relief into the shady peace of the footpath. Here, wild briar and elder looped overhead, shutting out the bright sky and muffling the birdsong of chaffinch and thrush. Halfway down this cool tunnel, Hawkweed stopped and leapt up the bank, pushing his nose through the rampant ivy that swarmed up to meet the hedgerow plants, and disappeared.

For a moment I stood there, confused.

Was this another game? Would he perhaps reappear silently

behind me to teach me a cat's proper stealth? I waited; but he did not show. Determinedly, I scrabbled up the bank, digging my toes into the shifting surface and dragging myself up painstakingly by root and stalk; but when I reached the top and pushed my face through the gap where I thought my grandfather had exited, all I could see was a wide, flat pasture, with some black-and-white cows grazing in the distance.

I jumped down into the grass on the other side of the bank and stared around.

No sign of Hawkweed at all.

I was mystified. I stared back at the hedge. Perhaps I had come out at the wrong place after all. The hedgerow was a chaos of plants: hawthorn and brambles, ivy and nettles, great, towering, sticklike plants bearing huge bracts of white flowers, docks and ferns and dog rose, and none of it appeared to offer any clue as to my grandfather's whereabouts.

I have to admit then that I experienced a moment of fear. What if my grandfather had deliberately abandoned me? What if I could never find my way home?

Then a bright red butterfly skimmed past my nose and all my anxiety was at once forgotten in the sheer joy of being a brand-new little animal who could leap and run and chase a butterfly across open pasture in bright sunlight, my muscles bunching and springing with the magical fuels of youth. It danced and teased, and I danced after it, not even really wanting to catch it, for then the game would be over. (And, besides, it might taste strange – all those legs and feelers waving around in your mouth.) I chased it some hundred yards across the cropped grass before it finally gave up the dance and fluttered up and away into the blue.

I watched it flicker over the fields, over the heads of the cows and into the trees on the far side, and wished I could follow it, just to see where it was going. It might be nice to fly, skimming through the air, gazing unconcernedly down upon the world, far, far below . . .

'Didn't catch it, then.'

A cold shadow fell across me.

I whirled around out of my reverie.

The old tortoiseshell had materialised beside me without the whisper of a single blade of trodden grass betraying his presence.

'You have a great deal to learn, Orlando. You need to keep your wits about you. Blundering about like an idiot after some silly scrap of colour on wings.'

I stared at Hawkweed, feeling rebellious. Why shouldn't I chase a butterfly? I was only a kitten. A cruel trick had been played on me, and by my own grandfather. I opened my mouth, ready to argue. But the old cat was smiling, the sort of hidden, fleeting smile that I was learning to distrust.

I narrowed my eyes. 'How did you do that – that disappearing thing?'

Hawkweed's smile widened for a second, then he tapped my nose with a conniving paw. 'Can't let you into all my trade secrets at once, can I, laddie? Or you'll think you know more than the old master, and then where will the rightness in the world be?' He cuffed me lightly around the head.

'Still want to know how I came by this name?'

He trotted off across the field and I stared after him, feeling the fur bristle on the top of my head. When it became clear that he was not going to stop and wait for me, I ran after him.

Hawkweed loped through the pasture until he came to the uncut margins of the field. Patches of wildflowers grew there where the earth was churned and heaped. He bent his nose into a patch of yellow ones and inhaled. He lay down and rolled amongst them. Then he sneezed.

I stayed well back, watching this odd display with some bewilderment.

Hawkweed stared back at me, his expression inscrutable. 'Come here.'

I approached cautiously. The plants he had rolled upon, though a little flattened, looked remarkably ordinary: a scatter of leaves and tatty little yellow flowerheads, scruffier than dandelions. I was not much impressed.

'So what do you see?'

'They're just a load of old weeds.'

My grandfather cocked his head. 'Look closer, laddie.'

I did as I was told.

The plants stood in little clumps, the flowerheads bobbing on their narrow stalks, stalks that rose out of a tightly packed rosette of hairy, undivided leaves. Both stalks and leaves were covered all over with little grey hairs.

'They're . . . furry.'

'Ah,' said my grandfather.

'There are rather a lot of them,' I added hopefully.

'Would you say, perhaps,' the old cat flicked a glance at me, 'that they look a bit – common?'

I quailed.

'Look closer, laddie . . . see here, where all the little runners creep out across the ground. Like little spiders they are, spreading their webs all over the field. Put down roots, they do, all along 'em, grow a whole new plant where they stop. Efficient, that is. A clever little beggar, this plant.'

The old cat bit off a flowerhead and pushed it towards me and as he did so, I noticed for the first time the strange tinge to the white fur on my grandfather's paws: a sort of yellow staining, like the markings on the fingers of the old man who tended the garden a couple of doors down. 'Chew that,' he ordered.

I patted the broken flower with a paw-tip.

'Don't play with the damned thing – eat it!'

I bent my head to the weed and gingerly took it in my mouth. It smelled bad enough; but it tasted appalling. My eyes watered. I shook my head to get rid of the taste, but it was acrid on my tongue. I swallowed, and at once the taste diminished. Was my grandfather poisoning me? Was this the old cat's revenge for my impudence?

Hawkweed watched me closely.

'There's a lot more to this little plant than might appear at first sight. Just as there is to everything in the world, Orlando. Perhaps you'll remember that whenever you see this fine example of vegetable life.

'This is *Hieracium pilosella* as a philosopher once termed it; but *Auricula muris*, Mouse-ear Hawkweed we call it today, and it is a noble and a useful plant. Rub it on a wound and the bleeding with stop, quicker than you can say "cat-spit". And that's not all.

47

'"To him that hath a flux
of Shepherd's Purse he gives,
And Coltsfoot unto him
whom some sharp rupture grieves.
To him that delirium seeks,
Henbane like drunkenness may seem;
But 'tis Hawkweed thou must take
if thou wouldst chase a dream."'

I regarded my grandfather, and then the scruffy little plant, with confusion. Then I said: 'You still haven't told me why you share its name.'

Hawkweed smiled into his ruff and shook his head sadly. 'You'll learn soon enough.' He winked at me and the scar tissue wrenched his face into a terrible grimace.

'What colour is piss, laddie?'

I laughed. 'It's yellow.'

'And what colour is hawkweed?'

I wrinkled my nose in confusion. 'Yellow . . .'

'Well, laddie—' Hawkweed pushed his face close to mine. Then he opened his mouth wide and roared so that my ears rang for minutes afterwards: 'We both have the ability to make you piss yourself!'

Six

WHAT MY grandfather had claimed was quite true, as I was to discover.

All the way home I had to stop to relieve myself. I urinated like a kitten, squatting ignominiously behind tufts of grass and stumps of trees, rather than the energetic way that Hawkweed rid himself of his water, with a contemptuous lift of the tail and a powerful jet of evil-smelling liquid. (This was a gift of which I was mightily jealous at the time; though when I was eventually to master the skill, I would find it brought me only difficulty and misunderstanding.)

I had never urinated so often or so copiously in all my young life, and with each embarrassing call of nature, I became more and more convinced that soon I would dry up entirely and shrivel away to nothing, and that my grandfather had laid some sort of terrible curse on me by means of the yellow flower. But when I unburdened my troubled soul to Dellifer later that night she just laughed.

'Poor little puffball! He's certainly got unorthodox teaching style, your grandfather. But Mouse-ear won't do you any harm, Orlando, my dear. In fact it's just what you need for your trade.'

I had no idea what she meant.

Anna watched Orlando squatting in the flowerbed.

'Oi!' she called. She tapped the window. He looked up, then guiltily away. A moment later he and the old cat burst into the kitchen and promptly had a disagreement about who sat by the Aga. 'Less of that,' she warned them. She fed Orlando, offering some to the tortoiseshell who as usual turned his nose up at it. 'What's your game?' she mused, blocking the way as he tried to leave. 'What do you two get up to out there?'

He walked round her without a glance.

She was still puzzled by him. She had enquired in the village, she had enquired in the Green Man. Oh yes, they said, he was a fixture. Everyone knew him, no one owned him. But Anna had noticed he always left the garden in the same direction, diagonally over the pasture and into the trees; so, that evening, with the low sunlight slanting through the rough grass, she set out to see where he went. His walk was a kind of rangy leonine amble. He knew quite well she was there. Once or twice he looked back at her, his fixed grin white in the complex shadows of his face. Reaching the edge of the pasture, he broke into an unhurried trot and disappeared into the rougher country beyond as suddenly as if he had fallen down a hole.

'Damn,' said Anna.

Right and left stretched an ancient hawthorn hedge, set in a steep-sided trough dense with nettle and dog rose. Perfect territory for cats, less so for someone wearing a cotton frock. Feeling as if the whole place was on his side – that he was in there somewhere laughing at her – she pushed through quickly and found herself in a green lane thick with wild garlic and sycamore saplings. Light fell, the colour of the old cat's eyes, across the central strip of rabbit-cropped turf. He was making off again, tail high, as Anna emerged from the hedge. She smiled to herself. He had forgotten she was there. Thereafter she followed at a relaxed distance while the lane took charge of them both, making its way up a wooded rise then down the other side, turning all the time towards the common, on the other side of which it encountered the nut-brown water of Brindley's canal and was lifted up briefly by a little red-brick bridge before wandering off to Drychester through low-lying fields. The old cat crossed the bridge, paused for a second to look around, then darted through the greying bars of an old wooden gate and jumped down on to the towpath, where perhaps a dozen narrowboats were tied up nose to tail.

Most of them had wintered badly. They were low in the water, with a list to one side or the other, and their once-cheerful colours, sandpapered by the cold downland winds, had a faded velvety look in the evening sunshine. Some had never been more than reclamation projects anyway, springlined loosely to the bank, their leaky decks and roofs cluttered with tins of paint, engine parts, bits and pieces of indeterminate use wrapped up in heavy plastic sheeting; grass had grown up around their mooring pins. Others, caught perfectly between conversion and decline, lay on the water with the charm of an Edwardian music-hall artiste. Everywhere you looked there were rose-and-castle motifs applied in curlicued panels, pelargoniums in coloured tin water-jugs, dignified old bicycles propped up in cabin doorways. Anna leaned over the gate and sighed. It was all rather tranquil. The willow-lined canal curved gently south and west. Net curtains flapped at open brass portholes. The air was softened by the distant sound of church bells, the faint shouts of cricket practice on the green; while near at hand, a radio played light classical music. As she watched, the old cat made a long back, slipped under a pair of mooring ropes, then sprang on to the deck of the *Magpie* – a seventy-foot narrowboat with battered strakes and upperwork faded to a kind of dusty terracotta – where he greeted its owner, and, after some head-rubbing and light cuffing, was given what looked like a fish.

'Well well,' whispered Anna. 'So this is where you belong.'

She climbed the gate and made her way down to the towpath. There, realising she was being watched by the owner of the *Magpie*, and seized by a sudden shyness, she dawdled along with folded arms until she drifted to a stop. All she could think of to say was:

'Is that your cat?'

The sun went in. Chilly airs ruffled the water. The cat looked up from his efforts – eating was a noisy and difficult process for him – and fixed her with knowing yellow eyes. Taking his dinner carefully in the good side of his mouth, he jumped off the *Magpie*, trotted a few yards down the towpath and disappeared into a hawthorn hedge. This left Anna uncompromisingly eye to eye with the man on deck. He was older than her – perhaps, she thought, in his early forties. Though slight, he had a compact look. Soft, longish black hair swept back from his forehead. His clothes – grey Levis and a black cotton sweater worn with the sleeves pushed up above the elbows – made him seem slighter than he was. His forearms were cabled and strong, very brown – tanned, Anna thought, not by holidays but by real time spent in the outdoors. He was very attractive. He had a book in one hand. Anna recognised nothing about him, nevertheless she felt a sudden, vertiginous rush of excitement, combined with a sharp certainty that she had seen him before. She couldn't explain it. The way he stood, perhaps, reminded her of someone she had once known. And yet he was more familiar than that.

'No,' he said. His voice was deep and rusty, as if he didn't use it much. He returned her gaze for a moment then added, 'No one ever owns a cat,' and went below.

Anna felt deflated. She stood on the towpath and folded her arms against the cold breeze. 'How rude,' she said loudly.

Later that evening, over a Bloody Mary at the Green Man, she was forced to admit to Alice: 'I was so angry I just stood there. I got thoroughly cold but he didn't come out again.' She laughed. 'I mean, it was so absurd,' she said.

She lowered her voice to approximate his. '"No one ever owns a cat." What does that mean? And this ridiculous silver earring.' She thought for a moment. 'And those big hands,' she added.

'Oh, you noticed them, did you?' said Alice.

'It was absurd,' Anna said again. 'I just stood there like a fool and let him be rude to me.'

'He's more shy than rude,' was Alice's judgement.

'You know him then?'

Alice ducked below the bar to fetch up a rack of clean glasses. 'His name's John Dawe,' she said.

'And?' said Anna.

'No "and" about it,' Alice said. She bent down again, coming up empty-handed this time to complain obscurely, 'The state they leave these things in,' and wipe her hands on a towel. 'This place is a tip!' she shouted into the back bar. There was no answer.

'So,' said Anna. 'He's John Dawe, he lives on a barge.'

'That's about it—'

'This is like getting blood out of a stone.'

'—except that they're narrowboats down there, all of them.

Cut's not wide enough for a barge. You don't want to let anyone down there hear you call them barges.'

'Alice!'

'Well what do you want me to say?' said Alice. 'Everyone knows him. He's lived on the *Magpie* at least since I was a kiddie.' She thought for a moment. 'Maybe longer. A bit of a mystery-man, John Dawe,' she mused, 'nice as he is. He's related to the Herringes, but no one's quite sure how he makes a living.' Then, in a more businesslike voice: 'He comes and goes. He's up at the hall now and then. Or she's down at the boat.'

'Who?'

'Stella. Stella Herringe.'

'He's welcome to her,' said Anna, remembering the bossy old voice on the phone.

'Oh he is, is he?'

'In fact they're welcome to each other.'

Alice giggled. 'John Dawe,' she said. 'I'd pay to have those hands on me.'

'Alice!'

'Well, wouldn't you?'

'He's a bit scruffy for my taste,' said Anna dismissively, while some renegade part of her thought: But his eyes were so beautiful—

'Stella's his cousin,' said Alice.

'She's a bit old to be that,' said Anna. 'Surely.'

For some reason she dreamt of Max again that night. It was the first time in some weeks. They were in the bedroom of the London house, and he was saying in that amused and infinitely gentle way he had, 'But Anna, you don't need me, you really don't,' as he packed his clothes with less fuss than if he'd been off on tour. The dream had a heartless clarity, an awful sense of foreboding, as if she was just discovering a loss which had already happened, which nothing could prevent – as, indeed, she was.

Ashmore Dreams

Spring

As Anna dreams regretfully of lost love, along the road at Eaton Cottages an old woman recalls a day in high summer just after the war, when her legs were long and slim and tan in the meadow grass behind the common. Between the stalks of poppies and scabious, she can just see the clocktower of the village church. Her lover's eyes are as blue as the cornflowers they lie among, and it is only in her dreams that she can visit him, now. Even so, she can still feel the hard muscle of his arm under her head, hear the beating of a heart returning to its steady pace after exertion. In the distance, a dog barks, on and on and on, as if barking is all it has left to it. She shivers. A cloud has passed across the sun, and she reaches out among the sheets for her lover, but he is gone, long gone.

At the vicarage, France Baynes finds himself flying far above the village. Down below, there is a football match. He knows all the players, and their wives and daughters and brothers and aunts, but the further he soars, the less attached he feels himself to his parishioners, until at last he is gliding among wisps of cirrus, his cassock belling in the cold winds of the stratosphere. He opens his mouth with a great shout of exhilaration and arrows towards the sun.

Nearer, my God, to thee.

Down on the narrowboats at the canal, dreams are flying thick and fast. They seem more tangled here, harder to decipher, flowing in tides of imagery, as mutable as the water on which their originators live. Here: a locked door in a darkened hallway; there, a multi-headed creature rises from a shining pool; flames lick at a pile of photographs – their edges char and curl, releasing the bright figures within like fireflies into the night air; a black cat twines around and around a man's legs, in and out, silky fur against naked skin. At last, the man lies down, and the black cat sits heavy on his chest.

Along Allbright Lane, dreams are forming, too.

A woman toils up a steep hill, her breath escaping in great clouds of steam. A man walks behind her. His face remains averted and in shadow. She is talking, laughing; animated: he does not respond, which makes her angry.

When she reaches the top of the hill, she turns to him, and trips. Her skirts – long, old-fashioned – suddenly blossom like some immense exotic flower, engulfing her head and trapping her arms. She spins, helpless, wrapped in shimmering colour. Below the fabric her body is naked. Pale and etiolated it seems a sickly stem for such a bloom. The man stares and stares, hands hanging limply at his sides.

The skirt gathers size, begins to fill with air. Soon, she is aloft. Her legs kick. Revealed between the pale skin of her thighs, her genitalia are as bright as blood, vivid as the reddest rose. It beckons to him, but deep in his private shadow, the man turns away and starts to walk back down the hill.

Seven

I FOUND IT hard to sleep that night. I lay irritably tossing and turning against my sister's flank. Vita, in turn, lay against Dellifer, every so often showing her awareness of my movements by jabbing a sharp elbow at me. Old Delly was fast asleep – I could tell by the rasp of her snoring. There was never another cat like her for snoring. Quite how such an awful noise could come out of such a frail cat, I couldn't understand. I imagined Dellifer's insides to be as empty and hollow as an old tin bucket, and her snores a vast bluebottle trapped inside it.

I listened to that inescapable noise for what felt like hours, but was likely only minutes, and tried to fall into rhythm with it, but whatever I did it rumbled on and on, oblivious to anyone else in the universe who might be trying to sleep.

Instead, after a while, I found myself listening to the sound of the wind in the trees outside the window. The world was full of air, it seemed; air that billowed softly in and out of every living creature: even the trees seemed to be breathing. I relaxed into this idea and in a short time became aware of how the currents of air stirred my whiskers and eyebrows, felt them move against the hairs of my ears and the exposed skin of my nose. If I tried hard enough, I thought, I might be able to feel the way the tides of the air moved outside, too.

So much life everywhere, breathing in and out, sharing the world! How strange it seemed then that the air that had sighed through the long grass in the meadow and the rushes round the pond, through the clouds and the cows and the bright yellow patches of hawkweed, should now be flowing through Vita and Dellifer's lungs, and through my own.

Everything was connected to everything else.

Thinking this, I began to feel rather odd, as if I was somehow outside myself, a little way above the sofa, gazing down on three sleeping cats: a long, thin white one, whose skin shone pink in the moonlight where the fur grew sparsely above her eyes; a small, barred tabby with white socks; and one of flaming orange and cream, who even now was yawning so widely I could see every sharp, white tooth.

My mouth snapped shut and suddenly I was staring out of my own eyes again. I shook myself and sat up in the darkness, my head spinning, and waited for the world to right itself.

Alerted by the movement, Vita stirred briefly and opened one pale eye, which glowed in the dark as mysteriously green and inaccessible as the display on the buzzing white box downstairs in the kitchen. She blinked once, then stared at me as if she had never seen me before in her life.

Disconcerted, I dropped my head and started to groom feverishly; and when I looked up again, Vita was fast asleep once more. I gave my paw a last considering lick, and found that the fur there now tasted somewhat bitter.

I sniffed at it.

The smell was horribly recognisable. That vile hawkweed! I blamed my grandfather. What a trick to play.

Complex little cross-currents of anger and recrimination chased each other through my head. One day things will be different, I promised myself, and settled back down against Vita. One day I'll show him. I worked on this idea for a bit longer until, wrapped around in a haze of fur and muscles not yet my own, I fell asleep. And as I slept I dreamed—

I dreamed, oddly enough, that I was awake. I was still in the back sitting room, amid a tumble of cushions, and beside me my sister slept on. Then I became aware that I could see very clearly indeed, although there was hardly any moon; indeed, everything I focused on appeared to be limned with a faint golden light, as if a sun had secretly risen behind the curtain of dark sky.

I rolled over on to my stomach, and then sat up. Beside me, Vita curled closer to Dellifer, as if to make up for the sudden loss of heat.

I leapt lightly down from the sofa, padded across the room and jumped up on to the windowsill to stare out between the curtains. The garden in darkness looked very different to how it looked during the day, somehow bigger, as if the moonshadows that layered each object added further substance, another dimension that might be explored. I had not been outside in the night before. Dellifer's advice was always to stay inside, 'out of harm's way'. When I'd asked, in all innocence, who Harm was, she had laughed. 'Harm's all around, baby cat,' she'd said softly. 'All around us, all the time,' and I had stared fearfully over my shoulder. For a very long time I had pictured Harm as a huge orange tomcat, with mangled ears and a mocking smile. Untrustworthy and prone to lashing out with an angry paw at any small creature in its way. A bit like my grandfather, in fact. Even though I now knew this was a fiction born of a kitten's fear, I still peered hard through the window in case such a silhouette should suddenly shift among the shadows.

Behind me, something in the room stirred.

My back prickled. A line of fur all the way from the space between my ears to the tip of my tail started to rise, apparently of its own accord.

I whipped around. At first I could see nothing out of the ordinary. Dellifer slept with her back to me, her flanks moving slowly in and out in time with her snores. Vita, too, was still asleep, but above her head, something glowed.

Something at once bright and cloudy.

Fascinated, I found that I was holding my breath. I slipped down from the windowsill and approached the sofa cautiously. I sat on the floor and stared upward. My sister's eyelids were flickering, backwards and forwards, very fast. Her paws twitched as if she was running. As her paws moved, so the cloud above her head moved, too, vague shapes and colours swirling in the air. I was transfixed. It reminded me of how a couple of weeks ago, I had watched some children walking down the road, clutching little plastic bags in which several golden-orange fish had switched back and forth, distorted by the substance in which they were immersed.

I stared harder and saw something move inside the globe. It was— *my* catnip mouse! But what was it doing in this strange bubble? Straining towards the cloudy mass, I could make out a blur of paws and the bright red toy flew up and disappeared. A second later a cat's muzzle quested after it, pressing against the limits of the globe, stretching it outward like a membrane. Another cat – with my toy! And the colouring around its muzzle was rather similar to Vita's tabby markings . . .

It *was* Vita, I realised with a sudden rush of recognition and fury; and at the same time, somehow it wasn't: for here she was, my sister, fast asleep in front of me, her breath misting the tiny mirrors on the bright cushions.

But I had no time to wonder about this peculiarity, for now the cloud was moving, up and away from me. Rather sadly, I watched it travel across the top of the room, skimming the ceiling, and finally passing through the wall.

I blinked. Then I raced through the door into the hallway, just in time to see the globe slip through the open fanlight and out into the night.

I knew from bitter and embarrassing experience that I could not follow it out of that fanlight, so instead, I rushed down the stairs, through the living room and into the kitchen. In there, the yellow light was stronger. The cat-door beckoned me. I stood by the flap for some time, staring through its scratched and misty transparence into the unreadable world outside.

Then I screwed my eyes tight shut and pressed my head through the cat-door, shivering as the hard plastic brushed my back and tail.

I was outside, at night, alone!

I opened my eyes.

The garden I knew so well by day was at night transformed into a shifting sea of shadow, and the darkness was punctuated by unfamiliar rustlings and distant cries. At once, I was strongly tempted to forget I'd seen anything odd at all and retreat to my warm sofa to sleep the night away, snores and all. At the same time, I was a cat, and curiosity soon got the better of me. I gritted my teeth and determinedly made my way out on to the road, feeling immensely brave, and at the same time immensely vulnerable in the face of so much dark space. In front of me, the village pond glimmered in the moonlight.

I looked very carefully right and then left and then crossed the road in a swift scatter of paws, until I was on the other side, panting among the bullrushes.

The surface of the pond shone like oil. Beneath the surface, in the roots of the pondweed, I could make out tantalising yellow shapes, just out of reach. I pushed my way out through a stand of rushes on to a floating island of sweet peppermint and for a moment was so overcome by its extraordinary scent that I had to sit down and close my eyes. When I opened them again, one of the yellow things had sailed close enough to the edge that I knew that if I dipped a quick paw into the water I might catch it. I wriggled down through the vegetation, keeping my profile low: something I'd learned, on those few occasions when I'd been able to sneak off for an hour or two, from a young cat called Ginge, who was an ace at early-season craneflies.

At the edge of the water I hesitated, sighting the yellow glow. Was it a fish? Perhaps even a golden fish? My mouth watered suddenly, and a tiny growl of desire started in the back of my throat. I swallowed it down for fear it would betray my presence to the fish, and then swiped a paw into the water. At once, the yellow glow dissipated into a thousand shimmering wavelets.

I glared into the water, mystified.

The ripples moved out across the pond, disturbing all the other yellow things, and it was only then that I realised that what I had tried to catch was nothing more than a reflection.

Slowly, I stared upwards into the night sky.

It was full of golden lights.

I nearly toppled headfirst into the pond in surprise. Goldfish in the sky? It seemed unlikely, even from what cursory knowledge of the world I had so far gleaned. Birds flew in the air: fish swam in water. The world was that simple, or so I thought then.

Then I remembered that I was dreaming, and therefore did not have to make sense of every strange thing I saw. After all, had I not experienced flying dreams myself? And everyone knows cats are not natural travellers of the sky. At once I relaxed, and as I did so, the golden shapes started to converge, slowly at first; then they began to stream towards me with heart-stopping speed.

I flattened myself on the mint and weeds, and the golden lights skimmed overhead, missing me by a whisker. It was if they were taunting me to follow them: but how could I, when they fled across the road, gained enough height to clear the hedge by the pub, and disappeared from sight?

Undaunted, I was off and running and the stream of gold seemed almost as though it hovered, waiting for me to catch up, then it drew itself up like a swarm of bees poised for entry into the hive, and barrelled through the gap between the houses and into the path down which I had that very morning followed Hawkweed.

In the gloom under the canopy they began to spiral and change direction. There appeared to be fewer of them now, I noticed, moving more slowly; while in the air above the path, little sparkles suggested that some of the golden lights had winked out of existence, as if lacking the will or the energy to continue their journey.

In contrast, I felt full of vigour. I bounded down the cobbles, water splashing where my feet slipped, leaping the bramble runners, the nettles and the thorny dog rose, and lunged up the bank after the lights. This time, I noted with satisfaction, I had no trouble reaching the top. I emerged at exactly the point at which my grandfather had vanished from sight. But the golden lights, too, had disappeared. Instead, at the top of the bank, I was confronted by a disturbance of the air and a strange scent: slightly bitter, rather acidic. I inched forward and suddenly the air pressure tightened against my whiskers. I pushed a little harder, and with a barely audible 'pop' the world seemed to release itself to me, and suddenly I found my head occupying a completely different category of space to the rest of my body.

'Outside' – if I can put it like that – the air brushed past me softly, with barely any resistance; but 'inside' the air hurtled past my head with brutal force. I felt my ears buffeted, my fur flattened against my skull. And it was cold, too: icy cold.

This was all very odd.

Oddest of all was the sight of the golden lights. They occupied the same icy tunnel as my head did: but they appeared to have greater resistance to the wind. They bobbled about in the darkness a foot or so above me, like soap bubbles constrained by some invisible surface. Seeing them up there, trapped yet still in some way still free, I felt an irresistible urge to chase them, to leap up into that night-coloured space and bat them with my paws.

At once, I felt myself moving. I watched my foreleg enter the windy place with some surprise: for as it did so, it appeared to grow. I waved the paw under my nose. It was huge, but it was definitely my paw, for it did what I told it to do. I thought about flexing my toes, to inspect my claws – as pinkly translucent as the shells in Anna's bedroom – and the enormous new paw spread toes each the dimension of a good-sized mouse, and from the end of each toe sprang talons like black stone. Curious to see if the rest of me would grow so large, I stepped the other foreleg inside.

The wind howled at me.

I wavered there for a few seconds, neither fully a kitten nor yet entirely the creature demanded by this harsh new environment; then suddenly the rest of my body followed of its own accord and I found myself standing in another world, in the midst of a shrieking gale.

My body felt very different in there: larger, more powerful. I looked down at myself, and saw that I was indeed a different beast: tawny and massively muscled. The blood pounded in my head. It was marvellously intoxicating to feel like this: but even so, I felt dwarfed by ferocious elements, as if, even in my brave new guise, I was still too small a cat to enter here.

I shivered, then braced my new shoulders and strode decisively into the jaws of the wind.

Eight

SOMETHING IN me should have recognised that by entering this savage place, I would be entering a new phase in my life and, in the process, making an unbreakable bargain with fate. But I did not stop to think, for it is hard for any cat to resist opportunity. On I went, with no idea of where I might pitch up, placing one foot before the next, head high, eyes watering, into a dark tunnel strung with dancing golden lights.

I made the most of those few minutes alone in the wild place. I let the wind riffle my new fur, used its strong currents to intuit my unfamiliar outline. I tested my muscles and tendons by harrying the globes. They evaded me as easily as the butterfly had; but the game was not yet serious.

I was just getting used to the odd gloom when I spied something in the distance. It was large: a dark, blocky mass which broke up the lights and the air currents, and I found that although I was concerned about what it might prove to be, I was unable to prevent myself from approaching. As I closed upon it, perspectives became more confusing, until I realised that whatever it was was moving quite fast towards me, a stream of golden lights racing out in front of it, as if in fear for their existence.

My fur stood on end, prickling all the way down my spine. My heart began to thump, for the shape was huge, and from the way it leapt and bounded, I knew it instinctively to be some great predator engaged upon a hunt. And no sooner had I realised this than I was overcome by a moment of worse terror: for there was nowhere for me to get out of its way. Surely it would crush me like an insect beneath its vast paws.

I had to turn tail and flee the length of the tunnel to save my life; but I discovered with sudden shock that my new body would not obey my thoughts. Instead, I found myself standing four-square to the advancing creature, my muzzle wrinkled in a ridiculous snarl of defiance.

Whatever is the matter with me? I thought wildly. And then the golden lights spiralled around my head, dazzling me so that I blinked and blinked, and when I opened my eyes again it was just to see the great dark shape gather itself like an oiled spring and leap high over my head. An acrid whiff of something hot and bitter accompanied its passage, and then it was gone into the darkness in pursuit of its prey.

Inexplicably brave in my big new form, I found myself following the great beast.

Its smell was familiar to me – familiar, and yet at the same time very strange, like something known and loved that has in some way changed its nature: like milk that has just turned sour, or fish that has been left in the sun for too long. But what milk! What fish! It was a huge smell, and its familiarity was the most disconcerting thing of all.

Bowled along by winds that in this direction assisted rather than hindered me, I soon caught up with the hunter.

It had managed to trap a number of the lights between an eddy of air and the side of the tunnel and was swatting them with huge, clawed forepaw. They fell, dazed, to the ground, where the creature caught them up in his razored teeth, tossed them into the darkness and swallowed them down, one by one. It stood there, chewing for a moment, then turned to stare at me. Light from the smoking spheres fell upon its face. Huge eyes shone like head-lamps in the gloom, yet even as the golden light fell upon it something in me recognised the twisted rictus, the permanent half-snarl of another cat's face.

At once, I felt like the small kitten I truly was, the bravado born of adventure dwindling in the blaze of the great cat's burning eyes.

'Who are you?' I felt myself saying, gripped by cold dread.

But the beast stared at me implacably and gave no answer. Then its huge jaws fell agape into a vast lopsided grin, a grin in which sharp white teeth gleamed like stalactites in a giant cave; a grin at once taunting and familiar, and I had the peculiar feeling

64

that I knew the creature before me well: while at the same time I did not know it at all.

Then it yawned and in the depths of its throat, I caught sight of something golden and quivering, slipping down and down, its glowing light dying even as I stared.

'Who are you?' I asked again tremulously.

Now the creature looked crafty. Its eyes narrowed. 'Don't you know me, laddie?' it crooned, and a great vibration rose up and seemed to lodged itself in my breastbone.

I shook my head wildly.

'No, sir, I do not.'

'Think again, Orlando.'

I stared and stared.

'Some outside refer to me as Hawkweed,' said the dark cat, and its voice was a deep well of sound. 'But here, they know me as the Dreamcatcher.'

'Grandfather?'

The great beast reared up, and I found myself cringing away, but all he did was to pluck one more dancing light out of the dark space above my ears. This one gave off no pungent smoke, but seemed as acquiescent as other globes were volatile. He hooked it with gleaming claws, flicked it with practised skill, and laid it at my feet, where it quivered under his great dark paw like a trapped bird. Cocking his head first left, then right, he considered it briefly. Then, as if dismissing it, he tossed it to me. Despite being taken unawares I managed to catch the thing – more by instinct than by judgement – between my teeth. If felt appalling. Quickly, I dropped it on the ground and trod on it quickly, before it could escape. I stared at it.

I could feel its horrible, slow pulse between my toes.

The wind battered at me with a roar, then subsided. Into the sudden silence, the old cat said: 'Well then, laddie. What now?'

I looked up at him. 'I don't know.' And I didn't. What would you do with a sac of gibbous yellow pulsing away under your foot?

The dark giant craned its head at me until he was so close that his fearsome, mangled face lost all definition.

'You EAT it, laddie!'

Even in the midst of my dream, I recognised the pattern of this coercion. I remembered the bitter taste of the yellow flowers I had been forced to chew down that afternoon. I remembered the bad consequences of that action.

'I won't.'

I waited for an explosion, but it didn't come.

After a while, the dark cat appeared to shrug. 'More fool you, then.'

So saying, it dragged the throbbing light out from beneath my unresisting paw, and tossed it high into the air. As it fell, end over end, spinning in the gloom, I could make out half-familiar shapes within the gold.

A child; another's hand; one toy: a minor battle.

I thought I recognised one of them as the boy-half of the fair-haired twins from the cottage down the road; then child, hand and toy were inside the maw of the dark cat, and disappeared from sight.

The great cat licked his chops. He washed his face. He ran his tongue over one side of his paw and rubbed it across a cheek, through his whiskers and down his muzzle. He sighed.

'Ah, a sweet one, that. You missed a treat there, laddie.' As if lost in some private, dreamy thought, he started to wash the other side of his face. 'The little ones are always the sweetest. Not strictly part of the job, though, if you know what I mean. Now some of the others—' the old cat went on, fixing me with a stern eye, 'the ones that smoke and sputter: they're the ones you want to watch out for, with their dangerous fumes, their corrosive intent. They don't taste half so good: oh, no. They're no treat at all. Quite the opposite. A bitter harvest to reap. A sour fruit from a twisted tree, those old ones. Especially the oldest of them all, filled up as it is with all its years of terror and hate. Now *that*'s a hard swallow to be made.' He paused. 'Not that you want to know about the worst there is in store yet, eh, laddie?'

'I don't understand what you're talking about,' I began hesitantly and gathered myself to face his rebuff; but the old cat just laughed grimly.

'Of course not, laddie. Of course not. Whyever should you, when your time has not yet come? Why should you have to experience these trials so early in an unblemished life? Not for you the onerous task, the duty to all. No burden to bear for young Orlando, eh, boy? What care you that the humans' dreams eat into our world; what care you if our highways are poisoned, if creatures sicken and die?'

I stared at him, unable to respond, not knowing what he wanted from me, but at last all he did was to grimace and then begin to retch painfully, a dry heaving which went on and on and on. I found myself wincing sympathetically. Hairballs could be a bastard, Ginge said. A real bastard. I hadn't managed to produce a proper one yet; but the process fascinated me.

One more retch and the old cat leant forward and with considerable effort ejected something pale and fibrous on to the ground between us. It should have been as dark as his fur; so I knew with some deep instinct that this was no ordinary hairball. What it was, I didn't know. I took a small step backwards.

The old cat spat and stretched his neck out as if it were distressing him.

'Days of roses still for you, laddie,' he continued at last. 'Chasing butterflies in the sun, sleeping as soft as a little mouse with no thought for the swift destiny that awaits. Leave all the work to your elders, eh, laddie? Let the old ones taste the poisons of this world, keep the place nice and safe for the rest of you.'

The old cat hunkered down heavily and the wind pressed its sparse fur against a skull that I suddenly saw for the first time was frail and ageing, even in its wild guise. 'Fifteen years I been doing this. Fifteen years. Kit and cat. There weren't no one to take the strain all that time. It's been a hard life, hard and unappreciated. Lonely, too. There's a few of us old beggars around these parts, but we're not much company for each other. What young queen wants to tie herself up with a dreamcatcher, eh? Well, a few, for a while maybe; but not the ones you want, no; always the dregs. That's what I've had in my life, laddie. The dregs. But what do you care? Why should it trouble you if your old granfer goes on chasing the damn things till I drop down stone dead, broken in heart and spirit? Ha!'

Hawkweed got up and shook out each foreleg in turn with little galvanic convulsions. Then he started to walk stiffly down the tunnel.

I watched him go. About twenty paces away, he turned and stared back at me. Dull golden light shone off his great eyes.

'Well? Come on then, laggard.'

Caught up in the weird internal logics of the dream, I found that I had little hesitation in following my unfamiliar grandfather deeper into this cold, windy place. When Hawkweed began to run, so did I. I felt the ground rushing past beneath my new paws and delighted in the power of my muscles as they propelled me effortlessly on and on.

After a while, I became aware of a subtle change in the light outside the tunnel through which we ran. It was an eerie effect, as if somehow I occupied two worlds: one which was dark and cold and urgent, full of blasting air; and another, less tangible but still visible if I narrowed my eyes: a world in which darkness gave way to streaks of red and gold and green; as if all colour that had once been here had somehow been pressed by the speed of our racing bodies out through the tunnel walls into the world outside.

Then we rounded a sharp curve and there, ahead, bumping against the unseen roof of the tunnel were a dozen or more yellow lights, vibrant in the gloom, giving off a faint, bluish smoke where they touched the boundaries of the highway. Sulphurous and acrid, it burned my nostrils, made my head ache. Hawkweed stopped beneath them. Their golden glow broke over his muzzle, haloed out around his ears. They limned his straggly whiskers and eyebrows with light, and gave back reflections of themselves deep within his unwavering eyes. An odd heaviness came over me as I watched Hawkweed scrutinise the globes, then stand up on his back legs to draw one gently out of the darkness. Pacing the small distance between us, he set it down in front of me.

This time, I did not back away. Rather, I found my paw reached out to secure and trap the thing. My claws extended themselves and sank gently into its surface, which initially gave way beneath my toes with a strange passivity; then I met a faint but definite resistance. I remembered then how, when slinking through the bushes in the back garden, trying to ambush Vita, I had once trodden on a much-deflated rubber balloon, lying bereft beneath the hydrangeas. How its surface, slick with dew and slug-trails, succumbed to the pressure of my claws, but in its new, shrunken state, somehow managed to repel a puncture. The globe felt a little like that, but less tangible, as if at any moment it might change its nature and squirm between my toes and away into the night. And as I felt that insubstantial but defiant pulse beneath my paw, I became aware in that moment of two things: firstly that the fear I had felt for the great cat beside me had somehow changed its nature, too; and secondly that I was going to eat the golden sac, despite the whiffs of acrid fume that now spilled from it.

I bent my head to it and felt the approving gaze of my grandfather upon me. Inside the yellow light, shapes swam indistinctly. I rolled it over with a paw and peered closely.

There!

Something twisted sinuously. I ducked my head back, perturbed.

'It ain't going to bite you, laddie.' These words emerged as through a half-stifled yawn.

I reapplied myself to my task.

As I watched, something protruded through the membrane of the globe.

An elbow!

Then, a foot!

I stared, fascinated. It appeared to be some sort of long, pale, many-limbed creature, but then as it moved again I realised that it had two heads. The heads separated, then came back together. The beast rolled; then half of it peeled away, and when I squinted I could suddenly see that what I had thought to be a single organism was in fact comprised of two, joined awkwardly at the hip.

I watched, amazed, as they rolled again, and then, quite suddenly, recognised the top half of the partnership. It was the man who lived behind the church. The young, rather heavy one who had chased Ginge off the comfortably warm bonnet of his beaten-up old truck, and had thrown a potato at me for digging for a beetle in his garden. (Even at the time I suspected the man had thought I was doing something else entirely.)

And now here he was, tiny and naked, determinedly positioned between a pair of long brown legs belonging to a young woman with ferociously short yellow hair.

I tapped the ball gently and it rolled along the windy ground.

The young man held on grimly to his partner as if completely unaware that his world was turning end over end. His eyes were wide open, triumphant and delighted by the good fortune his dream had accorded him; the woman's were shut.

'Don't play with the damned thing: eat it!' Hawkweed commanded.

I squared my shoulders. I pressed down with one paw on the globe till the image distorted. When it was unrecognisable, I lifted it gingerly to my mouth and held it behind the bars of my teeth. A faint wriggling reminded me of its contents. Something in terms of perspective and world order seemed wrong in eating down two human beings, however tiny, but I did it anyway.

It slipped down my throat far more easily than I would have imagined, and I could trace its passage, cool and slippery, to my stomach. It felt rather as if I had choked down a small frog. Except for the aftertaste, which was like nothing else I have ever tasted.

'Well done, laddie,' the old cat said, and his voice was warm with approval.

I glowed. I basked. It was a rare moment, and I was going to make the most of it. As well I might: there were not too many more like that to come.

'Your first dream swallowed. First of thousands: trust old Hawkweed on that; and probably one of the sweeter ones, too. Nothing quite like a bit of illicit lust to make it slip down easy.' He laughed unpleasantly.

I stared at my grandfather, bemused. Illicit lust. I had no idea what he was talking about.

No idea at all.

The next morning, I awoke, late and stiff-necked and feeling at odds with the world. The sunlight slanting in through the gap in the curtain made my eyes sting. The birds in the trees outside were singing their little heads off. At once, I was filled with irritation. With a groan, I rolled over to burrow under the cushions, and instead found myself nose to nose with my sister. The sun struck pale green lights deep in the iris of her eyes, making her expression quite unreadable. Then she gave a low growl in the back of her throat and reared up at me.

I rolled quickly on to my back and threw up my paws in defence. What a time to pick for a game, I thought wearily.

Then I stared.

Vita was saying something to me through a mixture of purrs and snarls, but I didn't hear a word of it, transfixed as I was by the sight of my own feet.

My paws had gone yellow!

I stared harder, my mind churning. Somehow, since I had last looked at them, the scallops of white around my toes had taken on that same ugly yellow staining I had noticed on my grandfather's fur.

And when I finally was able to focus on what my sister had to say as she launched her attack on me, it confirmed my worst fears.

'You left me alone!' she cried. 'You left me alone in the middle of the night. Orlando! Where did you go without me?'

The staining just wouldn't come off, no matter how hard I tried, though I punished the yellowed fur with the roughest part of my tongue. Ashamed, I hid the marks from Dellifer when she came to groom me, feigning an impatience I did not feel, so that instead of her brisk but comforting attentions, she tutted at my fidgets and shyings and left me to myself. I retreated to the old sofa, curling up with my paws tucked uncomfortably tight beneath me, and felt as if I had been set apart from the rest of catkind.

☯

'I won't be bullied in my own home by a cat,' said Anna.

The old tom had stayed away for a day or so, as if to register his displeasure at Anna's spying, then resumed his visits to the cottage. He no longer seemed at ease in the kitchen, however. He spat at Dellifer, ate nothing, and if Anna so much as spoke to him, would back into a corner and hiss until she returned to whatever she had been doing. She had put herself beyond the pale with him, and her attention was unwelcome.

'If you don't want to be here, you know where the door is.'

He yawned.

'This is ridiculous,' said Anna.

Eventually a truce was declared – or restored – between them. But he kept a weather eye on her, and was careful never to be followed again. She would sometimes see him leaving the garden via the old board fence on the left, into the garden of her neighbour on that side, Mrs Lippincote – known in the village as 'Old' Mrs Lippincote to distinguish her from her own daughter-in-law, who worked at the florist's in Drychester. Anna could hardly pursue him in that direction. One evening, drying her hair at the window of the spare bedroom (the electrical socket there was more conveniently placed than the one in her own room), she watched him slink across Mrs Lippincote's lawn and disappear into a planting of cotoneaster.

She rapped loudly on the window. 'I can see you!' she called. 'You needn't think I can't!'

He barely looked up. He was in no hurry. He knew he had got his own way. And to be honest, rapping on the window was no more than a gesture: though the old cat remained a puzzle, Anna was happy with her life at the cottage. She watched her kittens, she did her work. She ate well and slept late. If she thought about John Dawe, she admitted it to neither Alice nor Ruth.

Nine

SUNDAY EVENING, eight o'clock, and Anna – finding the refrigerator empty but for half a can of tuna, two cubes of feta cheese and some visibly suspect olives – had decided to have supper out. The Green Man was quiet and warm. Outside the wind bumbled and boomed over the downs, gathering its energies for the swoop into Ashmore, where it drove dense little squalls of rain across the duckpond, along Station Lane and into the deserted forecourt of the pub. 'How exciting!' said Anna, who had been content to let it blow her along too. 'The cats have been running about like mad all day!' It was so nice to be somewhere you liked. She looked with immense satisfaction at her drink, at the bar menu, at the firelight glinting on brasswork and polished wood, and told Alice:

'I think I'll have venison sausages.'

Alice said quietly, 'I know how those kittens feel. I've got the wind under my tail today, too. I'd do anything to be away from here.' She stared into the night. 'There's days you'd kill for something new.' Her eyes were full of some youthful expectation Anna could no longer share. 'Just one new thing.'

Then she shook her head as if to clear it. 'I wouldn't have the sausages if I was you,' she advised. 'The pot pie's nice.'

'Whatever you say, Alice.'

Alice – whose favoured cuisine was a bag of chips, and whose idea of waitressing was to drop the cutlery in front of you and say, 'There,' or 'OK?' – had just served Anna with home-made steak-and-Guinness pie, peas, and new potatoes, when a big car pulled almost silently into the forecourt outside. Headlights slashed briefly through the streaming rain: died. Doors slammed, there was a faint laughter, and a moment later the wind ushered in a rather beautiful woman accompanied by two young men. She looked excited, and she was still laughing and saying something about the rain. Her age was hard to tell. She had a way of tilting her head to look at the men – who were tall but hardly taller than her – which seemed always to catch the right light for her very black hair and startling green eyes. Her companions were in their twenties, elegant, anxious to please. Anna had seen numbers of young men like them in London. They were middle management, but not in the City: something more creative, perhaps, to do with marketing or publicity. They wore almost identical Paul Smith suits, and glided round the woman with the grace a good education gives. They sat her down by the fire. While one took her expensive raincoat and hung it up, the other was asking her what she would like to drink. She put her hands out to the fire in a sudden girlish gesture of delight, and smiled around with the vagueness of someone who is used to being looked after. In the warm light of the bar, you saw how good her clothes were, how good her skin was. You saw a tiny, perfect line of animation and irony at each corner of her mouth. You saw that despite her liveliness, the green eyes themselves were almost without expression.

'Who's that?' whispered Anna.

'Stella Herringe,' said Alice.

'Good grief,' said Anna.

'Don't stare.'

Anna looked down at her pot pie in confusion. 'But—' she began.

'Oh yes,' interrupted Alice with a kind of dour satisfaction. 'Fifty if she's a day.'

'I can't believe it. On the phone she sounded—'

'Well preserved, isn't she, our Stella?'

Anna shook her head. 'So much for first impressions,' she said. 'All this time I've thought she was some dowdy old monster who kept cats.'

This drew a puzzled look from Alice.

'Pardon?'

'Never mind.'

'Excuse me, dear,' called Stella Herringe. One of the young men had approached the bar and was standing there expectantly in his beautiful suit. 'We're ready to order now.'

Alice made a face only Anna could see. 'They're ready to order now,' she mimicked. 'As you can hear.' She went back to her place, picked up her order pad and, eyeing her victim with frank sexual displeasure, sighed heavily. 'If you're thinking of eating,' she warned him, 'the venison sausage is off.'

The rain eased, and village regulars began to arrive in twos and threes, taking off their coats and calling for drinks. A fat wet Labrador waddled into the middle of the room and shook itself energetically. 'That dog's barred,' called Alice, deadpan, to laughter. A game of darts began. Someone put money in the jukebox. Soon it was hard to hear yourself talk: over at their table by the fire, empty glasses collecting in front of them, Stella Herringe's companions glanced around impatiently and raised their voices. What were they talking about? Anna thought she heard one of them shout, 'I believe the company can afford to be quite open about that.' It fascinated her that they would sit in the public bar of the Green Man at all, let alone try to talk business there on a Sunday evening. 'After all,' the young man went on, 'it's a perfectly good product.' Stella Herringe gave him an indulgent smile, then shook her head. 'Not now,' she mouthed clearly. 'Not here.' She looked at her watch.

At half past nine, John Dawe came in.

He looked as if he had been walking all day. His face and hands were reddened by the wind, his black hair was full of rain. He hadn't bothered to bring a coat. He ordered German white beer which he poured for himself, taking care to stir up the sediment at the bottom of the bottle before the last drop or two went into the glass. Anna watched this little bit of theatre and thought:

'Oh, you again. So what?'

If he felt the weight of this judgement he gave no sign. Instead, he picked up his drink and found an unoccupied table in the corner near the jukebox, where he cleared a space among the empty glasses and crisp packets. He appeared not to have noticed his cousin and her friends; or if he had, he was deliberately ignoring them. What's going on here? Anna asked herself. I thought these two knew one another. I thought they were supposed to be close. She tried to catch Alice's eye, but Alice was in animated conversation with a local boy in cargo trousers and dreadlocks. Damn, thought Anna. Stella Herringe, meanwhile, her expression switching from irony to puzzlement, watched John Dawe drink his beer. She allowed the young men to distract her for a moment, turning to laugh and tilt her head for them. Her cousin searched his pockets for loose change, studied the jukebox menu, selected an old track by the Rolling Stones.

He *is* ignoring her, thought Anna, and she hates it.

Suddenly Stella Herringe looked her age; you sensed that her need to control her companions – to control men in general – came not from strength but weakness. For a moment her eyes were puzzled and hurt. Then she was on her feet, running over to John Dawe to greet him, pretending she had only just seen him there. She tugged at his hand, talking as animatedly as Alice. Would he come and meet her friends?

He smiled. He would. But as soon as he sat down at the table by the fire, she seemed to lose interest in him again. She was content for him to be there. Business – if that was what it was – took up her attention. This seemed to amuse him, and he stared into the fire with a smile playing about his mouth. After a few minutes she leaned towards him suddenly and embraced him, laughing. 'You mustn't mind him,' Anna heard her say brightly. 'He doesn't have much of an opinion about anything, my John.' The young men exchanged glances, chuckled in a dutiful, uncomfortable way. For a moment, as John and Stella stared at one another, you saw how similar they were, black-haired, fine-boned, full of ego and challenge and an energy always on the verge of anger. It was a balanced contest, Anna thought, a clash of personal magnetism. When they were together, they would always be like this. John, though he pretended to keep himself at arm's length, would always be drawn to Stella. And though he would never have admitted it, his very standoffishness was a way of attracting her. When he finally detached himself from her embrace, Stella laughed and said, 'At least fetch me another gin and tonic, you old grouch,' as if she had twenty years to his forty. His reply was too low for Anna to catch, but it seemed to amuse everyone. He scraped his chair noisily back from the table, and asked her friends what they would like to drink. There was an ironic edge, a kind of insolence, to this gesture which filled Anna with anger, though she could never had said why.

Neither could she have explained why, when he walked past her table on his way back from the bar, she got up, stood herself squarely in front of him, and said in a loud voice:

'I don't suppose you remember me, but I'd like you to know you're the rudest man I ever met.'

Around her, conversations stopped, heads turned. She was aware of Alice, caught in open-mouthed astonishment at the spirit optics. Why did I do that? she thought. Out of the corner of her eye, she saw the elegantly made-up face of Stella Herringe turning towards her in a kind of inevitable slow motion, that ironic half-smile at the corners of the beautiful lips. She had the sense that everything she had loved in the Green Man – the friendliness and warmth, the smell of beer, the fat Labrador with its head in the hearth, even the kind firelight itself – was at risk. And why? Why shout at a man you hardly knew, in a crowded pub? She hadn't been quite so horrified by her own behaviour since she was seven. She felt dizzy with it. Then someone laughed and called, 'You tell him, love. You set him straight on that.' Conversations started up again. The bar returned to normal. John Dawe stared at Anna as if he had encountered a madwoman on the street, stepped round her, and carried Stella Herringe's drink back to Stella Herringe's table under the puzzled eyes of Stella Herringe's business associates.

Anna had no names for the emotions she was feeling. She watched his retreating back for a moment, then, filled with panic because her own actions seemed so suddenly out of her own control, picked up her coat and ran out of the pub.

'Why did I say that?'

Out in the car park, squalls of rain blew through the glare of a single halogen lamp, to pock and ruffle the water that lay in broad shallow puddles on the tarmac. If you looked away from the Green Man, there was no sense of human habitation. A single vehicle, the dark grey Mercedes saloon in which Stella Herringe had arrived, stood in the rain. A few agitated tree-tops made themselves visible just inside the reach of the lamp: otherwise it was airy darkness, empty, rushing space. Anna huddled miserably in the doorway, struggling to get into her Barbour while the wind struggled equally hard to take it away. She felt childish, awkward, new to clothes. If she was quick, she decided, she could run home without it.

Oh, damn, damn, damn, she thought. Why on earth did I say that to him? I don't even know him. You can't just tell people what you think of them like that.

The rain and wind hit her like a wall. Halfway across the car park, kicking up fans of water as she ran, she knew that she would have to put the coat on after all. She stopped directly under the light and resumed the struggle. The sleeves eluded her. Wet fabric slapped her face. She looked back at the Green Man and there was John Dawe, silhouetted against the frosted glass panels of the door.

He'll see me! was her first thought, and she ducked out of the cone of light. But he didn't seem to be looking. Instead, shoulders hunched, hands in pockets, he walked unhurriedly over to the dark grey Mercedes, the rain plastering his shirt to his thick shoulders. He stood in front of it for a moment, walked round it first one way then the other, as if he was examining it in a dealer's forecourt, then brought his foot back smartly and kicked its offside front wing as hard as he could. Anna caught her breath. An alarm burst into life, hoo-hawing into the wind. John Dawe considered his handiwork for a second, a tight smile on his lips, then left the car park. Anna, who by then could think of nothing else to do, followed him with one arm inside her coat.

An hour and a half later she was shivering on the towpath of the Brindley cut, her feet soaked, and her shoes thick with grey mud.

She remembered the wind roaring in the tops of the chestnut trees at the edge of the village, then a narrow lane curving away blindly between untrimmed hedges. The landscape had wheeled and shifted around her as her eyes tried to adapt to the darkness. There had been lights in the distance, as of scattered houses. She remembered losing sight of John Dawe, only to glimpse him again, silhouetted for a moment against the sky where the canal raised itself suddenly on a shallow-sided clay embankment and ran arrow-straight for half a mile across the valley floor. She remembered not caring any more whether he saw her or not as she blundered along up there behind him with a frightening magnetic emptiness pulling at her from either side and rain billowing past like dirty net curtain. She remembered being unable to think for the buffeting of the wind. She did not remember these images in their proper order.

If she had little idea of how she had arrived here, she had even less of why. Why do you follow a complete stranger in the middle of the night? What happens next? Why, she thought to herself, do you have this weird feeling that you have seen him before?

The *Magpie* was dark and still.

John Dawe, unaware that he was being followed, had gone below and apparently fallen asleep without so much as switching on a light or boiling a kettle. A few minutes after his arrival, a beautiful if rather bedraggled cat, with long elegant limbs, fur a dense, tawny gold colour and eyes which reflected the night, had picked its way through the puddles and, rather obviously ignoring Anna's silent figure on the towpath, scratched for admittance at the cabin door. Receiving no response it had jumped on to the roof and after a moment's struggle, let itself in through one of the 'pigeon loft' ventilators near the bow. Forty minutes had passed since then, and Anna had stood like a statue for every one of them, while the storm blew itself out around her and stars began to appear between the rags of racing cloud in a washed ultramarine sky. Now she blinked and wiped her hand across her cheeks. She felt like someone waking up from an anaesthetic.

The pub will be closed, she thought. I've got to get myself home.

The lanes were littered with broken branches. Alluvial fans of sand and small stones remained where stormwater had poured across the road. Anna walked along for some time, telling herself, 'I won't think about any of this now.' After all, what could she think? She had shouted at a man she hardly knew in front of everyone at the Green Man, then for no reason followed him home. It was mad. Whenever he was around, it was as if some other Anna was in control. And then to stand like that in the soaking rain for forty minutes! The enormity of this preoccupied her: the next time she looked up, the moon had come out, and she found she had wandered on to the eastern side of the village, where the downs bulked up massive and unreadable against the night. Here, the lanes were a little wider, and she wasn't far from her own place.

She had just begun to feel relieved when she heard a kind of fluttering roar from the direction of the village. She was bathed briefly in dazzling light. A motorcycle lurched round the bend in front of her, its front suspension fighting with the pitted surface of the road, and shot past close enough for the hot airstream to pluck at her clothing. She jumped back, but by then its brake lamp was already flaring misty red as it heeled over into the next corner. A moment after that it was gone, folded away into the night as if it had never been, a spark of furious life in a silent world. Alice Meynell, some hapless boy pinned to the back seat of her Kawasaki, out looking for whatever adventure she might find in the rural night.

Ten minutes later, Anna let herself into the cottage, fed the cats, and went shivering to bed—

—where she was welcomed only by bad dreams, dreams like sea waves, in which formless shapes merged and broke, merged and broke in darkness. Anna was Anna: she was not Anna. She was in Ashmore, but it was not the village she knew. Faces moved above her, all around her, blurred but continually resolving themselves towards familiarity. If there were events in the dreams, they had become inextricably mixed with the events of the evening. Stella Herringe stared ironically across a room at John Dawe. 'I hate you,' Anna told him, as she stumbled after him in the chaos of the night, 'I hate you.' Clothes blew about in the wind, like rags. 'Hurry!' someone said. 'You must hurry!' Something awful was about to happen, and she made one last effort and work desperately, crying out, feverish and ill, only to find the marmalade kitten Orlando sitting on her chest, staring into her face with something that seemed close to concern. His eyes were huge as an owl's, and she almost thought she saw something move in them. Then he pushed the side of his head against hers and purred. His sweet breath tickled her ear. He smelled so clean and new!

'Hello,' she whispered. 'Hello, little thing.'

☯

Shapes spinning, colours braiding: green and gold and scarlet; moving apart and drawing back together, like wildflowers at the mercy of the wind. Mesmerised, I stared closer and the globe hovered, as though the weight of my gaze anchored it in place. Now, the shapes spun away from me, gaining perspective and definition. Figures in outlandishly long dresses circled one another formally in a space bright with candles, then there seemed to be a great rush of air and darkness replaced the light. Someone laughed. Harsh and high-pitched, it was not a pleasant sound. Rather, it made the hairs rise on the back of my neck. I looked away, and when I looked back, I saw a woman running as if in a storm. Her clothes whipped around her; no long dress now, but jeans and a wet coat, and her mouth was open, stretched wide in some expression of strong emotion.

It was Anna.

She woke up and stared straight at me.

Ten

THERE WAS a knock on the door next morning and it was Alice, with her motorcycle helmet in one hand and a bottle of red-top milk in the other.

'Delivery for you,' she said.

'You look tired,' said Anna. 'Come in and have some coffee.'

'I don't mind,' said Alice.

She was wearing jeans, and an ancient fleece-lined leather flying jacket over a Norwegian thermal vest. All these items had seen better days; someone had once tried to paint the flying jacket silver. Alice clumped through the cottage in her heavily buckled black boots, saying things like, 'That's nice, I always liked dried flowers when I was a kiddie,' and, 'I remember when this place belonged to old Arthur Dowden.' And then, 'Oh look!' She had found Vita.

'Try not to step on her,' said Anna.

'I'm used to animals. My sister's got two ornamental goats, a hamster, and her bloke's ferret. They used to keep rabbits as well.' Then she added, without a pause but as if in brackets, 'Oh, and they've got two boys, eight and nine.'

'Can a goat ever be ornamental?'

They sat on kitchen chairs pulled up to the Aga, drinking milky coffee while Anna first ate toast and marmalade then decided to poach an egg. 'My gran always coddled them,' said Alice. 'She preferred that to poached. Look! Look at this!' Clinging grimly to Alice's hand with her front paws, Vita had allowed herself to be lifted high in the air. She enjoyed it to begin with, then looked down and became thoughtful; while her foster-mother watched with anxious eyes, and Orlando tried to get at the butter.

'So,' said Alice, when Anna had finished her egg. 'What happened last night? What was all that about?'

'Let's put more coffee on,' said Anna, who would have been happy not to think about those events, let alone talk about them. She was still horrified by her own contribution. Her whole life, from childhood to university to TransCorp, had been a search for balance, decency, a quiet control over emotional events. It wasn't just that she now failed to understand her own actions – much more frighteningly, it was that she hardly knew the Anna who carried them out.

'I had Stella Herringe asking who you were.'

'Oh yes?'

'She was furious about her car.'

Anna shrugged. She didn't want to have to explain what had happened in the rain outside the Green Man – let alone afterwards – so all she said was:

'I'm not to blame for that.'

'Oh, she knows who did it,' Alice said. 'He's always had a temper on him, that one. They've been at one another for years. No, I think she was just fascinated by you.'

Anna shivered.

'What's up?'

'I don't know. Something walked over my grave.'

In fact she had experienced a clear, filmic memory of herself standing on the towpath by the *Magpie*, water streaming down her face as if she was made of stone. She had no explanation of her own actions, much less those of John Dawe or Stella Herringe. The last thought that had come to her before she slept was, I mustn't get mixed up with those two and their quarrels. Alice's opinion, it turned out, was very much the same.

'You don't want to take it to heart,' she said. 'What her and her cousin do is their business. Let them get on with it.'

Anna, who felt like hugging her for the common sense of this, offered her the coffee pot instead.

'No thanks,' said Alice.

'I don't really know why I made such a fuss.'

'Not to worry,' Alice said equably. She put Vita down, then removed Orlando from the butter dish and tickled him under the chin as he struggled. 'Gave everyone a laugh, anyway.' She stood up and stretched, revealing the safety pin that held up her jeans. 'Fancy a ride on the bike?' she invited. 'No. I can see you don't.'

Orlando followed her to the front door, trying to capture the buckles of her boots.

The weather stayed unseasonally bad. Lenses of low pressure passed over the village as regularly as jets at an airport, bringing strong winds, rain, even a little sleet: between showers the sky was high and pale, with a ceramic sheen and torn strips of cloud high up. Anna couldn't settle, so she cleaned the cottage from top to bottom. The cats, who were refusing to go out until the weather improved, hated the disturbance: as soon as they heard water pouring into a bucket or smelled furniture polish, they went to ground in the airing cupboard. Two hours later they crept out with the body language of the violated, sniffed everything as if it was brand-new and cheap, looked at the vacuum cleaner like dirt, then, fastidious and energetic, made copious use of the cat-litter so things smelled like home again.

'I don't care what you think,' Anna told them. 'It's my house.'

Two or three days of this, and she was as restless as Orlando. She switched the radio from station to station. She tried to read a book. She stared out of one window or another at the soaking garden, and for the first time found herself remembering nostalgically the little bars and cafés of central London. 'Well,' she reminded herself fractiously, 'you live in the country now.' But she wanted to shop. She wanted an almond croissant and a decent cup of coffee. In a gap between downpours she caught the morning bus into Drychester. If nothing else, she wanted to see what the kittens would do if she brought them back half a pound of whitebait.

Built on an eleventh-century lime-burning site, in a cup of the downs where they curved north and east, Drychester had made its fortune during the late 1500s, from wool, mutton, and a distinctive local stone much in demand by the country-house builders of the Tudor boom. Thereafter it had dozed like a woodcutter in a charmed sleep until the railway woke it and reinvented it as a modestly-popular Victorian spa. Now, like many an old market town on the cusp of the new century, it was busily turning itself into a centre for weekend leisure and heritage tourism, aided by the presence of Cistercian ruins, a network of gentle, engaging downland walks, and the railway station with its original cast-iron pillars and lamp-standards. A row of Tudor cottages hosted the different departments of the local history museum; a Queen Anne house the tourist information centre: while the old Shambles had become an extensive souk-like warren of little one-room shops selling everything from 'modern antiques' to speciality foods; a packet of Edwardian letters tied with faded purple ribbon, to half a pound of coffee ground for cafetiere—

'What was that, love, cafetiere?'

'Yes.'

'Half a pound?'

'Yes.'

'Costa Rica?'

'Yes please.'

On a wet day in Drychester everyone pressed into the Shambles to avoid the rain, filling its alleys with damp camel-hair and partly folded umbrellas. By twelve-thirty Anna was tired of shouting to make herself heard. She had bought the whitebait, and seen enough shellac records, 1920s cigarette cases and Festival of Britain tea services to last a lifetime, but wasn't quite ready to eat lunch. Standing in the Shambles bookshop leafing through a volume called *Canals and Narrowboats of Today*, she smelled scent – something subtle, expressive, musky, something hard to come by, Anna thought, even if you could afford it – and heard a voice say:

'It's Anna Prescott, isn't it? Whatever happened to those kittens, dear? Come and have some lunch, and tell me about them.'

It was Stella Herringe.

'Well,' said Anna, 'that's very kind of you, but—'

Ten minutes later they were facing one another across a table at Fletcher's, waiting for soup and filled croissants and – to Anna's dismay – calling each other by their first names. Stella Herringe settled herself and her shopping, treated Anna to an ironical but somehow satisfied smile, and then leaned forward to whisper, 'All these Jaeger jackets and Scotch House skirts! Very countrified. Very Drychester.' Anna, though she laughed and felt included, was suddenly aware of her own Barbour jacket and Levis. She said rather shyly:

'You look more like Manhattan than Drychester.'

Stella received the tribute with a curious mixture of complacency and mischievousness. She looked down at herself, then back up at Anna, tilting her head exactly the way she had done for her admirers in the Green Man. 'Donna Karan,' she said. 'Middle-aged but elegant. And exactly ten years younger than I ought to be wearing. I'm mutton dressed as lamb, dear, but I suppose you've already guessed that.'

She reached out suddenly and touched Anna's cheek. 'You should take care of that skin,' she said. 'I can recommend something.'

Anna was surprised and irritated by the intimacy of this gesture, disturbed by the dry, warm pressure of her companion's fingertips. She looked away deliberately across the steamy room, at the chattering seated women and hard-pressed waitresses, and only after she was certain Stella Herringe had lowered her hand, said, 'I think we're going to have a bit of a wait.'

Stella consulted her watch. She lit a cigarette – glancing ruefully at Anna as if to say, 'I know, I know. But what can I do?' – and called for an ashtray.

'And the kittens?' she said.

'I lost one. Along with the mother, of course, but you knew that. The other two are doing beautifully.'

'Oh good,' said Stella. She drew on her cigarette. 'You seem to have managed rather well without me,' she acknowledged.

Anna was unsure how to respond. Even if she had felt like taking Stella Herringe into her confidence, it would have been impossible: she couldn't begin to explain the unlikely circumstances in which her difficulties had been solved. So after some thought she decided to lie.

'I was grateful for your offer, of course. But I got them to accept baby formula in the end.'

'Good for you!'

'They're quite grown up now. Real little nuisances.'

'If they're a nuisance I could take the female off your hands as soon as she's mature. The male would be harder to accommodate. We might have to make other arrangements for him—'

'No, no!' interrupted Anna, appalled. 'I didn't mean that.'

Stella Herringe seemed to lose interest. She stubbed out her cigarette.

'They're just lively kittens,' said Anna. 'That's all.'

'Well, dear, just remember I'm here.'

Shortly afterwards, lunch arrived. Stella had barely glanced at the menu when it was offered to her. Now she said, 'Ah, *food*,' and concentrated her attention so thoroughly that Anna felt snubbed. Stella ate with the appetite of eighteen years and the fastidiousness of fifty, take small, quick, regular mouthfuls and dispatching them easily with her white teeth. Her eyes, unfocused, seemed to look inward. She addressed herself to her plate for some moments without saying anything, then, indicating the remains of her croissant with her fork, enquired. 'Would it be wrong of me to order another of these?'

Anna said faintly: 'They are nice, aren't they?'

'I think I'll have a parmesan salad as well,' Stella informed the waitress. 'I love food,' she said to Alice. 'Don't you?'

Some minutes later she was wiping her mouth on her serviette ('What we're taught to call a "napkin" in nice houses'), lighting another cigarette and suggesting, 'My car's not far from here. Why don't I drive you home?'

'Oh,' said Anna, 'no, thank you, but I—'

'Even better, let's go and have a look at these naughty kittens of yours, then I'll take you over to Nonesuch for tea. Mm?'

'I really shouldn't,' said Anna.

Somehow though she found herself sitting in the big grey Mercedes with its tranquil, cosseting interior, watching the hedgerows stream by on either side and – caught out so soon in a lie – wondering how she would explain Dellifer's presence to Stella Herringe. The sun had emerged from between sailing cumulus clouds in a scoured blue sky; the hawthorn leaves were bright fresh green. Stella drove well, if a little impatiently, ignoring the glitter of water on the road. She had a brusque way with corners, Anna noticed, as if she suspected their right to be there. While she drove, she liked to chat; and now that she had what she wanted where the kittens were concerned, she seemed less interested in them than in Anna. Without quite intending to, Anna passed from the guarded ('I suppose I'm just like anyone else, really') to the candid, providing details of her childhood in Warwickshire and Croydon, undergraduate life at University College, the beginnings of a career in banking and finance during the great stock market panics of the late eighties. But though Stella's curiosity was fierce, and she was good at listening and nodding, and saying things like, 'How extraordinary!' it was clear that none of this interested her in the slightest.

'What about men, dear?' she said eventually, with a kind of plaintive exasperation. 'It's no life without men.'

Anna drew the line at this, and – aware of the irony – returned as soon as possible to the subject of the kittens, which, though it had its pitfalls, seemed less invasive. 'I still feel sorry for their mother,' she said. Then, casting around for something to add: 'After I buried her and the dead kitten, some animal came and dug them up. It was horrible.'

Stella Herringe patted her arm. 'Don't talk about death, dear,' she advised. 'People hate it.' Then she said: 'What's all this I hear about you and John?'

Anna stared miserably out of the car. Any answer at all would mean acknowledging what had happened in the Green Man, establishing a link between her life and Stella Herringe's. It would mean – as she put it to herself – 'letting Stella in'.

'I thought he had been rude to me,' she said. 'But it turns out that he's just rather shy.'

Stella Herringe gave a shout of delighted laughter. 'Where on earth did you hear that?'

Anna, who had anticipated almost every reaction but this, blinked. She wasn't sure whether to feel relieved or angry. She had chosen the latter and was beginning to say, in the frostiest voice she could muster, 'I'm sorry?' when the sound of a mobile phone filled the interior of the Mercedes.

'That's mine, I think,' said Stella.

'It could hardly be mine,' said Anna, who had left hers behind with a sigh of relief when she left TransCorp.

Still laughing, Stella Herringe mauled her handbag about with one hand until she found the phone and, without driving the slightest bit slower, began to talk into it. After a moment or two she stopped laughing, and her voice became dangerously calm. 'Tell him he'd bloody well better get a move on then,' she said.

Then: 'I don't care. I don't care what his problems are. I asked him if he could sign by the end of the month and he said yes.' And finally: 'Look, dear, this is what I pay you for.' She studied her little Cartier watch. 'I'll be at Nonesuch all afternoon. About five minutes. Good. No.' And she rang off. 'I'm sorry,' she told Anna, 'but we're going to have to give the kittens a miss.'

This time, Anna felt only relief. 'Just drop me in the village,' she said. 'Anywhere will do.'

'No, no. I want you to see my house!' insisted Stella.

She seemed distracted, though. She drove very much faster; and about John Dawe nothing more was said.

Though the great house at Nonesuch was Tudor in origin – having been started from scratch in late 1482 by Joshua Hering, a Norfolk merchant who had made his fortune in and about the Mediterranean by way of enterprises described at the time as 'diverse' – it had been remodelled to suit the taste of successive occupants. Anna's first view of it was from the south, from which aspect the tall ranked windows of the Jacobean front (added in 1621 by Sir John Herringe, a nephew of Joshua's successor and the first to adopt the modern spelling of the family name) rose out of the surrounding gardens like something from a TV historical drama.

Nonesuch – known until the end of the sixteenth century as 'the New Build' – lay in the shelter of a shallow, wooded valley a little east of Ashmore village. One glimpse of the south front was enough for Anna to recognise a certain false modesty in Stella's original description of the house as 'the Tudor building on the left at the end of Allbright Lane'. It was rather more than that. Its convoluted design – carried out in Drychester stone and a delicious warm red brick and based, the story went, on a stylisation of Joshua Hering's initials – made for curious per-spectives and a crowded roofline rendered more fantastic by Flemish gables and groups of tall octagonal chimneys. The viewer's eye was always uncertain about Nonesuch – after a visit people were never really able to reconstruct its shape. The grounds were hardly less complex – hidden lawns and terraces, labyrinths of holly, fantasias of box and yew enclosing potagers and rose gardens between which wound, like tangled ribbon, pathways of herringbone brick – a pun endlessly repeated to assuage Joshua's Tudor ego.

Anna was entranced. 'How beautiful!' she said.

Afternoon light struck down on the Herringe arms, ochred with lichen, done in plaques on the gateposts. The Mercedes engine purred like a cat as it lifted them up the long rising drive which made its way between the gardens towards the great front doors.

'You're seeing it at its best, of course,' said Stella.

Once inside, Anna fell into an expectant but dreamy state in which the building itself seemed to affect her mood. Why should she feel sad in the airy, sun-filled space of the Great Hall, yet laugh despite herself when she saw the dreary two-light windows of the crypt (retained from a structure that had stood on the site fully a hundred years before Joshua Hering's time)? It was less the architectural features themselves that affected her than their juxtaposition. Nonesuch was a bizarre, mazy collision of styles and times, of corridors which had been turned into rooms, pantries which had been turned into stairwells, of solars and chapels and parlours. Every new addition or restoration or rationalisation was a few feet out-of-true with everything else.

'Cross a threshold here,' said Stella Herringe, 'and you've moved two hundred years before you know it. Take care in that doorway, dear, there's one more step than you'd expect.'

Anna stared up at a decorated ceiling. What kind of life had gone on beneath it?

'Old houses always feel so inhabited,' she said.

'Do they, dear? I suppose they do.'

'I would be overpowered by it,' said Anna.

Stella considered this view briefly. 'It's very modern to try and live without the past,' she concluded: 'But that's only a kind of repression, isn't it?' She seemed preoccupied. She hurried from room to room, moving off like an impatient tour guide the moment Anna caught up, and her voice was always echoing back from somewhere ahead.

Anna – disconcerted, and increasingly unsure whether Stella was talking to her or into the mobile phone which she kept shaking and pressing to her ear – struggled along behind, saying things like, 'Amazing,' and, 'Oh, but that's beautiful,' and trying to keep track of their progress into the house. It was colder near the centre, she thought: or perhaps she had only expected that. Puzzled by the ups and downs of her own feelings, and defeated from the outset by the curves and re-entrants of Joshua Hering's original ground plan, she soon felt completely lost.

'I thought these Tudor places always had a courtyard in the middle,' she said.

Stella ignored her. 'Look, I can easily get someone else,' she told the mobile phone: 'If that's what he wants.' She listened with exaggerated patience for a moment, then took the phone away from her ear and stared at it. 'Bloody things,' she said to Anna. 'You can't do anything with them and you can't do anything without them.' Then she opened a door.

'If you want a courtyard,' she said, 'have a look in there.'

Anna hesitated on the threshold peering in. Light from a casement window fell across the blackened floorboards of a large, sparely furnished room, to reveal the mural painted directly on to the plaster of the opposite wall. It was the view across a cobbled courtyard to a glassed-in arcade below a timbered upper storey – the gables of which were carved with Tudor roses and fleur-de-lys – seen through the leaded panes of an oriel window. There were no figures in the composition, but a shadow behind the leaded glass of the arcade suggested that someone, perhaps a woman, had just entered there. The courtyard light had been painted to seem as if it was coming from every direction at once, as if the artist had been instructed to make an illusion that would work at any time of the day. This cleverness undercut its own success. For a second, your eye was willing to be deceived: then it shrugged and gave up, turning with relief to the real things in the room.

'Go on,' encouraged Stella. 'You can go in and look.'

Anna entered reluctantly.

'Trompe l'oeil,' said Stella proudly, tapping the plaster with her knuckles to produce a hollow sound. 'Put in by the Haut-Herringes a couple of centuries ago. The original wall's behind it, complete with the Elizabethan window through which you could once look down into the real courtyard. They loved a joke in those days, they loved to be clever.' She stood away a little and waited for Anna to say something. Anna – partly to get her own back for the jibe about history and repression, and partly because she couldn't see how anyone had ever been fooled by the painting – laughed and said:

'I suppose they did. It seems rather naïve now.'

'Don't be too sure about that.'

Anna said, 'Oh, but look out of *this* window!'

She flung the old lights open and leaned out, to discover herself high on the east front. Long terraced lawns stretched away, broken here and there by groups of cedar trees and leaden statuary. From somewhere closer to came a smell of thyme and lavender, the sound of early insects bumbling through the grass. A breeze idly moved the tops of the great cedars, then went on to ruffle the beechwoods on the rise a quarter of a mile behind the house. Anna, standing in a kind of shocked delight at the window, said, 'I've seen this view before, I'm sure I have,' and then, laughing: 'But as soon as I think about it I know I haven't. Because I've never seen anything so beautiful in my life. *Déjà vu.*'

Then she said: 'If the courtyard really is back there, the house is only one room thick.'

Stella gave her a considering glance. 'Be careful at that casement, dear,' she warned. 'It isn't just the plaster that's unsound.'

Anna shut the window. '*Déjà vu,*' she whispered again.

Stella Herringe was waiting a little way along the dimly lit passage outside. Anna surprised her in a moment of respite, leaning against the wall holding her mobile phone laxly by her side and staring into the air in front of her. With no one to impress or dominate, she had allowed a vacant expression to creep on to her face, where it settled down to loosen the muscles, slacken the skin, accentuate a fold here, a gauntness there, until she looked all of her fifty years. On the oak panelling above her head hung a small, dark oil painting in a heavy frame from which most of the gold leaf was missing. It was clearly a portrait of one of her own ancestors, a woman two decades younger than Stella – lazy, used to power, wearing pearls and a tight brocade bodice – whose unbound black hair framed the same perfect bone structure. She was seated, and staring out boldly at the portraitist. One hand held the neck of a stringed instrument; the other was folded across it. They were strong hands, and her blue eyes were blank with greed.

Stella chuckled. 'Clara de Montfort,' she said, 'just after she married Joshua's grandson Edward in 1573.' She tilted her head. 'We're supposed to look rather alike. What do you think?' Anna thought the similarity shocking. Except for the difference in age, they might have been the same woman. But suspecting that Stella already knew this, she said only:

'I can see the family resemblance.'

'Ah,' said Stella. 'The family resemblance.'

She looked down at the mobile phone in her hand as if she had forgotten what it was for. 'She was a woman of great self-knowledge, that one.' A green light had begun to blink on the keypad of the phone. She touched it experimentally with the tip of her index finger. 'Great self-knowledge,' she repeated.

Suddenly she shrugged. 'The whole place is falling down round our ears, of course. Nobody's lived in more than a couple of rooms of it since the Second World War. I've had rather a nice little flat made at the back, where the north-east corridor used to be. Let's go and have some tea.'

Stella's apartment had an immaculate air, as if it was still waiting for someone to move in. Designed less as a home than as a 'living space', it featured spare, uncluttered white walls, furniture and fittings of stainless steel, polished hardwood floors. It was full of light. Ranked halogen lamps chased the shadows from a kitchen equipped with an eight-hob professional range and Westinghouse refrigerator; from a tiny bathroom with elegant shelves and a Japanese tub. Even the etched-glass risers of the staircase were side-lit, to bring out designs of stylised cats and herbs. Look beyond the untreated linen blinds, Anna thought, and you might be in Docklands or Clerkenwell: anywhere but Nonesuch. At first it seemed like an insult to the past. Yet in a sense Stella was only continuing the tradition of the English country house: like every Herringe before her, she had added to the building according to the fads and styles of her time.

As soon as the door of the flat closed behind her, she revived a little. 'Don't tell me,' she said, amused by Anna's expression. 'You think it looks like the lighting department at Heals.'

'It's quite a surprise.'

'That's what I told the architect,' said Stella. She lit a cigarette.

'Now,' she said: 'Tea!' She looked vaguely around the kitchen, as if uncertain where to start.

'Shall I put the kettle on?' Anna suggested.

'Oh god, dear, not for me. I was wondering where I'd left the gin.'

'Well I'd like some tea.'

'Help yourself to whatever you want,' said Stella. 'I won't be a moment.' Soon she could be heard pottering about in the bathroom. There was a sound of running water, the faint click of small items being taken down, rejected, replaced on the shelves.

Left to herself Anna opened and closed a drawer, turned on the water at the deep hospital-style sink. Ten or fifteen minutes passed. The kettle boiled. Anna poked around in the galvanised steel cupboards, where she found catering packs of Earl Grey tea and digestive biscuits, both unopened. She found several bottles of gin.

Everything's so clean, she thought. How nice to live so well.

When Stella returned, she looked ready for anything. Her green eyes were bright and clear, her skin seemed to have firmed up. She mixed herself a gin and tonic, sat down at the table and began to talk animatedly.

'Cosmetics!' she said. 'What would we do without them?'

'Surely not,' said Anna. 'I mean, you look—'

'Don't be fooled, dear. This is some of the most exclusive stuff in the world. If you could see it, I wouldn't wear it.' She sighed, and in a different voice complained, 'Women tend their fears with an intelligence that only ever makes them worse. We stand in terror of ageing, the loss of sexual attraction which is the loss of power, the loss of everything that makes a woman.' She leaned over quickly, captured Anna's hand, and passed her fingers lightly and rapidly across the skin of the inner wrist.

'Are you afraid yet?' she asked.

Anna pulled her hand away. 'Afraid of what?'

'How old are you, dear? Thirty-five? Thirty-seven?'

'I—'

'Sit there!' said Stella. 'Don't move!'

A moment later she was back again.

'It's never too early to start,' she said. 'And this will really help.' On the table between them she placed a pot of skin cream no more than an inch or two in diameter, beautifully packaged in a cool grey and pink carton. Anna, who had never in her life imagined herself buying anything similar, looked at it uncertainly. She wanted to laugh, but she knew what a mistake that would be. Instead, she began with care:

'I recognise the brand, of course. Who wouldn't? But I don't usually use—'

'I promise you, dear,' interrupted Stella Herringe, 'that it works.'

Anna gave up. 'It looks wonderfully expensive.'

'Doesn't it?' agreed Stella. 'Nevertheless,' she said, 'you're to have it.' She picked the little carton up again and folded the fingers of Anna's right hand round it, then, satisfied that Anna had accepted the gift, looked at her watch. 'I wonder,' she said, 'if you'd mind finding your own way home?'

'Of course not,' said Anna. 'It's such a lovely day—'

'Isn't it?' said Stella. 'Let me walk you back through the house.'

They stood for a moment on the steps outside the great door. The breeze had dropped. Afternoon light glittered off Stella Herringe's car. There was a sense of the space and heat of a summer evening, a kind of heavy softness of the air beneath the great cedars. Anna – who had in fact minded being asked to 'find her own way home' – was delighted all over again, and felt better immediately. The grounds of a Tudor mansion! Impulsively she took Stella's hands. 'It was very kind of you to invite me,' she said, thinking how much she would enjoy the walk down through the gardens. 'It's such a lovely place.'

She laughed.

'The only thing is, I expected there to be cats everywhere! After all, you're so interested in them.' She remembered something she had intended to mention over tea. 'I did hear just the one, when we were in the room with the mural.'

'I doubt it, dear. They never come in the house.'

'It was quite distant, but I'm sure it was a cat.'

Stella's face was suddenly expressionless. 'I never allow them in,' she insisted. 'It doesn't do, does it, to get too fond of them?'

Unable to respond to this (unable, too, to give the other response Stella wanted, 'I suppose I must have been mistaken . . .'), Anna felt she had become invisible, enabling Stella to look straight through her at the lawns and cedars, the driveway descending in its shallow, elegant curves towards the road. There was a moment of uncomfortable silence.

'Anyway,' Anna said. 'Thank you for tea.'

'You must come again,' said Stella.

Then she tilted her head as if to listen, twisting her body at its neat girlish waist to stare back into the shadows of Nonesuch.

'I think that's my phone,' she said. 'Excuse me.'

That evening, not altogether expecting an answer, Anna asked Ruth Canning: 'What could I say?'

'What indeed?' said Ruth, in the voice of someone who had called up in the hope of more interesting gossip.

'I knew I'd heard a cat. She knew too.'

'As she said, it may not have been inside the house. In my day, most of the AWC people had outdoor catteries. That was one of the big costs.'

'But if you love cats—'

'I'm not sure "love" is the right word here,' said Ruth. 'When you do rescue work, the animals you're taking care of are strays, or ferals, or discards. They're old, sick, difficult. They might have to be put down. You can't afford to get attached to them, and you don't mix them up with your pets. A lot of these old dears have learned the hard way. They take a witheringly practical approach.'

'Old dears?' said Anna. 'Ruth, that's another thing. She might be fifty, but she looks like the cover of this month's *Vogue*. As for the cosmetics, I've never seen anything like them. She's given me something that must have cost a hundred pounds a gram. I've only ever seen it in places like Harvey Nicholls. I couldn't afford it even when I worked for the bank.'

'Ah,' said Ruth. 'I think I can help you there. Speaking of money and banks.'

'Oh yes?'

'Do you remember me saying I thought I knew the name Herringe? Well I did, but I couldn't remember where from. It nagged and nagged – especially the AWC connection. There's only one thing I know about, and that's the City: so I went back through some of my old stuff. Sure enough, Herringe was a name that had cropped up more than once when I was researching articles on City institutions. There were a couple of Herringes on the boards of things, so I had another look, to see what I could see.' Moving from the internet to Companies House, then back to the internet again, Ruth had tracked the Herringe footprint through a bewildering web of holding companies, trust funds and offshore havens. It seemed to multiply endlessly, glimmering in the data like a seam of metal, associated with everything from petrochemicals to agribusiness. 'They aren't ICI, but they aren't poor either. They're in the Third World, they're in the First. Most of all, they're in money.'

'If they were in money I'd have heard of them,' said Anna.

Ruth thought this naïve. 'Who knows who runs anything?' she asked. 'A name slips away so easily into the cracks. After that it's proxy-directors, offshore operations, whole concerns run from a site on the Web or an address in some East-Asian office block. It spreads across the world until, somehow, the connections between companies become more important than the companies themselves. You'd find nothing unless you knew where to look.'

She paused, as if to order her thoughts.

'I'm not sure I should have put it quite like this. They're not hiding or anything. This is just the way business is done today. You know that as well as I do. Nothing's "above board" because there isn't a board any more – if there ever was.'

'Don't be coy, Ruth.'

'Hm. OK. Stella is both trustee and recipient of family money – not all of it by any means. But she's used it well. She has her own business interests too, and—'

'—one of them is a cosmetics manufacturer!'

'Exactly,' said Ruth. 'Engelion plc. Quite small, but very successful. Registered thirty years ago, with offices in Hoxton, although it appears to have led one or two lives before that, first as a wholesale fashion house, and then, weirdly enough, a firm of chemical engineers. To be honest, I got lost trying to follow it back. That's not my skill, of course, the bigger Herringe companies are fabulously old. You can trace them quite easily, all the way back to the 1600s and the beginnings of coffee-house capitalism.' She laughed. 'God knows what they did with their money before that.'

Anna thought of Nonesuch, with its entangled passageways and ancient cedars. They built houses with it, she said to herself. Or one house, anyway. And then, out loud, remembering the 'diverse enterprises' on which Joshua Hering had based his fortune: 'Nothing changes, does it?'

'Are you OK, Anna?' said Ruth.

'Of course I am.'

They talked for a few minutes about other things, then Anna said goodbye to her friend and put down the phone.

'Coffee-house capitalism!' she whispered.

Returning from Nonesuch in the late afternoon, she had unpacked the morning's shopping and then, turning out into a shallow bowl the whitebait she had bought from the Shambles market, watched with delight as Dellifer and the kittens confronted their half-pound shoal of tiny silver fish. Up had gone their noses, the moment the bag was opened. Up had gone their tails. Orlando and Vita had trodden on one another in their haste to bury their faces in the dish, then looked up at Anna speechless with love, gratitude and greed (not necessarily in that order). Dellifer, on the other hand, had approached the whole event more cautiously, crouching as far away from the bowl as she could and stretching her neck out to sniff at its contents, before dabbing at the fish with one paw and deciding that discretion is always the better part of valour.

'You ridiculous thing!' Anna had laughed. 'At least give it a try.'

In all this excitement she had forgotten the elegant little carton from Engelion Cosmetics. Now she took it out of her bag and placed it thoughtfully on the table in front of her. Separating the jar from its packaging and instructions, she found herself trying to make sense of Stella Herringe – the greed, the narcissism, the unsettling seesaw of conflicting moods. Childishness always on the heels of maturity. A need for approval one minute, for control the next. Weakness masquerading as strength – or, perhaps more accurately, a strength based on the very weakness it was trying to deny. Stella had arranged herself so coyly beneath the portrait of Lady Clara! Would it ever be possible to separate her from her own vanity?

The jar was heavy for its size, simple and nicely proportioned, made of a milky glass. Anna gave the lid a half-turn anticlockwise and the kitchen filled so suddenly with a thick, musky perfume that the cats looked up as if someone had called their names. It was a complex scent, layered and penetrative. A flowery first cousin to Stella Herringe's perfume overlay something harsher and more animal. Beneath that, a long way down, the ghost of chemicals, so faint you could never say for certain you had smelled them. Dellifer sniffed the air anxiously once or twice, jumped as if she had been prodded, then dived noisily through the cat-flap and out into the garden.

Anna smiled.

'Dear old Dellifer,' she said absently. 'Two new things in one day will always be too much for you.'

She touched the tip of her finger to the perfectly even white surface of the substance in the jar. It was surprisingly cold, as if she had kept it in the fridge. Though light in texture it had a strangely viscous consistency which made it feel as thick as oil. Anna unfolded the leaflet that came with it. 'Beauty,' she read, 'is a performance. It is the performance of your life.' The key to Stella Herringe's personality: youth as beauty, beauty as unrelenting display. What an effort it must take to maintain! 'To prevent your skin from losing elasticity,' the Engelion leaflet explained, 'anti-ageing precautions should begin as early as twenty.' A list of ingredients included 'ceramide derivatives to limit collagen decay, AHAs to retexture, and natural hydro-fixers including animal fibroins modified to retain 400 times their own weight in water'. Finally, it reassured: 'At Engelion we spend more than half our resources testing the product to make certain it is safe.' Anna wiped her fingertip on a tissue, replaced the lid securely on the jar. Stella Herringe had woken up one morning – ten years ago? fifteen? – and heard a clock ticking. Whatever she did now, Anna guessed, that sound rarely went away. Still living out the same long, dreamy moment of panic, she was stretched as tight as a face-lift across her own despair.

Anna understood perfectly. But it was, she suspected, too easy an understanding, one that would really mean nothing to her until – in one year's time? in five? – she panicked too.

Eleven

D AYS PASSED and the weather improved; but the dreams – if dreams they were – haunted me. My life appeared to have reached a turning point. Something I had taken for granted seemed to have been lost forever.

I enjoyed, as blithely as I always had, the things I loved most: the way briny tuna fired its way along the sides of my tongue: play-hunting my catnip mouse; the sun on my fur in the morning: but where before I had passed unthinking from one state of delightful immediacy to the next, now I found that when I was not entirely immersed in whatever I was doing, in those moments 'between' things – before I fell asleep; just after I awoke; when I sat on the bare patch of grass outside the back door without any specific plan in my head – I found myself preoccupied with suspicion and doubt.

Whenever I could, I avoided my grandfather, slinking silently under a bush if I saw a dark shadow in the long grass, fleeing swiftly into another room if the old cat entered the house. And I spent less time with Vita: unfairly, I now regarded her as dull – a childish nuisance, rather than my beloved nestmate.

Instead, I sought out the company of the young male cats who hung around behind the cottages, boasting of their conquests, their speed and skill and general hardness—

'Rats, now,' a large black and white cat, about six months old and known for no apparent reason as Fernie, would confide: 'They're *great* fun to hunt. A bit more fight in 'em than your average mouse or shrew. More sporting, if you know what I mean.'

Heads would nod vigorously. They rarely disagreed about

anything that really mattered. The group dynamic tended to favour conformity, rather than difference, and I had decided against sharing with it such philosophical difficulties as whether dreams could have physical consequences – like stained fur – opting instead for safer ground: hunting, fighting and feeding, or a combination of all three. No one noticed the yellow marks on my feet: the self-absorption of the young is legendary. Besides, personal hygiene did not figure very high in their priorities.

'Ah, but they don't taste that good, do they, rats?' Ginge would shake his head sadly. 'Rather bitter.'

'Blackbirds, though: once you get through the feathers—'

'Thrushes too—' This from a small brindled cat who encouraged the others to call him Feisty, although I often heard him summoned by his owner, a little girl with long brown hair and big green and white shoes, by the name of 'Oscar'.

'A really good *robin*—'

I would join in enthusiastically, though I had never yet actually caught and eaten another living creature. It did not occur to me that neither had most of the others. Ginge and Fernie, though, spent a considerable amount of their time hanging out with some older cats down near a place they referred to as 'the canal'. They described them with awe, and I had soon made a picture in my head of an exotic, tattered bunch of ne'er-do-wells who lay in the sun-streaked rushes by the waterside, stripping their shining claws and spinning tales of blood and guts.

Such connections conferred senior status upon Ginge and Fernie. But because I was a well set-up young cat who could run and leap as fast and as high as others a month or two older, I soon found myself further up this little pecking order than I might otherwise have expected, and it pleased me immensely, giving me as it did somewhere to belong, without complications.

Thus it was that I left my kittenhood behind, along with the sister I would now chase off with a snarl and a cuff rather than allow her to infiltrate my fragile male domain.

One day I slipped through the back door to hear Dellifer comforting Vita in the kitchen. Vita sat there miserably, head down, toying boredly with a piece of wilted spinach: 'Never mind, darling,' Dellifer said. 'He'll grow out of it.'

Grow out of it! At the time I was highly miffed.

But she was right, of course. It was, after all, her job to be right.

Yet it must have seemed to Vita that I never would. Her days without a playmate with whom to share her kittenish energies, her ravenous need for adventure, stretched out dull and interminable. Dellifer, her own youth receded to a distant blur, had no patience with mock-fights and tail-biting. 'I'm far too busy for that sort of nonsense,' she would say crossly, and then would go and arrange that oddly long white form along the sunny windowsill in the breakfast room and stare blankly out into the garden. Expressly forbidden to wander beyond the confines of the garden, Vita took to lying disconsolately in the flowerbeds, her only companions ladybirds and centipedes, none of whom seemed inclined to play the games she craved.

Those days rolled past in a haze of warmth and scent: first the patio roses and the foxgloves; then the delphiniums and mallows; the lady's mantle and the montbretia; and all the while Vita waited for me to remember she was there.

Late one afternoon, on my way to join my peer group at the garages, I was practising pouncing techniques on a fantastically iridescent rosechafer beetle I had found on the dusty path behind the house. I had now perfected a leap into which I had incorporated an elegant half-twist, the added torque of this manoeuvre transferring considerable power to my landing paws and to the eventual 'kill'. I was looking forward to showing off this new weapon in my hunting arsenal: I thought Fernie, in particular, would be impressed by it.

Thus engaged, I did not notice a long dark shadow bend sinuously around the corner of the house and slink up behind me.

'Hello, laddie. Been avoiding your old granfer, have you?'

Shocked out of the perfection of my inner game, I landed awkwardly. The rosechafer picked itself up out of the dust and, lifting up its great green wingcase like an old woman raising her skirts, legged it into the long grass with considerable relief.

'No, of course not, Granfer,' I lied.

The old cat's muzzle split lopsidedly into an unattractive grin, but his eyes remained hard and cold. 'Glad to hear that, laddie. Wouldn't like to think my own blood was trying to dodge me. Especially when there's important work to do.'

He cuffed me lightly across the top of the head, but whether by design or accident his thumb-claw nicked the edge of my ear.

I winced. 'How do you mean, Granfer?'

'Come with me, laddie, and find out.'

The old cat set off at a deceptively fast lope across the gardens so that I had to run to keep up with him. We passed the garages where Ginge and Fernie, Feisty and Stripes and Seamus were leaping up at a snail upon the brick wall. When they saw us, they all stopped what they were doing and stared. For a moment, I had a vision of them as kittens playing together in a carefree world, a world from which I was excluded; then I trotted obediently after my grandfather, the weight of five pairs of eyes upon my retreating back.

Hawkweed led me behind the cottages, along the side of a wire-netting fence surrounding a tennis court, across a well-manicured lawn scattered with metal hoops, across a gravelled driveway, over a rickety close-board fence, in and out of the intricately planted bean canes in a vegetable garden, and through a tiny hole in the hawthorn hedge that bordered the common.

In the middle of a stand of crab apples and goat-willows, he stopped and sat down so suddenly that I nearly ran into the back of him.

'Well, Orlando,' – and at this I shivered, for my grandfather rarely called me by my given name – 'do you have any questions for me? Anything that might have concerned you since that night we ran together?'

My mind went blank. I stared down at the ground. Woodlice bumbled through the soft leaf mould. One of them ran up to my foot, turned round and scurried back the way it had come. I looked up suddenly.

'I do have a question, Granfer.'

'Well ask it then, laddie: don't delay. Life gets shorter every second you waste, though you're too young and stupid yet to realise it.'

I looked him in the eye. 'Why, since that night I came with you in your dream, have my paws gone yellow? And how can I make them white again?'

Hawkweed laughed evilly: 'That's two questions, laddie, and a statement that begs a few more. *That night you came into my dream*, eh? What a fool you are, laddie, to think it a dream. I see we have a long way to travel together: a long way indeed. But all you want to ask is why your feet have gone yellow?'

I nodded emphatically. At this precise moment it was the *only* thing I wanted to know.

'That's not just a stain on your *fur*, laddie.' The old cat leaned forward and leered at me. His snaggled teeth were startlingly white and sharp. 'It goes right through to your soul.'

I felt my mouth fall open, at first, I thought, in shock: but then a shout of laughter broke out and flew into the air. I closed it again quickly and the laugh was abruptly silenced. My grandfather was staring at me, and I noted with a certain grim satisfaction the light of surprise that had appeared in those baleful yellow eyes.

Hawkweed recovered himself with alacrity. 'You may laugh now, laddie, but you'll be laughing on the other side of your face soon.'

As I was considering this possibility, wondering whether this was how one laughed when one's face had been smashed about as my grandfather's was, my world turned upside-down. In an eyeblink, the old cat had launched himself upon me and was gripping my throat between teeth that stopped just short of drawing blood. I could feel the pinpricks of those sharp points through my fur, the power of those jaws around my windpipe. Just one bite, one prolonged application of pressure, and I knew I would be choked to death. Black stars danced in my eyes and the inside of my head felt soft and heavy. My legs, which had been resisting frantically, began to relax. Then something in the balance of the world changed and the compression around my throat receded, and as I began to come back into myself, I heard a voice deep in my head, intoning:

'Enough of this foolish defiance. There are things in this world which I know and you do not, and it is time for you to learn them. There will be times when you want to run away and forget you were ever the wiser; times when the weight of your knowledge will bow your head down and make your heart stiff with grief. Other cats will spurn you: some will fear you; many will despise you – I know, for so it has been for me. But you cannot – you must not – turn aside from your fate. I, for one, will not let you.

You may be young and thoughtless now, but soon you will be old and careworn, like me. Enjoy the time between the two, Orlando: the transition is precious and fleeting: and you have a great deal to learn if you are to survive the pitfalls of the journey.

'Now, close your eyes and pay attention to what I say.'

I did as I was told, but deep in the recesses of my body my heart raced like a cornered mouse. The voice droned on above and beyond me, and soon I was not listening to it at all: rather, with my head pressed hard against the ground, I found I was listening to the blood beating around my body, the thump and pulse of my heart, and then my senses became attuned to different, deeper rhythms below me; below the leaf mould and the centipedes, the worms and the mites; and at the same time above me, in the trees, the clouds and the sky. It was as if I could feel the heartbeat of the world: powerful, firm, inexorable. The voice went on, and I found that as I lay there, my own heart beating steadily in time to the rhythm of life itself, the words fell into my head like some complex backbeat.

'. . . wild roads, Orlando. The animals' highways. Invisible to the eyes of humans, they run wherever there is life: they *are* life, laddie – they carry it through the body of the world, and without them we are nothing. If they fail, all life fails: if they wither and die, then so do we. We are all wild things on the face of the world, and how we live and fight and dream together determines the health of that world. Listen to me, Orlando, and learn.'

And, in a strange sing-song voice I had never heard my grandfather use before, Hawkweed told a tale passed from one cat to another through the history of the world, and there amongst the scrubby undergrowth of a small English wood, caught in the beating heart of that world, I listened.

'Long, long ago, before the world was born, the Great Cat lay lazy in the darkness and groomed Herself. And one day as She groomed, the realisation dawned upon Her that She was lonely. She licked and smoothed and considered this matter. Aeons passed, and still She groomed. She groomed until Her fur gleamed; She groomed until Her tongue ached; and still She was lonely. For millennia She licked Her gleaming flanks, and at last as She licked, so hills and woods and plains emerged where before there had been stripes and spots and whorls; She licked until rivers and seas and lakes became established in their beds and courses. She made a world for Herself, of Herself; a world to cherish and groom forever. But still She was lonely. So She reached down into the wildest part of Herself and She dreamed. Dreams are powerful things, and the Great Cat's dreams were the most powerful of all; for they were true dreams that bore with them the gift of life. She lay lazy in the darkness and She dreamed of creatures who would inhabit Her world and keep Her company: She dreamed of birds and fish and insects, mice and rabbits, frogs and magpies; voles and fleas and fledglings, hedge mice and moles; ducks and corncrakes, shrikes and shrews and stoats; all manner of beasts. She dreamed them into being: and then She dreamed of Herself, enjoying the world She had made, and out of Her dreaming eyes there leapt the cats.

'All the wild things of the world ran and hunted and played; and when they were tired they slept and in turn they dreamed: natural, ingenuous dreams that mirrored the running and hunting and playing of their days. But the Great Cat dreamed too long, and soon She became trapped in the toils of the first nightmare. Before She could swallow it down, something else struggled up through Her dreaming mind, and swam towards the light of the world. And as it fought its way out, it learned. It learned the power of the Great Cat's dreaming, and it, too, coveted the ability to make the world anew in the form of its dreams. And so it was that humans entered the world – as wild as all the other creatures, but with the wildest power of all: a ferocious imagination.

'The humans imagined themselves kings of the world; and so they became. They hunted and killed as many of the other creatures as they could find, and even though the Great Cat dreamed hard, She found She was powerless to stop their destruction, for they were so many, and She was only one. And so She dreamed into existence the wild roads, for Her creatures to travel out of the sight of humans and carry with them the natural energies that would keep the world alive and well.

'But She had reckoned without the wildness of humankind. No matter how "civilised" the humans became, still there was a part of them that was drawn to these highways. When they slept, their dreams would rise up out of them and fly out to join with the other wild things on the wild roads. And there they caused terrible harm: for the wildest dreams of the wildest humans were too powerful and corrosive for even the wild roads, or the cats who travelled them, to contend with. Dreams of greed and lust, hatred and revenge: they invaded the highways; and where they settled, the fabric of the roads was fatally damaged, poisoned and twisted by their force. Where the worst dreams corroded the highways, they burned right through, so that the clean energies of the world spun away into the darkness, and creatures sickened and died. And as the best of the world was poisoned and dissipated, so the balance was spoiled, and fear crept out into the night. Fear gave way to anger, and anger generated violence, and violence brought death and pestilence in its wake.

'And so it went on, night after night: the humans dreamed and the highways succumbed to a more powerful and more savage force.

'The Great Cat looked down upon Her dying world in despair, and She sighed. Her breath drifted out over the wild, forgotten places of the world, where it passed like a breeze, until it fell upon a small, insignificant-looking yellow flower, a flower borne up by a furry green stem and leaves covered in a soft mousy down – and it was these hairs that caught and held the Great Cat's breath. All the yearning that She felt for Her world to be safe was drawn down through its leaves and stem, down into its roots. And when it reached the roots, Her sigh spread to the next plant. And where roots could spread no further, the plant sent downy seedheads to drift upon the winds to establish new plants, here, there and everywhere it could avoid the invasions of humankind—'

'It's hawkweed!' I interrupted, scrambling upright.

The cat who shared its name now regarded me steadily, his ruined face stern. 'It was indeed that plant which placed its mark upon you. You've been initiated to your task, laddie: now it's time to learn what it means to be a dreamcatcher. Do you understand?'

I could feel my brow furrow. With my eyes open and my airways operating normally, back in the recognisable world again, the story seemed implausible and infantile, the meanderings of an old cat trying to persuade an idiot youngster to save him an unpleasant chore. Moreover, I suspected some perverse, unfair motivation, and probably another cruel trick. My throat ached where the old cat had gripped it. I examined the tell-tale stains on my paws, then stared belligerently at my grandfather.

'I wanted an explanation, and all you give me is a fairy tale—'

The old cat silenced me with a look. 'If you had not interrupted my *fairy tale*, laddie, you might have learned its true conclusion. Since you have, you deserve to remain at a disadvantage. Let that be a lesson in itself, Orlando: do not leap in where a little thought might save the day.' He clicked his teeth in disgust. 'There's no respect any more. You youngsters think you know it all, when you hardly even know how to lick your arse clean.' He turned away, splayed his back legs and started suiting action to words.

I watched out of the corner of my eye, a little revolted by my grandfather's crudity. I was, however, rather sorry that I had interrupted: obviously there was more to the tale than I had realised. While Hawkweed groomed, I tried to make sense of it all; but yellow flowers and murder and horror and enormous cats and a world made from fur and spit all got tangled up in my head so that I was left more confused than I had been to begin with.

By the time the old cat completed his cleaning routine the sun was starting to sink between the trees like some great distant fire, sending scintillas of red light shooting through the silhouetted branches.

Hawkweed surveyed the sky thoughtfully. 'Time for a more practical lesson,' he declared.

The moon rose over the hawthorns to light our way as I followed my grandfather with some trepidation into the middle of a gorse thicket. Scents wafted up out of the earth as if the night had released another, secret world; one filled with smells of extra-ordinary interest, smells that made my skin twitch and my nose strain. Rabbits! At this stage in my life I had never actually seen a rabbit, let alone caught one; even so, the image rose as instinctively into my mind as the scent rose from the ground. Soon my head was buzzing with excitement. It was dark, and here I was, out on the common with Hawkweed, surrounded by the scent of warm, wild prey.

The smell got stronger. Soon I could feel it deep in the bones of my face, fizzing around my sinuses, suffusing my skull. Saliva flooded my mouth. Blinking, I swallowed hastily before my grandfather caught me drooling.

'Get down, laddie!' Hawkweed hissed suddenly, dropping to a crouch, and I flattened myself hard against the earth. He moved along with jerky little jabs of his legs, elbows as high as his shoulder blades, like a badly wound clockwork toy: but his head and spine remained in a straight, straight line, and his eyes did not waver; only the tip of his tail twitched out of true.

The next thing I knew, there was a confusing flurry of movement. Light and dark furred shapes spun like dervishes. Stifled growling, as of a furious cat with its mouth full of something which squirmed and fought: then an eye-watering shriek that fled for a moment out into the night skies, only to be cut short by a terrible crack that echoed off the nearby beech trunks. Then nothing but an eerie silence.

I squinted into the gloom, the fur on the back of my neck and spine itching with curiosity. Cautiously, I edged forward.

Something in the darkness ahead began to hiss and bubble and I drew back, suddenly afraid that what I had just heard had not in fact been Hawkweed getting the better of a rabbit, but some other terrible predator which had lain quietly in wait for just such an opportunity to ambush my grandfather.

And when the moonlight fell squarely on the figure in front of me I was still not entirely sure this was not the case: for the creature that raised its head was a fearsome sight indeed. Its face was masked with gore, through which its teeth gleamed like the teeth in a death's head. Its eyes glittered with inimical lustre.

'Chow down, laddie,' it said. 'You'll need to line your stomach for our next task.'

The rabbit, neck broken and belly open to the night, steamed gently into warm air. I had never experienced anything like it before – chicken and game casserole, tuna chunks and minced turkey in gravy all came out of the can with a distinctly homogenous chill to them – so the sudden heat of fresh rabbit-blood on my tongue took me so greatly by surprise that I leapt backwards as if bitten. Hawkweed appeared to take no notice of my discomfort, engaged as he was in eating the rabbit's head. He wrapped his jaws expertly around the skull, positioning the cutting edges with practised care, and bit down hard so that a second snap of bone echoed into the trees. This was followed by such grotesque crunching sounds that I thought I might just wander home while my grandfather was thus distracted and see what Anna was serving for supper that evening. Tinned food seemed rather more tempting than all this gory ravaging. For the first time I found myself wondering whether the lads at the garages had been scrupulously truthful about their hunting exploits. No one had ever mentioned the sound of a skull cracking, the snap of a neck breaking; the mess and heat of it all.

He who hesitates is lost.

I could have turned at that moment – while Hawkweed busied himself amidst convoluted tissue and dark cavities – and run swiftly and silently back through the gorse, out on to the dark common and along the road to the golden light at Anna's kitchen window; I could have slipped through the cat-door into a world of central heating, processed food, ownership and dependence for the rest of my life. But just as I was about to turn intent to action, my grandfather's eyes rose up over the corpse of the rabbit and glared right at me, and I felt myself flush with shame. All my self-will slipped away.

'Well don't hang about, laddie, or there'll be none of the damned thing left!' So saying, Hawkweed applied himself to his meal again and the rest of his unwelcome pronouncements came to me though muffled chewing— '. . . least you can do to show your appreciation of your old granfer's efforts . . . still show you spineless youngsters a thing . . . might just give you some backbone . . .'

I approached. Now the smell of the prey was not so strong, for the night air had cooled the carcass. What lay before me now, gleaming softly in the moonlight, bore no resemblance at all to the image of the rabbits I carried in my head. I closed my eyes and tried to think of it as something that might have slipped out of a can. Not being able to see it helped, and soon I was tearing away at the rabbit as if I had not eaten in days. It tasted different to the food I was used to: salty and tangy in a way that made my tongue buzz with sensation; then after a while I was shearing and swallowing without even registering the taste, and my fur was sticky with blood. Sated, I reeled away.

Hawkweed was sitting at a spectator's distance, with his tail curled neatly around his hind paws. The sleeked fur of his head looked newly groomed and his snaggled teeth glinted in a grimace that lay somewhere between a leer and an ironic grin.

'The warm ones are the best, ah yes; the warm ones are the best.' He leaned forward. 'That'll be the easiest kill you ever eat, laddie, but just remember: the first one's free.'

Half an hour later, I had finally managed to strip my whiskers of the last of the rabbit-blood and Hawkweed was becoming impatient.

He shook his head sadly. 'The Great Cat Herself was never so clean. Shake a leg, laddie, and let's be off. They'll all be dreaming by now.'

The moon had sailed clear of even the highest trees so that their shadows preceded us as we walked across the marshy corner of the common, crossed a small stream and made our way into the woods.

The wild road we entered on this occasion was very different to the one I had dreamed of. It was smaller, for a start, and the winds inside it were neither so strong nor so cold. However, the sensation of pushing my way through the initial resistance felt exactly as I had originally imagined it, and once inside I could feel my body responding to the demands of this strange place, taking on the larger, wilder form I recalled so well. I regarded my huge new paw with grim satisfaction, and felt the blood of the great cats flow through me. This time, though, I felt oddly comfortable with this curious state of affairs, as if I were returning to my proper element.

Already, there were golden lights in the highway.

I gazed at them, remembering.

I remembered the thing that had hovered over Vita's head. I thought about the shapes I had seen in it, and in those others on the wild road.

I thought about the one I had eaten.

I considered the yellow on my paws.

I recalled the story of the hawkweed and the Great Cat's sigh, and although the connections still eluded me, dancing as erratically in my head as the golden globes danced against the roof, I could feel the shape of a theory forming—

'There!' Hawkweed leapt ahead of me, head as alert as any pointer's watching the kill fall from the sky. 'See there, laddie: that's one!'

I started, my mind shaken once more into randomness, the thoughts falling this way and that, like a child's snow-globe turned upside-down.

'Wh— what?'

'Now you earn the rabbit, laddie. Now's your chance – bring it down; go on!'

Up above me, hovering in the gloom, was the largest golden light I had so far seen. It wobbled in the air currents, distorting to left and right, as if something inside it were struggling to get out. Its edges had started to flare into the fiery corona I had learned to recognise as belonging to those dreams most destructive to the highways. And indeed, where it bounced against the side of the wild road, it burned and smoked, releasing a horrid stench into the air. Already I could see the damage it had done, for the outside world shone more brightly beyond it than it should. I could feel the way the energies around me, inside me, were drawn to that thinning, as if they wished to pour themselves away into the night. What then? I thought, still confused by my granfer's lesson. If the wild road were to burn through, here and now, would we be ripped out into the world outside, unnatural in our giant forms, there to wisp away to nothing? Or would we fall choking on the ground, two small domestic cats, defeated by forces beyond their control?

'Go on, Orlando!' My grandfather's voice broke through my grim reverie, and his face was avid and urgent. 'Catch it, laddie; embrace your fate!'

I felt my spine prickle, as if every hair there were rising to meet a challenge: rising not from fear, but because of some other emotion, something that burned inside me, something that buzzed in the deep cavities of my skull. The golden globe smelled like prey. It gave off the bitter tang of the hunted and the terrified.

At once I was all predator.

Unbidden, my hind legs gathered and, muscles bunching and releasing, I leapt high into the swirling air and took the thing cleanly in my jaws.

It squirmed briefly in my mouth.

I laid it upon the ground of the highway and held it down, quite professionally, I thought. I was just examining my catch more closely and congratulating myself on the dexterity with which I'd carried out the whole manoeuvre, when the yellow sphere pulsed like a trapped jellyfish. I dug my claws in tighter—

As I did so, something dark rushed up at me, so that I jerked my head away. It was a dog! A dog inside the golden light! I recognised it with the instinctive dislike of his species, but still I managed to hold on. A scarred muzzle was pushing at the membrane of the globe, distending it. I trod down harder, and the muzzle withdrew. I rolled the sac under my foot, and saw a human running. The perspectives were all wrong: the human was tiny; the dog running after it, mouth agape, a soundless bark wrenching spasmodically at its head, was vast and threatening. Suddenly, the human fell over and its skirts flew up, revealing veined and lumpy legs, stockings ripped – by teeth? The dog, triumphant, stood over the fallen figure with menacing intent. Its jaws worked furiously, but no sound came out. I could see the whites all around the human's eyes, the muscles stretching fear across its face. It was the woman who ran the local post office, an old human whose clothes smelled musty and of long-dead cats, who could be counted on to open a can of sardines for you if you mewed outside her kitchen door. Overcome by horror, I sank my teeth into the globe, felt its outer surface break beneath the carnassials I used for shearing through food. Something wriggled against my gums, then it burst in my mouth with a foetid rush.

Appalled I leapt back, shaking my head from side to side to try to rid myself of the taste. Little globules of yellow spilled across the highway.

'No!' A cry of utmost dismay from my grandfather.

I whirled around.

'Catch it! Catch it!' Hawkweed's voice was pitched high with panic.

Bewildered, I turned back to do as I was told, only to see the tiny black dog shrugging its way out of the clinging shreds of the golden globe. Or rather, the once-tiny black dog: for as it emerged from its prison into the winds of the wild road, it was growing, and growing . . .

'Kill it!'

I stared in horror, as the creature grew from the size of a shrew, to the size of a vole, to a rat—

Then I was knocked sprawling to the ground. Hawkweed hurled himself at the dog, catching it awkwardly by the leg; but as he did so, its swelling muscles prised his jaws open and it escaped again. Now it was the size of a small cat and where it touched the highway, its fur singed and smoked, and the tunnel walls caught light.

'Help me, Orlando!'

Suddenly my paralysis evaporated. I wanted to flee in the opposite direction, putting as much distance as I possibly could between myself and this wild road, my grandfather, the horror I had accidentally released. Instead, I found myself leaping at the snarling beast, jaws wide and fury flaming through my veins. I remembered the rabbit. I clawed my way up the dog's shoulder until I reached its neck and sank my teeth down into the bones there. My head bumped against Hawkweed's. Together we bit down with the primordial power of *felidae* jaws and the beast howled. Foul juices ran down my chin. Then there was a sharp crack and the thing fell limp beneath us.

It was as large as a pony.

At once, the acrid flames that licked the walls of the wild road smouldered and died, leaving scorch and thinning in their wake. The creature on the ground beneath us seeped slowly away, until only the foulest of smells remained.

In a cottage on the main road of the village, the widow Lippincote turned in her sleep and pulled straight the bedclothes that had become twisted around her feet as she fled from the avatar of her nightmare. After a few moments, her breathing eased and she started a new dream: one of summer meadows and a young man with cornflower-blue eyes, running his hands up legs that were smooth and young and varicose-free.

Chest heaving, I turned to face my grandfather.

'I don't understand.'

'They're dreams, laddie, the golden lights. Only cats see them. Cats like you and me. Everyone dreams, Orlando: cats and humans and horses and elephants. But some dream worse than others. Some dreams, they're as light and sweet as butterflies, but some are dark and vile. Those are the ones you have to watch for: they're the ones that do the damage. It's human dreams that do the worst hurt, laddie. Humans think they're civilised—' He laughed bitterly. 'They think they're better than us: stronger, wiser. Oh yes. But dreamcatchers, we know the truth. We've seen it all – the gluttony and the lust and the terror, and the things they do in the name of those emotions: the stealth and the hate, the violence of it all. Civilised? Hah! What they don't ask, people, is where their wildness went.' His eyes flared briefly in the reflected gold of another dream as it drifted by. 'Doesn't just vanish. Oh, no. Nothing ever vanishes, laddie. Nothing is ever lost.'

He fell silent, considering this proposal. I shifted uncomfortably. Biting the dog had made my stomach twist with repulsion. I thought I might throw up. But my grandfather was not yet finished with his lecture.

'Humans are every bit as wild as the animals they despise. Wilder, I believe. Wilder and more dangerous than the maddest dog—'

'Then why,' I butted in, 'did we just save the old woman from that one?'

Hawkweed regarded me with disgust. 'We didn't save *her*, you fool. *That*'s not our job.' He clicked his teeth angrily and his eyes glittered. 'We're here for the wild roads, for the health of the world, to keep the highways safe from the corrosive power of their bloody dreams. If we didn't do this, my lad, you'd soon see a difference. It can start small if the damage is slight: lack of sleep and niggling tempers, minor illnesses that just won't clear up; little creatures running slower than usual. Soon it's arguments and fighting; children hit for no good reason; animals run over for the sheer hell of it; a malaise fallen over an entire area; even the weather becoming unnatural. But once you get the really nasty dreams out there, the true nightmares, then it's plague and violence and death, laddie. Plague and violence and death.

'We do the Great Cat's will, Orlando, keeping Her highways clear and healthy. And how does She reward us?' He retched and spat. 'She curses us, laddie. That's how.'

Back home later that night I passed the food bowl that Anna had put out for me in the kitchen. Tuna imperial, my nose told me, the one with shrimps and other seafood mixed in with the fish. I bent to sniff it, but suddenly the sight of a piece of squid obtruding from the mixture reminded me of the rabbit; and when I remembered the fur of the rabbit, suddenly the taste of the dog was in the back of my throat.

Gagging, I raced back through the cat-flap, feet slipping sideways on the slippery quarry tiles, made for the first flowerbed I came to, and threw up with considerable gusto. I stood there for several minutes afterwards, heaving and blinking. Up had come most of the rabbit: I had expected that. What puzzled me was a mass of longer black strands.

They looked like dog hairs . . .

Ashmore Dreams

Summer

Now summer dreams are flowing along the Brindley canal, pooling in the quiet places where the current runs slow, seeping under the bridge, swirling upstream around the lock-gates.

Venetia Hall, an elderly painter who lives on one of the narrowboats and has that day returned from her annual visit to the Tate, finds herself swimming, a young girl again, in water almost tropically warm. It is night, but garden candles burn in tall cressets, illuminating apple trees full of cascading roses. Around her, lilies, floating on pads as large as plates, have opened to spill their heavy perfume into the summer air. She can hear laughter and voices and the clink of glasses; music drifting lazily from the bandstand. She turns to float on her back, and it is then she realises that her feet have become entangled in the lily roots, and that the man she has been swimming with has disappeared from view . . .

Up on Village Road, the McEwan twins, each, alone, have dreams of flying out of their dormer window. Separately, they step from the ledge, spiral and fall . . .

Fred Burbage and his wife Enid have been bickering more than usual recently, and always over the tiniest of domestic matters: now, he turns over in his sleep, his hands gripping the pillow as if it is his wife's throat; and tomorrow morning when he wakes it will be with relieved surprise that he finds Enid still snoring gently beside him.

Another dreamer is visited by a long-backed fox, its fur all burnished copper, save for a grey patch on one flank. Its eyes are knowing, and wary. When it opens its wide black mouth, the dreamer hears it speak: 'Take care of what you dream,' it tells her, 'for when you dream, your fears eat the world. Someone must warn you of the damage you do, awake and asleep. We care, and are watching.'

Twelve

Outside the post office one sunny morning shortly after her visit to Nonesuch, Anna spotted Alice deep in conversation with John Dawe. They were standing on the other side of the village street, a little way down from the old almshouses. Alice had got in as close as she could and was talking animatedly. Though they were of a height, she had somehow arranged herself so that she was looking up at him. As a consequence she had to lift one hand to shade her eyes from the sun, and this gesture had given her upper body a relaxed, attractive tilt. She laughed at something he said; then, seeing Anna, waved and called:

'Hey! Come and talk to us!'

Anna thought about it for a moment. Then John Dawe turned his head towards her and smiled tentatively, and that was that. She half-waved at Alice and, blushing, let her feet carry her rapidly away. Later, in the Green Man, she admitted:

'I don't know what comes over me when I see him. God knows what I must look like to him.'

'Mad,' said Alice. 'I suspect he thinks you're mad.'

'Well, at least I'm not rude and violent and satisfied with myself,' said Anna. 'And what does he know about cats anyway?'

'Play us another tune,' recommended Alice. 'We're bored with that one.' She went off down the bar to serve someone. 'The fact is,' she said when she came back, 'you fancy him.'

'*What?*'

'You fancy him.'

Anna drank her drink. 'Don't be ridiculous,' she said.

'Suit yourself,' said Alice sunnily. 'But you'll find I'm right. You may not *like* him, but you already fancy him something awful.' She wiped the bar.

All the way home, Anna puzzled over the implications of this. It was true, she decided: she was attracted to John Dawe, in quite a simple, physical way. She liked his shyness, so easily mistaken for bad temper. She liked his sudden smile. She thought frequently about his tanned, powerful forearms. But for some reason that only made her angrier with him. How dared he have such an immediate effect on her? It felt intrusive. She might understand it if he was Max Wishart, or some other old lover – but someone she had never met before?

Nothing was solved.

Anna began to work energetically, if haphazardly, on her garden. When he could spare the time, Orlando was delighted to help. He sat around yawning louchely in the sunshine while Anna put in the hours, occasionally jumping on the bits of leaves and stick she pulled up in handfuls from the borders. Anna found herself grateful for his support: to her, even weeding was an adventure. Generally she worked from a book, or asked over the garden fence the advice of Old Mrs Lippincote. Her neighbour on the other side, Mr Thompson (an active old man, pink-faced and boyish at eighty-three, who wore thick woollen worsted trousers and still drank a pint or two of Guinness at the Green Man every morning), promised to help her plant her own vegetables, though he clearly expected to do much of the work himself. He was often more available than Old Mrs Lippincote, who would only talk during the ten minutes she took for 'morning coffee'. She was, she intimated, too busy the rest of the time, re-doing her daughter-in-law's washing.

'And I wondered about this?'

'Gold bless us, my girl,' said Mrs Lippincote, 'it's sweet william, where were you born?'

'I did think it might be,' Anna apologised.

'The fact is,' she admitted to Alice Meynell in the pub that night, 'I've just pulled up a borderful of biennials. I can't tell the plants from the weeds.'

'Who can?' said Alice.

'I think I'll clean out the garden shed instead.'

As a result of this decision Anna found herself in possession of a bicycle. A ladies' black sit-up-and-beg, with skirt-savers and faded, creaking wicker baskets front and rear, it came out into the light with all the other junk, covered in cobwebs and dust. She wouldn't have been seen dead on it at Cambridge. Now she hosed it down, oiled the working parts, and, after an abortive attempt to train the kittens to travel by basket (Orlando, unimpressed, shrewdly refused to join in; his sister stayed in place a moment or two before trying to climb up Anna's forearm to safety), was soon riding round the lanes, up towards Cresset Beacon and the high point of the downs. The bicycle clanked mournfully on the steeper hills, but otherwise seemed sound. From the top, she watched cloud-shadows race across the valley, while the wind blew her hair into her eyes. She loved to be out and about before Ashmore was awake, bowling along the towpath of the Brindley canal or down past the village shop – from behind the tiny counter of which Hilda and Reggie Candleton sold frozen fish pie and first-class stamps, Kodak film and ice-cream for the summer visitors – in the thick yellow sunshine.

She was happy, though after Stella Herringe had given her the Engelion cream, she sometimes found herself staring into the bathroom mirror in the late afternoon. She would gently touch the side of her face, a brand-new look, tentative and questioning, in her eyes as she searched for evidence of the Annas of the past – Max Wishart's Anna, or TransCorp Bank's Anna, or the Anna who had lived briefly in Muswell Hill with Barnaby and Ruth Canning and a rather beautiful Japanese boy called Kenzo who wanted to be a performance artist.

But generally things went well. The kittens were becoming proper young cats, with never a day's illness. The weather continued to improve. Two or three afternoons a week, Anna put on a flowerprint cotton frock and sailed off to the Candletons' to fill her bicycle baskets with shopping; or – conned by Alice Meynell, who claimed she couldn't very well do it on a Kawasaki ZZR – delivered the newssheet of the Ashmore & District Summer Fête to front doors as socially distinct as Stella Herringe's at Nonesuch and Hetty Parker's at number six Eaton Cottages, the Victorian terrace opposite the pub. She drank cups of tea with Francis Baynes, the vicar, who was some years younger than her, believed that the Church did too little to encourage the innate spirituality of what he called its 'constituency', and always seemed to be reading *A Glastonbury Romance*.

She drank the Hewett sisters' elderflower cordial, which was, so the Hewett sisters said, a legend in three parishes.

In this way she got to know the villagers, and they began to look out for her, perhaps as a welcome contrast to Alice, who, at the age of eight, had grown out of bicycles forever and announced the fact by driving her father's unattended Land Rover down Station Lane and into the pond.

Anna was in the garden one afternoon when the doorbell rang.

'Damn!' she said.

She put on her sandals and went to answer it. Stella Herringe's cousin was standing there.

'I wondered,' he said, 'if you—'

Anna shut the door.

She walked up and down behind it for a moment or two, biting her knuckles in embarrassment and hissing, 'Go away. Go away.' When she opened the door again, he was still standing there. The weather being hot, he had rolled up the sleeves of his oxford-cloth shirt. His Levis had seen better days, as had his oiled-leather Bluntstone boots; slung over his shoulder was a faded canvas-and-leather knapsack as old-fashioned as Anna's bike. He had clearly been out walking, and she couldn't bear the healthy look of him.

'My name is John Dawe,' he said.

'I know that,' said Anna.

'I felt as if we'd got off to a bad start,' he said, 'and I wondered if you would have supper with me to—'

'Of course I won't,' said Anna. 'Not until I know—'

She shut the door again. She had been about to say, 'Not until I know why you have this effect on me. Not until I know who you are.' But it was worse than that. What she really wanted to say, she now saw, was: 'Not until I know who I am. You confuse me, and make me breathless, and I feel out of control near you, and all I want to do is follow you around. No woman does that any more. No woman wants to feel like that.' Orlando, who had run in from the back garden to see what was going on, rubbed against her legs purring, his tail held high. 'You can go away too,' she told him in a venomous whisper. She studied the yellowed lining-paper which had begun to peel off the walls of her tiny hallway. 'I want to be in *control*,' she said. She opened the door a crack and peered out. John Dawe was walking away towards the centre of the village. Orlando, hugely delighted by all this, darted out between Anna's legs and began to follow him down the road.

'Come back!' called Anna.

As a consequence, three things happened at once. John Dawe stopped and turned round uncertainly, raising one hand to keep the sun out of his eyes. Orlando, consumed by shyness, retreated to a position just outside the front gate, where he sat down thoughtfully and began to lick one of his paws. And several ducks which – encouraged by human activity to expect stale bread – had left the pond to waddle about on the grass across the road, eyed the cat and returned cautiously to their natural element, where quarrels broke out among them.

'All right,' Anna said. 'I will have supper with you.'

John Dawe looked as confused as the ducks. He swapped his knapsack from his left shoulder to his right, walked back a little way, his blue eyes fixed on hers, and knelt down in the road to stroke Orlando's head.

'This is a nice little cat,' he said. 'Is he yours?'

'"No one owns a cat",' Anna quoted contemptuously.

'And will you meet me at the pub, or on my boat?'

Anna, angry all over again – although at least now she understood why – said: 'I would rather meet you on your boat, of course.'

'Why did I say that?'

'I could have a guess,' said Alice.

'And what am I going to wear?'

'Trousers, I would.'

'Alice!'

'It's no good pretending you don't want something you've just been at considerable pains to get,' said Alice. 'Not with me. Look, now try this,' – she put a half-pint glass down in front of Anna – 'and tell me it's not the best summer ale you ever tasted.'

Anna drank the beer. 'What do you mean, "pretending"?' she said.

'Hold your nose and pour it down, then. I don't know why I bother.'

'Alice.'

Alice flounced off to the sink. 'What I mean,' she said significantly, 'is that there are those of us who have never had the chance, try as they might.' She came back with a floor cloth and used it to wipe the perfectly clean patch of bar around Anna's drink. 'There are those of us,' she said, 'who are gagging for it.'

'I haven't been at "considerable pains",' Anna defended herself. 'How can you say that? You saw what happened in here the other night.'

Alice laughed bitterly. 'I certainly did,' she said.

'Alice, what am I going to *wear*?'

'You can borrow this if you like.'

'Alice, that's really kind of you. But it wouldn't work so well without the pierced navel.'

Alice cheered up. 'We could always get you done,' she said.

In the end, though, Anna went up to London by train from Drychester. She arrived at Victoria at ten in the morning to find the streets already grey and humid, the traffic reluctant and confusing, the air full of thunder. She looked up at the cap of cloud over Pimlico and the river, and took a taxi to Knightsbridge, where she saw some beautiful things, but nothing – as she put it later to Alice – you could wear to supper on a narrowboat with someone you didn't really like. Two or three hours later, badtempered and sticky, she was forced to admit defeat. She ate lunch on the fifth floor at Harvey Nicholls, then, rather than go home empty-handed, wandered the food market at random, buying exotic produce for herself and the cats. She called Ruth Canning, with the idea of suggesting tea or a drink, but no one answered the phone. It was dark by three in the afternoon. Lightning flickered silent and eerie inside the clouds. Then, as Anna scuttled across Sloane Street among a crowd of other people trying to catch the attention of a cab-driver, she thought she saw someone she knew.

'Stella! Stella Herringe!'

It wasn't Stella but a much older woman, in her late sixties and really quite frail. A stroke had left one side of her white, heavily powdered face hanging lax and unbiddable. The eye on that side was dull hazel, instilled with panic; the mouth dragged down.

'I'm sorry,' said Anna. 'I can't think why I thought . . . Sorry.'

The woman looked at her for what seemed a long time before turning away.

Unsettled for the rest of the afternoon, Anna gave up the idea of a taxi and jumped on a bus instead, intending to go to Sloane Square and have a look in the King's Road shops. Anxiety made her get off at the wrong stop and she wandered about in the dreary triangle between Chelsea Barracks, Belgravia and the railway, until the sky opened and a steady, vertical rain drove her back to Victoria, where she stood on the concourse soaked and impatient among all the other disgruntled shoppers.

'I'll never like London again,' she told Alice, and two days later, at half past seven in the evening, walked reluctantly down to John Dawe's mooring dressed in jeans and an old Jigsaw jumper, carrying a bottle of Chardonnay that had cost twenty pounds in Harvey Nicholls' food market.

'Hello?' she said.

No reply.

It was very quiet down there, and all the boats seemed empty. The day had stored its warmth in the packed earth of the towpath, which was now giving it up gently. The subtle light, more suited to dawn than evening, blanched the summer colours out of the landscape and softened the *Magpie*'s terracotta upper-work to pink. Despite that, everything looked quite clear and sharp, the boats, the trees, the curve of the little bridge reflected on the absolutely motionless surface of the water. Anna didn't quite know what to do. Should she just go aboard? She had thought of phoning him to cancel, but there was no Dawe in the telephone book.

'Hello?'

She took a step or two back towards the bridge. As if at a signal, the *Magpie* creaked and rocked a little against its spring-lines, the doors at the stern of the boat banged open and a cat jumped out. 'For God's sake, Lydia,' she heard John Dawe complain in his rusty growl, 'can't you have some patience?'

The cat gave Anna a filthy look and picked its way forward to sit at the stem of the boat. After a moment or two it began to wash ostentatiously.

John Dawe came up the little steps from the interior. His eyes were as blue as cornflowers, and through a rip in his grey jeans, she could see that the skin of his thigh was as tanned as his forearms. A strong smell of fish came up with him.

'Fresh tuna,' he explained.

'How nice,' said Anna.

'She thought it was for her.'

'Ah.'

This seemed to be as much as they could manage. They stared at one another uncertainly, and she half-offered the bottle of wine, as if she had to give him something to be invited aboard.

He took it from her, unwrapped the tissue paper and held it up for the cat to see.

'Perfect with fish!' he taunted.

The cat turned its back.

'She's pretty enough,' he said, 'but she has the moral sense of a barracuda.'

Anna laughed. 'What lovely fur,' she said. 'It's like gold.' She added: 'I think I once saw her in the dark.'

John Dawe didn't seem to hear this; or if he did, ignored it. 'Good parentage, bad lot,' he said. 'Half Abyssinian, half Siamese. From the mother, indolence and sentimentality. From the father a loud voice and violent appetites. Just enough brains to be dissatisfied with everything. She'll never be happy, but she's certainly a star.'

'You talk about her as if she's a person,' Anna said.

This seemed to annoy him.

'Their lives are only different to ours,' he pointed out. 'Not less important.'

'I didn't mean that,' said Anna.

There was a silence.

'Well,' said John Dawe eventually, 'I ought to cook the fish.'

'That wine should still be quite cool,' she said.

The *Magpie* had been built a mere twenty years ago, so its tumblehome sides announced, by L.T.C. Rolt of Banbury. Anna felt obscurely disappointed. There was an engaging shabbiness to its exterior – but it was the shabbiness, she thought sadly, of a

1970s bungalow where you had been expecting the more dignified decline of the Victorian workman's cottage. She didn't know what to make of the interior at all. If it had been less cluttered it would, paradoxically, have seemed smaller. Ducking down the little steps, she had the impression of a single long, low, poorly lit space, the varnished roof of which seemed to stretch away into a distant gloom. Bits of furniture outcropped here and there: a foldaway bed, old-fashioned cane chairs one either side of a small table, a little grey solid-fuel stove the flue of which went up dangerously between packed bookshelves. It was clean, but fantastically untidy. Books overflowed the shelves and on to the floor. Bedding trailed off the bed. Every surface was covered with objects.

There were bowls full of small fossils and bits of flint, a glass case containing a small stuffed ray, a heavy old artillery compass, two or three chess sets with bizarre or incomplete sets of pieces. There were items assembled from feathers or leather, or carved from ivory: bird's eggs, Egyptian-looking trinkets, browned old bone; dusty, once-colourful, gypsy kinds of things all mixed up with modern items – a saxophone, a Sony laptop with its modem cable plugged into a mobile phone, software CDs, an expensive sound system playing some kind of South American ambient music full of bird calls and muted drumming. It looked like the room of an intelligent teenage boy.

While John Dawe busied himself in the tiny galley area, Anna wandered up and down with a glass of Pineau in her hand, picking things up and putting them down again. What did he do all day in here?

'I haven't had Pineau since I was last in France,' she said. 'I'd forgotten how nice it was.' When he didn't answer she added, 'Can I help?'

He was so used to doing everything by himself that this seemed to confuse him. Eventually he said: 'You could clear some space on the table.' And then: 'These boats are a bit cramped for co-operative cooking. It's better if one person does everything.' He was right. The cabin was so narrow she had to keep pushing past him, murmuring, 'Sorry,' or, 'Can I just—?' The fact was, no one had been doing anything much on the *Magpie*. What a mess, she thought, trying not to look at the unmade bed.

A minute or two later he said, 'I think we could eat this now.'

He had seared the tuna, and now served it with sautéed courgettes and a rocket salad. They sat in the cane chairs, which were too low for the table. John Dawe was a self-sufficient eating companion, attentive but silent, passing the salt or pouring wine without comment.

'This is nice,' said Anna.

He seemed surprised. 'I'm glad,' he said. Then he added: 'I don't cook often. Fish is always easy, isn't it?'

Thinking of Max Wishart's culinary talent – which had been a natural extension of his easy sensuality – she said: 'I never got the hang of it.' Max had spoiled her, she realised. She had let him cook all those wonderful meals and learned nothing from him. He had been attentive, thoughtful, and in the end unreliable: a honey trap. John Dawe was an altogether spikier proposition. He would be difficult to get to know, but perhaps more rewarding for that.

He laughed. 'Ten minutes each side,' he said. 'A bit of oil. That's the secret of tuna.'

His manner was a kind of carapace, she thought: under it, he was not so much shy as, like his own voice, unused. He had got out of the habit of sharing himself. They soon finished the wine. As they ate, the cat made its way back in, sitting quietly at the cabin door while it tried to gauge his mood. Finally it approached, and rubbed its head tentatively against his leg.

'You're not getting anything,' he said. 'So you might as well stop selling yourself.' But Anna noticed how affectionately he caressed the fur of its throat as he spoke.

'You're very fond of her,' she said.

He looked up from his food and shrugged. 'Am I?' he said. 'I suppose I am. But I doubt that's why she stays.'

'Oh, surely—'

'We can't know how they see the world,' he interrupted. 'Perhaps it's a mistake to imagine they love us in return. Perhaps to them we're just a source of warmth, food, shelter.'

'I know my cats love me,' said Anna.

While he made coffee, she examined his books. They were a mixed lot. Paperback popular science rubbed shoulders with university texts in foreign languages. He seemed to be interested in everything from physics to shamanism. She recognised a title here and there – *The Golden Bough*, *The Book of the Dead*, *A Brief History of Time*. There were books on ancient Egypt, the vanished native-American cultures, the Inuit peoples of the Arctic. There were, curiously, books on ocean navigation, as if he had considered taking the *Magpie* to sea. There were a lot of books about dreams. She opened at random a volume called *Dream Time*. 'Listen,' she said, ' "Dreams go by contraries. To weep in dreams betokens bliss." Now you know.'

He laughed. 'I wish it was so simple,' he said.

Anna shut the book. 'You do love cats, don't you?' she said. 'I mean, not just have ideas about them?'

'I suppose I do,' he admitted.

'Then can we call a truce on the subject, do you think?' she said.

He smiled. 'I was going to ask you that.'

He looked so relieved that Anna touched his hand, and felt the tension go out of things, and it was like a normal evening for a while. They took the coffee outside to the twilight, and sat in the warm air, listening to music and talking. Lydia, now forgiven, came out to watch the swifts and housemartins as they hawked for insects above the surrounding fields, until at twilight they were replaced by bats, and she remembered business of her own, and was off. John Dawe went inside to change the CD, then again to fetch another bottle of wine. He brought out a lamp, and a jacket for Anna to put round her shoulders. Anna, relieved that they seemed to be getting on again, felt bold enough to ask him about himself. Educated at Marlborough and Cambridge, he had become interested in dreams early on in his career. A doctorate in anthropology followed, and for a few years he had taught cultural studies at a Midlands university. In the end, though, the students – who, interested only in their careers and already confusing the world 'dream' with the word 'ambition' – had begun to bore him, and he had lost interest in that side of academia. His own dreams had puzzled him increasingly. From the age of thirteen, when he first lived at Nonesuch, they had been curious, vivid, really rather undreamlike.

'They're more like plays or masques,' he admitted to Anna, 'the same situations rehearsed over and over again in different costumes. As intense as bad TV but as fragile as a cobweb. Sometimes I wake from dreams like that and I'm certain they're memories of other lives.'

'Very scientific, said Anna.

The attempt to understand his own dreams – or at least to find out if anyone else dreamed in the same way – had led to a fascination with dreams in general, and that fascination had rapidly become the structuring principle of his life. 'For quite a long time I was obsessed. Dreaming was life; the rest of life was just standing around waiting to dream.' He had given up teaching and travelled extensively, in India, Africa, the Near East, East Asia. 'I even spent time above the Arctic Circle, listening to the Inuit talk about their dreams. It wasn't enough. Perhaps you never can learn enough: I come back here every so often and try to fit it all together, and there's always a piece missing, so off I go again. Climb a mountain. Stand in the Valley of the Nile at dawn. Try a new drug. Write down the dreams of everyone I meet. You only get to know the world by being in it, and in fact perhaps it would be better to do just that – *be*, not *know*.' He laughed. 'This is a distinction only male academics make,' he explained. After a pause he added softly: 'And the dreams just go on.'

'And are you any nearer understanding?'

'The obsessed,' he said, 'always believe that the inside of their obsession is bigger than the outside. Climbers, poets, scientists at the cutting edge, people who collect things – they always think there's a whole world in there to be mapped and understood.' He shook his head. Though his face was softened by the lamplight it was no easier to read. 'It's only your own obsessiveness you're exploring.'

Max Wishart had always taught her that it was an evasion to describe yourself in terms of your ideas – a way of hiding yourself. Anna now understood why. Max was a skater across the surface of things. Even his music had come easily to him. He had never allowed it to keep him awake at night. He would never burn his fingers on it, or allow it to stretch his spirit. The attraction of John Dawe was that he found his ideas worth the effort. He was committed. This made him seem odd and difficult and distanced, but, in a peculiar way, more reliable – he wouldn't, you felt, drift cheerfully away in pursuit of the next sensation. At the same time it made him so hard to open up! How could she get him to talk about Stella Herringe if he wouldn't first talk about himself?

'And you always come back here, to the boat?' she asked him. 'Not to Nonesuch?'

This invitation he refused. 'Not to Nonesuch,' he said. 'Not since I was twenty.' He offered the wine bottle. 'Have some more of this.'

Anna held out her glass. 'But what do you *do*?' she pressed (meaning perhaps, What have you done with your life?). 'What's the end product of all this travelling, all these—' lost for words, she made a vague gesture '—*intellectual adventures?*'

He filled her glass. 'More adventures?' he suggested. When she didn't laugh, he added: 'A book, I suspect. But not soon, and not a fun read. Look for *The Dream as Cultural Index*. You won't be any wiser than I am when you've finished it.'

'Why bother then?' said Anna irritably.

'To understand myself.'

'What a helpful contribution to the world,' said Anna. She found him pretentious one minute, confused the next. 'Rather than living,' she went on, partly out of spite, partly in an attempt to force his hand, 'you seem to have spent your life collecting ideas about life.'

He smiled. 'That truce didn't last long,' he remarked. Suddenly he looked tired. He lifted his hands. 'And what about you?' he said.

'I was in London before I came here.'

'And what did you do in London?'

She thought for a moment how she might answer this. The coat she wore smelled of him; the yellow lamplight spilled out across the water, even and warm, to faintly illuminate the willow trees on the far bank. 'I worked in the City,' she said; and when he didn't respond but only waited to see what else she would say, demanded with a sudden impatience: 'What do you want to know? I was just like anyone else, I went to university then got a job.'

No answer.

'Do you understand money?'

He shook his head slowly.

'Well, I moved it around the world at night, to take advantage of the exchange rates. A thousandth of a percent here, a thousandth of a percent there. In the morning there was more of it.'

As if by magic, there always had been more of it.

'I was never a high-flyer,' she was prompted to admit, 'but I did well enough.' She managed not to add, 'for a woman,' and looked into her wine instead, as if she might see herself in the twist of light at the bottom of the glass – walking briskly across the atrium of the TransCorp Bank on Old Broad Street wearing the clothes she wore then. As if she might remember herself more clearly. 'We would move money around all night, and then drive madly off to Stepney and have a fried breakfast at six in the morning in Pellicci's. The other traders were all men, and I got on well with them. It was very competitive but I quite liked that then.' She laughed. 'I never thought of it as money, only numbers on a screen. I moved numbers around on a screen and one year's bonus was enough to buy me a little house by the Thames.' A little house that had cost five hundred thousand pounds. She shivered to think of that world now. It all made such a tangle in her consciousness, such a complex knot of pleasures and anxieties.

She said: 'Have you ever had money?'

He leaned forward, his face a mask in the lamplight. 'Not what you would call money,' he said grimly. 'So tell me: when people ask you who you are, is this how you always answer? Is this how you would want yourself described, as someone who once had a career in the City?'

'Of course not.'

'Well then,' he said, as if she had demonstrated some point he wanted to make. She didn't know how to answer that, so she left a silence. Into it, he asked, in quite a different voice:

'Why are you here, Anna Prescott?'

'I'm not going to tell you that,' she said, adding immediately, 'I suppose I wanted a rest from my old life, and I thought Ashmore would be—' She had meant to say 'nice' or 'kind' or 'safe', but he was already interrupting her.

'No, I mean here. Why did you come here tonight?'

She stared at him. 'I don't know,' she admitted.

'So you're an adventurer, too.'

She laughed. 'Touché,' she said.

He stood up. 'It's turning cold. Would you like to go back inside?'

'Very much,' she said. She lifted her hands to him.

Bats flickered through the damp air between the willows, absorbed by the invisible world: echoes, then echoes of echoes, shivering away into the great emptiness of the water meadows. Small clouds raced through a sky the colour of a grapeskin, where the new moon floated in its prismatic ring of haze. A breeze ruffled the canal, and in response the *Magpie* moved gently against its springlines.

'Careful,' said John Dawe. He helped her to her feet. His hands were dry and warm. For a moment Anna was so close to him she could smell his skin. She thought of sand; walnuts. She thought he would kiss her.

Instead he said lightly: 'Stella was determined I should apologise. She said you'd been up at Nonesuch.'

Anna stared at him. 'Is that why you invited me here?'

'Of course not.'

She pulled away from him. 'It is,' she said, wonderingly. 'You wouldn't have been interested in me if she hadn't.' Suddenly she was furious. 'It is! What do you want from me, you and your cousin?'

When he didn't answer she was surprised to hear herself say coldly: 'I like you, John, but there are too many problems here.'

And then: 'I think I'll go home now.'

'Wait. You can't—'

'I can do anything I want.'

She pushed past him and stepped awkwardly back on to the towpath.

Sixty or seventy years ago, when Ashmore was still a proper farming community, cottages had come right down to the water here, their gardens divided from the water only by a low wooden fence. Nothing was left of that. Thinking she would be home quicker if she went directly across the fields, Anna pushed blindly through the straggling hawthorn hedge which had replaced it.

Suddenly she was among the couch grass and bracken, the rotten, lichenous apple boughs of an abandoned orchard, her feet soaked with dew. The trees creaked in a gust of wind, which drove dead leaves through the hedge and across the surface of the canal. John Dawe ran after her between the grey boughs then stopped. Anna heard him call her name once, but he didn't follow her. She was glad. For a moment, when she looked at him, all she had felt was panic.

When she got home her house was deserted and cold, and she blundered around inside it like a stranger, switching on all the lights in the hope of making things familiar. The cats were out, their dishes empty. Obscurely disappointed, she put down fresh food and water for them; she did the washing up. 'I should go to bed,' she told herself, but she couldn't settle. She made a cup of instant coffee and huddled over the Aga with her hands in her armpits more for comfort than warmth. If she closed her eyes she could see John Dawe's puzzled face. She could hear herself shouting at him. She thought: I have to understand why I'm doing this.

Then she thought: But what is it they want from me?

Slipping out of his leather jacket, she brought its comfortable, age-softened folds up to her face. I was right, she thought, his skin does smell of sand and walnuts. Then embarrassment washed over her. 'I've still got his coat,' she said aloud to the empty kitchen.

This seemed to settle something. She got up, went out into the front garden, and looked up at the sky. The air had cooled further, clouds were scudding energetically across the moon. There was a faint smell of foxgloves, mallow, night-scented stock. In the morning there would be ground-mist in the hollows of the common: then another brilliant day. She found her bicycle propped up under the window, its shadow black against the cottage wall. She wheeled it into the silent road, mounted, and clanked off towards Station Lane. 'This is mad,' she told herself. As if in response, a mallard called drowsily from the crack-willows at the other side of the pond.

The canal boats lay motionless and untenanted. Only the *Magpie* showed a light: one dim yellow porthole. Anna manhandled her bike down on to the towpath and let it fall. Through the porthole she could see John Dawe, sitting at his table in the lamplight. He had shoved the supper plates and salad bowl to one side to make room for a book, a tumbler, a half-empty bottle of Jim Beam. She tapped the porthole with her fingernails. As if he had heard something without quite registering it, he stopped reading for a moment and ran his hands tiredly over his face. She tapped the glass again. This time he looked directly at her, and she heard him laugh. A moment later he was up on deck. He appraised Anna, then the abandoned bicycle.

'It's three o'clock in the morning,' he said.

'Yes.'

'Your feet are soaked.'

'What?'

'Your feet.'

She looked down at them, shook her head impatiently. 'What does that matter?' she said. 'Why do we keep doing this? I don't know why I keep doing this.'

He smiled faintly. 'No.' he said. 'I can tell that you don't.'

'That isn't any sort of *answer*,' she wailed. 'John, all this see-sawing back and forth, it's mad. We're at each other's throats every five minutes but we can't just walk away. We barely know each other but I already feel as if I'm trying to escape something. I don't *understand* myself any more! Do you feel that?'

'I'm not sure what I feel,' he said.

'That's not enough, John,' she said. Suddenly it felt like three in the morning. Her legs ached, and she was exhausted. She took his coat off. Held it out. 'Do you want this back?'

'Do you want to give it back?'

'No,' she said.

'Would you like to come in?'

'No. Not now.' She looked round for a moment, then made a small gesture, as if the night, the water, the trees on the far bank, were enough to explain something. She thought of saying, 'I just came back to tell you I was sorry,' but found she didn't want to go that far, and turned it into, 'I just want to understand what's happening here,' instead. 'I just want us to stop doing this.'

'Then perhaps we will,' he said gently.
She turned away.
'Shall I telephone you?' he said.
'I'd like that.'

Thirteen

Tɪᴍᴇ ᴘᴀssᴇᴅ, and as it crept by so did my horror of the dreams and what they contained. In fact, in the last several forays I had made out on to the wild roads with my grandfather, nothing very dramatic had occurred and I was beginning to accept as another fact of normality the idea of apprenticing to be the local dreamcatcher. I even found myself taking some pride in my night-work, the clean despatch of the small dreams we encountered.

Most of them were harmless things: children's night-fears, full of monsters that at first appeared grotesque and terrifying, but once bitten dissolved to nothing, like a mayfly on the tongue. With Hawkweed I learned how to run down and trap the more elusive human dreams of guilt and shame and anxiety. I did not understand, then, most of the images I came upon in this way, for many were blurred and shifted shape as fast as I bit them. Others were as bright and defined as the pictures I saw on the black box in the living room when we curled up on Anna's lap on a lazy weekend evening.

Between us, my grandfather and I ate them all down, allowing nothing to escape, and all the inhabitants of Ashmore and its environs slept easy in their beds, their nests and dens.

One late summer afternoon, after a week of baking sun, the lads and I were lying scattered in whatever shade we could find behind the garages. Heat haze rose shimmering from the concrete.

We lay there and dozed, too hot even to talk, until there was an outraged howl from Ginge, who, defying the sun, had climbed up to sit on the bonnet of a black truck, eyes closed, a beatific smile upon his dreaming face.

'Ow! It bit me!' He leapt off the vehicle and glared at it accusingly. 'It bit my bum,' he complained, turning round and round to assess the extent of his injury. 'It bloody hurts.' He twisted desperately in the other direction, but his bottom got no closer. Eventually he fell over in a heap and peered through his legs.

The rest of us gathered around, curious, and not a little amused. Ginge was a show-off: we shared a certain grim satisfaction in his discomfort.

'Go on then, Ginge,' said Stripes, pretending deep concern. 'Let's have a look.'

Someone sniggered. Ginge's head shot up, but the culprit's face was carefully masked. Ginge was a big cat and could give you a fair bite.

'My ma says you can do yourself irreparable damage, sitting on a hot car,' Seamus added earnestly. 'Says you can fry your bollocks so that they're never the same again.'

'Best have a look, Ginge,' Feisty urged.

Ginge regarded them with dubious eyes. Then he turned slowly and lifted his tail. Even through the dense orange fur of his rump a distinctly pink flush was clearly visible.

Fernie sucked his breath through his teeth. Stripes shook his head. 'Nasty, that,' said Feisty.

'Can you see it?' Ginge demanded, twisting again. 'Is it bad?'

'Terrible.' Even I was involved now.

'Oh no—' Ginge was starting to lose his sang-froid.

'Only one cure for that, mate,' Fernie stated solemnly.

Ginge looked hopeful.

Fernie leaned in confidingly. 'Sweet cat-spit from a virgin's tongue! Best go see young Liddy down at the canal.'

The other cats howled and fell about.

The blush on Ginge's bottom flooded out over the rest of him until it burned, hot-pink, like a beacon.

'Heard she's quite a one, Ginge.'

'Too wild for you.'

'Too posh, more like.'

'Thinks she's some kind of princess, she does.'

'Got herself some romantic airs.'

'She wouldn't lay a tongue on Ginge's arse!'

'Says she'll only go with a proper wild cat, one that's proved himself out on the highways: no green boys for her—'

'I ain't green—'

'Nor pink ones, either!'

At this jibe, Ginge lost whatever composure he retained and flung himself at Fernie. Seamus, always one who enjoyed a good scrap, leapt on top of them both. Stripes, with a war-cry, joined the fray. It looked like good, clean fun: so I dived in as well. Soon there was one great whirligig of fur and the air was full of howls.

The heat was like a hammer. Enervated, we finally fell apart, helpless and exhausted.

Each of us found a shady spot and started licking our fur back into place. Ginge lay on his side a little way apart from the rest of us and peered with apparent fascination at a distant tree. A tickle began in the middle of my skull. I had been thinking of revealing my secret life to my friends for some time, but something had always stopped me. Latent common-sense, perhaps; or fear of my grandfather. Now, I could feel the words bubbling away in my head. I pushed them down, tried for modest silence, but bravado got the better of me. Looking around to make sure everyone could hear, I dropped casually into the silence: 'I've been out on the wild roads.'

The others stared at me.

I waited for their startled approval.

Then:

'You ain't.'

'Liar!'

This was too much to bear.

'I have,' I said hotly. 'Loads of times. With my granfer.'

At the mention of Hawkweed they went quiet again. Stripes rubbed his ear furtively. It was something he often did if he felt uncomfortable, or if the weather were changing.

'He's a dreamcatcher, ain't he?' Fernie said, squinting at me through the bright sunlight.

Seamus made two scratches in the dust. He looked fearful.

'So?'

Ginge stuck his chin out. He knew he'd lost points: wasn't prepared to lose more. 'They're filth, dreamcatchers. They attract evil, like flies to shit.'

For a moment I was stunned. I felt the hackles rising all the way down my spine like teeth of fur, and it was only when they reached my tail that I realised I was furious: furious on behalf of my grandfather, the dreamcatcher who kept the wild roads of this region safe from the harm of human dreams: furious on my own behalf, as his apprentice.

I opened my mouth to respond, and was surprised when a roar came flooding out.

Ginge's ears went flat and his whiskers trembled.

Fernie stepped between us. 'Enough fighting for today, I'd say.' He turned to me, a calculating light in his eyes. 'You're not the only one who's seen the wild roads. I have too. So, been out with your granfer, have you? What do you do then?'

For a moment I havered, caught between the urge to fight and the compulsion to impress them. Vanity won; but just how honest should I be? My so-called friends could be unpredictable. Volatile hormones spun through their bodies seeking an outlet. One-upmanship was not encouraged: there was an agreed hierarchy, and stepping out of line could bring savage reprisals, even exile from the group. Rodomontade was tolerated, so long as it was entertaining, but the fact that I'd kept my excursions secret from them might well earn their displeasure.

I decided to hedge.

'Well, you know – hunt and stuff.'

At once I knew I had their interest.

'Hunt what?'

'Oh, this and that. Rats and things.' I could see this hadn't impressed them. Hastily I added: 'A dog, once.'

'A dog?' Fernie sounded sceptical.

'You've got to be kidding!'

'Dogs can't use the wild roads—'

'They're too stupid!'

'Anyway, the Great Cat would never allow a dog on to the highways – She made them for us—'

'Now we know you're lying!' This from Ginge.

'I'm not. We did. It tasted . . . bloody awful.'

The swear word brought them back to me.

'Yuk! A dog! Fancy hunting a dog.'

'Well, we didn't hunt it, exactly—'

But that was enough for them: now they were off and flyng.

'Wow! I bet that old Alsatian at the yellow cottages tastes bad—'

'Or that little yappy one down the lane—'

'Can't imagine *that* on a wild road.'

'Perhaps if we all banded together we could get it on to that little highway past Glory Farm,' Feisty suggested.

'It doesn't really work like that,' I said hesitantly.

'How d'you mean?'

'Well, the dreams. They come out of dreams, see.'

'How could a dog come out of a dream, stupid?'

I shrugged. 'I don't know exactly. This one did. It started really tiny and it . . . grew.' When I tried to explain the dog-dream like this it sounded plainly ridiculous, a desperate and ill-constructed lie; even I began to question my memory of the events.

'Don't believe you—'

'A *dog*!'

I felt I was digging myself a deep hole.

'Are you sure it wasn't a mouse?'

I began to wish I had, and could hide myself in it forever. It was all or nothing now: if I backed down I'd lose my place in the hierarchy, probably get chased off, ridiculed.

'Right then,' I said forcefully. 'If you don't believe me, I'll show you.'

'Yeah?' sneered Ginge.

'Anyone who's got the nerve for it can meet me back here tonight when the moon's full up. I'll take you dreamcatching.' I stared challengingly around the group.

Seamus wouldn't meet my eye. Feisty shifted uncomfortably from paw to paw. Fernie grinned cynically. Stripes examined something interesting upon the ground.

It was Ginge who broke the silence.

'All right, then. I'll be here. Looking forward to seeing what a liar you are.'

Midnight saw a furtive group of cats gathered by the garages. Moonlight gifted them with long, attenuated shadow-selves. Of Seamus and Feisty there was no sign.

'Seamus is superstitious,' Stripes said matter-of-factly. 'He's scared of dreams and stuff.'

'And poor little Oscar's mummy won't let them out in the big bad night,' Fernie jeered.

'Let alone the wild wild roads,' added Ginge, swaggering up and down with his tail up.

'How's yer bum, Pink-Boy?' Fernie asked evilly. 'Ready to earn a licking from the lovely Liddy?'

I led the little group past dark-windowed houses and their sleeping occupants, through silent gardens and across the empty road. I could sense the presence of dreams in the air, and sure enough, by the time we reached the common I could see a soft trail of golden lights skimming the tops of the hawthorns, drawn by the network of highways that criss-crossed this wilder heart of the village.

Weaving through a rough boundary of brambles and furze, we passed from the civilised world of cultivated gardens, neat closeboard fences and carefully pruned privet hedges into an area of land that had – apart from the temporary effects of volunteer parish working parties trying to keep some of the winding pathways clear for dog walkers and blackberry pickers – rebuffed the modern world. Largely unchanged since medieval times, the common acknowledged no owner, made concession to none other than its own. Here, amongst the goat-willows, gnarled crab apples and blackthorn, ancient hollies loomed dark and massive, leaves hostile with prickles from crown to root. At Christmastime, heedless of such defences, villagers came to steal their boughs and berries; but hollies have long memories, and the satisfaction of knowing that their assailants will soon be in the ground themselves, nourishing the soil for another generation of trees.

Ginge looked about him apprehensively. 'It's pretty dark in here, isn't it?'

'Does little Pinkie want to go home?' Having been out on the wild roads already, Fernie wasn't frightened: scoring points off the younger cats' fear was only adding to his enjoyment.

I gave him a hard stare. 'Leave him alone.'

Fernie looked surprised. 'Or what?'

I stood my ground. 'Or I'm not taking you in with me.'

'Suits me.'

'Oh leave off, Fernie,' Stripes said wearily.

The wild road we found was a small one, framed by blackberry runners heavy with hard green fruit. To the uninitiated it might just have been a rabbit run; but I had been here before.

Fernie shouldered himself in front of me, pushed his head into it and looked around. Ginge, arriving a moment later, was confronted by the sight of what was apparently half a cat hanging in mid-air, its head, front legs and chest in some other dimension entirely, and jumped backwards with a little exclamation of shock. Fernie withdrew from the highway and regarded him with satisfaction. 'Now you see me—' he winked at Ginge '—now you don't—' and leapt into the wild road, leaving only the tip of his tail visible to the outside world.

I sighed at these theatrics. 'Come on,' I said to the others, 'before he does something really stupid.'

Inside, it was at once icy and dusty and a freezing wind blew all around us. For me, this was something I barely even noticed any more, but the others looked less comfortable. Ginge, a small and tawny sand-cat, shivered in the gale; Stripes, belying his domestic name, had taken on the form of some small, spotted jungle cat. Fernie, revelling in his prior experience, was larger entirely, with tufts on his ears and fangs that glistened in an ear-to-ear grin.

'Where are these dreams of yours, then?'

I looked around, but the air was dark in all directions. Trying to appear decisive, I set off into the gloom, Ginge close behind me, Fernie and Stripes bringing up the rear.

The dreams were elusive that night, of all nights. For half an hour, we paced the highways, Fernie's taunts growing ever more derisive, and I was beginning to think of turning back, and leaving home forever. Then we came to a junction where two other highways joined the flow and there, bobbing gently above our heads, was a cluster of small golden globes. I turned triumphantly to my companions.

'Watch what I do,' I said softly. 'Stay here quietly, or they'll scatter.'

I dropped into a hunter's crouch and silently approached the dreams.

Stripes turned to Fernie, his face quizzical. 'What's he doing then, Fern?'

Fernie stared into the darkness, eyes narrowed. The gloom

reflected back off his pupils as dark, unrelieved black. 'I haven't the faintest idea.'

Ahead of him, all Ginge could see was the large cat whom he had known in another life as his friend Orlando making a balletic leap into the roof of the tunnel, jaws opening and closing with a snap, then performing a neat flip and jerk movement as if to bring quarry to the ground.

With the dream squirming pleasantly underfoot, I raised my head. 'Come and see,' I said.

Intrigued, Ginge stepped forward. A bitter whiff raced past his nose, an acrid, unfamiliar smell. 'What've you got there, Orlando?' he called into the darkness.

'A dream, Ginge; just a dream. Come and have a look.'

'I can't see anything, Orlando.'

'Well, open your eyes, then.'

'They're open as far as they'll go,' returned Ginge; and it was true; his eyes were as round and wide as dinner plates.

Stripes and Fernie pushed past Ginge.

'You're a fraud, Orlando; nothing but a bloody liar!'

I stared at the usually mild-mannered Stripes, bewildered. I opened my mouth to protest and turned to indicate to them the half dozen or so dreams still bobbing in the air currents above us. But as I did so, the globes began to dance in an agitated manner, then to stream wildly away from me; and when I turned back to my friends their faces were lit briefly by the golden lights. In their eyes, in the split second during which the dreams illuminated them, I could read a shared expression of dawning terror. Then there came a great roar and a rush of blizzard wind and suddenly in the highway, seeming to fill all available space and gaining on us by the second, was a great black shape, in the midst of which glowed a red maw framed by shining white incisors.

The chill that permeated my chest was not one of horror, but of recognition.

Then Hawkweed, the vast and savage Hawkweed of the wild roads, was upon us, anger radiating from him like a fire, his breath steaming hot and rancid in the freezing air.

At once, Fernie, Ginge and Stripes took flight, legs everywhere, falling over each other in their panic to get away. And who could blame them? As they ran, their wild forms sleeted off them, shimmering wisps of primal energy sucked back into the fabric of the highway. Dwindling second by second from magnificence to their undistinguished domestic forms, they hurtled away into the darkness.

Hawkweed turned to me, his face twisted with disgust. 'What are you doing here, Orlando? Without me? With those—' he stared after the diminishing trio '—those *houseflies*?' The word held the utmost scorn.

I hung my head. 'They didn't believe me,' I whispered.

Hawkweed curled his lip. 'And you thought you'd show off to them? Show them what a hero you are? Hunting down all the little dreams of the village like some mighty spiritual warrior?' He craned his neck, thrusting his great head up under mine. At such an angel he appeared even more grotesque than usual, the preternatural light of the highways gleaming off his eyes so that they appeared at once blank and milky. I backed away, more than a little afraid.

'I meant no harm by it—' I began.

'No HARM?' Hawkweed's roar echoed off the walls of the tunnel.

'No harm?' he said again, more softly. He laughed. 'The world is full of harm, and it's our job to lessen that harm wherever we can. You're the son of a dreamcatcher's son, Orlando, and you have eaten the weed. For you there is no escape, no way to shed or share the burden. Wherever you go it will be with you always and you will feel its presence.

'Only you can see the dreams, laddie. Don't you understand that? Only you.'

Fourteen

AUGUST FALTERED, then failed. Then, after two weeks of miserable weather, Ashmore was rewarded with an Indian summer. The village spread itself once more with a satisfied sigh under blue skies full of broad white cumulus clouds. No one could remember anything like it since the summers of the postwar idyll. On three notable occasions – all Sundays – Hilda and Reggie Candleton ran out of ice-cream to sell. The tourists, having traipsed through Drychester all morning, came out in the afternoon to drink summer ale at the Green Man and examine the Saxon grave-slabs in Ashmore churchyard; then drove off in a generous daze to try and get a glimpse of Nonesuch through the cedars. You could see their camera lenses flashing in the sun.

'Cultural paparazzi, dear,' said Stella Herringe, when Anna pointed them out. 'Middle-brow cultural paparazzi.'

When weather permitted, they had had 'tea' on the lawn – or one of the lawns – two or three times a week. Stella insisted on it, and Anna – who, despite her first reactions, had begun to love Nonesuch – had no will to resist. By then she was trying to see Stella as a lonely woman with an unfortunate manner, someone whose good points – an absent-minded generosity, an acerbic wit – were there to be enjoyed by the persistent observer. This was easier at some times than others. Despite her youthful looks, Stella often seemed tired and bad-tempered. Sometimes, after an afternoon's gin and tonic, even her looks deserted her: her strength of character ebbed away with them, leaving only a kind of wilful self-pity. But her intelligence was never in doubt, and neither was her curiosity. As Nonesuch worked its relaxing magic, Anna's resistance lessened: across the bright days, Stella stripped her bare with the simple repeated question, 'And what about men, dear? It's no life without a man.' Anna told all. Out of some dim sense of self-preservation she saved Max until last, and regretted him the very moment his name was off her lips.

There was no price to pay at the time: Stella only smiled with a gossip's cunning – she had, after all, dug her way to the pearl inside the oyster – and cried, 'Max Wishart! Oh but I know some people who played with him, at the Queen Elizabeth Hall in 1997! The Downing Ensemble? Anthony Downing and his friends?'

All drunks, thought Anna.

'I've met Anthony,' she was forced to admit, and left it at that. She felt depressed without knowing why. Except that it had nothing to do with music or musicians. She felt as if she had let herself down.

As a reward, perhaps, she was given the run of Nonesuch, or at any rate parts of it. 'Now you must,' Stella insisted, 'as long as I'm here and the door's open, you must just make yourself at home. No one's loved this place as much as you for years.' Anna, taking her at her word, wandered the unlocked solars in a childish daze of pleasure. A bar of creamy golden light fell diagonally across the Chapel Corridor. Dust motes hung like dandelion fluff, a whole afternoon suspended with them in the heat. At the tiniest shift of humidity, Nonesuch creaked like an old ship. Occasionally she felt as dizzied by its complexity, as oppressed by its weight of history, as she had that first afternoon. But in time these sensations became like clues, guides to a more intense experience of her own pleasure at being there, and she grew to welcome them. It was as if she had accepted – or been accepted by – the Nonesuch past. Annoyed by the false light of its trompe l'oeil courtyard, she avoided what she had learned to call the Painted Room. Sometimes, she still thought she heard a cat crying, but it was a long way off.

'Oh and by the way,' Stella reminded her one afternoon, 'I hope you're using your skin cream. If not, just try anything you find.' She made a vague gesture with one hand. 'There are boxes of the stuff around.' There were – at least until the Ashmore & District Summer Fête had come and gone, and along with it the traditional yearly Nonesuch cosmetics stall, piled high with

Engelion seconds. 'It's just shopsoiled packaging, dear, or mis-labelling,' Stella explained. 'Or perhaps we tried out a new jar and no one liked the shape. Nothing wrong with the stuff inside.'

Alice Meynell had other ideas.

'They'll put any old muck on their faces,' she told Anna, 'the silly bitches round here. My old Gran, now, she never had cosmetics on her, not once. Before she died she was like a road map to her own life. All those lines! But they had a wonderful dignity, and her skin felt like a kid glove, it was that smooth.'

She shook her head in wonder, then looked angry again. 'She had a life, my old Gran. It kept her young, however she looked. What have this lot ever done but stare in mirrors?' She thought about this, then said: 'You don't want to worry about all that.'

'I wasn't,' said Anna guiltily. The night before, she had taken down the little Engelion jar, touched her index finger to the cold, smooth, slightly resistant surface of the stuff inside, and stared at it for a long time. Then, catching sight of her own expression in the bathroom mirror, she had wiped her fingertip on a tissue and put the lid back on.

She said: 'It's nice to look nice though, isn't it?'

Alice dignified this with a laugh. 'It is, is it?' she said. 'And why would that be, I wonder?'

'Oh well, you know,' said Anna. She pushed her glass forward. 'Can I have another half of this, please?'

She was seeing John Dawe as often as she saw his cousin. Rather comically careful with one another, reluctant to develop things further, they went to the pictures in Drychester. He invited her to an exhibition of Egyptian art at the British Museum; she suggested a visit to the South Bank. She wore his jacket to the Green Man. But if she liked him increasingly, and came to depend on him as a kind of quiet physical presence in her life, she was no more certain of him – or of herself – than she had been the first time he invited her aboard his boat. He came and went, she didn't know where. Even when he was in Ashmore, there were times when he was so inner-directed he seemed absent. 'Oh, but physics is a kind of mysticism!' he said to her one evening in the pub. It was a statement almost meaningless on its own, the conclusion of some train of thought that excluded her. At times like that, his identity seemed to her to be based on a weakness, thought not feeling, the struggle to assemble himself from a set of ideas, in wilful ignorance of whatever he already was.

'Knowing is one thing,' she tried to tell him. 'Feeling is another.'

He leaned forward to touch her arm. 'I know that's true, Anna,' he said. 'But somehow I just can't *feel* it.'

She burst into laughter. 'John, you bastard!'

They still fought. Sometimes there still seemed to be two other people down there. But they had begun to rely on one another. They had admitted, quietly and determinedly, each in their own way, that there was more to be had by knowing one another than by keeping apart.

Stella Herringe was much more certain of herself than her cousin. She thought less, acted more. 'Who you are, dear,' she advised Anna, 'is what you want. When you know what you want, you know who you are.' Anna was unable to reply to that. Her puzzlement increased one afternoon, when, making her way dreamily along the Chapel Corridor (built and rebuilt many times since Joshua Hering's day but with its fine Jacobean ceiling joists clearly visible), she heard raised voices some distance off.

'I won't have it,' the first voice said angrily, and then, after some answer too quiet to catch:

'I don't care about that.'

It was late afternoon. Thundery light flickered across the lawns of Nonesuch, pooled in the blue shadow of the cedars. Indoors, the heat had been lodged for days behind the warped oak panels and horsehair plaster, filling the house with the overpowering smell of its own history.

'And yet you spend the money, dear,' the second voice said. 'Someone has to care.'

A door slammed. Footsteps moved rapidly away. There was a bright, empty laugh and then silence. Anna stood for some time, waiting for something else to happen, but all she heard was her own breathing. Her senses were so sharp she could feel her upper body rocking with every beat of her heart. What tied these cousins together in such an uncomfortable knot? As parts of her life, Anna's instinct was to keep them separate. But as the summer drew to a close this became more and more difficult.

Ashmore and the surrounding villages lay suffocating under the spell of heat and humidity. Thick overnight mists hung in the low-lying fields either side of the Brindley cut, giving way to hot, dazzling days. The afternoons were heavy with the smell of corn, elderberries and dust, the evening airs breathless and soft. Summer had piled itself up against the door into autumn, John Dawe said, and soon its own weight would push it through. It was the time of year, he said, when you knew nothing could last.

'That's very cheerful,' Anna told him.

To escape the heat, they took the green lanes up on to the downs, where the world seemed huge and they could walk about all day under a windy sky full of white clouds. The sandy soil of the gorselands smelled like cinnamon. If they could escape the heat, they couldn't escape each other. They talked and talked, but in the silences she felt how close he was, felt as an irritant every dry touch of his sleeve on her arm, felt her heart jump when something he said caused her to see him in some new light. Trying to explain the choices she had made in her life, she heard herself say, 'You do know what I mean, don't you? I know I'm not saying this well, but you do know what I mean?'

He stopped and held her by the shoulders and laughed. 'Anna, I haven't a clue what you're talking about.'

'Oh dear. I know. Isn't it awful?'

'Look,' he said. 'A hawk.'

Or a dragonfly. Or deer, moving gracefully behind a screen of trees. He was always showing her things. He was always redirecting her attention.

'I see them! I see them!'

Do something, she wished. You stupid man.

Tell me what we already know.

In the end, he did do something, but he waited until it was evening and they were almost home, leaning on an old gate, watching rabbits crop the greying turf in the field beyond. He stopped talking, and she did too. They stared helplessly at one another for a moment. Then they were too close to do anything but kiss. She had waited for that kiss for what felt like centuries.

Relief made her weak. She clung to him for a moment – transfixed by the clarity of the world, the feel of him, the hot, baked smell of the earth in the field – then returned the kiss quite savagely. He said, 'I've wanted to do that for so long.' She whispered, 'Why didn't you, then?' She laughed softly. 'Never tell me anything about physics or rabbits or the environment again,' she said. They kissed again, for longer. This time as they separated, Stella Herringe's Mercedes came round the corner from the direction of Ashmore, travelling at high speed.

It passed them, rocked to a halt a few yards on, then reversed rapidly. Stella wound down the window and stuck her head out. She was wearing a Hermès headscarf, heavy sunglasses and an animated smile. 'How nice to see you!' she called. She pulled off the scarf, shook out her hair, opened the driver door and stepped out into the road, all in the same motion. An exotic perfume filled the heavy evening air.

'Hello!' said Anna.

'Hello, dear,' said Stella, and walked past without looking at her. She was wearing a short A-line skirt. 'John!' she exclaimed. When she lifted herself up on her toes like a small girl to embrace her cousin, she had the calves of a twenty-year-old tennis player, firm and honey-coloured, without a sign of a vein. 'John!' If he seemed reluctant; she seemed nervous. Their closeness short-circuited itself the moment they touched. He always seemed to be about to shake her off, with a kind of absent-minded distaste. 'And where have you been?' she chided him. 'You knew there were papers to sign this week!'

John Dawe shrugged. 'I had other things to do,' he said.

Stella turned her head to look up at him. She gave her little laugh. 'I'm sure I believe you,' she said.

Two young men in grey suits got out of the back of the Mercedes. Were they the same two Anna had seen in the Green Man? She wasn't sure. They stood in the road for a moment, looking around as if they had heard about hedges before but never seen them. Then one of them said to Anna, 'Hi, I'm Oliver and this is Mark. Was that a jay we just saw in the tree over there?'

'I don't know,' said Anna.

Stella called, 'Don't get out of the car, dears! I'm not staying.' She had walked John Dawe a little way off, holding him by the sleeve, as if she expected him to run away from her. 'Look,' she said to Anna, 'would you mind awfully if I borrowed him for a moment?' Then, as if Anna might have some definite but not entirely reasonable objection to this: 'We'll only be sitting in the car.'

Anna tried to catch John's eye. 'Of course not,' she said when he didn't respond. Before she had completed two words out of the three, Stella was ushering him towards the Mercedes.

Anna folded her arms on top of the gate and stared across the empty field. She blinked. The warm wood felt hard and smooth under her hands, as if it had petrified long ago. 'Well I thought it was a jay,' she heard Mark say to Oliver; or perhaps it was Oliver to Mark. When she turned round a minute of two later, all four of them were in the car, talking earnestly. Oliver and Mark seemed to be trying to explain something to John Dawe. Stella was looking amused again. Suddenly, she started the engine. John got out of the car, slammed the door behind him, then put his head in through the open window.

'You could have talked about this at any time,' he said.

'John, dear—'

'For God's sake leave me alone.'

He walked off towards Ashmore.

Stella smiled at Anna. She let the car roll forward. 'It looks as if you can have him back now, dear,' she said. 'If you can catch him.'

The Mercedes accelerated and vanished round the next bend. Through its rear window Anna could make out the very similar heads of Mark and Oliver, facing one another in silhouette. They didn't seem to be talking. When she looked back, John was already a hundred yards away and walking hard. She ran after him.

'Why on earth are you behaving like this?'

His eyes were completely empty.

She stood in his way. 'Stop. Don't do this,' she said. 'It's so childish.'

Eventually he shook his head like someone waking up. He laughed harshly. 'Families always know how to turn the screw,' he said. 'Well, I can't be bothered with her.'

'I don't know what you mean.'

He shrugged. 'It doesn't matter,' he said.

'Won't you explain?'

'It doesn't matter.'

They walked in silence. Then he said: 'I knew you'd been spending time up at Nonesuch. She was careful to mention it.'

'What do you mean, "careful"?'

He shrugged, in a way that made Anna feel cold.

'John, it's the most beautiful house I've ever seen. And she's very kind. I'm always delighted to go.' She let a few seconds go by, then said: 'You're quite alike, you two. I mean in looks.'

'Not in much else,' he said.

'I can see the Herringe looks in you,' Anna said.

He turned his head away. 'Yes.'

When he didn't say anything else she added: 'She's very young for her age, isn't she?'

An expression she couldn't describe to herself went across his face. 'I suppose she is,' he said. Then he added: 'I wish she hadn't seen us together.'

'What do you mean?'

He stared at her. 'I mean I wish she hadn't seen us together,' he said.

By this time they were standing on the bank of Ashmore pond, looking over towards Anna's house framed between the willows. The water was absolutely still. A dragonfly hung above it like a blue enamel brooch; darted a little way; hung again. John Dawe bent down to look for a stone to skip across the pond. Anna, who felt suddenly that if he broke the surface of the water, something else would break, touched his arm. 'John, what is it?'

'I wish you wouldn't spend so much time up there,' he said, and seemed to have difficulty continuing. 'Look,' he managed eventually, 'Stella can be . . .'

'What?'

'She's not what she seems,' he said.

This wasn't enough for Anna. 'I won't stop going there unless you can give me a reason,' she said gently.

'I can't,' he said.

After that, neither of them could find a way to alleviate the silence that stretched out between them. You idiot, she thought, say something. But if John Dawe wasn't prepared to give an explanation of his relationship with his cousin, Anna was equally unprepared to admit that she required one. So in the end they walked round the pond, and he left her at her gate, and they parted without arranging to meet again.

When he didn't call the next day she felt angry and then miserable, a condition which she alleviated by cycling all the way into Drychester to buy a quarter of Gruyère cheese from the Real Cheese Shop. When he didn't call the next day after that, she went down to the Green Man and sat around in the public bar reading the *Guardian* women's page and getting on Alice's nerves.

Alice was unsympathetic.

'Men don't call,' she said. 'You ought to know that.'

'Perhaps he feels pursued.'

'Perhaps he does,' agreed Alice. 'Perhaps,' she suggested with some asperity, 'he's doing what you ought to have done a bit more of, from the start.'

'What?'

'Treat 'em mean, keep 'em keen,' said Alice.

'Max always felt pursued,' Anna said. A further thought occurred to her. 'Perhaps Barnaby did too.'

'Barnaby was a cat, Anna. He was a cat.' Alice took the newspaper out of Anna's hands the way you would take a comic away from a child, folded it up in a haphazard fashion and pushed it out of reach. 'Are you going to drink that beer or not?'

'I think I'll have a margarita instead.'

'Not in my bar you won't,' said Alice with some determination. 'Not in the middle of the afternoon.'

After she left the Green Man, Anna went home, made coffee and worked. Figures scrolled down her computer screen. She worked all afternoon and into the evening. At half-past seven Orlando came in and upset the small jar in which she kept paper clips. 'Don't do that,' she told him absently. He jumped down, purred round her feet for a minute to two, then she heard the cat-flap bang as he went out again. Eventually she got up and went into the kitchen and looked in the refrigerator. It was nine o'clock. Rather than cook, she switched on the TV and walked about her small front room listening to the news while she ate bio yoghurt from the pot with a dessert spoon. There had been reprisals in the Balkans, record temperatures in Illinois. Here at home the good weather would hold. When the news was over, Anna put on her shoes and walked down to the canal. She stood on the bridge and looked over to where the *Magpie* lay in darkness, yellow lamplight in its portholes, water lapping against its hull. Two voices carried to her on the still warm air. John Dawe had a visitor. If she hadn't been so afraid of finding out who it was, Anna could have walked a few yards down the towpath and looked in at the light porthole.

When she got home again, the red light was blinking on the answerphone. There was a call from a double glazing company. There was a call from Ruth Canning. Ruth's voice filled the cottage, warm and affectionate, a long way away from all these difficulties. The children were well, financial journalism was slow; Sam had been offered a new job. 'Give us a call,' Ruth ended. 'We miss you. There was something else I meant to tell you, but I can't remember what it was. Something to do with that Herringe woman?' There was a brief pause. 'Damn. Oh well, I'll phone you if I remember.'

Anna rang the Hackney number, but no one answered.

'They'll be in bed by now,' she told the empty cottage. 'Which is where I should be.'

She stood in the hall and looked up the stairs to her bedroom. In the daytime, when the bedroom door was open, the staircase was dark and the door made a welcoming rectangle of light around the attractively composed shapes beyond – the corner of her bed, part of the pine dresser, a bit of blue sky framed by the bedroom window. Now it was the other way round, and she walked up under the bitter sixty-watt light into darkness.

Next day, the *Magpie* was gone.

Anna welcomed the gusty winds, the outbreaks of rain that swept in over the next week, as an excuse to eat comfort food, put on comfort clothes, and trudge up and down the towpath with her hands in her pockets. The line of canal boats lay much as she had first seen it, locked in a slow struggle with the seasons. The *Magpie*'s empty mooring was like a lost tooth in a jaw so familiar it must be your own. She couldn't keep her tongue out of the gap:

she missed the boat as much as she missed its owner. She missed his clutter, his rough attempt at making his life comfortable.

'You're unaccomplished,' she had once said to him, thinking of Max's easy familiarity with the good, ordinary things in life – food, wine, shopping. 'You're unaccomplished at living.' And then, touched his forearm gently: 'Everything is such a struggle for you.'

Now she thought: I love that. I love that about him.

Anna couldn't concentrate. She made long, late-evening calls to people she hadn't seen for years, most of whom put down the receiver at the end of the conversation without knowing quite why she had phoned. She began garden projects she knew she couldn't complete. Within days of his leaving, her dreams were rank with sex. She dreamed of sex between cats, one black and one brown – there was no need to guess who was who. Awake, she couldn't imagine him biting the back of her neck like that. Her dreams were steeped with him. She admitted this surprisedly to the practical Alice, who grinned.

'I'm off work in half an hour. Come out and have a ride on the bike. Do you good.'

'All right,' said Anna.

'What?'

'I'd like to.'

'Bloody hell.'

Alice brought her home late, with a loud rushing sound in her ears. They had been to London and back, and had Smirnoff Mules in a bar in Catford. She got clumsily off the bike and held on to her front gate. When she closed her eyes, she could still see the world hurtling towards her, grey with speedlines, at a hundred and thirty miles an hour. The horizon lurched sixty degrees to the left, snapped upright, then tipped the other way. She was still astonished by the violence and excitement of it all, the noise, the vibration, the airstream like a constant slap in the face, the raw competition of forces that held the Kawasaki in place at any given moment. There had been moments of such precariousness that she screamed with terror; and moments of such relief that she screamed with laughter. Then an instant of machine grace, when they seemed to be flying.

'You see?' said Alice.

Anna clung to the gate. 'Alice, I can't hear you!'

'It definitely helps. I mean, admit it. Sex can't compete with that.'

'What did you say?'

Alice grinned. 'I'm off now,' she mouthed.

'I can't hear anything at all.'

Two days later she put her head round the door of the Green Man and he was sitting there on a stool at the bar as if nothing had happened, reading a newspaper. Firelight winked off the bar furniture and spirit optics behind him. He looked up and began to smile. Anna slammed the door, then went and stood in the car park, where she trembled with surprise and fury. 'Well I'll just go home, then,' she told herself, and rushed out into Station Lane. She got as far as the pond and – with some idea that it might make her feel better – decided to have a walk round the churchyard instead. That was where he caught up with her.

'Wait!' he called.

'I won't,' she told him, though by then she had come to a halt anyway and was staring in a preoccupied way at the Herringe family graves lying between the great dark yew tree and the flint-knapped walls of the church.

'Anna—'

She bent down to scrape lichen off some of the older stones. Laminated and flaking, reduced to mere fingers of Horsham slab, they protruded at odd angles from the tangled grass. A little under half of them belonged to women, though the women had not, it seemed, belonged to themselves. 'Wife of,' she read. 'Mother of.' 'Hys lovinge sister.' You could barely read the names, but quite a few of the dates were intact. She stood up again.

'Don't call me Anna,' she said, dusting tiny dry flakes of lichen from her fingertips. 'Go away.'

She was careful to keep her back to him. If he wouldn't leave, she promised herself, she would; but a kind of hypnosis held her in place. They were both as nervous as ponies. She was going to walk away. She was going to refuse to speak. She was going to shout at him. She had no idea what she was going to do, only that she would never need to turn, or look, to find him: she could feel him there, heat, smell, everything.

Perhaps he guessed. He touched her shoulder. 'Anna, why are you acting like this?'

'You dare ask that!'

'How will I know, without asking?'

This reminded her too much of Max Wishart.

'Don't be clever,' she said.

He hated that. 'And don't pretend you're angry just because I am,' she warned him. He spread his arms then let them fall to his sides helplessly. She thought he looked tired around the eyes. 'You went off without a word,' she said. 'You kissed me and then went off without a word.' Before she could stop herself, she had added, in a voice she hardly recognised as her own, it was so full of need: 'You wouldn't put me before Stella.'

He looked startled. Then he said: 'She owns me, Anna.'

'What?'

He said gently, 'Anna, I live on a canal boat, read, travel around. I'm writing a book no one but academics will ever read. I know a lot about dreams, and shamanism among the Inuit. Does that strike you as a way of earning a living?'

'I thought—' She realised she hadn't thought at all. 'Then what do you do?' she asked.

'No one in the Herringe family has needed to work since the Industrial Revolution. We're a bit like royalty: we spend three years at Oxbridge, take second-class degrees in useless subjects, and the ambitious ones get a job in the firm.' He shook his head. 'The really ambitious ones end up running it. I wasn't one of those. I collect a cheque every six months from a trust fund set up when I was born.'

Anna hated the bitter defensiveness of this. 'You make yourself sound like some sort of dosser!' she said. 'But you got a doctorate, not a second-class degree, and you held down a demanding job for years. Since then you've been working on a project you love. You've been all over the world. Why are you making yourself sound so feeble?'

'That's not the point.'

'I begin to think it is,' said Anna. 'All you do is denigrate yourself. I've got no patience with it. Other people would be proud of what they've achieved. Anyway, I don't see what that has to do with Stella.'

'Stella administers my trust.'

'So?'

'I've known her since I was twelve years old,' he said, after a pause. 'Nonesuch had already come down to her. She was in her early twenties then. So hungry, so determined, so flawed and fragile underneath it all! No one in the family could deny her anything.' He examined these statements as if, like the house itself, they had complex internal architecture – as if, in saying one thing, he was really struggling to articulate another. 'She filled that place like a light. She always got what she wanted. She still expects that, especially from me. She's demanding, but she has no real underlying strength. That makes her difficult to deal with. Do you understand?'

'I don't know what you're talking about.'

He shrugged. 'Perhaps I don't, either,' he said bleakly. 'There are various ways she can limit my income, that's all.'

'But I can't see why she should want to!'

He looked away. 'She's easily made jealous,' he said.

'Of me? Oh, I don't believe I'm hearing this!'

'Anna—'

'Family money. Sibling rivalry. It's a bad historical novel, John. I'm not going to be drawn into this.'

'It doesn't have to make any difference to us.'

'It already has,' said Anna quietly.

After that there didn't seem to be a great deal to add. John Dawe looked angrily away into the distance. Anna, miserable, confused and unable to assimilate these changes to her view of him, simply went back to examining the Herringe graves. Presently she said: 'They all lived a very long time, your ancestors.'

He glanced with hatred at the leaning stones. 'Only the women,' he said. 'The women always outlive the poor bloody men.'

She looked up at him. 'All these resentments, John. You should stop blaming Stella for your life.'

'If you knew—'

'I'm going now. I'll call you.'

He stood by the family plot and let her walk away.

Fifteen

AFTER THE embarrassing fiasco on the wild roads of the common, I found that I was no longer an accepted member of the band of cats I had come to think of as my friends. When they saw me coming they would run off with great loping strides, tails high in the air like taunting question marks, just slowly enough for me to note that their avoidance was deliberate; just close enough that I could catch a word here and there of name-callings aimed only at me. 'Air-Catcher' they called me; 'Loony', and most hurtfully, 'Yellow Paws'.

So they had noticed, after all.

Ginge and Fernie appeared to have taken control of the gang, and in an insultingly short space of time had brought two newcomers into the group to replace me: a pair of grinning, brindled male kittens who had strayed much further from home than their owners would have liked. I was already stung by this rejection; but it was the sight of the two new members being initiated into the group's rough and tumble play-fights that finally confirmed for me my own exclusion.

For a while I tried to make new friends, but the other village cats had already formed their own cliques, all with their own nicknames and games and little territories, and had no wish to welcome a larger-than-usual ginger kitten with an odd smell to him. Indeed, word about me seemed to have got around: many cats made it clear with hisses and curses that my presence was not required. Lonely and miserable, I took to making long, solitary forays into the surrounding countryside.

I wandered far away from the area which I had explored as part of the gang: down into the wastelands at the bottom of long, rambling lawns where the tenuous cultivation of part-time gardeners had lost any grip on the land, and brambles and nettles and self-seeded saplings were forming a vanguard for the wildwoods beyond.

Down there, I watched the summer come and go. Down there, where the air was cool and the tangle of undergrowth was alive with the scent of prey, I danced and hunted; and dozens of voles and mice succumbed to my pent-up fury. I crunched my way through them, bone and sinew, with grim determination, but I never took them home. They were my private vice; my own small triumph over the world.

On a mixed diet of wild prey and tinned food, I grew quickly. Already a strong cat, my daily journeys and hunting exploits made me firm and flexible and turned kitten-fat to lithe muscle. My head became lean and my profile striking. Looking at me in the light of early morning, Dellifer often commented on how I was coming to resemble the young Hawkweed. I could not imagine how this could be. Almost, I was affronted.

But I was not just developing in physical ways. I had begun to learn about the world: for it is quite one thing to be shown the world and its secrets by someone else, another entirely to discover them for yourself. As a result of my wanderings I saw things no other cat of my age had noticed: how skylarks rose into the air at dawn from the cornfields below the escarpment; how they hung invisible against the sky, borne up by the power of their song.

As the mists cleared in the mornings, allowing the pale sun to strike through, I saw how each single wet leaf had become a mirror which shone light back into the air, and I wondered at the complexities of the world.

On a day on which enough rain had fallen to bow the grass into a silvered sea, I looked back over my shoulder to see how my footprints marked a weaving trail from the byre at Glory Farm, out past the solitary sycamore where the crows gathered in its branches like wind-caught stripes of black plastic, to the stand of beeches on the crown of the hill.

I saw badgers in the ambiguous dawn light blundering along the side of the new dual carriageway, still confused by the bisection of their animal highway by this stinking, oily tarmac and the alien vehicles that hurtled along it. And all too often I came upon barely recognisable creatures ground to a mess of red meat and fur on the sides of the road; worse still, a cat I had once met in a farmyard some miles to the south of the village wandering vaguely around on the verge. It kept falling down then struggling up again, its legs trying to obey scrambled commands, only to collapse once more. Even from several yards away, I could tell that something was very wrong with the side of its head, and when I called out to it, it stared blankly at me for a moment, then pitched forward and lay still. When I sniffed at its face, I could tell there was no life left in it any more. I remembered how the two of us had once spent a companionable afternoon in the back of an abandoned haycart, watching the chickens pecking stupidly in the yard, before I had bidden it farewell and continued on my travels.

I shuddered and turned away, feeling at once elated at still being alive; and at the same time hollowed out, inadequate in the face of such pointless loss.

And through all this time, weaving their way in and out of the long nights, the dreams ran like the world's unconscious memory of itself, secret and vivid and visible only to me.

I often lay out in the long meadow grass and watched the streams of golden scintilla ghosting up into the dark air: tiny and frantic, the dreams of insects; slow and languorous, the dreams of sleeping earthworms.

I examined the dreams of ponies and dogs, saw in them how they kicked up their heels to run, unfettered and ownerless, across windy moors. I watched the dreams of domestic fowl; how the hens dreamt of the cockerel, and he of them; how garden birds dream-fought over nest-sites and bacon rinds; and it struck me how curious it was that we should all be bound together by the commonality of our dreams; humans and animals, birds and burrowing things, all dreaming together of mates and territory and food, the ordinary stuff of life.

Having come to this simple conclusion – a deep truth I believed it then – I thought that nothing in the world could surprise me; and that such simplicity of motivation could do no great harm, whatever my grandfather said. Mine was the arrogance of the young, blind and sure. I had a lot more to learn.

It was, I see now, this arrogance, this inability to make a deeper connection, that alienated me from my own kind. Turned away by my friends, the world turned me also away from myself, so that my thoughts fled away from me, streaming out into the deep pink sunrise, into the forms the rabbits left upon the dewy grass, the sound of rain falling deep in the woods.

Then one day, exploring the hinterland of the village to the north, I threaded my way through stands of soft wet bracken and tall grasses, and emerged on to the towpath that ran beside the canal.

I had heard a lot about this place, but for a long time had deliberately avoided the area for fear of running into Ginge or Fernie or another of the local cats. Now I realised with some surprise that I no longer cared whether I did or not: my kittenhood felt such a long way away that the events that had led to my exclusion seemed paltry and inconsequential to the cat I had now become.

Even so, I approached with some caution, sniffing the air. Milling scents marked the area as the territory of a number of vigorous tomcats. I stood there, alert in the sharp morning light, muscles braced for a swift departure if it became necessary, and stared out over the canal. The houseboats basked lazily in the still water, and the sun struck off their colourful paint and bright-work. Pansies bloomed in pots on the roof of one of the narrowboats; on another an unmanned fishing line dropped from the bow to an idle plastic float. Washing had been strung amongst the rigging of a third, but there was no breeze to stir the hanging shirts and jeans. Of the owners, those creatures neither of dry land nor water, there was no other sign. It was the most tranquil place I had ever seen.

I sat on the edge of the towpath, eyes half closed against the sunlight, and let the quietness wash over me. How long I stayed like this, I could not say: it could have been moments only; or an hour. This slow passage of time was interrupted by the steadily growing sensation of being watched. I felt the gaze that fell upon me like the weight of an insect on my fur; but when I looked around, I could see no one at all. I shifted position, craned my neck. Still no one.

I sat up, stretched each of my legs in an apparently uncon-cerned manner, and walked nonchalantly along the towpath, my neck bristling under the unseen onlooker's stare. When I reached the darkest of the moored houseboats, I stopped. There was a new scent in the air, a scent that made my nose twitch and my blood fizz. Puzzled, I stared around, but saw nothing but coiled ropes and shining metal, coloured railings, the shadowed deckhouse . . .

Slowly I looked up.

On top of the deckhouse, lying in a pose altogether contrived, yet wholly instinctive, was a tawny gold cat, a cat of maybe seven or eight months of age. She might be barely out of kittenhood, but any trace of kitten-fat had either vanished or had been subtly redistributed to imbue her slim figure with just a hint of seductive feminine roundness: softly, at the angle of jaw and cheek; here, at the shoulder; or *there*, a perfect curve of haunch. She licked her fur with the intentness of one at once aware of scrutiny, yet completely absorbed in her routine: it was as if the energy of her grooming consumed itself, only to generate itself once more as some powerful and mysterious magnetism that drew the eye and froze the limbs of any observer.

I was captivated. And when she lifted her head and focused on some point just beyond and to the left of me, the light fell full upon her features, and it seemed to me that her face was like a flower opening to the sun, and at the moment I felt I lost my heart entirely and irrevocably.

Her gaze shifted fractionally. She appraised me, her nostrils flaring briefly, then bent to lick with precise grace between the toes of her outstretched foot.

'I haven't seen you before,' she said after a few strokes, knowing that I was still rooted to the spot. Her voice was cool and low, the vowels softened by a discernible country burr.

She considered for a moment. 'But then again, it's entirely possible I just didn't notice you. After all, it's not as if you're much to look at.'

I was stung, I will admit. I wasn't used to dealing with beautiful little queens with sharp tongues. Flummoxed, I stared at my feet. My face burned with sudden disappointment.

When I looked up again I found that she was looking at me, head on one side, and a wicked little half-smile lurked beneath her whiskers. 'What's the matter, eh? Cat got your tongue?' She gave a little howl of laughter.

I felt as though someone had stuffed my brain with dandelion heads. I shook myself. 'You're very rude,' I observed.

'Mmmm, I find it saves time and effort.' She spread her claws and examined them minutely. 'There are so many idiots around, and they all seem to want to talk to *me*.'

'I don't regard myself as an idiot,' I said stiffly, my eyes fixed on her extraordinary face, 'though there are some who might disagree with me.'

'Do stop gawping.'

'Sorry.'

'And don't apologise – it's so irritating.'

I had no idea what to say: all avenues seemed closed to me. So, 'Don't you like anyone but yourself?' I pressed on, and found myself horrified at what had slipped from my mouth.

But all the vision did was to smile again, eyes averted: a smile that promised the disclosure of secrets. Then she said: 'Since I don't even know your name, I regard that as an impertinent question.'

'Orlando,' I said quickly.

'That's rather a smart name for such a foolish cat.'

'Look,' I said with sudden force, 'if you can't be friendly, why talk to me at all?'

'Ah, so you do have a bit of spirit. Tell me, *Orlando*,' – an involuntary shiver ran down my spine to hear my name enunciated to such sensual effect – 'what are you doing here, down by the canal?'

'Just exploring.'

'A bold explorer, are you?' She managed to look down at me through her eyelashes, a gesture I found most provocative.

'I think so.' I thought for a minute. 'I've walked the countryside around here for miles in all directions. I've seen some amazing sights.' I could see by the glaze that fell over those luminous tawny eyes that this line of discussion was failing to capture her imagination, so I added desperately: 'I've wandered the wild roads too.' For this, I was rewarded by a sudden spark of interest. She leaned forward.

'Do tell,' she purred.

So I told her of my experiences on the highways – how the icy winds blew constantly, howling away into the darkness; how the world outside could still be seen, dimly visible through shades of grey that whirled and flowed, shadows upon shadows, as I barrelled down the tunnels; how magic fuels entered me so that my spirit became that of a great cat, and I could run forever without exhaustion, powerful muscles bunching and stretching to eat away the ground.

I said nothing about the dreams.

All the while her eyes never left my face.

'I've probably travelled the wild roads more than any other cat in this region, other than old Hawkweed, that is,' I finished smugly.

At this, a shudder ran through her elegant frame. 'Hawkweed, you say?'

'My granfer.'

'The dreamcatcher?'

I nodded, then watched in dismay as she recoiled.

'And you go out on the wild roads with him?'

'I'm still learning—'

'Typical. The only cat worth talking to in this whole forsaken area and he turns out to be an apprentice dreamcatcher, that most raggle-taggle, untrustworthy and depraved of creatures.' And with this extraordinary pronouncement, she turned her back on me, laid her head down on her paws and closed her eyes.

I was nonplussed. The sun slipped behind a cloud, and the true temperature of the day abruptly made itself known. I felt its cold shadow fall across my heart. Looking up at the implacable back above me on the deckhouse, I implored: 'At least tell me your name.'

But the golden shape did not stir.

Sudden realisation dawned on me. 'It's Liddy, isn't it? You're the one Ginge talked about—'

At this, she turned around, regarded me over one slim shoulder. 'Actually,' she sniffed, 'my name's Lydia. Only the ignorant call me Liddy.'

I returned her gaze. 'Well,' I said, 'ignorant I may be, but there are many more who use that version of your name without the respect you seem to think you deserve.'

She looked at me as if I had suddenly begun to smell disgusting. 'How so?'

I composed my face to careful neutrality. 'I had heard, from a number of Ashmore cats, that a fine remedy for many ills is the sweet lick of a virgin's tongue.'

She wrinkled her brow in puzzlement.

'A very specific virgin.' I watched her closely. 'Liddy was the name they mentioned. Definitely.'

Her eyes went wide. Her mouth fell open. Then: 'How dare they – how dare *you*! Anyway, I'm not—'

Refusing to allow her the satisfaction of the last word, I stalked across the towpath, inserted myself into a gap in the bracken, and disappeared from view.

When I looked back, at a safe distance, and well hidden from view, I could see her staring after me, an unreadable expression on her face.

Half an hour later, in a clearing of willow on the edge of the common, my head was still buzzing from the encounter. My body sang to me. It was a most peculiar feeling. I felt more powerful, more alive, than I ever had on the highways, if less in control of myself than I would dare to be in those wild places. My blood danced and frothed in my head, full of messages I didn't want to hear. It whispered of gold and spice, of feverish delights and primal acts. What a beauty she was, it bubbled, and a challenge, too. Ah, Liddy, Liddy, Lydia . . .

Then again, I could not decide whether her rise to my barb had meant that she was a virgin or not. Was she a queen, or an untried princess pretending to be a queen? If so, why would she behave so? It was too confusing for an inexperienced lad like myself. The thoughts flew around my skull like trapped butterflies. I felt furious with myself for my pathetic efforts to impress her; furious at her for her imperious dismissal, her withering contempt.

Ah, yes, my blood whispered: *maybe she despises the dreamcatcher in you; but what does she truly know of the power of the wild roads? You should drag her there and let the great cat in you have its way . . .*

On they went, these thoughts, speaking to me of acts that

sought no permission, acts of violent satisfaction; but I swallowed them down like trapped dreams. They, too, left a bitter aftertaste.

That night, when the moon sailed high overhead, I found myself back on the towpath, as if my feet had walked me there entirely of their own accord. Standing at the water's edge, in the fringe of grass and rushes, I stared out at the planished surface of the canal. The houseboats sat upon the water like great birds with their heads under their wings. I walked along beside them until I came to the one I thought of as Lydia's. Its small windows were dark and lifeless.

Nothing stirred, or made a sound, except for the blood that ticked and boiled around my head.

I sniffed the air and caught the smell of caulked planking, stagnant water in the bilges, a faint trace of spices as from a dish of curry not completely eaten; humans, male and female; and – there! *Her* scent, rank and heady, an intact queen in her first flush of power. The scent filled my brain, flushed through it like some exotic substance, making me dizzy and stupid.

Lydia, Lydia: Liddy!

I stared into the darkness, overcome. She was there, though out of sight. At once I felt furious: with her arrogance, her teasing, the hauteur with which she had turned her back on me. My muscles twitched with intent, but even as I contemplated leaping on to the deck of the boat, it shifted slightly in the water, like a sleeper stirring. Ripples of water undulated between the hull and the bank. Timbers creaked softly, like a yawn in the wood. On the other side of the canal, the two swans who had created the wavelets sailed serenely past, white ghosts against the intense black of the water.

I watched them go, my head light, a heavy fire around my pelvis. Then I turned from the boat and, cocking my tail high into the air, sprayed the area around the mooring post with a copious stream of urine. This act gave me considerable satisfaction. It was as strong and true a jet as ever I had seen old Hawkweed produce. The grass broadcast the acrid scent so that it hung in the night air like a war pennant.

Orlando's mooring, it stated. *Orlando's houseboat*. And, by inference: *Orlando's queen*.

Moments later, my body started to shiver with apprehension. The fur that ran from the tuft on the crown of my head to the very tip of my tail was suddenly stiff and bristling; my spine itched.

For good reason.

Out of the shadows, from the bracken and the ferns and the long grass; from the decks and wheelhouses and galleys of the sleeping boats, came cats. There were perhaps a dozen of them, all different shapes and sizes: all different colours. A patchy black-and-white bruiser with half an ear missing, some non-descript tabbies and tortoiseshells, their markings camouflaging their outlines in the undependable light. One silver tabby, its coat a riot of furls and flames; another ginger cat like myself, only smaller and meaner-looking, its face as sharp as a door-wedge. They were a motley crowd, it was true, but what they had in common was the singularity of their focus: me.

And up on the deck of the nearest houseboat, Lydia: looking down upon us all with her paws and tail demurely folded together, and her pretty pink mouth quirking into a grin. Her nose twitched. Hopeless, avid males, the lot of us, we stared back, hearts skipping a beat, ready and willing to sacrifice ourselves to her favour. Her nonchalant gaze at last upon me; and then she winked. She might as well have dropped a flag for the commencement of battle.

Snarling, the big black-and-white with the tattered ear launched himself upon me. At such unnatural proximity I could see two of him: a nighmarish effect for a cat whose first serious fight this was. The play-fights of my youth and the lessons I had learned then dwindled to insignificance. Miraculously, other instincts took over. Without a second's conscious thought I found myself lying on my back, claws extended to rake and tear, and then the black-and-white was gone and a cloud of tabby fur was in my face and I was up and spitting, dancing high on my toes, my limbs filled with liquid fire.

After this, the battle became a blur. I remembered sinking my teeth into an opponent's shoulder, the howl of outrage and the twist of pain that accompanied this action. I recalled someone else's teeth meeting in the soft flesh of my ear: how I had rounded upon my attacker in a bloody mist and was rewarded by the glimpse of fear in another's green eyes, the fleeing brush of a white tail. At one point I saw ginger fur in front of my nose and for a moment was unsure whether this was some part of myself, adrift and oddly placed. Then the scent came to me: unfamiliar and hostile, and I bit down and was sharply gratified to hear a shriek of agony. Through it all a high-pitched howl wove about me, through my ears and round my skull and back out into the night air: a fierce, resistant war cry that spoke of determination and defiance, desire and frustration and raw red fury.

It was impossible to tell how long all this took. It felt to me as if time had been slowed down to a sticky slug-trail of events; but to an onlooker, the battle was no doubt over in moments, and cats who had been in the thick of the action, biting and scratching and yowling their heads off one second, were suddenly sitting calmly in ones and twos, licking their wounds with unhurried poise, or disappearing into the undergrowth, embarrassed at their lack of prowess, their sudden loss of nerve.

I sat in the middle of the scene, bleeding from a dozen different bites and cuts, but my head was high and my vision was clear. Swatches of multicoloured fur littered the ground. Some of it was probably mine. And as I thought this, a cold wave of loss swept over me. I had the feeling that I had somehow, in the midst of this fight, lost a part of myself.

Disorientated, I stared around, and indeed there it was – a forlorn tuft of ginger fur, pale against the ground, and the night air was cool against a patch of uncovered skin at the base of my neck. I felt a dull, aching sorrow for the loss of that small mouthful of fur: daily grooming had made me intimate with every square inch of my coat, and it was impossibly sad to think that bit would never be licked clean again. Had I examined this feeling more closely, I might have realised that it was not the tuft of fur I was mourning for at all, but something far more integral and interior.

I looked up then, and Liddy was watching me. There was a glint in her eye: of fear, elation or contempt? Then one eyelid closed again with deliberate languor. She stood up, turned around, and her tail rose into the air like a question mark. The last thing I saw was her tawny rump in all its glory disappearing down the galley steps.

No invitation could have been clearer.

With a single bound, I found myself on the deck, following her delicious scent into the belly of the boat.

Down there, it was warm and musty, alive with smells. But my nose was interested in only one: the enticing rapture of Lydia. It drew me as if I was attached to her by an invisible wire, a wire that penetrated my nostrils and ran, silver-white with heat, along my spine and into my erect penis. The tiny barbs on its exposed tip tingled in the pressing air.

At the far end of the boat, in the soft lighting of a single gimballed brass lamp, she stopped and looked over her shoulder at me, her golden eyes dark and clouded with lust. She growled softly, a husky rumble which thrummed in the spaces between my ribs. Dropping her front end, she waved her rear provocatively, and I could help myself no longer. With a growl of my own, I leapt upon her back, catching the thick skin at her neck between my teeth to stop myself slipping from her sheer and glossy coat.

Ah, the bliss of that moment. Even now I can return to it, perfect in every detail in mind's eye. I shall treasure it always. I may have to—

Two seconds later, a door in the galley opened and a tall, dark man walked out, rubbing his eyes.

Lydia tensed.

I, who until that second had been entirely intent on locating and penetrating the exact target of my desire, looked up.

Above and behind the man's head, and still attached to it by a thread, like a child's balloon on a string, caught by the low doorway and bobbing unsteadily in the dim light, was a dream. It was large and fiery gold, its edges tinged with a dark corona of red and black.

It spoke to me. Not in words, of course: but far more invasively. It spoke to me of violence and destruction. I recognised its type from my granfer's lectures: 'Watch out for those with an edge of fire to them,' he'd said. 'They're the ones that want to destroy: the ones born of terror and loathing.' If I were to let it go, I knew it would make at once for the highways, wild with all the images it contained, there to wreak terrible damage. If I let it go, a wild road might die, and with it every natural creature that used that right of way; more: a whole network of roads might be caught in its death throes, a whole village – my village – fall under its dark influence. I could not ignore it.

I felt as if I were being physically torn in two. My physical body, my heart, my cells, wanted, with primal, selfish desperation, to continue my congress with Liddy; but the dreamcatcher part of me, like a parasite in my brain, drove towards the strong dream.

Like a fool, I havered.

And then – as if the dreamcatcher in me had taken control of my limbs, and all else – I fell gracelessly from Lydia on to the wooden floor.

The dream trembled with the anticipation of the chase. It pressed itself through the doorway, and gaining the main body of the narrowboat, sailed free of its originator, up the stairs and out into the night.

With an apologetic glance back at Liddy, I turned tail.

The dream was easy to follow. Its fiery corona left a trail of afterimage in its wake, and the weight of its cargo kept its trajectory low and unstable.

It progressed up the towpath for a few hundred yards, then drifted over the canal, shedding light like some grotesque sun. I pounded after it. I crossed the canal at the little brick bridge, skidded down the steps on the other side, and followed the dream around a gorse thicket, through a haze of young birch, across a field of sleeping cattle, over a five-barred gate, down a long, pot-holed lane and eventually found myself confronted by a tall, dense yew hedge.

The dream, apparently unconcerned by my pursuit, wobbled over the top of the hedge and disappeared from view, rising as it went.

I ran leftwards, looking for an opening; but finding none, turned and ran in the opposite direction. Still nothing. I tried brute force on the yew, but the ancient hedge was having none of it and repelled me with ease. My heart pounded with frustration. First, to ruin my mating with Liddy; now this! I could not give up so easily: something vital, I felt, was at stake here, and not just my pride.

Redoubling my efforts I fled down the length of the hedge, finally coming upon a tall wrought-iron gate. A flick left, then right, and I was through the ornamental fretwork and standing amid a vast expanse of gravel, bordered by lawns and flowerbeds that stretched away as far as the eye could see. Far ahead, betrayed by a dull orange glow, I saw the dream float into the branches of a vast cedar, and lodge there, twisting uncomfortably.

I crossed the dewy glass, leaving a trail of silvery footprints. I came to the foot of the tree and stared up. I shuddered. I'd done a little tree-climbing in my time: a couple of small spruces with horizontal branches like ladders to their tops; the apple tree in the next-door garden in which a pair of nuthatches had made their nest; and once, for a bet, I and Ginge had made it halfway up the big oak tree by the church, both chickening out at exactly the same point. This cedar, in comparison, was a monster.

I walked around its great trunk a couple of times, staring up into sturdy black branches that started such a long way up the bole. The dream swayed in the top of the tree, as if struggling to escape. I sighed. I walked backwards, keeping my eye on the dream, shifted slightly sideways to get the best possible line, then ran at the trunk and leapt as high as I could, all four paws outstretched, toes spread wide, claws extended. The bark was thick and heavily striated: all my claws sank in and up I went. Almost sick with commitment, I reached the first branch. Already the ground was a long way below me. If I looked up (which seemed preferable to looking down) I could still make out the glow of the dream high above. I climbed for several minutes, slowly and steadily, refusing to think about the lethal distance I was opening out between myself and the ground, resting where I could on the spreading branches. At the height of about thirty feet, a sudden panic as to how I would get down again flitted across my mind and I seized upon the thought before it could grow larger, and chased it off into the dark, bony cavity of my skull where I kept such fears, refusing to examine it further.

At perhaps fifty feet, the dream came clearly into focus. It was still a long way above, almost as far again as I had already climbed, but I gritted my teeth and ascended stoically.

Some minutes later, I found myself at the junction between the trunk and the branch in which the dream was caught. Going up,

I soon found, was far easier, for all the stress it had placed on my muscles and sinews, than the precarious traverse I now had to make. Typically, the dream was lodged amongst the small twigs at the end of the branch, where it tapered to a fan of spiky blue-green foliage and a cluster of tightly furled cones. With obsessive care, I shuffled out towards it. The foliage danced and whispered.

The movement was all the dream had been waiting for. One moment it appeared trapped for all time; the next it had sailed free of its sylvan cage. Furious to see my prey escaping, I forgot where I was and leapt at it. I connected with the dream, sinking my teeth and front claws deep into its soft casing, and bit down. Warm, rancid juices trickled down my chin and lodged in the short, thick fur of my chest. A jumble of extraordinary images pressed themselves against me. For a second, I found myself engulfed in a tangle of human arms and legs, moans and sighs, heat and humidity and unfamiliar sexual organs; then my hind feet were scraping frantically for a foothold, and I was airborne.

My eyes popped open in horror. I stared around wildly, my vision obscured by the flickering corona of the dream. The tree was somehow *below* me. The dream was carrying me. I hung on harder, and the pressure thus exerted caused the contents of the globe to spew out, so that the dream jiggled wildly, lost upward momentum, and started to fall. From here, I found I had an incongruously clear view of the house and its grounds. There were formal flowerbeds and several ornamental trees, and as if hidden behind the towering old brick and timber structure, a complicated-looking arrangement of dark shrubs. To one side, a tennis court and some outhouses; the glint of moonlight off a car's roof. As we floated down closer to the house itself, I could make out, between the complex slopes of roofs and tall chimneys, what appeared to be an enclosed courtyard – a confusing place of shadow and metallic gleams, as if someone had piled dozens of cages there; then the dream shifted in my grip and all I could see was a pair of humans coupling, the woman astride a man tied to a bed with what looked to be cords made out of her own black hair. I blinked, confused, and the dream wriggled again, allowing me a sight of the skies above.

There, the moon gazed down, unperturbed by the drama going

on below. Silver-edged clouds drifted past that blank face, their passage unruffled and serene.

Great Cat, I thought suddenly. *Great Cat, whose silver eye sees all, help me now!*

I had never before been prompted to seek divine intervention; indeed, had considered all of Hawkweed's tales to be no more than moral entertainment for foolish kittens; but now I felt a desperate need to believe I might be saved.

The dream began to plummet. As it did so, the faces of the man and woman rushed out at me, lips fused together so that they appeared to form a single freakish entity. As one, they turned to regard me, their pupils dilated to gleaming black pits – with terror or passion or enmity at my intrusion? It was impossible to tell. I thought I recognised them, though the fiery corona distorted their colouring, throwing wild shadows across the plane of their faces. I bit down harder. The woman sighed and her lips came free of the man's. Her eyes locked upon mine and I felt a second of the purest fear; then, in a writhing arc she pushed past the tear in the dream's sac and boiled out into the air, dispersing in tiny pixillated bursts of light into the darkness.

As if it were the presence of the woman alone that had formed its ballast, the dream stopped its downward trajectory and began to float unsteadily, like a rudderless boat.

I took a moment to secure the claws of my hind feet upon the globe and looked down again with trepidation. I was perhaps ten or twelve feet above the ground: soft grass, an easy landing.

With grim determination, I sat my jaws to work once more upon the casing of the dream, and with a gush of foetid air it surrendered itself to me. We hit the ground together with a gentle thump. Secure upon the earth again, upon the saving body of the Great Cat! I could hardly believe my very great luck. With the momentous feeling that I owed the world something in return for my life, I resumed my task. I bit and swallowed. Even though the main image of the woman in the dream had escaped, there were still afterimages: the couple in a remarkable diversity of sexual positions, ripples of sensation and musky smells that reminded me of Liddy . . . I fought the thought away, and chewed grimly on until at last it was all gone.

I lay there after that, weak with exhaustion. Exhaustion gave way to despair and a nagging sense of futility. Why had I left Liddy to chase this particular globe? Served up bliss on a tea plate and all I could so was to abandon it for the wilder temptation of a human dream! And then to risk my life so heedlessly, climbing to the top of the tallest tree I had ever seen, for no good reason. If the dream had stayed trapped there, it would surely have dissipated in time, of no danger to anyone and certainly too far from any wild road to wreak any of the havoc I had sensed in it. I shook my head sadly.

Liddy was right: I was the most untrustworthy and depraved of creatures.

It was a sad, drained Orlando who pressed himself through the cat-flap at Anna's cottage much later that night. I dragged myself across the kitchen to my food bowl and stared at it empty-eyed.

I was still standing there, head down, dog-tired, some minutes later when my sister came trotting down the corridor. Seeing me, she stopped dead, nose twitching at the stew of rank pheromones in the air. She started to hiss. I stared at her, bewildered.

'It's only me, Vita,' I said softly.

Vita bared her teeth at me. 'You smell,' she declared.

Then she turned and fled upstairs.

Sixteen

For the next few days, I stalked around the cottage and the gardens, tail lashing, a permanent half-growl rumbling quietly at the base of my throat. I felt at odds with myself and everyone else. I had gained access to another world, a place where all I had ever wanted would deliver itself up to me with a purr and a wave of musky scent; and had stupidly turned my back on it and run away. I knew I could never find my way back.

For this reason, I avoided even thinking about Lydia. I avoided the canal. I avoided Hawkweed and the highways.

Dellifer and Vita avoided me.

'You live your own funny little lives,' Anna said to Dellifer, 'don't you? You cats?'

Dellifer purred contentedly.

'What do you think about, all day long?'

It was Saturday night: comfort night. Orlando was out. These days, in fact, he was rarely in. His whole demeanour was that of a cat with important business. He rushed about. He rushed his meals. 'But we don't care about him,' Anna said. 'Do we, girls? Because we've got comfort night.' She had fetched fish and chips for an early supper, and now, while Vita dozed contentedly in the kitchen, waking occasionally to lick the ghost of grease off her paws, Anna and Dellifer were sitting on the sofa in Anna's tiny front room, watching *Casualty* on the television. Anna sighed happily. She had beside her a cup of mocha which she had made half-and-half with drinking chocolate; and a moment ago one of the more competitive of the young doctors had been rushed into his own emergency room with a suspected rupture of the spleen after an ill-considered rock-climbing weekend. What more could you ask? Dellifer yawned, and rearranged her long, scrawny body on the sofa so that her head rested on Anna's forearm.

Suddenly she raised her head.

A moment later, Anna did too.

'What's that awful smell?' she said: 'Orlando!'

She phoned Stella Herringe.

'He's done it everywhere,' Anna said, 'and I've got no idea how to clean it off.'

Stella laughed. 'My dear, he *is* a tom,' she said. 'If you don't want a smelly house, you'll have to have him snipped. How old is he?' and when Anna told her, 'Well, he's a little early, but there it is. You can get it done in Drychester,' – here, she gave a strange laugh – 'but it's so straightforward you could probably do it yourself.'

Anna discounted this bizarre possibility. 'I suppose I'll have to have them both done,' she said.

There was a silence, then the click of a cigarette lighter. Stella inhaled and said in the same breath: 'Oh no, dear.'

'But—'

'Has she come on yet?'

'I don't know. I'm not sure what to look for.'

'You'd know,' said Stella. Another laugh. 'Well, look, think about it. It would be such a waste. She'll just make the most wonderful kittens.' Then, before Anna could object that she had enough kittens in the cottage already: 'And I'll take them all off your hands at six weeks. Earlier if you like. How's that for an offer?' She blew smoke into the receiver at her end. Anna could almost smell it. 'Or you can bring her up here and I'll organise the whole thing. But do have the little boy done, because we don't want him as the father.'

Anna barely considered this. 'It would be hard to split them up now,' she said. 'They're so used to each other.' To soften her refusal, she added: 'I'll have to think about it.'

'You do that, dear,' said Stella. 'But let's not have an accident.' She left rather a long silence, and then to Anna's surprise said in a more hesitant tone, 'Have you seen that awful cousin of mine this week? Or is he off at some symposium on the spirituality of Eskimo Nell?'

'Do you know,' lied Anna, 'I'm not sure.'

'Not sure if you've seen him, or not sure where he is?'

Anna laughed uncomfortably.

'Never mind,' said Stella. 'Look, I thought I'd have a supper party a week on Friday, and of course you're invited if you want to come. Hello? Now's the time to say, *How nice, I'd love to, dear.*'

'Sorry?' said Anna. 'Oh, of course I'll come. Thank you.'

'Good. Eight for eight-thirty. And, dear? If you talk to John before I do, tell him I'd love it if he could be there too. Will you tell him?'

'I will. Of course I will.'

The phone went down at Stella's end.

Anna stood with the handset to her ear for some seconds. She thought: I'm not sitting in night after night watching TV with my cats. I'm not. For the first time since their disagreement in the churchyard, she dialled John Dawe's number.

'Can we be friends again?'

'My God, I thought you'd never ask.'

Emptying out with relief, her heart pounding, Anna said carefully, 'I'm working quite hard at the moment, but if you like, we could meet at Stella's dinner party next Friday,' and waited to see how he would answer.

☯

Anna seemed to be upset that I had sprayed inside the cottage. She chased me out of the kitchen door, flapping her hands and shouting at me, by which I understood my presence was not welcome inside the house. I went and sulked, holed up on the dark, dry earth under the bay tree. I dozed. I slept. Every time I felt a dream brush soft as feathers against my mind, I woke and shook it away. Later, with the moon shining through the fragrant leaves above me, Anna came out and called my name. She stood there on the step, the golden light behind her making a halo of her hair, and stared uncertainly into the darkness. In one hand she held a dish which she rang repeatedly with a spoon – clearly, I noted with suppressed fury, to signal my suppertime. This went on for some minutes, while I wrestled with greed and an inchoate desire for revenge, until eventually with a sigh she turned and went back inside.

Unseen, in the depths of my refuge, I glared with ferocious satisfaction at her retreating form. It felt like a victory of sorts, until I heard the unmistakable sound of the cat-flap being locked.

Shortly after that I realised I was starving.

Later, at the Green Man, Anna told Alice: 'He didn't know.'

'So?'

'It means he really hasn't been there. He hasn't seen her since I shouted at him.'

'I don't know why you're so happy.'

Anna emptied her glass. 'Yes you do,' she said. She went over to the jukebox, put coins in, and pored over the menu. She knew what she was looking for.

'You're jealous of her,' called Alice from the bar. 'I know that.'

Anna thought of John Dawe the first time she had seen him, in his grey Levis and black cotton sweater, insisting, 'No one ever owns a cat;' then on the *Magpie*, grimly searing tuna, shaking oil and vinegar for salad dressing; finally in the graveyard, admitting his dependence on the Herringe money. She thought of Stella, whose voice had been edged with such an unaccustomed anxiety when she said, 'If you talk to John before I do—' She thought of herself on the phone, lying to Stella, lying to John. The not-so-small dishonesties of love. She grinned at Alice over her shoulder.

'That too,' she admitted.

A group of regulars, pushing open the door of the Green Man a few minutes later, found her dancing dreamily away in the middle of the floor, to the old Rolling Stones track John Dawe had selected that strange rainy night with Stella in the bar. As she danced, Anna was thinking, he ignored her easily enough then. She was thinking, why should the Herringes have him, them and their money? I can make money, too. She was thinking, he'll clean up very nicely if I can just get his self-confidence back.

'You made the house smell!' Vita declared gleefully when Anna finally let me in for my breakfast. 'I ate your supper.'

Of course, it was not long before I was drawn back to the canal. How could I have thought I could keep away? My love – my lust – for Lydia called me.

The narrowboat cats regarded me warily. I recognised most of them as the opponents I had tangled with on that fateful night; indeed, some of them still looked a bit the worse for wear. One or two hissed their hostility and danced sideways on their toes to demonstrate that they were ready for a second bout, should it so please me. But when I failed to rise to the challenge, staring back at them blankly with the sun shining off my slitted eyes, they soon cheerfully ignored me, and sloped off to sit around in tight little huddles licking their fur and laughing quietly, I suspected, at my expense. Any threat I might have posed to the social order had obviously dissipated; I wondered, even, whether the delightful Liddy had shared with them the shameful circumstances of my precipitous departure.

Of that little queen, however, there was no sign.

I sat there, quite still, for several hours. The sun sailed overhead, bright and impassive, slipped once or twice behind high clouds, and began to drop towards the horizon. Chilly shadows chased one another across the surface of the canal, and still nothing stirred. Eventually, I settled down with my head on my paws, and waited for night to fall.

I may have dozed: for when a voice disturbed my rest, it was full night. It was a female voice, yet it seemed to be coming from behind me. I was disorientated. The narrowboat, and its occupants, lay dark and quiet in front of my nose. I started up and looked around.

Only to find a long-legged tabby-and-white cat regarding me with her head on one side and a strange half-smile on her face. She had a small silver hoop in one ear, and a spiky crest of fur on her head, rather like that of a jay.

'I said, you should give it up.'

I stared at her. 'Pardon?'

'I said you should give it up. Call it a day. It's stupid, waiting around for hours and hours for Miss Lydia just to have her wrinkle up her little pink nose at you. She is,' – the tabby-and-white paused, searching for the right expression – 'a prize coquette.'

Then she winked at me. The white patch that looped across the left-hand side of her face became a perfect snowy disc. She was without doubt the oddest-looking cat I had ever seen.

'A what?'

'A coquette, a vamp, a philandress.'

I was none the wiser.

The tabby-and-white sighed. 'Honey, she's a tart.'

I demurred, but the odd-looking cat carried on, impervious.

'She is – how can I put this? – anybody's.'

I have to admit I was shocked.

'Whereas some of us,' she considered, 'are extremely choosy.'

'You don't seem like the other cats around here,' I said at last.

'I know. I'm not from round here.' A broad grin spread across the patched face. She rolled her eyes, 'Thank the stars.'

I regarded her with a frown. 'You're not very polite.'

The tabby-and-white cat threw back her head and laughed, a generous sound that echoed off the moored boats. The silver ring jounced merrily in her ear. 'Polite? What's polite? It's just something for those with nothing better to do. Polite is for cats who care what others think. Me, I don't give a damn.' She cocked her head. 'You know, for a dreamcatcher, you are a bit of a fool.'

For a moment, I was deeply affronted. Then I said, 'If I am a fool, then you are a freak.'

Her eyes gleamed dangerously. 'A freak? What do you mean?'

I nodded towards her earring. 'To mutilate yourself like that.'

She laughed, rather bitterly. 'You think I have done this to *myself*? Then you really are a fool. A man thought he owned me once and he did this to me to prove it to himself. I left, of course. No human can own a cat. My mother taught me that: no one ever owned her.'

An edgy silence developed between us as I thought about this. Then something else occurred to me: 'How do you know I'm a dreamcatcher?'

The long-legged cat shrugged. 'My dear, if anyone knows anything round here, everyone knows it. To be a dreamcatcher, well—'

'I know.' I hung my head. 'It's not my fault, though,' I rushed on. 'It was my granfer made me eat that stuff, and now I seem to be stuck with it. Look at my paws . . .'

She bent to sniff at the yellow-stained fur around my toes, and a strange look came into her eye. She had very shiny eyes, I noticed suddenly; shiny and rather wicked.

'Ah. Hawkweed.'

I stared at her. Did she mean my grandfather or the little yellow flower? 'What?'

She laughed at me. 'You act as if you're ashamed of it. Where I come from dreamcatchers are like royalty: all the girls want them. A dreamcatcher's family always know when trouble's coming, that's what my mother said. And she should know: she mated with one.'

'Your father's a dreamcatcher?'

'Sure. One of the best. Or he was.'

'What happened to him?'

She avoided my gaze, bending her head round to tease goose-grass out of her haunch. The movement of her tongue made the spiky crest rise and fall like some kind of warning signal. When she raised her head again, her eyes were distant.

'He disappeared one day: out the door one night on his usual rounds, and never came back. There's more to it than that, but it's not something I talk about, especially with someone whose name I don't know.'

'Orlando,' I said quickly and immediately pressed on: 'Did he disappear on the wild roads?'

The strange cat surveyed me coolly. Then she shrugged. 'Who knows? To be sure, it is none of your concern. You are a very determined cat: really, quite pushy.' Then, seeing my uncertainty, her eyes lost their topaz glint and she grinned. 'My name is Millie. Short for Millefleur, which means yarrow, or something in French. My mother liked to give the impression that she travelled a bit, you see. She didn't, of course, but you can't catch a dreamcatcher by being dull. It is nice to meet you.'

She extended a paw in mock-elegant manner, then changed her mind and affectionately head-butted me instead.

'Do you want to come dreamcatching with me?' I asked suddenly. It was the first thing that came into my head; I still don't know why I asked her, or why I should have forgotten my mission so easily.

Millie smiled delightedly. 'I can't see the dreams, even if I eat the weed,' she admitted. 'They say it skips a generation, you know, the gift.' A roguish light came into her eye. 'But I love to hear about the dreams. Humans, they're so bizarre!'

Being on the highways on my own had been a tense adventure, one that made my heart hammer in my ears. Being on the wild roads with Hawkweed was more like being on trial, as if the old cat were in league with the highways and had brought me there as to some ancient testing ground, where the compass winds would probe with icy fingers beneath my new wild fur to root out the essence of my character, to examine the tenacity of every moral fibre.

Being on the highways with Millie was a whole other experience.

As we entered my favourite wild road, the one that led off the old footpath running past the Green Man, I watched her caper in delight as her wild form came upon her. Silver and black bars wrapped themselves around her fur; from her ears great tufts sprouted like shoots of spring barley; her paws grew to the size of lily pads; and her body was one great smooth coiled muscle. On the highways, Millie was quite a different proposition to the odd little cat I had met upon the towpath. She saw me watching her and a huge fanged smile split the grizzled mask. Reflections of golden dreams danced in her eyes, so strange that none but I could see them.

'Well, what are you waiting for?' she rumbled. 'Catch me some dreams.'

So I leapt and pounced and leapt again. Up I soared, into the roof of the highway, paws splayed and talons spread. A dream fled past to my left, and at once I was upon it, worrying it like a mouse before flipping it up into the air again. The golden globe wobbled and fell, straight back into my waiting maw. I landed on my hind legs and at once sprang back into the air. I landed on all fours, two dreams pinioned beneath my front paws. I pirouetted; I spun like a dervish. On and on I hunted: a twisting leap here; a killing blow there.

Dream after shining dream succumbed to my lethal jaws and spilled their sticky juices down my ruff. The air was rank with the smell of them, hot with the energy generated by a dreamcatcher's dance of life.

One by one their golden lights failed and died, until at last the road was dark and empty once more. Empty except for an apprentice dreamcatcher and the rumbling purr of my new friend, the lynx.

'Now we will go back into the tame world and you can tell me about the dreams of the people of Ashmore,' it said. 'And when you have done that, I will reward you.'

The purr of the lynx reverberated through the highway like a force of nature. And then, quite abruptly, it stopped, and where there had been the most powerfully companionable noise in the world, now there was a complete absence of sound, as if I had been sucked into a vacuum.

I looked around. I was alone. Confused, my head full of other people's imagery, I gazed into the darkness, just in time to see the flick of a bob-tail disappearing through the wall of the wild road.

Outside, the stars were scattered all over the sky as if someone had thrown them down in haste. There was a distinct chill in the air.

Millie, her wild self now only a memory, a shimmer echoing down the length of the highways, was stretched out in a patch of wild poppies, paying meticulous attention to a long, slim, extended leg. Where her barbed tongue tracked through the fur, it gave back a silvery sheen to the stars, and with each stroke the silken flowerheads nodded their approval. There is a little in life so reassuring as grooming. For a cat who has just slipped out of the adrenalised haze of the wild roads back into the cold, still exposure of the mundane world, where the vast, remote dark sky wheels overhead and perspectives are surreal and untrustworthy, the warm, rhythmic rasp of tongue over fur and muscle is a gentle reaffirmation of self: the persistent re-creation of identity.

For me, watching Millie's head bob and draw, bob and draw, it was like watching the Great Cat Herself steadily licking the world back into shape. With each stroke I felt my heart slow, my pulse gentle; I felt the dancing dream-images in my head coalesce to harlequin patterns of pastel light.

She looked up. 'So, now, my little dreamcatcher,' she said. 'Tell me what you saw.'

And so I settled myself beside her and recounted what I could recall of the dreams I had eaten, without pause to make any sense or order of it all. I told her of curious figures and sequences; of running, and screams; how the light fell on the skin of an orange; how mould spread like a wave across a woman's skin; how an empty boat rocked gently in a lake of pale liquid gold; I remembered bare brown skin and a shining dark eye, very close up. How, seen through a small window, a dove rose vertically into blue air by a church spire, the bright sun turning its feathers to brilliant white and, circling, how it disappeared from view, only to re-enter the windowframe on the other side, a bird black with shadow. Of corridors lined with hundreds of doors, all closed. Of glowing embers and a broken violin. And made her laugh when I told her of a woman I had seen in her dream, a woman whose eyes were the most extraordinary green, her hair as black as a crow. She was watching her reflection in a mirror as her head became the head of a cat.

'She should be so lucky.'

'In her dream, she felt she was.'

'Transformation is magical,' Millie said simply.

I stared at her, surprised by the sudden gravity of the conversation.

She smiled. 'Everyone likes to be more than they are. That's why I love to be on the highways. That sense of greatness, all that power and potential.' She flexed her paws so that her claws popped, sharp and glinting, out into the moonlight. 'On the highways, Orlando, you are a lion. Did you know?'

Now it was my turn to smile. 'And you, Millie: you are a lynx.'

'A lynx is good,' she considered. 'Did you know that hundreds of years ago humans believed that a lynx could see through walls?'

I snorted. 'A cat on a highway can walk through walls. That's no big trick.'

'And they believed that its urine crystallised into precious stones!'

'Now you're making things up—'

Millie started to laugh. 'People are mad, Orlando: quite mad! They used to think that squeezing the juice out of a civet cat's arse made them smell good! Can you imagine?'

'Never!' I scoffed.

'It's true!'

She rolled on her back and wriggled in delight. The starlight glimmered on the silver ring in her ear and made crescent moons of her eyes. Then all of a sudden she became still and her bellyfur glowed submissively white against the dark ground.

'You were a lion when you fought the narrowboat cats, too,' she said, and her voice was as low as a bumblebee's drone. 'I watched you beat them all, one by one by one.'

The long, long legs parted minutely, in a gesture both vulnerable and lascivious. A warm pheromonal musk filled the air.

My mind went blank.

'Don't need to fight anyone for me, honey,' she said softly, a light purr trilling at the back of her throat.

In the distance a cricket chirred and a night-bird sang, and my blood beat faster. It would be so easy to fall upon this willing female, to roll her roughly over and bite the thick skin at the back of that long unfamiliar neck and to lower myself into her receptive warmth. Too easy. And far too difficult.

All I could see in my mind's eye was a tawny cat, gold to the bone, angular of face and slim of shoulder, beckoning me into the depths of her boat.

'I can't, Millie,' I gasped. 'I just can't.' I leapt to my feet as if scalded. I could not bring myself to look at her. 'I'm sorry. Really, I am.'

And with that I turned and ran.

Millie rolled on to her side and watched the young marmalade cat go, and the jaunty piebald mask she wore to encounter the world fell away to reveal a face both bleak and inexpressibly forlorn.

Seventeen

So that she wouldn't be tempted to go to London to panic-buy clothes she couldn't afford and didn't really need, Anna left all her decisions until Friday afternoon. This strategy of delay becalmed her in front of the bedroom mirror two hours before she was due at Nonesuch, with most of the contents of her wardrobe on the floor around her feet. She was not so naïve as to assume that frock-anxiety signified only itself: beneath it lay a reluctance to go to the party at all. Despite her efforts, the complexities of her relationship with John had somehow spread to include his cousin: knowing what she knew about *their* relationship, she found herself suddenly reluctant to meet Stella.

There was more. A kind of shyness lay between her and John. From the beginning, part of their antagonism had been sexual, an oblique acknowledgement of the physical tension between them. They had been like two rather dangerous animals, puzzledly trying to defuse one another's defences sufficiently to mate. Every touch of his startled her. She knew he was startled too. His eyes widened when he saw her, he couldn't hide that. The kiss in the lane had eased nothing – indeed it had probably been the kiss, rather than the meeting with Stella, which had caused their latest quarrel. Since then she had been having a disturbingly recurrent fantasy in which – at the turn of some darkened corridor of his cousin's house, his eyes intent yet wary – John Dawe reached out to explore the hollow of her collarbone, then ran his long, strong fingers lightly downward.

When she wasn't worrying about what to wear, she was wondering what she would say to Stella. When she wasn't worrying about Stella, small thrills of sexual anticipation were chasing themselves across the surface of her skin. She shook them away.

'Don't be so ridiculous,' she advised herself. 'It's only a dinner party.'

She pulled out a jacket of brown and grey velvet. Bought at fantastic cost from Voyage on the Old Brompton Road, at the height of her career with TransCorp, it would save the day, as it always had. It was her favourite garment. But at some point when they were younger Orlando and Vita had found it, and, deciding that they loved it too, covered it in fine tabby and orange cat-hair. She threw it on the bed in despair.

'I should have donated you both to Stella,' she said out loud. 'It would serve you right.'

In the end she decided on a long, strappy black dress from Whistles, plainly but nicely cut. It would be the first time she had worn it in two years. A side-slit revealed rather more leg than she had remembered, but as soon as she saw herself in it, she knew. A more confident Anna Prescott emerged to stand before the mirror. Her face, long and oval, finely featured with its strong eyebrows and steady brown eyes, gazed solemnly back at her. 'Not bad.' She twisted her hair up and pinned it casually so that tendrils fell to her pale shoulders. 'Not bad at all.' Suddenly she was grinning and twirling, imaginary glass of champagne in hand, taped viol music echoing softly off Jacobean walls, and a silent dark man watching her every move as if she were the centre of his universe.

She looked at her watch. Seven thirty, and the light was going out of the air. She had half an hour in which to bathe, put on her make-up and get into the local taxi, driven tonight by an old boyfriend of Alice's who chain-smoked and drove rather too fast, his free arm resting across the back of the front passenger seat.

'Wow,' he said, looking at her legs. 'Party at the Big House, is it?'

Anna nodded.

'Nasty old night,' he said.

It was a nasty old night. A few stars hung above the afterglow, smudged by flying streamers of cloud. A black westerly was bringing ripe horse chestnuts down from the trees in such numbers that they bounced off the bonnet of the Ford like small munitions. '"Wild west wind"!' quoted Anna to herself, wondering what the evening held for her. At Nonesuch, the cedars shook themselves like great slow animals; rain fell suddenly, blackening the soft stone of the gateposts, disfiguring the Herringe arms as the taxi passed beneath.

'We're in for it now,' predicted the driver as he pulled up by the lighted porch. Anna, handing him three pounds, said: '"Thou breath of Autumn's being."'

'You what?'

'Could you come back for me about midnight?'

'Pumpkin time, eh?'

Anna grinned.

The heavy, iron-bossed front doors hung open, surfaces limned with gold light. There were complex smells of food and wine: she felt her nose twitch like any cat's. The supper was being catered, by a firm from Drychester which usually did weddings. 'I'm damned if I'm going to cook, dear,' Stella had warned Anna. 'And you'd be damned if you ate it.'

Staff from the caterer's met Anna in the big hall and were quietly surprised by the Voyage jacket (quickly defurred with some Sellotape) which Anna had decided to wear anyway as cover-up over the sleeveless dress. She was surprised in her turn to be led not into Stella's little minimalist flat, but towards the centre of the house and into the Long Corridor instead. There, with Clara de Montfort staring down at her in cold amusement from the row of ancestral portraits, Anna protested: 'Is this right? This can't be right.'

But it was. They were going to eat in the Painted Room. She walked in, feeling less sure of herself than she had, and there was John Dawe, waiting for her, dressed in a loosely tailored black suit and a mid-grey shirt. Something gave her the idea that he had spent an afternoon similar to her own – putting on a tie, perhaps, then discarding it. Putting it on again, with a different shirt. She went up to him straight away and said: 'You look nice.'

'You look nice, too.'

'Shame about the boots.'

He looked down at his Bluntstones. 'They give the game away,' he admitted. 'But I did polish them.'

He offered her a glass of wine. She took it, and held it in her hand. Puzzled and impressed by one another's best clothes, unsure how to progress further, they stared around the Painted Room, lit by a myriad of church candles, as if neither of them had seen it before.

'I hate that mural,' Anna said, eyeing the trompe l'oeil, with its counterfeit window frame and flatly painted view of the original cobbled courtyard. The light in it seemed to have changed since she first saw it, so that the gables on the far side of the courtyard were grey and diffuse, the intervening air smeared with rain. 'Don't you? Especially since they've hidden the real courtyard behind it. Why would you do that? Brick up a lovely old Elizabethan window and then paint a false one over it? How could anyone have mistaken that for the real thing?'

'I don't think that was the point,' John Dawe said gently.

'Well it isn't clever,' Anna heard herself insist. 'I think the Herringe ancestors were just intellectual snobs. And that! Is that supposed to be a person there, in the arcade? It's just such bad drawing!' She stared into her wine. Her voice seemed quieter to her than its own echo, which went about hollowly up there among the roof beams. That, she thought, is what you get for avoiding the issue. She lifted her chin, looked him in the eye. 'I don't care how you live,' she said, more definitely than she had intended. 'The other day – I was wrong to have an opinion.' And then, just so he couldn't miss the point: 'How you live is up to you.'

John Dawe studied this abrupt apology as if uncertain how best to acknowledge it. Then he smiled. 'I don't care how you live, either,' he said.

Anna gave him a cross look. 'That's very generous of you, I'm sure.'

They were saved from further confrontation by the arrival of Stella Herringe, who came in through the door smoking a long, dark cigarette, and turning to call back down the corridor to her third guest of the evening.

'Anthony Downing! Of all people,' she was saying, in her most mischievous voice. 'But so typical of him!'

If Stella had spent the afternoon in a dialogue with the mirror, it didn't show. She had chosen a one-sleeved evening gown in pewter lamé. With her black hair in an elaborate French pleat to lengthen her pretty neck and Manolo Blahnik kitten heels to give her an inch or two on Anna, she looked like a single, perfect flower in a narrow vase. It was, perhaps, a little too cold, too studied: then you saw her bare shoulder, round, inviting, smooth as butter. She gave her attention to the Painted Room, as if she, too, had never seen it before, the trompe l'oeil courtyard full of a watery light of its own, the candles, the long Jacobean table with its gleaming cutlery and snowy napery.

'But here they are!' she marvelled over John and Anna, as if some puzzle had solved itself. 'They're already here!'

The third guest stepped into the room.

Flickering candlelight played off longish, untidy blond hair, a long, mobile face split by an enormous grin.

It was Max Wishart.

'Anna—' He crossed the room in two bounds, wrapped his arms around her so that she was crushed against the white linen of his dress shirt. Her wine glass tilted: wine slopped uselessly on to the wooden floor. His smell, which she had forbidden herself to remember, surrounded her like the climate of another country. It made her feel raw and new, transplanted, responsive to pain. Her life in Ashmore, so carefully fostered to protect her from her own emotions, had peeled away like the scab from a wound. Her defences had not held up.

He was holding her at arm's length and regarding her with an expression both delighted and bemused. 'Anna. Anna Prescott. Here, of all places! How in the world are you?' Simultaneously, in quite a different room, he was holding her in the same way to say goodbye. Trapped on the vertiginous contour between these two events, Anna found herself unable to think, unable to speak. Everyone else in the room must have seen this, she thought. She felt caught out: on view. She felt shamed in some way. This moment had lain in wait for her all along. Somehow Stella Herringe had sought it out and ambushed her from inside it.

'Max. Max Wishart.'

Her own voice sounded flat and false to her. She disengaged herself from him awkwardly, feeling the weight of John's gaze upon the two of them. The beat of her heart was painful. It was so terribly unfair.

'Fine,' she lied. 'Nice to see you.'

Max looked puzzled.

John Dawe looked puzzled.

'Now we must all sit down!' said Stella Herringe, who didn't look puzzled at all.

It was like being forced to open the shoebox of things you put away after every finished relationship – the matchbooks, cinema tickets and blanched photobooth snaps – only to find that while your feelings were no clearer, they had become just a little faded, just a little remote. Max stood there and the connection was instant. He stood there, and he was a million miles away. He had just got off the plane from New York – where he had been on a 'bread and butter tour', as he put it, 'playing second violin to a flautist whose name I'm too embarrassed to mention' – and was clearly surprised to find himself here at such short notice. He looked down at Stella, who only smiled and murmured, 'I was so glad you could come!'

He seemed thinner than he had the last time Anna had seen him. Perhaps he had been working too hard. Otherwise, he was Max – tall, smiling, generous with his intelligence and wit, clever but never superficial, murderer of hearts and cats, everyone's favourite dinner guest.

Dinner was a strange affair. The wavering light from the church candles glittered confusedly off an assortment of Victorian glasses and Jacobean silverware but failed to illuminate the catering staff, who moved about the dim room beyond like ghosts, coming and going suddenly and without apparent reason. Stuffed quails came and went, followed by champagne granités and a rack of lamb, trussed like a victim and accompanied by so many cleverly presented vegetables that Anna felt quite without appetite in their presence. 'Have some of the parsnips juliennes,' Stella urged her, ladling a spoonful of the glistening strips on to the huge, ornate dinnerplate. The food lay there, mythic in dimension, never diminishing despite her best efforts, which were, she had to admit, pathetic in the extreme.

'I'm sorry,' she heard herself saying. 'I'm just not very hungry tonight.'

Stella, laughing, speared the pinkly bleeding lamb from Anna's plate – 'too good to let it go to waste, dear' – and despatched it with fastidious gusto.

She had assembled her guests in a kind of pocket of time. They sat, the three of them, staring uncertainly at one another across the dazzling white tablecloth, trying to think of things to say; while Stella looked from one to the other with a small expectant smile on her face, and the history of Nonesuch seemed to revolve around them like a shadowy carousel.

'So, Max,' John Dawe said, 'you're in the music business.'

If his tone was a little sour, a little calculated, Max didn't seem to notice. The smile with which Anna had seen win him the attentions – wanted or unwanted – of so very many women, spread itself slowly across his face. The skin crinkled around the corners of his apparently guileless blue eyes.

'You might say that.'

Stella had seated them rather oddly, Anna thought. She had placed herself, reasonably enough, at the head of the long table; but rather than seat Anna and John to face one another across the shorter expanse, as you usually would with a couple, it was as if she had imposed a carefully premeditated distance between them. At the same time, by placing him at the opposite end to herself, she had accentuated her link with her cousin: two members of the Herringe family presiding over the little soap opera going on in the middle.

'Max's a baroque violinist,' Anna said. 'He won't tell you, but he's one of the most respected in Europe. If he wasn't so lazy he'd be more famous that he is. We're old friends.'

'Oh, a little more than friends, dear,' said Stella, reaching across the table to squeeze Max's arm, 'if all I hear is true.'

Despite herself, Anna blushed. 'We lived together for a while,' she said. 'People do.' Everyone comes with baggage, she thought. Why should Max and I have to defend ours? Why is she making such a fuss about this? Then she thought, she's doing this deliberately. She's going to try and use my history with Max to lever John and me apart. Why *should* I have to defend myself? She glanced across at John for help, but he was looking at Stella. The whole arrangement of the table made it difficult to catch his attention; and that had been deliberate, too. Out of a kind of astonished rage – not so much at Stella's scheming as the pathetically old-fashioned assumptions behind it – she found herself smiling at Max and saying with a lot more warmth than she felt: 'It's good to see you again.'

'The violinist and the currency dealer!' Stella said. 'How extraordinary. You do look rather wonderful together. What went wrong?'

That's really none of your business, Anna thought angrily. She was opening her mouth to say so when Max interrupted mildly, 'You know, I don't think it was really a matter of anything going wrong: just a matter of moving on.' He appealed to Stella. 'It's important to move on, don't you think? You can't just immure yourself in the past, can you?' He glanced casually around the Painted Room. 'Though this is lovely past to live in, if you must.'

At this, Anna's heart filled with gratitude: for once, someone had made Stella look ill at ease. To cover her annoyance, Stella examined the ruins of the previous course. 'Do any of you want pudding?' she said. After a moment she rang the little silver bell at her elbow and two of the shadowy caterers appeared. Dessert turned out to be a concoction of whipped cream accompanied by a salad of exotic fruits. 'It's my own recipe,' Stella announced, 'and my only contribution.' She sat back with an expectant smile. Among the figs, lychees and blackheart cherries lay something apple-like, soft, and slightly rotten-smelling.

'What's this?' Anna asked. Even the food seemed to have been designed to put her at a disadvantage. She prodded a slice with her spoon. 'I don't think I've ever come across it before.'

'It's a medlar,' John said. 'From Stella's orchard.'

'You have an orchard?' Anna asked in surprise.

'Oh yes, dear. What would Nonesuch be without its orchard? It's walled, and very old, and rather overgrown. We keep half a dozen medlars amongst the apples and pears. The stock is sixteenth century, I believe. You eat the fruit only when it's decayed.'

'"You'll be rotten before you be half ripe, and that's the right vertue of the medlar,"' John quoted. 'All those glorious Elizabethan images of decay and sex.' He met Stella's eyes. Something unspoken passed between them, and even as it did, Anna saw a movement in the picture behind them. The rain-dirtied courtyard light darkened further towards evening. The shadowy figure in the arcade beneath the Tudor gables seemed to come into focus, shifting in some subtle preparatory way. She blinked, but when she looked again the painting was as dull as it had ever been, and all she had seen was the shadow of one of the catering staff flicker across it. A candle guttered, as if in a breeze.

Max said: 'Rotten before you're half ripe. Sounds like one of my dreams.'

'More like a nightmare,' said Anna. 'Decay and sex.' She shuddered.

Stella Herringe gave her a brief, considering glance. Then she said; 'John's your man for dreams. He thinks if you dig around in dreams enough you can unearth all life's little dark secrets.'

'But how Freudian,' said Max. He looked genuinely amused.

'John's is a more spiritual approach, I think.'

John glowered at her. 'You make me sound like Gipsy Rose Lee,' he said.

Stella turned her head to give Max the benefit of her blue eyes and challenging little laugh. Before this gesture was complete she had murmured – almost lightly, almost in passing – to her cousin: 'Well, you do look as if you have a touch of the tarbrush, darling. Not in every light, of course.'

John clenched his jaw. With some idea of saving him from his own temper – though by now she would happily have seen him turn on his cousin – Anna interrupted quickly: 'I've been having the strangest dreams.'

She hadn't thought much about this, but as soon as the words were out of her mouth she saw how true they were. 'In fact, I haven't been sleeping at all well.'

Ever since John kissed her, bizarre images had filled her sleep, only to evaporate as she woke hot and upset, tangled in her sheets in the middle of the night. Of those that remained by morning, some achieved a peculiar clarity, often frankly sexual but edged with violence or horror, and quite unlike the unfocused tranquillity of her usual dreams; while others seemed to have so little meaning that the word itself was irrelevant. 'Here's an odd one,' she said, hastily selecting the most innocuous example she could recall. 'I'm sitting in a room looking out of the window and I see a bird soaring into the sky beside a church spire, the sun turning its feathers to brilliant white. Then it starts to circle, disappears from view, and I think it must have flown away. There's no real sense of loss. I don't seem to have any feelings in the dream. But then the bird re-enters the window frame on the other side—'

She paused. 'Only now it's become completely black.'

Max gave her a thoughtful look. 'Might it not be a different bird?' he asked.

'Oh, no. It's the same bird. Always the same bird.'

Stella, who had listened to Anna with a kind of greedy anticipation, leaned across the table and said excitedly, 'I think we should all tell a dream, don't you?' then, in a completely different tone of voice, to John Dawe: 'Well now, dear. What do you make of that?'

John put his elbows on the table, cupped his face in his hands. 'It's interesting enough,' he said, as if he was already tired of talking to amateurs. After a moment he looked up at Anna and said: 'Dreams aren't a simple code.'

'Oh, cop-out, cop-out,' exclaimed his cousin.

He ignored her. 'Dreams are an ad hoc language. It's not just that they have a different grammar to the ones we use in everyday life: it's that every one of them has a different grammar to every other.' It was a reproach, Anna saw; he was reproaching her because she had inadvertently helped Stella turn a lifelong passion into a parlour game. 'You can't just perform simple substitutions. Symbols don't cohere, they shift and break up. They don't have to mean the same thing twice. You can't even be sure what's signal and what's noise.'

'That just sounds so clever,' said Stella. 'Doesn't it?'

'But surely you can hazard a guess?' wheedled Max, to whom everything was a parlour game anyway. 'Otherwise why bother? People want an interpretation, not a discussion of the interpretive method itself.' He winked at Anna. 'Myself, I'd say it was a dream of lost innocence.'

John Dawe gave him a sarcastic look. Then he poured himself a second brandy, drank half of it in one swallow, and asked: 'And just how do you reach that conclusion?'

'Well, I'll tell you,' said Max.

Max Wishart, Anna thought, as she watched him consider his answer, who are you now?

He wasn't quite the Max she knew. Despite the passion for red wines, and bouillabaisse, he looked underweight and drawn. Little sheaves of lines had developed at the corners of his eyes and mouth. He looked less blithe, less self-sufficient, than when she had seen him last. Perhaps his life had not been so continually successful as he expected; perhaps it had been less friendly to him. This thought she savoured, though she knew it to be spiteful. Max, happily unaware, sat back and stretched his long legs out under the table so that they brushed against hers. Flustered, she tucked her feet under her chair. He didn't seem to notice.

'I would read the white bird,' he said, 'as an image of purity.'

John Dawe leaned back in his chair. 'You would,' he said, more to his wine glass than Max Wishart, 'would you.'

'Oh yes. The window of the house, the eye of the soul: you know? So this is something very personal to Anna. The bird is herself. Is the landscape herself too?' he asked himself in parenthesis. 'Well, we can't know that. So anyway: your little white bird returns blackened from its trip around the sky. What can have brought about this disaster? The only other signifier in the picture is' – here he grinned at Anna – 'the phallus represented by the church spire.'

Stella laughed. 'We know all about that,' she said.

John looked contemptuous. 'One interpretation is as good as another at this sort of level,' he said roughly. 'Why don't the three of you play Trivial Pursuit and be done with it?'

'Dear me,' said Stella to Max. 'He didn't like that.'

'What is your interpretation, John?' Anna asked softly.

He shrugged. 'The sky is a venue, a field of possibilities, a space in which to act. A life,' – here he acknowledged Max's inter-pretation with a nod – 'perhaps Anna's life. The white bird flies out, only to return, in a gesture of completion, as its own diametric opposite.' He spread his hands. He looked around as if nothing more needed to be said. There was a puzzled silence. 'Don't you see?' he appealed. 'There is only one bird here.' He gave Anna an intense look. 'You have dreamed,' he said, 'the two halves of a whole.'

'Nice,' Max Wishart admitted softly. 'Very nice indeed.' The two men exchanged a smile.

In the comfortable pause that followed, Anna thought about her own life, which she now saw not as a seesaw of good and bad, success and failure, happiness and unhappiness, gain and loss, but as one whole, healed thing. The two birds were her own heart, the yin and yang of her, the warm fluttering systole and diastole of life. It was an image too difficult to maintain, but even after it had slipped away she felt buoyed-up and at ease with herself for the first time since the split with Max.

Stella Herringe toyed with her wine glass, and would not look at the others. 'But what about the spire?' she demanded. 'That's all very well, but what about the spire?'

'Oh, I think that might just be Ashmore Church,' said John carelessly.

Everyone laughed, even Stella. The cheese board arrived. The catering staff attended to the failing candles, coming and going with their long white wax tapers like cathedral attendants. '"The sapient sutlers of the Lord",' quoted Max obscurely. John seemed to approve of this, because he raised his glass. Stella's table warmed a degree or two, and the supper party with it. John and Max had a loud argument about what John called 'romantic religion'. Everyone drank more brandy. Max, egged on by Stella, produced for their entertainment a recurring dream he had.

'I'm sailing alone in a carved and varnished boat on a calm ocean. I can go anywhere in the world. It's wonderfully relaxing.'

'And?' said John. 'Then?'

'Nothing,' said Max. 'Do you see? That's the beauty of it. Nothing else happens at all!'

'Lucky you,' said Anna pointedly, but Max was already turning to Stella and urging her, 'Come on, my dear, you started this, and now it's your go. What dream have you for us?'

'Oh yes!' said Anna. She clapped her hands.

'My cousin is afraid to sleep,' John Dawe said. 'For one reason or another. She doesn't miss it. Insomnia's something of a family tradition.'

Stella laughed. 'Herringes hate to waste time when there's so much to be done in the world,' she told Max.

'Just like Margaret Thatcher,' said John.

'You must be able to remember one dream,' Anna urged. 'I've gone and Max's gone. It really is your turn.'

'Tell them the one about the cats,' said John in a cruel voice.

Stella greeted this with a blank look. Suddenly she said: 'I'm walking uphill with a man. When I reach the top there's a strong wind blowing. It blows so hard, it inflates my skirts and I rise up into the air like some balloon with my feet dangling and an intense sensation of pleasure.' She looked pleased with herself. 'There. I don't think we need analyse that, do we?'

'And what about the man?' said Anna.

'Oh my dear, you know men. He just walks away.'

'Touché,' applauded Max Wishart. 'Is this a dream of higher things? Are we to envisage you rising at night from the contaminating earth, like an angel, or a holy fog?'

John snorted into his brandy glass. 'An angel,' he said.

This seemed to hurt Stella, who looked away. His indifference, so obviously displayed, left her tired and old. It was an effort to gather herself together again, but after a moment, she said, 'What about you, John? What do you dream of?'

He put back the rest of his brandy. 'There are cultures which believe that at least half of our life goes on in dreams. That dreaming is the soul's adventure – no, the soul's project. That the effects of those dreams are as real as any event that takes place during the day. There are cultures which believe that the dreams you have at night can affect the health and well-being of the entire daylight world.'

He looked round table, pushed back his chair and got unsteadily to his feet.

'I don't dream to amuse you,' he said. 'Sorry, folks.'

'Well that's a nice neat hole to hide in, said Stella. 'The dignity of the expert.'

Anna leaned across the table and touched John's forearm. He had taken his jacket off and rolled up his sleeves. He was clenching his fist so hard that the muscle was like a block of wood. 'Come on, John,' she said. 'It is your turn.'

He stared at her in a betrayed way then, lifting his hands, palms open, in surrender, sat down again.

'All right, then. Here's the dream I had last night—'

'He writes them down,' Stella interrupted, 'in a book he keeps beside the bed.' She smiled sleepily across at Anna. 'Don't ask me how I know that.'

'—I was sitting here, at dinner. The table was laid just as you see it now.' He made a gesture that took in the whole of the

Painted Room. 'There were candles everywhere, just as there are now, throwing odd shadows on the walls. That bloody awful painting lay there in wait for us all, the way it always does. In some way, I knew it was this evening. Here's the only difference: I was sitting where Max is now, and opposite me sat a woman.'

'Ah,' said Stella. 'Which one?'

'I never saw her face.'

'Another cop-out!' Max cried happily.

'Do you think so?' John asked him. 'Is that what you think? She sat opposite me and she held my hands in hers. Have you ever been rendered powerless by a touch? I was so sexually attracted to her that I could barely breathe; and I knew, even though I couldn't see her face, that she was tremendously beautiful.'

Stella began to smile. It made her look twenty or thirty years younger.

'I was afraid of her. She had asked me for something I was unable to give. I wanted to give it: don't think I didn't. I had refused less out of fear than out of sheer sexual paralysis.'

He stopped. 'Have you ever felt that?' he asked Max. 'Have you ever wanted someone so much you simply couldn't take them? Only men ever feel that,' he added bitterly. And then before Max could say anything: 'I felt a tingling sensation in my arms. When I looked down, I could see swirling silver patterns appearing on my hands, starting at the fingertips and spiralling past my wrists; then up my forearms in great complex, knotted patterns, almost Celtic in form, the lines crossing and recrossing as if to bind me. And these patterns were so entrancing that although I knew they bound me to her, I could never break them.'

He looked down at his hands, as if he could see the patterns there now. 'I knew I would have her for the rest of my life,' he said brutally. 'I knew I would never have her. In some way, she had made herself available and unavailable to me in exactly the same gesture. She was a shaman. I was bound.'

Anna's chest felt constricted. She realised she had been holding her breath.

'My, my,' said Stella softly. Her skin glowed in the candlelight; her eyes were bright.

Max looked round the table, let his gaze rest on Anna. 'Someone's clearly got designs on you,' he said to John.

Anna blushed and looked away.

John sat bolt upright. 'What was that?'

'I said, someone's got designs—' began Max.

'Not that,' John interrupted him contemptuously. 'Listen. That. I thought I heard a cat.'

The room fell quiet. Anna shivered. 'I heard a cat in here this summer,' she said. 'But Stella never has them in the house.'

John Dawe got unsteadily to his feet, pushed rudely past Stella at the end of the table and announced, 'I've got to piss.'

In the wake of this gesture, no one could think of anything to say. And when, after fifteen minutes or so, it was clear that John wasn't coming back, supper lost its momentum. The atmosphere of the Painted Room would no longer support conversation. In the silences that stretched out between increasingly dull attempts, Max interested himself in the mural. Stella poured more brandy, and stared listlessly ahead of herself, her lips moving as if she was rehearsing some old argument with her cousin. Anna poured herself some mineral water: something – the brandy, the tension, the smell of stale candle smoke – had given her a headache. She didn't think things could get much worse. Then Max turned to her and said carelessly:

'And how's my favourite cat, then?'

Anna couldn't think what he meant. 'Pardon?'

'How's old Barnaby doing?'

'Oh,' she said. 'I see.' She frowned. Then she said flatly. 'He's dead. He was run over the week after you left.'

When she looked up and saw the stricken expression on Max's face, she knew she had gone too far. But nothing she could think of adding would make the situation any better.

'Sorry,' she said.

'It's a myth, of course, about them having nine lives,' said Stella, as if she was one of an elect few who had seen through this old wives' tale. 'Just a misreading of the reincarnation themes which leaked out of Egypt via the Mediterranean cultures in the millennium before Christ.' She stared at Anna. She was very drunk, Anna realised. 'Take my word for it,' she said. 'They were fertility symbols, nothing else.'

Anna's head started to spin.

This woman is mad, she said to herself, then out loud: 'Excuse me.' She walked quickly out of the Painted Room and with what she thought was remarkable presence of mind considering the rush of brandy to her head, managed to find the little bathroom attached to Stella's apartment. There, soothed by the cool white walls and minimal fittings, she sat perched on the toilet with her head in her hands and cried with rage and mortification. The whole event had been a disaster.

She washed her face. When she looked in the bathroom mirror, her eyes, dark with misery and self-loathing, stared at her over the top of the pristine white towel. How could she possibly go back inside that room without killing Stella Herringe? She looked at her watch. It was almost twelve.

She retrieved her jacket from the caterers and stepped out into the cold, damp autumn air. Of John Dawe there was no sign.

The taxi came for her just after midnight.

'See you didn't turn into a pumpkin, then,' said Alice's ex.

'It was the coach that turned into a pumpkin,' she reminded him, 'not Cinderella.' She looked down at herself. 'But have it your way.'

Back at the cottage, she tore off the long black dress and stuffed it disgustedly into the back of the wardrobe. She changed into an old, but comfortable, brushed cotton nightdress, made herself a cup of chocolate and curled up on the sofa with Vita and Dellifer and a Joanna Trollope novel she had bought in the bookshop in Drychester. She was just ebbing away from herself, slipping comfortably into the story, when there was a knock at the front door. Vita leapt off the sofa excitedly and ran aimlessly about. Dellifer tucked her nose under her paws and made a huffing noise as if irritated at the disturbance. Through the diamond of bossed glass in the front door, Anna could make out a face, framed by blond hair.

It was Max Wishart. He had a cat in his arms.

Anna put her book down carefully, pulled her robe around her and opened the door.

'I found this rascal sitting in the middle of the road,' he said, offering her the cat, which turned out to be Orlando. 'For a minute I thought it was Barnaby.'

Orlando, who never much liked being picked up, squirmed briefly in Anna's hands, jumped to the ground and legged it out of the door and into the front garden. He sat there for a time licking his fur in an affronted manner, then vanished into the bushes.

'You never used to let Barnaby out at night,' Max said.

'That was London,' Anna said firmly. 'This is Ashmore. Things are different here.'

'I can see that.'

'Why are you here, Max?'

'Stella invited me.'

'No, I mean why are you here, now, at nearly one o'clock, in my cottage? Max, we haven't seen each other for two years. What did you think we might have to say to one another?'

'I came to apologise,' he said. 'For this evening.'

Anna regarded him steadily. 'That's new,' she said.

'Anna—'

'The man I lived with would never have apologised for anything. He'd have just slipped away in his usual bloody solipsistic dream. *Moi?* Hurt anyone? How could I? I'm Max.' She turned away from him and began to shut the door in his face. 'I'm too ornamental for that. And you are, Max, you are. Barnaby was more use than you.'

He held on to the door. 'Anna, listen—'

'Bugger off, Max.'

'Listen: I deserved that,' he said.

She stared at him. 'There's something the matter with you, Max. Isn't there?' When he didn't answer, she said, 'You'd better come in. Do you want a cup of tea?'

Once inside, he didn't seem to know what to do with himself. He looked around at the CD shelves, the TV, as if he had never been in a house before. He picked up the Joanna Trollope, put it down again. He tickled Dellifer under her bony chin and said, 'Well now, and what's your name?' (Dellifer purred politely, but Anna could see she hadn't fallen for it.) He came into the kitchen and stared at the kettle on the Aga.

'Look, Max, you don't have to follow me everywhere. For heaven's sake go and sit down.'

'I hardly know Stella Herringe. I had no idea why she wanted me there.' He saw that Anna didn't believe him. 'I've got fans,' he said. 'You know that. They come to the concerts, they buy the CDs, they—' He shrugged tiredly. 'She was very insistent. I assumed it was something like that.'

Anna laughed bitterly. 'Oh, I bet you did, Max.'

'Anna, listen to me—'

'Oh, I know, Max. All that stuff at the dinner table was perfectly deliberate. She set me up, and I fell for it. All those years at TransCorp, dealing with men who would have killed each other – let alone me – for my job, and I allow some old bitch to manipulate me back to my teenage days – no confidence, lots of guilt, not knowing how to defend myself. Well, it won't happen again, you can be sure of that.'

Max looked at her intently. 'You've got between those two, and it's a dangerous place to be. That's all I wanted to say.'

'No it isn't,' said Anna. 'Max, I lived with you, remember? What is it? Why did you come here?'

When he still didn't answer, she said: 'I can take care of myself, Max. Here's your tea. Please come through and sit down and drink it and then go.' But although he wandered obediently out of the kitchen, she couldn't get him to sit down. He stood in the tiny room, the teacup in his hand, while she bustled around him trying to tidy things up. His head brushed the central ceiling beam. Eventually he said: 'I'm sorry it didn't work out for us—'

'It didn't "not work out" for us, Max. You walked away from it.'

'—and I'm really, really sorry about Barnaby.' Suddenly, tears filled his eyes. He looked blindly around for somewhere to put down his cup. She got up and took it from him. She held his hands. His strong, calloused violinist's fingers lay passively in hers; they were cold.

'Anna, I'm ill.'

'Max!'

'They don't know what it is. They're doing a spinal tap next week.' His face crumpled. He said in a strained and muffled voice: 'They think it may be MS.'

'Oh, Max—'

'What's life worth, Anna? What's it worth when this can happen to you?'

Anna threw her arms around him. Whatever he had been to her – whatever he had done to her – he was just a man now, in need of help. How thin he had got! She could feel the bones of his shoulder blades under the palms of her hands, even through the wool of his coat. She could feel him tremble. 'Sh,' she whispered. 'Max, shh.' She put her hands on either side of his face and made him look at her. 'It will be all right. I promise you.'

He clung to her like a child.

They were standing there like that, in the middle of her front room with the lights full on and the curtains wide open, when she saw a face at the window.

'Max!'

She tried to pull herself away, but he only buried his face in her shoulder and clung on harder, so that they tottered about together in a ghastly two-step of despair and frustration.

'Max!' she said harshly. 'Let go of me!'

John Dawe stared in at them for a moment. Then he was gone.

Eighteen

ANNA STOOD on the doorstep listening to the wind. There was no sign of John Dawe. All she could think was: I must catch him, I must talk to him, I mustn't let him think the wrong thing. She went back inside, where she found Max slumped on the sofa with his eyes closed.

'Look,' she said, 'I'm sorry, but I've got to go out.'

He didn't seem to hear her. His face looked grey and tired and he couldn't stop stroking the cat. Dellifer, looking uncomfortable but flattered, accommodated him with a kind of dusty purr.

Anna bent down and put her hand over his. 'Max? Are you all right?'

He opened his eyes.

'Max, you're being a bit rough with her.'

'I'm sorry,' he said.

'I'll be back as soon as I can,' said Anna, as if he had asked. She tried to get her Barbour jacket off the back of the kitchen door and pull on her wellington boots at the same time; dashed upstairs in a futile search for her torch, her house keys, her purse for which she would have no earthly use in Ashmore village at two in the morning.

'Make yourself another cup of tea or something,' she told Max. 'Anything you like. There's plenty of food—'

'I'm OK,' he said, stroking the cat. 'I'll be fine.'

She stared down at him. He gave her a vague smile. She had a feeling of her life flying apart with his.

'For goodness' sake, Max!' she begged. 'Do something with yourself!'

Ashmore had no streetlights. This was a blessing on a clear night, when Cassiopeia and the Plough arranged themselves like chains of paste on jeweller's velvet, and even an untutored eye could sometimes make out the smoky red dot of Mars; less so on a cloudy one, when you were looking for a man. The village pond, ruffled yet contemplative, presented a grey curve to the street. There were no lights in the houses. Anna squinted anxiously right and left but saw nothing to convince her John Dawe had passed either way. There were only two places, she decided, in which to look for him. He would go to the *Magpie*, and sulk; or back to Nonesuch, to be comforted – if that was the word – by his cousin.

A couple of hundred yards up the road, at the junction by the church, she bet on the latter, and was rewarded by glimpses of a dark figure moving purposefully north.

'John!' she cried. 'John!'

He gave no sign that he had heard. She went after him down Allbright Lane at a sort of trudging, indecorous trot, her rubber boots slapping painfully against the backs of her bare calves. A stitch bent her double. A single gust of wind roared off the edge of the downs, flailed in the hedgerows, tore her voice out of her mouth. It was gone as soon as it arrived, leaving behind a steady, streaming rain. John Dawe walked fast, with his hands in his pockets and his head down into the weather, but as long as she kept running she made up ground. This went on for some minutes; then he must have heard her calling out, because he looked back over his shoulder and he began to run too. It was the most hurtful response she had ever experienced.

'*John!*' she shrieked.

He hesitated, then shrugged and reluctantly allowed her to catch up. As soon as she got close – perhaps with an idea of keeping some distance between them – he began to walk backwards away from her. He was out of breath. 'I'm not talking,' he said. 'I don't want to talk.' His clothes were soaked, his face white and drawn. He kept his gaze focused away from her, and an angry, inturned smile on his face.

'John, it's not what you think.'

'So what is it?'

'He's an old friend, John, and he's not well.'

'He's an old lover. You said so yourself.'

'I'm a grown-up, John. You are too. Only children come without a past.'

He started to say something, shrugged.

'What?' she said.

'Nothing.'

'There is something,' she said. 'What is it?'

She tried to take his hands, but he moved away. She began talking quickly, in case he took flight again. 'Max and I meant something to one another once. Now he's frightened and he needs help. Look,' she appealed, 'I never wanted to see him again. But in a way I'm glad this happened, because it could bring him back into my life as what he ought to be – an old friend.'

If she had made up any ground she lost it here. 'How nice and modern,' he jeered.

She looked down miserably. 'He's no threat to you.'

John Dawe shook his head, as if that wasn't the issue, and the two of them just stood there again until after some time he said: 'Look, I know I haven't any right to be jealous. I just hoped we meant something to each other.' This struck her as disingenuous.

'It's too late for coat-trailing,' she said. 'Of course we did.'

'"Did"?'

'Oh, grow up,' she advised him bitterly, adding before she could prevent herself, 'Stella brought him here, not me. Ask her why. Ask her why she spent the evening trying to get a lever between us!' He stared at her for a moment then deliberately turned and walked away. She let him go. 'Run back to the family, then!' she heard herself shout. 'I'm so *sick* of men!' He turned a corner, and the high black hedges covered him from view.

'You bastard,' she whispered.

She stood there for some time in her nightdress and wellingtons, shivering and uncertain of her feelings. She was upset and hurt. But she was irritated with herself too, and angry with John: so in the end – though the sanest course would have been to go home, apologise to Max and make him comfortable in her tiny spare room, then curl up to sleep with her cat – she gathered her resources, pulled the clammy Barbour jacket around her, and plodded after him. Fifteen or twenty minutes later, at a bend in the road, Nonesuch offered itself to her out of the sodden darkness.

Two in the morning and the great front doors – designed by Bramber Herringe and his wife Juliette after a visit to India in the last decade of the seventeenth century, to be hand-built somewhat later by local craftsmen – were firmly closed. The caterers' van had departed, leaving muddy tracks on the grass where it had been manoeuvred carelessly into the drive. Stella's Mercedes gleamed with rain in its usual parking space. The lady of the house was at home, then: asleep, perhaps, dreaming the balloon-dream, unaware of the events she had set in motion. Of John Dawe there was no sign.

Anna rang the doorbell, and when no answer came, set off round the base of the house to see if she could find a way in. The curiously angled roofs and gable ends of Nonesuch bulked above her, black against the racing clouds. Apart from the rhythmic drip of rain from the lower branches of the great cedars, the gardens were eerily silent. Vindicated at last in her choice of footwear, Anna stumbled across the soft earth of lawn and parterre. There were no lights on in Stella's apartment; the windows of the Painted Room were dark. All the ground-floor doors were secure. Many of them, she knew, needed no locks. They had been warped or rusted shut for years, or gave entry to disused pantries and closets which were themselves bricked off from the rest of the house. But as she made her way along the back of the house, she came upon an open French window, and heard voices from the room inside. She thought that one of them said, 'I don't remember,' to which the other answered:

'You will. You must.'

It was Stella and John. They were quarrelling. For a moment, their voices became indistinct, as if they had moved away from the window. Then she heard, quite loudly:

'None of this means anything to me. It's all in the past. Why can't you leave me alone? Why do you always meddle in my life?'

Anna backed cautiously away. The French window opened on to a stiff, formal little arrangement of clipped and topiaried box-hedges – the Herringe knot garden, with its inevitable sly encodement of the family initial: here, she hid herself. Nothing happened for a moment. A long white curtain bellied in and out of the room in the damp wind. Then there was a clever little laugh, some inaudible exchange, a feminine shout of rage. The sound of a glass breaking against the wall. 'Do what you like,' said John Dawe. 'It's only money.' A moment later, he rushed out, pursued by his cousin. Almost immediately, the knot garden brought him to a halt. He stared at the hidden shape in the box hedges, as puzzled as a pony, while Stella approached him with care, as if he might kick or bolt, to lay upon his shoulder the infinitely patient hand of a woman who has grown up with animals of all kinds. She was still wearing the pewter lamé evening gown. Even with the rain making rats' tails of her unpinned hair, she looked amazing.

'This is *our* past,' she said. 'No one can share it with us.'

John shrugged her off. 'Yet you go off to London and drag back this bloody violinist. He's in her house. I saw them there. It looked as if they were kissing.'

'And that's such a good thing,' she said. 'Isn't it? If you think?' She stepped in close to him and, before he could react, ran the fingers of her left hand lightly down the side of his face. He stiffened for a second under her touch, but then it seemed to relax him. 'Because she's not a permanent part of the pattern. London's their world. They'll go back to it. They're safer where they belong, aren't they? Isn't that true?' She looked intently into his face. 'She's a flimsy little thing, John: she's on a visit. Enjoy her while you can.'

The clouds parted briefly to reveal a sky as iridescent as fish-skin. Moonlight poured down on Stella's face and seemed to spread a fine web of lines and wrinkles there.

'I'm the strong one,' she said. 'You always come back to me. I'm the only you always need.'

'What does she mean?' said Anna loudly.

Stella gasped and covered her face with her hands.

Anna stepped out of the dark. She hadn't meant to speak. She hadn't meant them to know she was there.

'John, what does she mean?'

He stared at her. His eyes were flat with surprise. The three of them stood there in a triangle in the knot garden in the bright moonlight, two at the centre, one at the edge, and everything was held suspended, like sediment in clear water. Everything between them was held in abeyance. Their shadows were fixed. Then the clouds fell back across the moon, and Stella Herringe let drop her hands. She smiled. She said:

'Look at her, John. Is that what you want? Wincyette and wellingtons?'

The cousins regarded her silently. Anna could sense contempt radiating towards her like cold fire.

That's not fair, Anna thought. I came out as I was. I just put these things on: I didn't choose them. In London, I was proud of how I looked. In London, success had given her a fine finish, added a kind of sleekness to her hair and skin. Success was more than cuts and cosmetics: it was confidence, running daily through you like a hormone, to rebuild and reaffirm. I lost that when I left, she thought. I lost that when I lost Max. True or false, this admission was like opening a door. She tried to turn away from what came through, but in the end could only stand helplessly, cold water trickling down her back, her feet chafed and hot in her boots, and allow Stella's scorn to usher it towards her, something huge that came rushing out of nowhere like a physical blow. There was an epileptic flash in her head. Then double vision. Some prior defeat, some old humiliation, imposed itself on the present and began to play itself in starts and flickers, like a damaged video recording. In quick succession she saw a room, a window, a frieze of trees black against enamelled winter skies. She heard raised voices, a man and a woman; she heard her own voice hoarse with shouting. Was it Nonesuch? Was it the Painted Room? But how absurd! She felt faint and sick, staggered, bent at the waist to vomit—

Only to feel a powerful grip first upon an elbow, then her waist. John Dawe's face, knotted with emotion, was thrust into hers.

'Do you need me, Anna?'

'What?'

Her tongue filled up her mouth. She was still stuck somewhere in the past. Figures danced in her head, they were in outlandish costumes and bizarre wigs. Firelight; moonlight; cats wailing. Then it was all gone, and she was staring at John and Stella with a contempt of her own. What are you? she thought. A woman trying too hard to look young; a man who never found the adult focus of his life.

'*Do you need me?*'

She pushed him away. 'No,' she said. 'What I need is a hot bath, a dry towel and a whisky.'

She turned her back on the knot garden and walked away.

John Dawe must have made some move to follow her, because Stella suddenly shouted: 'Go on, then! Give up on the last four hundred glorious years. Go after her, if you think that's what you want. But don't come whining back to me the next time the money runs out—'

There was a scuffle, a slap, a scream.

Anna quickened her pace. She would not look back. She felt the cousins staring after her for a moment, then the corner of the house cut them off. It was a relief to be away from them. She wrung water out of her hair, turned up the collar of her coat. By the time she reached the end of the drive, she had stopped trembling. She cast a brief glance up at the great gates, the rain-blackened Herringe arms. Behind them the walls of Nonesuch leaned away at strange angles among the dripping cedars. How oppressive it all is, she thought. I'll never come back. Not after this.

She thought: if he loved me he wouldn't have let me go.

And then: What did she mean, 'four hundred glorious years'?

John Dawe caught up with her about half a mile down Allbright Lane, where the trees joined overhead to make a dark, groined tunnel. She heard a shout, then the sound of heavy footsteps behind her. She winced away in surprise, calling out, 'No! No!' but he pulled her to him and kissed her hard. His hands were tangled in her hair, he was cramming her mouth painfully against his. Rainwater dripped from his face on to hers. 'I don't want you,' she tried to say. She closed her eyes and shuddered helplessly. She felt a savage wash of triumph. *Do you see, you old cow?* some part of her thought: *Do you see this?* She was appalled. Several minutes later, breathless and confused, she rested her head against his shoulder, felt the thin, quick pulse of his heart through the wet cloth of his shirt. The rain fell on them unabated.

'Am I mad?' she heard him wonder aloud. 'I think I must be.' Then he said: 'I've drunk more than I should.'

'That's all very flattering,' she said. She heard herself add: 'You never have to go back there, if you don't want. Tear the cheques up. You can earn a living anywhere.'

'Is it so simple?'

'Yes.'

'There's more than money involved. She knows me too well. Like all family, she knows which buttons to press.'

'How fascinating, that you work by buttons. Did you hit her? Back there in the knot garden?'

He gave a short laugh. 'She hit me. When I stepped out of the way, she got off-balance and fell down.'

'Goodness,' said Anna. 'Fancy trying to get mud out of that dress.'

He stared at her thoughtfully. 'That's not kind.'

'I don't feel very kind at the moment.'

They walked in silence for a while. Then Anna asked, 'Why did you go back there?'

He shrugged. 'I was angry with you.'

'I thought you must have been.'

'I saw you and the violinist together—'

'—and you couldn't think of anywhere else to go but Nonesuch. My, you're independent.'

'What's your history with him?'

'I'll tell you that,' she said, standing in front of him to make sure she had his attention, 'if you'll tell me your history with Stella. Otherwise, no more questions.' He tried to kiss her again. 'No,' she said. 'Tell me.'

It took him some minutes to frame a reply. They resumed walking; passed a row of dark cottages, the village school, the vicarage. Anna's house was almost in view when he finally said:

'You wouldn't understand.'

She laughed. 'It won't do, John. Try me.'

He shook his head.

'I'm sorry,' he said. 'This isn't fair on you.'

'Just what is it, exactly, that isn't fair?'

'Oh, I don't know. Family history, I suppose.' He laughed. 'Only here there's no family, just history.'

'Four hundred glorious years?'

'Four hundred glorious years. Pathetic, isn't it? All those

desperate old matriarchs in the graveyard over there, outlasting everyone else by sheer willpower, driving their feeble sons to an early death! And those portraits in the Long Corridor! Not one of them had an ounce of compassion when it came to getting what they wanted.'

He seemed to consider this.

'It's all so *binding*,' he said.

'You're not a Herringe,' Anna reminded him, 'you're a Dawe—'

'Bloody good job, too!'

'—And you aren't feeble, and you're certainly not her son. Kiss me again.'

'I will.'

They went the rest of the way with their arms around one another. By the time they got back the moon was out and the rain had stopped. Her cottage remained as Anna had left it. The front door hung open. The uncurtained window, still yellow with light, revealed Max Wishart sprawled on the sofa with his mouth open, like someone in an American Gothic painting. There was a sense of disarray, of ordinary life suspended. At the gate sat Orlando, as sorry for himself as only a wet cat can be, giving his sodden fur a half-hearted lick.

'You look like a loo-brush,' Anna told him. 'Have you gone mad? Why didn't you sit inside?'

'We've all been a bit mad tonight,' said John Dawe.

He knelt down to stroke the cat. In return, Orlando sniffed and sniffed at his boots, his hands, his trousers.

'Look at him!' said Anna. 'He likes you.'

'He can smell Liddy.' John Dawe got up again. 'She hasn't been home lately, and I'm a bit worried about her. I think I'll go home and see if she's back. She's a tart—'

'—but you miss her,' Anna finished.

'Bless her crooked little heart.' They smiled at one another. After a pause he asked: 'Will I see you tomorrow, Anna Prescott?'

'You will.'

'And the man asleep on your sofa in there?' he reminded her.

'He's an old friend, John. Nothing more to me now. Nothing less.'

He nodded. 'I will have to take your word for that,' he said.

'You'd be a fool not to.'

She watched him walk off down the road, then, shooing Orlando along in front of her, went inside and closed the door. The cottage was cold. Max had woken up at some point and, unable to find anything else, taken the old woollen blanket off the cat's favourite chair and draped it over himself. His long legs hung over the armrest of the sofa. If she listened carefully, she could hear his steady breathing. He seemed more at ease with himself, but how could you tell? She wondered what the future held for him. 'Goodnight, Max,' she whispered. She crept past him, turned off the lights and, slipping carefully into bed next to the snoring Dellifer, fell into a deep if dream-filled sleep.

Early the next morning she woke puzzledly, to the sound of voices.

The whole cottage smelled of coffee and fried bread. In the kitchen she found Alice Meynell – whose idea of cooking was to have the stove turned as high as possible – banging pots around in a haze of superheated fat, the cats weaving round her feet with their tails up and hopeful expressions on their faces. Max Wishart sat at the table, an empty plate in front of him, watching her with an amused expression on his face. Alice's flying jacket lay on the floor in a corner. Despite the change in the weather, she had chosen to wear underneath it a pink mohair crop-top which left three inches of bare skin above the waistband of her black leather motorcycle trousers.

'I made myself at home,' she said. 'Do you want coffee?'

Anna took the proffered mug and held it in both hands.

'You look recovered,' she told Max.

Before he could open his mouth, Alice said: 'He needs a lift to the station. I said he ought to have some breakfast before I took him.' She examined Max as if she had never seen a man before and added off handedly, 'Egg on bread, nothing special.'

'You're taking him on your bike?'

'Well, the Rolls-Royce is being mended just now.'

'Do you think that's wise?' Anna asked Max.

Max Wishart lifted an eyebrow. 'Do you remember me as wise?' he said. He was still tired round the eyes, but he seemed less depressed. He had the air of a man who had made decisions about himself in the night. He looked at his watch. 'London calls. If I want that train I think I'd better kiss and run.'

She smiled at him. 'You were always good at that, Max.'

'Wasn't I, though?'

Anna went out to say goodbye, stood with her arms folded under her breasts. The motorcycle exhaust steamed in the cold air. The sun was out, and she could see the edge of the downs again. Balanced incongruously on the back of the Kawasaki in his suit and overcoat – his knees cocked at strange angles, Alice's spare helmet on his head – Max looked up at her and said: 'Take care of yourself. You know what I mean.'

'You take care of yourself too, Max—'

They tried to kiss, but the helmet got in the way.

'—and let me know what happens.'

'I will,' he said.

'As soon as you know.'

'I will. Come and see me play next month. I'll send you tickets. Queen Elizabeth Hall: three viols and a soprano. Very beefy.'

He thought for a moment.

'The programme, that is. Not the soprano.'

Shortly after they had gone, Ruth Canning phoned.

'How's life in green welly paradise?' she said.

'Bloody,' Anna told her.

'So we can expect you back in Hackney when?'

'Don't tempt me,' said Anna. 'What's all that shouting?'

'Half term. Oh, and we decided to put the computers in the boys' room and boys in the loft. For some reason it's meant a lot of carpentry.'

'Everyone has their cross to bear,' said Anna.

There was the shortest of pauses. 'Oh, we do OK, me and Sam,' Ruth said. Suddenly she shouted, 'Put that thing down and leave your brother alone!' Another pause, in which a child's voice could be heard debating the point. 'Or I'll kill you,' she answered it reasonably. 'Is that clear enough?'

Anna said: 'Are you all right, Ruth?'

'Oh you know. Sam wants to change his job again, I want to go back to work full time, the boys want a Dreamcast, we all need a bigger house. Nothing a lottery win wouldn't cure. Listen,' she said, 'I can't talk long. I called because I picked up something rather peculiar last night, talking to Charlie Royle in some appalling gastropub somewhere. Remember Charlie? Got sacked from Benedict-Beiderhof for being too clever with hedge funds, and landed his own column for some broadsheet's business page two days later? Well I thought I'd have a sniff round him to see what he knew about the Herringe operation. As soon as I mentioned the name, all he wanted to talk about was Engelion Cosmetics. They'd been doing so well everyone thought they were going to float. There was a lot of quiet support for going public. But suddenly they've been blacklisted by some animal rights organisation, and people are pulling back. No one wants to buy shares in another cruelty scandal.'

'Blacklisted? What on earth for?'

'Testing on rabbits. Charlie was full of it. Though I know for a fact the bugger spends his weekends down in Hampshire, shooting anything that moves.'

Anna frowned. 'But Stella's worked for animals all her life.'

'Look, this kind of thing is really easy to track down on the web. I'll give you some addresses, and you can follow it up for yourself if you want to. I'd do it,' she said rather sadly, 'but I just haven't the time. God save me from motherhood, wifehood and the *Financial Times*.'

'Ruth – thank you.'

'Look, I've got to go. Bedlam's broken out. Sam's supposed to be looking after them, but all that means is he encourages them to watch football all day, and it makes them hyper.'

'Are you sure you're all right, Ruth?'

'Right as rain,' said Ruth. 'Take care.'

Anna put the phone down and stared at it thoughtfully. John Dawe's voice came back to her from the night before. 'Not one of them,' she remembered him saying of the Herringe women, 'had an ounce of compassion when it came to getting what they wanted.'

Alice Meynell returned a couple of hours later. She sat outside on the Kawasaki, blipping its throttle in an irritating fashion, every so often tilting her head to one side as if listening for something in the note of the engine. When Anna went out to talk to her she shut it down, dragged off her helmet, ran a hand through her blonde brush cut. She looked pleased with herself.

'You've been gone a long time,' said Anna.

'Oh well,' Alice said lightly. 'You know, London's not so far. I thought I'd take him all the way.'

Ashmore Dreams

Autumn

Dreams of dissolution and decay seem to come with the season, as the year turns towards its stagnant time, the leaves fall and rot, the berries wither on the brambles. But this year the dreams are persistent, with a nightmare edge to them.

Hilda Candelton stock-checks in her sleep, a task she will perform the next day in preparation for driving into Drychester to the cash and carry for winter supplies. Carefully, she lists the tins, the cans, the bottles, the packets, but there is a pungent smell amongst the vegetables: and one rotten potato can infect all the rest. With a sigh she reaches into the paper sack, feels only the earthy tubers, whole and hard. So what is making the terrible smell? She tumbles the contents of the sack out on to the floor.

Amid the rain of potatoes falls an animal, hitting the tiles with a dull and frigid thud. It is small and hairless, and its eyes are shut. Its limbs are curled around its torso. Its skin is covered in a fine, dusty mildew, but pale white shoots are already beginning to sprout from its chest. Hilda picks it up and cradles it and takes it back up the stairs to the bedroom to show Reggie.

In a big house on the other side of the village a sleeping woman touches her mouth. She parts her lips, investigates a tooth with one finger. It wobbles. She prods at it again, and it comes away in her hand. Her eyes fly open and she stares at it in disgust. As she does so, another tooth comes loose and slips down through her long black hair and into her lap. Her hands fly up, horrified, as if to hide the damage, but the unrooted teeth flow round her fingers.

They fall softly, like snow.

Mrs Anscombe, a big woman in a salmon-pink anorak, feeds the ducks at the pond, watching the birds fight over the bread she casts upon the weed-netted waters, and soon there is none left. With a sigh, she starts to pluck at the anorak until it disintegrates into tiny gobbets of material. The greedy ducks swallow the pieces down avidly until there is none left, and, beaks working furiously, demand more. Poor Mrs Anscombe, a martyr to all, tears at her flesh.

Soon there will be nothing left of her, either.

The orchard is enclosed by a high brick wall, the courses of which were cleverly inlaid with twined initials, all looping curlicues and flourishes, as if the designer's intent was as much to obscure as to lay a signature. Marvelling at its artistry, she sets a foot into the curve of an 'S', takes hold of the top of the wall and hoists herself up and with an effortlessness that surprises her even as she sleeps, she slips down over the wall into the damp grass on the other side. The mist swirls up, disturbed, around her knees and shoulders and presses itself clammily against her skin. The fruit is all about her – its scent so powerful that she experiences it as a physical taste on the back of her tongue. Sweet, very sweet; then as musty as death. She reaches up and suddenly a single medlar lies in her hand, soft and brown, as small as a curled mouse. When she bites into it, it bursts upon her tongue, all juice and rotten flesh, and she hears a man's voice cry out in agony.

Nineteen

A DAWN MIST had crept stealthily into the garden, under the now-leafless beech hedge and through the gaps in the hawthorn, before the sun was fully up. Vita, awake for an hour already and bored enough to contemplate a foray, stared uncertainly out through the transparent perspex of the cat-flap.

In the middle of the patch of grass and moss that Anna called the lawn, a large bird was strutting up and down in a vague but muscular fashion, its head snapping backwards and forwards in that way that particularly dim-witted avians have, as if they own no more self-will than a clockwork toy. Its plumage glowed artificially vivid against the winter grass: a fabulous tapestry of gold and amber, crimson and an oily, iridescent green. Long barred and tawny feathers curved out from its golden rear, like the tail of a comet curving away from a sun. Around the neck it wore a collar of close white feathers as if some human being had declared ownership of it; but for all this the bird stalked the lawn as if it were staking a claim. Watching it, Vita felt a chatter of fury rise up in the back of her throat, and before she knew it, the chatter had escaped out into the still of the morning. Suddenly, as if it had heard her – through the deadening blanket of mist, through the shrubs and the pots and thick perspex of the Cat-O-Matic – the bird fixed her with an unblinking black eye.

Vita stared back defiantly. Her haunches tensed. In her vivid imagination she saw herself with surreal clarity – all vim and muscle – springing out through the cat-door to cut through the veil of fog like a fiery meteor and—

Just as her heroic daydream faltered, there was a flurry of activity from the beech hedge: an urgent rustle of fallen leaves; a blur of colour and electric speed, and in that instant a long-legged tabby-and-white cat sailed across the lawn, to land in a bounce of paws upon the trespasser.

An ear-splitting rattle filled the air. It echoed off the neighbouring houses. It echoed off the branches and off every twig in the beech hedge. It reverberated in Vita's skull. Her eyes went round with amazement. How could such a din come out of a mere bird?

The cat had stretched its jaws around the golden bird's throat. Unsurprisingly, the captive looked deeply upset. Its beady eyes swivelled desperately and its beak kept opening and shutting, and still the terrible, mechanical sound came racketing out. The tabby-and-white, obviously as unsettled as Vita by the noise, shifted its grip on the thing and after a few failed coughing sounds, the rattle ground to a rusty halt.

Small dark neck-feathers drifted to the ground like the antithesis of snow.

With the trespasser safely occupied, Vita stepped smartly through the cat-flap and trotted across the lawn to get a better view. After its initial horror, the bird was now putting up quite a fight, writhing and flapping with a kind of grim, demonic energy.

The hunter, meanwhile, stared blankly and determinedly into the bird's neck as if calculating its next strategy. Its breath misted up into the winter air. Vita watched as the tabby-and-white blinked once, twice, a third time. Then, as if its meditations had yielded a plan, it started to perform a manoeuvre that seemed to owe its existence to some balletic but arcane form of martial art. With an exquisite shift of balance, the cat reached a long hind leg up and over the bird's back, reached forward and pressed down hard with a spread-clawed foot. All at once, the bird's contortions subsided. A gleam of pure panic switched back and forth across its beady eyes, as if it believed for the first time in this ungainly debacle, that it might in fact be in mortal danger.

Vita watched this manoeuvre with considerable interest, noting it for future use. Then she corkscrewed her head in and under the sagging bird to stare at the visiting cat.

'Hello.'

Effortfully, the tabby-and-white rolled its eyes to regard her. White cornea glared all round burning topaz irises. It mumbled something indistinct but not entirely friendly in tone, and returned its attention to the bird, for they were obviously now at a deadly and difficult impasse. As the strange cat bent its head again, Vita noticed something small and silver shining in its ear. Any interest she had had in the fracas was immediately forgotten.

'Oh!' she exclaimed with desperate envy. 'That's pretty!'

Puzzlement knit the tabby's brows. The bird, sensing a momentary distraction that might signal its last chance of escape, went from limp subservience to frantic dynamism. With a sudden wrenching thrust it tore itself free of the cat's choke-hold and stumbled backwards, its scaly brown toes scrabbling for purchase on the damp ground like a pair of vast spiders. Free at last, it ran awkwardly across the scorched grass, feet lifted high in the hysteria of unexpected freedom, until at last it gained sufficient momentum to take off. It flew with lopsided and overstated effort over the hedge and fell into the safety of next door's apple tree, where it propped itself up against the trunk and stared back down at the cats. Its great golden chest rose and fell with shock and relief.

The tabby-and-white watched the bird go, its narrowed eyes full of species loathing. Then it turned to Vita. 'You have lost me my breakfast, you idiot! Whenever will I have such a chance again? My father once told me, "a pheasant makes beautiful eating". Now I shall never know. Damn!' It paused, then glared at Vita. 'What is your name, moron?'

'Vita,' said Vita, watching the silver ring jounce and spark.

'*La Dolce Vita. La Stupida Vita*, more like.'

Vita was unperturbed. 'I haven't the faintest idea what you're on about, but what I do know is that you wouldn't have wanted to eat a great dusty feathery thing like that old bird anyway,' she said dismissively. 'Delly says they're full of parasites, birds. Besides, what's the point of having to catch your breakfast when you can eat lovely fresh wet things out of a tin?' Her eyes went sly. 'I know: if you tell me where I can get a pretty thing like the one you have in your ear, you can come and eat with me.'

The other cat stared at her. 'You want my earring?'

Vita nodded.

'You're mad. Quite mad. A cruel man did this to me because he thought it marked me as his property. It hurt a lot, and then it festered. And now you want me to do the same to you?'

Vita's eyes were fixed on the ring. 'I'm not afraid of pain.'

The tall cat sighed. With an articulate back foot the strange cat reached up to its left ear, flicked out a gleaming claw and hooked it beneath the metal. It felt around there for a moment, as if searching for a weakness in the link, then gave a sharp pull. The earring came away cleanly, leaving behind it a single drop of crimson. She dropped the ring at Vita's feet.

Vita sniffed at it with fascination. Then she stared at the other cat. 'But how do I put it on?' she wailed.

The tabby-and-white smiled. It was not an altogether friendly expression. 'That's your problem. I can make the hole—' she pushed her face close to Vita's 'by biting you, and you will bleed and bleed and spoil my appetite. So first I claim my breakfast.'

So saying, she stalked over to the cat-flap. A proper house. It had been a while, on her long and arduous quest, since she'd been in a proper house, she thought. She looked back over her shoulder to see if Vita was following. 'Come on, little mouse,' she said encouragingly.

Vita gave the earring a last hard stare. Then she picked it up carefully with the side of her mouth and trotted up the lawn.

As soon as Millie entered the kitchen she knew whose house this was. His smell was everywhere like a signature upon the air. There – on the edge of the cupboards where he would rub his cheek while waiting to be fed. There: by the food bowls and up against the door-frame! And subtly permeating the entire scent-map, cutting a swift synaptic pathway through the harsh artificial-lemon of Anna's cleaning fluid (which she had used a dozen times on the same patch of dining-room carpet), through the plug-in air freshener ('Bouquet of Spring Flowers') and vanilla-scented candles, and straight into her cerebral cortex, was the unmistakably rank musk of a mature tomcat.

Orlando.

She breathed his name silently and a frisson of sexual tension trembled up her spine.

Vita turned around. 'Did you say something?'

Millie blinked. Had she made a sound? She didn't think so. 'I – no.'

'Oh.' Unconcerned, Vita sashayed over to the food bowls. Wedging the earring carefully beneath the mat on which they stood, she stuck her face in the blue one. Between mouthfuls, Millie could make out the following: 'Here . . . tuna . . . salty . . . my brother's . . . help yourself . . . never miss it . . .'

Millie crossed the grey and white linoleum cautiously, checking for escape routes. The brine in which the fish swam called to her enticingly. The green bowl – Orlando's – was full of his scent. Millie felt her breath catch painfully in her throat. Warring emotions spun through her head: fear of discovery and attack; excitement; hunger; and a sort of confused resentment at Orlando's rejection. The resentment hardened to a small dim fury, fuelled by the tang of salty fish. Stealing Orlando's food seemed, suddenly, a rather attractive form of revenge.

Without further thought, she buried her face in his tuna.

Fog had cleared to reveal a swathe of hoar frost across the short broad-bladed grass of the common, leaving it crisp and brittle underfoot. Savouring the quietude of being the only creature out and about at this early hour, I stood motionless beneath the spread bare arms of a gnarled oak, my coat fluorescing in the raw light, and watched my breath cloud off into the air. Behind me, stretching away to the perimeter of brambles and hawthorn, my footprints showed damply green where the warmth of my pads had melted the frost.

I had been looking for my grandfather, but had ascertained that Hawkweed had not passed this way today. I had been spending a troubled time on the wild roads recently. From out of nowhere, it seemed, had come a rash of bad dreams: little night terrors and phantasms that had chased each other down the highways, swirling and spiralling to avoid my furious pursuit. I would go after them in a mechanical, dogged fashion, pinning them down, biting them up and swallowing them with merciless efficiency. Today, it had left me tired and listless, and with an unpleasant aftertaste. I found myself nurturing a small flame of anger at having to deal with the nightmares of Ashmore all on my own. I was, after all, only an apprentice dreamcatcher and my grandfather was surely falling down on his duties that I should find myself so overworked. Where could he be?

It had been some time since I had seen hide or hair of the old cat; and then he had avoided my eye, dropping his mangled head into a slouch as he slunk past the gate and stalked, swaybacked, up the road past the church, before turning into the junction of Allbright Lane. It was as if he didn't want to involve me in whatever it was that he was up to; but more likely, I thought with a sudden flare of annoyance, he was off on one of his mysterious journeys, safe in the knowledge that his student would protect the village's wild roads. He suspected, I am sure, that I could now no more turn my back on a dangerous dream than he could stand in the path of a speeding car.

I stared down at my stained paws in disgust.

I have to admit that I felt trapped. Trapped by the circumstances of my birth; by the trickery of my own grandfather; by the peculiar powers of the hawkweed; and now, worst of all, by my own conscience.

No wonder Liddy had been so contemptuous.

I felt the unfairness of the matter like a stab of indigestion, sharp, between the ribs. A few moments later I realised that there was, in fact, an acute pain between my ribs; and just as I realised this, I vomited.

Something – something hard and uncomfortable, something awkwardly shaped and horrifyingly familiar – came rattling up out of my stomach, caught for a second in my mouth, then spattered out on to the ground, to fall with an audible sound at my feet.

As the steam cleared, I regarded the ejecta with alarm. In the middle of a patch of liquid bile, gleaming against the melted, glistening grass, was a human tooth.

'By the eyes of the Great Cat, Vita!'

Dellifer, who had slipped quietly into the kitchen while Vita was deeply preoccupied with what she thought might be a mouse running along the top of the butcher's table, stared at her charge in complete horror.

Vita, having spent the best part of two days avoiding just this sort of situation, ducked her head and tried to run for the cat-flap; but Dellifer, despite her age and her bulk, was just too quick for her. In a flash, she had blocked Vita's escape route and had grabbed her by the collar.

'Whatever have you done?' she said. 'Just look at your ear.'

This command is a difficult one for anyone to carry out without the benefit of a reflective surface, and so Vita stared at the ground without a word.

Dellifer thrust her thin white face closer to Vita's head, sniffed, screwed her face up in consternation.

'Mutilation, that is,' she growled. 'The work of the devil.'

Vita twisted her head in the older cat's grip and grinned. 'Not the devil. Only Millie.'

Dellifer's eyes narrowed. 'That little harlot. I might have known. You thought I hadn't noticed you'd sneaked her into the house, stolen food and played in the mistress's bedroom, didn't you? There's nothing happens here I don't know about, missy. I may be getting on, but I've got two eyes and a good nose: and I could smell her as soon as she set foot in here, that little queen, with her strange ways. Whatever will the mistress say?'

Dellifer blinked sadly. She set a lot of store by the cleanliness and good behaviour of her youngsters: such was her job after all, the trade that defined her to the rest of the feline world; the reason old Hawkweed had chosen her above others to raise this two grandchildren.

'It's pretty,' Vita said defiantly.

'Pretty? Since when was making a hole in yourself and coating your ear with dried blood considered pretty? If that's pretty, you must think your granfer a splendid sight indeed.'

Vita wrinkled her nose. 'Eh?'

'Hay is for horses, child. Say "pardon",' Dellifer corrected reflexively. She tutted. 'Look at the state of your poor ear.' She rose up on her hind legs and gripped Vita's head firmly between both front paws. Then she licked the area gently until the blackened flakes were all gone. The earring, resting neatly inside the single hole Millie had made at Vita's teeth-gritted demand, sparkled all the more provocatively for her attentions.

At last, Dellifer let her charge go and tutted again. 'Shall I pull it out for you, my dear?' she offered suddenly, with a glint in her eye. She flexed her toes and an array of surprisingly well-kept claws sprang into view.

Vita looked horrified. 'No!' She backed up against the fridge. 'Besides, I want to show Orlando: he never takes me seriously;

228

thinks I'm just a baby.' She wagged her head from side to side to feel the jewellery brush her ear.

Dellifer's eyes became misty. 'Oh dear,' she said. 'Oh dear, oh dear, oh dear.' She brushed a paw across her face, and when she looked back at her charge again her eyes were hard and clear. 'Vita, listen to me, and listen well. You'll never gain true beauty by suffering or inflicting hurt, missy: the world holds pain enough, and to add to it wilfully and for such small reason, is both reckless and wicked. Beauty comes from the inside, that's what my mother always told me; and I have learned by hard lessons that she is right. What does it matter if your fur is as silky as a mouse's ear, or your eyes as bright as a star; if your whiskers are as long as summer grass or your paws as neat as daisies, so long as your essence is spoiled and tainted? Such outward things are just empty fancy that fade and fall as the years sail by. It's only those whose souls please the Great Cat who can ever be considered truly lovely: the ones with a light inside themselves, a light that blazes out clear and true as a beacon to those in need. Wisdom is what makes you grown, Vita my dear; and wisdom's hard to come by. Earning it takes years of experiencing the world and judging which actions to take based on that experience. It's not age makes you grown; and it's certainly not some silly gewgaw a-bobbling in your ear. Don't you go bothering your brother with your self-indulgence. There's a cat who's out there learning those hard lessons, my dear: he's got more on his mind than such fripperies. A lot more.'

But Vita had given up listening to this tedious moral lecture almost immediately. The idea of being considered reckless and wicked just for the sake of a tiny little earring was so plainly ridiculous that she thought Dellifer must be quite mad. She sat there with her face composed in a rigid expression that was supposed to convey concentration; and as soon as her guardian finished speaking, she trotted out of the kitchen, through the cat-door and into the garden, where she had just remembered there was a waterlogged plant pot in which she might be able to see her reflection.

I stared at the tooth for a long time. Then, with a shudder, I picked it up and carried it the few paces to the base of the oak and carefully buried it in the soft mulch there.

When it was safely hidden from view, I lay down on top of it, as if the weight of my body would somehow keep at bay the implications of its violent and unusual appearance.

After a while, I dozed; then finally fell into a disturbed and fitful sleep. And as I slept, I dreamed:

I dreamed I had entered a wild road that somehow ran above the ground, where I found myself hovering like a silent kestrel searching for prey. When I looked about I could see the village, though I was looking at it through a mist: everything was slightly hazy, but if I blinked and concentrated I found that the object I was looking at would come into better focus, leaving my peripheral vision as misty as ever. It was an odd sensation, but after a few moments I forgot about it and began to enjoy my unusual vantage point. From here (wherever I was) I could see all the way down the road to the cottages on the corner, to the stand of ash trees that obscured the bend there, and beyond that across the wide green fields that stretched to Glory Farm. In the opposite direction I could make out the spire of the church emerging from the dark yews of the churchyard, and, much further away, and with hardly any cottage in between, the gates of the old manor house. Between the church and the common, where Anna's cottage and its two neighbours should have stood, set back a few feet from the road behind their chintzy little gardens of herring-bone brick and aromatic herbs, there was nothing but open ground, grazed by a number of scruffy-looking sheep.

I squinted.

The facade of the cottage opposite the pond looked curiously new and unstained; and the roof-windows where the children sometimes leaned out and catapulted nuts at passers-by were missing. Then I noticed that the illuminated box that stood on the corner, into which people went and talked, had also vanished, leaving nothing in its wake but a bank of hazels, newly budded catkins hanging like lambs' tails.

The road, too, was different: somehow unfinished-looking and dusty, full of small stones and deep ruts. And not a single car to be seen anywhere: not parked along the side of the road, nor gathered outside the school, nor even emerging from garages or driveways. There was no sign of the big black car next door, nor the gleaming blue vehicle of the family up the road; and in the area I recognised as the pub car park there was only a large wooden cart and a broken-down old horse chewing in a resigned fashion on a patch of thistles.

The familiarities of the scene jarred painfully. It was my home; and yet, somehow, it was entirely strange to me. But how could it be my home, if there was no home to go to? I pondered this for a while before the consequences of such a situation sank in. If this was not my home, and I could see now way back to that place I regarded as my home, I would never see Vita again; nor Dellifer, nor Anna, nor my grandfather; nor the lads by the garages; nor Liddy; nor even the little long-legged cat with the interesting smell.

At this realisation I felt a moment of pure panic, followed by a wave of terrible loneliness.

I was just giving in to this rush of self-pity when my eye was caught by a movement from a low stone wall on the opposite side of the road. A small white cat had leapt up there and had started to clean her face. She looked rather as Dellifer might have done in another life, I thought dreamily: more rounded where the old cat was thin and angular, but with the same tilt to her cheek, the same slightly upturned eyelids. As I watched, she licked a paw and rubbed it prettily down the side of her head, as if aware of being the centre of a male cat's attention. She was young and neat and daintily proportioned: apart from a vast swell of belly which filled the entire width of the wall.

Kittens! I thought, and a maudlin sorrow flowed through me. My own mother had once looked like this cat, though she had not been white; she, too had once sat on sun-warmed stone and groomed herself in this careful fashion. Her tongue had probably run right over me and Vita, blind and tiny inside her. I felt a little moan escape me; and as I did so, the white cat looked up and stared straight at me.

She had eyes the colour of forget-me-nots, eyes the colour of the wide summer sky. Dellifer's eyes.

She jumped down from the wall, and with her tail high in the air and her feet planted with neat precision, began to cross the wide dusty road towards me.

At that moment, something came hurtling around the corner past the ash trees, and the sound of its passage split the silence of the village like thunderclaps on a clear day. Great gouts of dust shot up into the air, obscuring its true shape; then, horrifyingly, it appeared right in front of me. Four huge galloping horses, their eye-whites showing stark against their dark faces as they strained against the cruel metal of their bits, came crashing into view; and behind them, attached to them, came a vast black coach, its sides so spattered with mud as to largely obscure the ornate family crest worked in colourful detail on its door.

'Run!' I cried, but the white cat paid me no heed.

She never stood a chance. It seemed she did not even hear the carriage as it bore down upon her, for in the middle of the road she stopped and mewed up at me, as if in greeting. Seeing the little cat in their path, the horses skittered wildly, determined not to crush her with their great hooves; but the sight of these vast creatures so suddenly upon her appeared to shock her so badly that she leapt sideways in panic. For a second I saw her – startlingly white amidst all the black – and thought she had escaped injury. Then the first of the enormous wheels went over her and I could see her no more.

At once the carriage came to a shrieking halt and one of its doors burst open. A woman wearing a long dark cloak over a rich burgundy gown flew out into the road, her white hands covering her mouth in a gesture of the utmost horror. Without a care of her gown, she dropped to her knees in the dust and ducked her head to stare underneath the carriage. Two liveried servants came running to her aid, tricorn hats in hand. Taking no notice of their shouts, she reached gingerly around the wheel and after a moment straightened up with the white cat cradled in her arms.

I held my breath.

For a few seconds, maybe four or five, the pregnant cat struggled, her hind legs twitching as if she believed herself in another existence to be running out of harm's way. Then all the life went out of her in a rush and she sagged, a limp ghost of a cat against the dark fabric of the cloak.

The woman's hands were busy. Her fingers were prodding at the distended white belly as if she might somehow save a life; but when she realised that the little cat had indeed been carrying young her hands fell still, clutching the dead creature to her like some hideous trophy. Already, it had left a dusting of white hairs against the deep black velvet of her dolman.

All my breath hissed out of me. The little white cat had died and it was my fault. My fault! She had seen me – where I was – and come to speak to me; and now she was dead.

While I was thinking this, a sudden wind whipped up out of nowhere, shaking the catkins in the hazel hedge so that they danced and twirled, making the branches of the ash tree rattle; and then the woman's wide hood fell back upon her shoulders, to reveal a long, pale face, with skin as translucent as porcelain, framed by hair as black as night.

It was a face I recognised.

And as if she felt my eyes upon her, the woman, as the little white cat had done before her, stared straight up at me, her gaze as cold and hard as emeralds. My body went chill from the inside out. Whether or not she was truly able to see me, I did not know; for as she looked up and searched the air above her, I awoke with a start, my heart hammering painfully against my ribcage. But the image I retained in the nighmares that came whenever I fell into any sleep deep enough to enable me to dream for the next week or so was not the horrifying sight of the little white cat being crushed to death beneath the wheels of the great black carriage, but the sight of that face, mouth open wide in some transcendent emotion – amazement, maybe; or triumph.

Despite her porcelain beauty and apparent youth, there was not a tooth left in her head.

Twenty

IT WAS rare that Dellifer made excursions into the outside world, but today she crossed the dandelioned and mossy lawn, past the untidy lavenders and the stark rose bushes, noting even in mid-stride how in the space of just a year the wood of the plants had extended another inch or so up the stem; another inch of dead wood in which the thorns would thicken and harden to great uncompromising claws; another inch which would, for all the care Anna lavished, never produce another shoot or bud. That was how she felt, she thought suddenly: an elderly cat, long past her best; sucked dry by litter after litter of motherless kittens, with her blood thinning and her joints stiffening, and less and less life left to run in her. Nine lives! What sort of nonsense was all that? She smiled to herself, and for an instant there was a glimpse of the young queen tomcats had fought over down the generations. Or maybe it was the memory of one tomcat in particular that brought that smile to her face.

For all her years, though, she leapt up the fence and on to the top of the old shed, with its peeling white boards and air of neglect, with a grace born of long experience of judging height and distance. Something had called her out there; something that made her skin twitch and her nose alert; but now, gazing about her, she couldn't imagine what it might be. She took in the cottage, with its warm red bricks and crumbling mortar; the leaded windows glinting in the chill sun; the curl of smoke from the fire in the snug, and sighed. Her job here was done: she had raised the two kittens to something approaching adulthood, and it had to be admitted that they no longer needed her. There seemed little reason to stay: sentiment, maybe; or a promise long given that might never be kept, and possibly a certain self-interest; for of all the places she had passed through on her journey, she would miss this cottage and its inhabitants most. The woman had been kind to her, despite difficult circumstances; and her charges had not been the most troublesome of her long career. Young Vita was turning into quite a handful, but it was only to be expected, at that awkward age. The fancies would soon pass, once she had kittens of her own. Having children made you more aware of the priorities in life, Dellifer thought. She'd never had any herself, not in this life, but she'd looked after enough of other cats' litters to know the truth of the matter. And through it all, she kept producing milk. One of the Great Cat's little miracles, she often said. Though it might have more to do with the strange-tasting food the woman at the big house had fed her during the long, strange stay. All those kittens . . .

Dellifer blinked away her thoughts.

She settled deeper on to her paws and sank into that restful state which cats achieve so easily and humans hardly at all, when the body relaxes itself into the flow of the world and the mind becomes a tranquil pool; and sat, as the sun went down and the first glow of the moon spread itself across the sky, as unblinking as a sphinx on a desert plain.

I, meanwhile, was approaching a place I had long avoided. I hadn't a thought for my kindly foster mother in my head: no, I was intent upon other concerns entirely.

I made my way to the canal from the common, through mazes of highways and the thin, dank foliage of winter, following a scent-map as familiar to me as my own heart.

The dream of the death of the little white cat under the wheels of the black carriage, of the bizarrely young, yet toothless woman, had disturbed me in a way I could not define to myself. Even now, some days later, it nagged at me, buzzing at the edges of my mind like a great black and gold bee, freighted with information I could not decode.

Was Liddy beyond the reach of harm? I had to know.

I came out on to the towpath a little further up from my usual track, and emerged from the brambles and dead bracken into a place of silence and obscurity. It was the canal's most elusive hour, when all things are undependable and it is hard, even for a cat, to tell what is shadow, what wave, or wood. Dark shapes sat at unexpected angles, in different configurations from my last memory of the place. Pale gleams between the blacker areas suggested empty moorings, abandoned berths. Nothing moved: not a breath of wind, not a rill of water. I sniffed the air.

A patchwork of scents came back to me: tar and oil; cats of all kinds; humans, too. Usually, I would have picked the golden thread of Liddy's scent out from among the others in a second; but so many nights out on the highways catching and gulping down the horde of nightmares that had descended on Ashmore over the last week had left my senses slow and befuddled. I sniffed again.

There!

Her scent. Liddy's. It was faint, but even so it was as clear as a crow in an empty sky to a cat obsessed.

Liddy's houseboat lay in its usual place, though the neighbours on either side were gone. Fuelled by inexplicable optimism and a sudden deep calm that wrapped my racing heart, I trotted to the edge of the towpath and called softly into the night.

'Liddy! Liddy, come out . . .!'

Nothing stirred on board the narrowboat.

I walked from one end of it to the other, before I caught a new scent. New, but not unfamiliar. I dropped my nose to the ground and followed it, trying to pinpoint its origin. The scent was human: that much I could perceive at once; female, too. I opened my mouth and inhaled deeply. Anna! I could smell Anna. I felt a shiver run through me, a mixture of emotions and images: a gentle hand in my fur, a face looming close but unthreatening above me; food offered and accepted freely, a familiar voice calling in the dusk. But underlying the smell of Anna, another, older scent, fusty and indeterminate, like something that has been stored for too long. I sensed a faint recognition of this scent too: something in my head insisted I had encountered it more recently even than Anna; which seemed peculiar, since I had seen no one else all day . . .

I was still brooding confusedly on this when there was a movement above me.

Liddy!

I looked up with a leap of the heart. Moonlight licked off a shiny eye. I found that I could not speak. I craned my neck for a better view of my beloved and from above there came a hiss.

I backed off a little way, stared along the darkened deck. The hissing stopped, and the narrowboat yielded only indistinct shadow to my scrutiny.

'It's all right, Liddy, it's only me, Orlando. I came to see if you were all right, and to apologise. I let you down, and I'm sorry, truly I am. I shouldn't have run off like that: I don't know why I did it – I just couldn't seem to help myself. Dreamcatching is a terrible burden, Liddy, and it has made me miserable thinking about that night. I know I don't deserve another chance, but, oh, Liddy, if you only knew how terribly I've missed you, I'm sure you'd take pity on me and let me see you again . . .'

From the deck there came a sort of cackle.

I examined the shadows with indignation. 'There's no need to make it worse than it is,' I said, feeling miffed. 'I do have some pride, even if I've come crawling back here. You might have the grace to hear me out without making fun of me. I've tried not to think of you, but it's no good. I even hurt a friend because of you, and I didn't mean to do that, either.' I hung my head. 'The truth is, Liddy, I'm hopeless around females. I just don't know what to do, or say, or even think. I feel confused all the time. All I need to know is that you like me, just a little; that you could try to forgive me.'

Silence.

I sighed. 'Please say something, even if it's only goodbye. At least I'll know where I stand. I think you owe me that much, Liddy, truly I do. Just tell me you hate me and you never want me to come here again and I'll leave, even though it will break my heart.'

There was a scuffling noise on the deck of the boat, and as I stared in the direction of that noise, a new smell came to me on a breath of breeze. My nose twitched. Not Liddy—

Pale radiance filtered through the thick clouds. I saw a flicker of movement above me, then light gleaming on curved yellow teeth. It was a rat! Infuriated, all thoughts of my beloved subsumed, I leapt from towpath to deck in a single athletic surge, but the rat was quicker. As soon as it had seen my haunches bunching for the spring it was off, its long bare tail slapping along the wooden deck like a length of wet cord.

There was a splash, and then the rhythmic sound of water displaced by determined movement. I ran to the edge of the deck, only to see the rat swim to safety on the other side of the canal.

I stared after it, heart sinking as the implications became clear. A rat, on board Liddy's home. No cat would allow such a thing.

She had gone.

A prolonged examination of the boat, of the steps to the living quarters and around the door at the end, where a cat would rub its cheek to mark its territory; the food bowl crusted with days-old food: all reinforced my fears. Liddy was gone, and by the faintness of her scent, might have been gone for some days. I had no idea of where she could be, of whether I would ever see her again.

I sat dejectedly at the foot of the steps and thought about this for a time. Then, perversely, I felt my heart lift.

She had gone, but it was still possible that she might not entirely hate me. It was better than nothing. It was just enough to keep me going.

With a new impetus of energy, I ran up the steps two at a time and jumped lightly down on to the towpath.

The canal cats were by nature an undependable lot, creatures neither of solid ground nor truly of the waterways. And, just as they belonged to no one element, neither did they belong fully to themselves or to the humans on whose boats they travelled. Some of them liked to play up to this contradiction, swaggering like pirates up and down the towpath, seducing females and picking fights, secure in the knowledge that if things got too hot at this anchorage, they could just skip town on the next barge, if they could find people – an equally shiftless breed – with sufficient mental rigour to engage in the lengthy process of disconnecting their gas and water and sewage and mooring lines, and threading their assiduous way through the other craft and out into clear water, to drift slowly down to the next docking-place. Some of the narrowboats never moved from their berths from one year's end to the next; some had likely forgotten their original function entirely and would spring a leak at the very thought of sailing open water once again; others tied up and were immediately fretful, still searching for the perfect mooring. It was an aimless, carefree existence and it made for easy acquaintance but little close friendship, as I was soon to discover when I started trying to question the cats I could find over the mystery of Liddy's whereabouts.

The first cat I met was a tattered, brindled specimen, who wore his facial scars like a badge. I thought I remembered him from the fight; and indeed some of the wounds looked barely healed, but when he spoke, the brindled cat – who liked to be known as Charlton ('never Charlie,' he instructed me fiercely) – shook his head. 'Don't know who you mean, mate,' was all he would say when asked if he knew Liddy.

'Liddy,' I repeated stubbornly. 'Lydia, she prefers. You must know her: she's the local beauty, or so I was always told.'

Charlton raised an eyebrow. His short white whiskers bristled. He thought for a while as if consulting a long mental address book. 'Nah,' he said at last. 'No Lydias. Mind you,' he leered, 'they don't always tell me their names.'

I was persistent. 'That boat over there. That's where she lives. Except there's no one there any more.'

But the brindled cat shook his head. 'Sorry, mate: can't help you.'

And off he went up the towpath, sway-backed and stumpy tail held high, and disappeared into the shadows under the bridge, a notorious place to score an old fish-head or a less-than-choosy queen.

I walked up and down beside the dark canal for half an hour or more, but could see no sign of other cats. I could, however, feel their presence; could sense eyes watching me from covert quarters. Frustration ticking in my head, I sat down on the towpath and made myself comfortable. Clearly, there was no point in going after them: they'd just burrow down into their boats like worms down a hole; but if they got the idea I wouldn't leave until I'd had my information, perhaps they'd come to me, if only to speed my departure.

It was a good plan. Evidently rattled by my patient repose, a pair of young scruffs braved a nearby companionway. They lacked the bluster of such brigands as Charlton, being both young and smaller, and far less bitten about the head and ears. Nervously, they jostled one another at the rail.

'You ask him.'

'No, you.'

'It was your idea.'

'You're older than me.'

'Only by twelve minutes.'

After some further bickering and head-butting the older of the pair cleared its throat as if loosening a hairball.

'Excuse me – sir.'

I opened a lazy eye a little wider. 'Me?'

'Er, yes, sir.'

I sat up and flexed my claws. There was a further flurry of activity on the houseboat, and a lot of whispering in which I thought I caught the words 'battle' and 'champion', then the second cat piped up: 'You won't hurt us, will you, sir?'

The older cat cuffed its brother round the ear. 'Don't be stupid. Of course he won't hurt us.' He raised his voice as if to convince himself. 'After all, we've done nothing to him: we were only spectators.'

I grinned to myself. They were only kittens.

'Get down here,' I said sternly. It felt strange addressing other cats in such a patriarchal tone. I wasn't that much older than them myself; but I rather liked it.

The twins, each an indeterminate russet colour, almost fell on to the towpath in their eagerness to comply. They would probably turn out to be burly little cats in their time, but for now they still had their fair share of kitten-fat and puffball fur.

'Nutmeg,' said one.

Whatever did he mean?

'Cinnamon,' said the other at once. They started to giggle anxiously. 'Our owner bakes a lot of cakes—' Nutmeg started, but I cut in hurriedly: 'I'm looking for a friend. She lives on that boat over there.'

The kittens followed my gaze, took in the dark shape of the houseboat, and stared at each other. They looked up and down the canal, at the blank spaces of empty moorings. They trod the dusty earth of the towpath with neurotic paws. They milled, muttering, around each other in tight little circles until I lost track of which of them was which.

'Don't know,' said one at last.

'A lot of cats have gone recently,' said the other.

I stared at them. 'What do you mean, gone?'

'Been taken.'

'Oh, Nutmeg!'

'Ssssh. They have. They were taken—'

'We don't know—'

'—by the Basket Beast.'

'The what?' I was incredulous.

Nutmeg looked defensive. 'Well, that's what I call it. It's got a basket.'

'It's a stupid name—'

'No, it's not—'

'You say!'

Nutmeg bit Cinnamon and Cinnamon promptly retaliated and I had to separate them. 'Calm down. Tell me properly: what did you see?'

Cats had been disappearing from up and down the towpath for the past few days, they told me. And not just any cats, either: only young ones; only females; no neuters. Nutmeg and Cinnamon had lain out under the deck tarpaulin one night to see who came along. They were very frightened. Most of the humans they recognised: the young couple from the prettily decorated narrow-boat near the head of the dock, reeling back from the pub as usual; an elderly lady painter who lived by herself with the smelliest, raggediest tomcat of them all; the fat man who didn't like cats at all and would throw water on any who sang near his boat; the tall man from Liddy's boat.

I sat up straighter. 'What about his cat?' I asked quickly. 'You must have seen her: she's very—' I paused '—attractive.'

The twins shuffled embarrassedly. 'Oh, her,' said Cinnamon.

Nutmeg snickered. 'We saw you get into that fight over her,' he said.

The kittens elbowed one another delightedly. When they looked up again, my face must have fallen still and urgent.

'What about her? Where is she?'

The twins conferred wordlessly. Then Cinnamon hunched his

shoulders as if to receive a blow. 'She was the last,' he said. 'The Basket Beast took her last of all.'

I questioned the youngsters long and hard, but was unable to glean any more useful information other than that it had been a human who had taken Liddy: that the figure had been tall, and had come by night.

The vanishings were not the only disturbances, either, they said. Even before the female cats were taken, everyone had been experiencing nightmares – both boat-owners and felines; even the few dogs that lived on the canal had not been immune, so it must be bad, for everyone knew dogs only ever had dreams about food and running. I scowled. 'I know all about those,' I said grimly. 'They've kept me very busy lately.'

People, they said, had become strangely agitated. They sat up late into the night with books and magazines and strained their eyes by the soft light of the gas mantles; anything, it seemed, to put off the bad dreams. That was why some of the houseboats had moved on: the humans were saying they didn't feel comfortable at Ashmore any longer; they couldn't relax; and what was the point of being happy wanderers if they weren't happy where they were? That, announced Cinnamon, was what their old lady had been saying to her husband: they should weigh anchor and go on up the canal to Winchfield. He'd moaned about the whole palaver of it, but eventually he agreed to move on: only this morning he'd said he felt positively hag-ridden, Nutmeg declared, stumbling over this odd phrase.

I left the twins and carried on down the towpath towards the bend in the canal where the moorings petered out; but everywhere was dark and silent and no one else came out to speak to me.

Dejected, and with my skin crawling with anxiety, I turned for home. Where was Liddy? Who had taken her, and where was the tall man, her owner? Perhaps, I thought, in an attempt to calm my worst fears, they'd just moved up into the village for a while, to have what humans call 'a holiday'. People did inexplicable things like that: abandoned one perfectly good place to spend time in another. Head down in thought, I entered one of the paths that led back to the common, stepping neatly over bramble runners and exposed roots.

But what about all the others?

And why had only young, unneutered females disappeared?

Was it a coincidence? Or was it something far more sinister?

Millie regarded Vita despairingly. 'You're quite sure this is what you want to do?'

The little tabby cat nodded emphatically. 'It's time,' she declared. 'I'll never be truly grown up till I've experienced the world: even Dellifer said so. And it was only after Orlando went with grandfather on to the wild roads that he became so insufferably adult.' She jiggled her head to feel the silver ring brush the soft fur on the inside of her ear. Then she said. 'You like my brother, don't you?'

Millie stared at her. She could think of nothing to say that was not an outright lie.

Vita watched her with a curious expression, which seemed to consist in equal measure of astonishment – at having hit the mark with what had been, in fairness, something of a random shot – and gratification.

'How can you tell?' Millie asked eventually. 'For all you know, I might never have met him.'

'I watched you at his food bowl,' Vita said gleefully. 'You almost fainted. Your eyes went all fluttery—' She mimicked an impassioned swoon.

'I was hungry, that's all,' Millie's voice had a dangerous edge to it.

Vita, too naïve to know when she was on the edge of a precipice, laughed. 'Even so, if you don't take me on the highways, I'll tell him you love him,' she said, and had to dance swiftly out of the way of Millie's raking claws.

The long-legged cat, furious with embarrassment, was not to be evaded. She caught up with Vita and cuffed her till her ears rang. 'If I take you on the highways, I do so because I choose to do it,' she said severely. 'I do it because even at this age you are still a stupid kitten and you need to learn a lesson: so if it's experience you're after, I can promise you will soon acquire some. But I warn you now: you may not like it.'

Vita looked mulish. She drew herself up. 'You can say what you like.' I'm not a baby, and I'm going to prove it to everyone –

243

to you, and my snotty brother, and to nagging old Dellifer. I'm fed up with being treated like some pathetic little orphan who can't be trusted to fend for herself. I'm the same age as Orlando, and probably not much younger than you, so there's no need for you to be so overbearing. Just take me to the entrance. You don't even have to come in with me if you don't want,' she finished. By now, her chin was jutting belligerently and a liquid shine in her eye threatened a temper tantrum of considerable proportions.

Millie knew when she was beaten. 'OK,' she shrugged. 'But I'm coming in with you, like it or not.'

She led Vita through back gardens full of silent shadow and silvered foliage, over and under fences, through holes in hedges and around trees. Vita followed the taller cat closely, her eyes wide open and as empty as the night.

At last, on the edge of Ashmore Common, Millie stopped. She sniffed the ground. She interrogated the dead and sodden bracken with her paws. She pushed her face against something Vita could not quite see; and suddenly she had no head.

Vita stared and stared.

Then, just as abruptly, Millie retracted herself from the highway and her head popped back into view.

'It doesn't smell right,' she said.

Vita glared. 'I'll go in alone, then.' She approached the invisible doorway. As Millie had done, she sniffed at the wet grass and the trodden earth; she observed the bracken. Other cats had been here: that much she could tell, and one of the scents seemed familiar, though the mélange was too confusing for her to separate out a single strand. Experimentally, she pressed her face where Millie's had been. For a few seconds, nothing: just cold air and the smell of wet leaves and mould; then a slight resistance as if somehow the air had taken on substance, become thicker and grown a skin. Resolutely she pushed.

'Wait!'

Millie grabbed Vita's tail and hauled her unceremoniously backwards.

'Look,' Millie said through gritted teeth, 'something's wrong in there. I can just tell, all right? So if you're determined to get yourself into trouble, then you'll have to take me with you. So. First things first.' Her tone brooked no dissent. 'You will hang on to *my* tail at all times,' – she stuffed the tip into Vita's protesting mouth – 'which will have the benefit of keeping you both safe *and* quiet. You will go at my speed, you will neither pull nor let go; and you will not bite it in childish excitement. Right?'

Vita nodded grudgingly.

'Wild roads are wild places. Do not be surprised to see some strange sights there. And,' she fixed Vita with an uncompromising stare, 'you will experience a change when you enter the highways. There's no call to be alarmed by the transformation: it's a mark of the Great Cat's for us, that She releases the greatness in all of us when we enter Her roads. So, accept the change that overtakes you, no matter how peculiar it feels. Be humble and grateful for such blessing, and do exactly as I say. And if I start running, then you'd better pray your little legs can keep up with me. Let's go.'

By the time I returned to the cottage, the thick blanket of clouds had parted and the moon was shining through overhead, the Great Cat's silver eye beaming like a searchlight across her domain, as perplexed as I was by the mystery of it all. It illuminated the garden so that sharp shadows jutted from the flowerbeds and made monsters of the terracotta pots. As I wove amongst the rose-stumps, there was a high keening cry from behind me. I spun around, senses balanced precariously between the urge to fight or run, and found an apparition staring at me from the top of the shed. Its eyes were as round and as sheeny as puddles, and of such a lambent silver it was as though there was nothing in its skull but moonlight struggling to be released back into the night.

I gazed at it in shock before recognition struck me. 'Dellifer – what is it?'

The older cat regarded me uncomprehending, its opaque white inner eyelids shuttering back and forth like some overdriven mechanism. At last they sprang apart, and the pupils dilated to take full measure of the light until at last they were able to focus on the marmalade of my coat. 'Orlando, Orlando! Thank creation you're here. The most terrible dream—' She shook her head as though to jar it loose.

More bad dreams. I shuddered.

'Vita, Vita . . . oh!'

'What's happened to Vita?'

'I don't—' her voice wavered on the edge of hysteria '—I don't knooooowww!' Her wail of anguish cut through the night with appalling clarity. In the elm tree next door, pigeons shifted uncomfortably on their roosts.

I leapt up the peeling boards in one fluid movement. I stared at my foster mother. I didn't know what to do. It was so unlike Dellifer to over-react to anything. She was always relentlessly sensible: she was our touchstone, our security blanket, the closest thing to a parent we had . . . I butted my head against her cheek, then with sudden decision began to groom her. Some way through this process I was ambushed by the realisation of how much smaller than me she seemed to have become: I had to bow my neck in order to reach her. In turn, Dellifer raised her head meekly to my attentions. Roles reversed, we sat thus, while the shudders of aftershock running through the old cat's muscles began to subside and her breathing became slow and even.

'Now tell me slowly, Delly: what has terrified you so?' I shouted, to make an impression on those old ears.

'You'll think me foolish, dear. It was just a dream. Not a pleasant one; no, not at all pleasant. I can't even remember what it was about now. There was a lot of running and shrieking; tall rooms; something terribly in pain . . .' Her face contorted itself in the attempt to remember. 'And then . . . and then . . .' She sighed. 'It's no good, dear, I just can't think.'

'You said something about Vita—'

Dellifer's eyes became round with panic. 'Oh my. Vita! Yes – I left her alone. 'She peered over my shoulder towards the cottage. 'Orlando, I fear something terrible may have happened to her while I slept up here, dead to the world!' And with that she leapt down from the shed, her old limbs jarring at the shock of the landing, and ran stiff-legged to the back door. By the time I reached her, she was scratching distractedly at the cat-flap.

'What is it?'

'It's locked!' she wailed.

I shrugged. 'She does that at night now, Anna,' I said soothingly. 'We'll be all right; and Vita's probably snoring her head off on the bed upstairs.'

But she wasn't.

When Anna opened the back door the next morning, Dellifer and I scurried past her and searched the house from top to toe. Of Vita there was no sign. In the kitchen, though, I stopped dead in my tracks. Someone I knew, though not well, had been in my kitchen. I stalked around the quarry tiles with my nose an inch from the ground, as if tracking a very small beetle. Near the food bowls the scent was strongest, even though I could tell that Anna had washed them both this morning and refilled them with dried lamb-flavour pellets. I sat there, all at once overcome, staring into the green and blue dishes as if they might somehow contain an answer. First Liddy; now Vita. A dreamcatcher was supposed to know everything that happened along the convoluted web of his highways; yet here I was, still only an apprentice, with no idea where the two cats who mattered most to me in the world might be. I sniffed the air again; and suddenly all the bad dreams I had swallowed in the last horrible week returned to me in a flood, filling my mouth with harsh and bitter flavours, befuddling my senses; until I could not even tell whether the trace of scent I had discerned was cat or human: only that it was female.

I was still sitting there, deep in thought, when Dellifer came bustling in, her fur all over the place from burrowing behind furniture, and a wild light in her eye.

'There's no time for breakfast,' she admonished me severely. 'Your sister's missing.'

For a moment I was angry that she had misinterpreted my reverie; then, inexplicably, I found myself thinking about the little tabby-and-white cat I had met by the canal, Millefleur: Millie. How I had last seen her, with the starlight glittering on her earring and her white bellyfur shining up at me, and the blood buzzing so hard in my head I hadn't known whether to abandon myself to the glorious invitation of her scent, or to run till I could smell her no more . . .

When I looked up again, Dellifer was regarding me with a disturbingly knowing expression. I suddenly felt myself transparent to her gaze, my every thought wide open to her view.

Slowly, Dellifer shook her heard. 'To think that only yesterday I was priding myself on having brought the pair of you up so well that my job was done. They always say that pride comes before a fall, and 'twas a lesson long coming to me. I've never had a child disappear from home before, from under my care. Lads – you expect them to wander; but little Vita . . . Whatever will your granfer say?'

'He should be here,' I said forcefully. 'He's supposed to be the dreamcatcher. Something strange is happening in Ashmore, and he should be here to help us.' Guilt and fury made me vicious. 'Instead, he's out there wandering around without a care in the world, probably giving all his scattered queens a good seeing-to, and leaving me to chase his bloody dreams.'

At the mention of the dreamcatcher Dellifer began to swell visibly, the fur bristling up from her head and neck as if she were being inflated. 'Damn Hawkweed for his selfish, wayward, cussed nature! Never kept a promise to me in his life: can't imagine why I thought he might honour the one he made me this time. I was living perfectly comfortably – nice, smart family; very good quality carpets and central heating – when he comes to me, wheedling. "This is the one, Delly," he says. "This time I'm sure. Poor little orphans, and one of them the new dreamcatcher: I swear. Come and take care of them, Delly, as a personal favour, just for me. See them through the hard times, and then when the lad's come to age enough to take on the task, you and I can be together and there'll be no more roaming for me, no more careering around the highways at all hours of the day and night, no more chasing those damned dreams. And for you, no more litters to raise. Our jobs will be done, Delly. The two of us can be together at last: we can settle down in the bliss we deserve. And if the milk still comes (bless the lady for that at least, amongst all her other doings) well, I'm getting on now, my dear," he says, "and there's nothing quite so nutritious as mother's milk. It won't go to waste!" And he laughs and laughs. Dirty old beggar . . .' She rambled to a halt, breathing hard with indignation.

It was the longest speech I had ever heard from my foster mother, but its import burned through me like poison. I stared at her, eyes wide.

'So it's my turn to shoulder the burden, is it?' I said bitterly. 'Now that I've been trained up as the Dreamcatcher of Ashmore, so that you and that old renegade can retire into a life of ease.

You didn't raise me, Dellifer: you sacrificed me. I'm as damned now as Hawkweed ever was!'

And I fled through the kitchen and out of the cat-door with such violence that I left fur stuck in its hinges.

Dellifer stretched up to where the tuft of marmalade fur lay ensnared in the cat-flap and sniffed at it. Spicy, and dusty at the same time, the scent of it was enough to transport her as effectively as any wild road to a place in her life where a tiny ball of orange fluff, and one of darker tabby, butted at her belly, their eyes squeezed shut and their tiny pink mouths mewing piteously for her milk.

All at once she found she could not swallow. Her eyes became so tight and sore it was hard to blink: but as cats are unable to weep, Dellifer could only open her own pink mouth to release a howl into the morning air that had dogs barking the length of the village's main street and people pausing in their gossip in the post office to wonder at the sound.

Twenty-one

THE YEAR had tilted towards winter. The geese abandoned the pond to its year-round inhabitants, the coots and mallards. Fewer people drove out from Drychester to the Green Man for Sunday lunch. The inhabitants of Ashmore woke cold, and made a note to have their winter-weight quilts dry-cleaned. Down in the valley, the canal filled with willow leaves, which lay for a week fading to white before they drifted away; the water slowed, took on the colour of a bottle that has been in the ground. It was bitterly cold in the surrounding meadows at night. When Lydia did not return to the narrowboat, John and Anna walked the length and breadth of Ashmore together, calling, 'Lydia? Liddy?' to no avail. They posted notices on fences and trees.

'She'll be back,' he said glumly. 'Who else would put up with her?'

'You know you love her.'

They were meeting almost daily by then. They sought out things they could do together. They ate Thai food in a rural pub near Westley ('Ah,' he said, 'coriander and cricket trophies: nothing like it!'); they joined the Film Club (which, being the interest of Francis Baynes, the vicar, offered mostly subtitled Eastern European films about the martyrs of Mystic Christianity). One cold morning he got her to help him strip and repaint the *Magpie*'s faded terracotta upperwork. After an hour Anna found herself staring speculatively at his hands. In the end she had to look away. 'Please just take me to bed,' she wanted to say: 'There's nothing in the way of that now.' But something held her back. Perhaps he was holding himself back too. What would he be like to live with? she wondered. The boat would be impossible for two, it was narrow, damp, there would be too many cats; and the idea of John Dawe – his untidiness, his restlessness, that obsessive energy which, thwarted, would turn so easily into the kind of sullen, self-destructive anger she had seen him direct at his cousin – trammelled by her neat little cottage seemed equally unlikely. Nevertheless, she found herself trying to imagine some sort of life the two of them could share. She stopped what she was doing in the late afternoon to think about it. Standing at the bathroom mirror before she went to bed at night, she congratulated herself wryly:

'You don't look so bad, for someone with no obvious future.'

They avoided talking about it, but wherever they went, the events at Stella's dinner party went with them. Stella was always in their minds, too, a difficulty postponed, almost consciously unacknowledged. It was an unspoken rule that they never mentioned her.

They did their Christmas shopping in Drychester indoor market, where, after agreeing to meet up again at Pizza Express for lunch, they drifted easily away from one another in a daze of consumption. He bought her a brightly coloured Peruvian ear-flap hat. She bought him a bottle of honeyed wine. He arrived at the restaurant first. She arrived laughing. 'Along with the condiments,' he said, 'Pizza Express are delighted to put a real flower on your table every day.' As she sat down he took the flower out of its vase and presented it to her solemnly. 'This is for you.'

'Don't be silly.'

He smiled.

Later she said experimentally: 'You don't ask me about Max any more.'

'No,' he said, 'I don't.'

He put his hand out across the table. She held it.

'Alice Meynell took him back to London that morning,' she said. She wanted him to be certain about these events; the meanings of them.

She left a pause in which he could make a comment if he felt like it, then added: 'She's been up there a couple of times to see him, I think.'

John was amused. 'Has she now?' he said.

'I think I'd like more chilli oil.'

The closer they got, the more cautious they became. They were aware of Stella, of course, brooding up there in her hideout among the cedars. But it was more than that: neither of them could forget how fragile things had been the last time, and this forced courtesies upon them they might not otherwise have observed. He had a cellphone on the *Magpie* – she left messages with his answering service. He left messages with hers. Though both of them, perhaps, wished it otherwise, they never called on one another unexpectedly: until one day she woke to find him on the doorstep with the milk.

'It's early,' she pointed out.

'I thought we might go for a walk.'

'Excuse me.' Anna stuck her head outside and inspected the weather. 'As I thought. Foggy and cold. I hate December, it just looks like a lot of damp sticks. And anyway, what would we see, in this?'

'We could walk up to Cresset Beacon,' he said, as if he hadn't heard her. He had his ancient leather-and-canvas knapsack with him; this he opened, to allow her a brief glimpse of its contents. 'I've got a picnic.'

'Anyone can pack a flask and some apples,' she said carelessly, 'and something wrapped in kitchen foil, and call that a picnic.' She thought she might have seen a woollen blanket in there too. She had another look at the weather. 'Not today, thank you,' she said briskly, beginning to close the door.

'Trust me,' he promised, 'and you'll have sunshine.'

She looked up at him. 'Oh, all right then,' she said, without believing a word of it.

The fog was so thick you expected it to have weight, consistency, substance of its own. It padded the arms of the old fruit trees in the cottage gardens, muffled the sound of the closest voice. Cars made their way through the village as cautiously as cows through a new gate; the fog swung closed behind them, and they moved away mooing nervously at one another. Few people were out and about on foot. The postman was the rattle of a gate, the clatter of a letterbox. Old Mr Thompson, bundled up in worsted trousers, two pullovers, and a quilted bodywarmer, waved his stick at Anna and John as they passed, though whether in greeting or reproach it was impossible to tell. Down near the common, where the fog lost texture and took on the colour of milk, Anna saw a marmalade cat dash suddenly between two trees.

'Was that Orlando? It was!' She stared anxiously into the middle distance: nothing. 'Did you see him? Did you see him?'

'No.'

'I don't like to think of him outside in weather like this. What if he got run over?'

John Dawe smiled. 'By whom?' he asked. 'No one's going more than ten miles an hour.'

'Well, lost, then,' she said, 'like Liddy. What if he got lost?'

'Cats have their own lives. You can't just coop them up to stop them getting into trouble.'

'I suppose not.'

They walked for a while in the padded silence. Anna, who had been thinking of Barnaby as well as Orlando, said: 'Do you suppose they really have nine lives? Cats, I mean.' When he didn't reply, aware of the risk she took in bringing the name out into the open between them, she took the opportunity to add: 'Stella doesn't. At the supper party – after you left? – she called it a "misreading of popular reincarnation themes that leaked out of Egypt in the millennium before Christ". She said cats were just fertility symbols.'

John shrugged. 'Stella has a metaphysics all her own,' he said. 'Mostly, she believes in Stella.'

'But what do you think?'

'I think the cat symbolises Atum-Ra, lord of life. "From Atum-Ra issued Earth, Air, Fire and Water. And from each element its presiding deity." One god, four elements, four demiurges: if you like, you can add that up to nine. Prayer, a tree of life, an emergent cosmology, all contained inside the one symbol – Mau, the cat. Stella's interpretation pales by comparison – it's vague and reductive at the same time, like most anthropology.'

'Cats are fertile though,' Anna said. 'Aren't they?'

He kicked at a stone, which skittered away across the road to be swallowed abruptly by the fog.

'"I am one who becomes two; I am two who become four; I am four who become eight; I am one more after that,"' he quoted at last. 'Can't you feel the force of that? Can't you feel how thin it makes the words "fertility symbol"? There must be more to it. Love, invisibility, power, healing, protection.' He thought a moment. 'There are no metaphors here,' he decided. 'At Deir el-Bahari, in the Missing Dynasty, in some perfectly literal sense, five drops of cat's blood would immunise a child against illness.'

This was too much for Anna. 'Those Egyptians,' she said. 'With medicine that advanced, no wonder they had to believe in reincarnation.'

'Don't you?' he said.

'No,' she admitted, 'I don't think I do.'

'You're lucky,' he said. 'My dreams are full of it. Since I was a little boy. I still dream of Nonesuch every night. It knows me, that house: it knows who I am. Who I've been. Do you ever feel as if there's some truer, more complete world than the one we occupy, some different story of things? You're a part of it, but you don't know why? You're part of it and you don't even know where it is?'

All she felt was that she had to slow him down. 'John,' she said, 'I—'

He smiled and moved his hands, in a gesture of defeat. 'Of course not,' he said. 'Of course you don't. No one in their right mind feels that. But I do. My soul's a jigsaw made of years. All this is only the smallest, newest piece. It's barely real.'

'Thanks a lot,' she said; but he didn't hear, so she laughed as best she could.

'I ask myself why nature would go to the effort of creating all those lives – all those souls, all those billions of different personalities in the world – if, when the body died, they just disappeared into nothing. Wouldn't you say that was wasteful?'

'Reincarnation as recycling,' she said. 'Very green.'

He rubbed his hand over his face. 'I'm not explaining myself well here.'

'No.'

The lanes had brought them out above and to the north of Ashmore. Here, where the land fell away into steep pasture, the fog had a luminous quality to it, as if it were full of light. It was no easier to penetrate, but John Dawe leaned over the nearest stone wall and stared into it anyway. He said:

'The thing is this: the first time I saw you, down on the towpath, I knew without a doubt I'd seen you before.'

'Well, you probably had,' said Anna. 'It's a small village.'

'I don't mean that,' he said patiently.

'Then what?'

'I thought I had seen you in another life,' he said, and walked off quickly uphill as if he already wanted to divorce himself from this news.

Anna, thrown into a panic she couldn't explain, caught up with him and called his name and touched his body just beneath the shoulder blades. In exactly the same instant, they emerged from the fog into dazzling sunshine. It was like a flashbulb going off; or an electric shock. Anna, who thought confusedly that she had been burned, dropped her hand. While she was blinking and rubbing her eyes, filled suddenly with an extraordinary sense of peace, he took her roughly by the tops of the arms.

'Turn round!' he said urgently. 'Look!'

Fog, burning white, its surface shifting and roiling like a slowed-down sea. Somewhere below, she imagined, Ashmore lay smothered and gasping for breath, never suspecting the airy ecstasy of light above. A little way down the valley, the tops of some birches and a stand of pines cleared the surface; a bird flew up out of the trees, then, losing height suddenly, disappeared again.

'Its amazing!'

'It's a temperature inversion,' he said. 'On mornings like these, a layer of warm air keeps the fog in the valley. Look at me.'

She looked at him.

'I always keep my promises.'

'Do you?' she said.

She took his hand and with one finger traced the word 'Mau' on his palm. 'I thought I recognised you, too,' she admitted, 'the first time we met.' She shivered, looked out across the illuminated mist. 'What can it mean? What can it all mean?' The very thought of it brought a kind of vertigo. It was like tottering on the lip of some endless fall into thin air, and reaching out for help, and finding none, and realising even as you toppled that the fall was into yourself. 'Even if I remember you,' she heard her own voice say, 'I don't remember anything else.' Still, she clutched at him as hard as she could.

The followed the footpath to the Cresset Beacon viewing point, climbed a stile and sat down on the wooden bench there. The air was still. There were spiderwebs among the bracken, still laden with dew. In another hour, the sun would have peeled the fog off the lower downland. Anna leaned against John Dawe, and he put his arm around her. For the first time she felt neither nervous nor angry in his presence. He felt familiar at last.

'I wonder if we've—' she said.

'What?'

'Nothing.' She had meant to finish '—been here before?' but she didn't want to articulate any of it, she wasn't ready to admit anything to herself. 'Why don't you kiss me?' she said instead.

He kissed her for a long time – then, brushing hair away from her face, seemed content just to look at her. His fingers were rough from work on the boat; his eyes were as tawny as a cat's. Staring into them, she felt her blood beat up in her. How knowing he had been, all along. He took her hands and pulled her to her feet.

'Come on,' he said.

'I—'

'Come on.'

A little unsteady with anticipation, she let herself be led away. At the back of the hill lay a hollow like a cup in the earth, encircled by old rowan trees and hornbeams. He knelt down there, took the woollen rug out of his bag, and spread it on the ground. She could only seem to stand and watch, hypnotised and helpless. He peeled her out of her scarf, her coat, her gloves; out of her old Artwork cardigan. She didn't care that it was December air on her skin, December light among the trees. She was full of a languid curiosity to see what happened next. She was hot where he touched her, or where she thought he might touch her next. When he entered her, it was astonishingly familiar and intensely new. It was so easy. 'Oh,' she heard herself say. She opened her eyes for a moment and saw the trees above her, the ancient winter light of the hollow. If she had been able to think, she might have thought, have you brought me here before?

When she came, it was in such a rush of sensation that she was barely aware of him. Had he come too? She gazed up at him, only to find him gazing down. The hard edges of his face had softened. He looked younger. He looked delighted.

'Hello,' she said, as if she had been away. 'Was that all right?'

This made him laugh. 'Anna, Anna, Anna,' he said.

A fox walked into the circle of trees.

It emerged silently from the shadows, the exact colour of copper beech leaves, with a splash of cream at the throat and down into the rough fur of its chest. Had it come to watch? What did it make of them? It stood there, its breath a faint vapour in the bright morning air, regarding them with intelligent, unblinking yellow eyes. When it had seen enough, it turned and leapt away, vanishing suddenly between the hornbeams, shedding as it went what seemed to Anna, in her state of dis-orientation, to be rings of rainbow light. There was a patch of grey fur on one of its haunches.

'Look!' she said. 'Look!'

John had seen it too. 'The *genius loci*,' he whispered. He sat up. 'The spirit of the place.'

She pulled him back down to her. 'I'm cold if you move,' she said. While she thought to herself: It was the fox. It was the fox!

Three miles away, where the fog coiled at its thickest around a tall-chimneyed, gabled house, a woman for whom sleep came hard wailed into her pillow, but in her dream no sound emerged.

Ahead, through a blinding, icy mist, she saw two mouths meet and fix upon one another with fervent, unmistakable hunger. It was a hunger she recognised: she had lived with it herself for so long now that it had become a permanent ache. But something about the scene was not right – for the head that reached up to take the kiss was mousy and nondescript, not glossy and black. The mist swirled and parted, and for an instant she saw more clearly: two bodies, naked, entwined—

The fury that rose in her was so powerful that she could feel herself generating it with a physical force, a welling fountain of hatred and bile.

Something moved in front of her then, blocking her line of sight.

A red mask reared up, a lolling tongue, a jaw lined with teeth—

'You can't keep doing this,' accused the fox.

'What?' she snarled. 'What do you mean?'

'Wreaking your havoc.'

She glared at it. 'I'll outlive all of you.'

'Surviving at the expense of all that is natural is no survival at all.'

'What do I care for what you call natural?' Her eyes glittered angrily. 'If I cannot have what I want, it can all wither and die and go to hell—'

It was like birthing a monster. The Dream burst from her, all glowing blacks and reds, all teeth and claws and murder.

The fox ran at it, ears flat with desperation, but his legs were not made for leaping. It evaded him easily, fleeing away into the icy tunnel, and where it touched, it burned . . .

John Dawe had found a comfortable place to sit among the roots of a rowan tree. Anna lay with her head on his thighs. The sky was an uninterrupted cerulean blue with vapour trails high up: the air was like glass. From this side of the Beacon they could see all the way to Westley. Church spires and threads of chimney smoke rose against the rolling downland; there were oak-hangers on the rises. They had put on their clothes, eaten the picnic, which included the contents of the foil packages – two delicious beef and onion pasties that John had cooked himself, early that morning, and finished the contents of John Dawe's flask. ('I'm not sure,' she had concluded, 'that Calvados goes all that well with hot chocolate. Whatever you say.') They had talked companionably about everything that came into their heads. Now they were content just to be there with one another, part of the limpid silence of the morning. After a while Anna felt so secure that she was able to say:

'And so what about you and Stella?'

She knew the moment she closed her mouth that she had made a mistake. The fact was, she didn't want to know.

'You don't have to tell me,' she said quickly.

'No, no, I don't mind,' he said. 'When I first met her, she was twenty-two years old.' There was a long pause, as if he was organising his thoughts. 'Stella! You wouldn't have believed her then.'

'I'm not sure I believe her now.'

'She was twenty-two, I was thirteen. We were related on my mother's side, that was my Herringe connection. She was a sweet woman, my mother, but never competent. As for my father—' He shrugged. 'He seemed like a fool, but what do I know? She went downhill after he died, and I ended up at Nonesuch. The Herringes were very good about it, but they didn't quite know what to do with me.

'They didn't know what to do with Stella, either, and that in itself was a bond between us. She was mad to achieve something in her life, and they had no idea how to handle that.' He smiled thinly. 'This was the sixties, remember. So there she was, stuck in the middle of nowhere, all that energy going to rot and waste. She had no outlet until I arrived to soak it all up. I was like blotting paper. Quite soon she was all the family I needed.'

He looked out over the downs, his eyes narrowed, as if he could see himself there, at Nonesuch all those years ago.

'I don't know which I loved more, her or the house. Can you imagine a twenty-two-year-old girl in charge of all that? Stella made her own rules even then. We did what we wanted, ate what we wanted, we lived from room to room like gypsies, while the staff followed us about. She still had a staff then. We took an Old Dansette with us everywhere we went, and I watched her dance to the Rolling Stones in a slant of sunlight in some fifteenth-century solar I never found again. She wound us – everything we did – into the history of the place. I loved that history, because it was in itself a kind of dusty attic, a secret passageway, filled with all the fantastic bric-a-brac of ancestry and inheritance. I loved the idea of a convoluted but unbroken line that ran from Joshua to Stella – and even, in some measure, from Joshua to me. All the time, I realised later, Stella was watching me for something beyond that, some other response; but in the end, like everyone ordinary, I was a disappointment to her. I hadn't understood the lesson. I hated to disappoint her.'

'She's very strong, isn't she?' Anna interrupted, because she was jealous and wanted him out of this dream of adolescence. 'One of the strongest people I've ever met.'

He stared at her. Eventually he gave a curious laugh.

'Stella Herringe hasn't a tenth of your strength,' he said. 'She's demanding, she's wilful, she's driven, but underneath it she's insecure and desperate. Her needs always undermined her intelligence. The Herringes never knew what to do with her for that reason alone: they sensed she was undependable, and old money has such an instinct to protect itself! In addition, of course, she was a woman. She came out of a minor Oxford college at twenty-two years old expecting to move up the family hierarchy, join the players, run one of the high-profile businesses. They were still on the mainland then. They had manufacturing concerns. They were in armaments, steel, the nascent North Sea oil industry. Stella saw herself in a boardroom somewhere, ousting the old men who drink the Herringe port. But the trustees made sure all she got was me, Nonesuch, and a run-down chemical company to play with. She built that into Engelion, and it was a brilliant achievement; but apart from some trust-fund politics and a few semi-active directorships, Engelion is all she has. It was never a sufficient powerbase from which to take what she thought of as her rightful place in the family. The power lay elsewhere, if it lay anywhere at all. Stella had already begun to break herself against that discovery when I was young. I heard her walking the passages at night, ranting to the ancestral portraits on the walls.'

He shook his head.

'She's terrified of ageing, she's terrified of death. She's obsessed with Nonesuch and its past. She's gone so far into herself now that she has to be looked after. What do you think that fatuous pair Mark and Oliver do? They make sure she signs the right papers and doesn't drink too much gin. They put petrol in the Mercedes when she forgets, and make sure she doesn't run it into a tree. They're from some even more distantly related branch of the family than I am – and that's how they treat her, like some great aunt three-times-removed. They make her feel young, and in control, and she laps it up.'

He took Anna's hands. 'Don't you see? It's a mistake to think of her as strong. It's weakness that makes her so dangerous. She sucks you in, and before you know it you're propping up her fantasies. Then, when you try to get away . . .' He sighed and looked off into the distance. 'And yet somehow, there's more to it. There's more to Stella, but I only ever understand it in dreams.'

He sighed. 'And she was so extraordinarily beautiful back then. When she was in the room I couldn't take my eyes off her; when she wasn't, she was all I could see.

'I felt like Pip in *Great Expectations*. You know? She held all that out to me: how could I have resisted it?'

He shook his head. 'Unlike Pip, of course, I got what I wanted.'

'I don't know what you mean,' said Anna; although she thought she did.

'Anna—'

'I don't care about all this.'

He was about to contradict her when she said in a rush, 'No, I really don't. I love you. We could have something together.' She took his hand in both hers, curled it into a fist, put it against her heart. 'I know it. I feel it. But you have to let go of Stella. You have to stop feeling bound to her, by the money, whatever—'

'It's not the money,' he said dully. 'Not only the money.'

'Then what is it?'

'What do you think?' he said. 'What do you think happens between a bored, power-hungry girl twenty-two years old and an adolescent boy?'

Anna got to her feet quickly. 'That's awful,' she said.

'No it isn't, he said. 'It isn't awful at all. Not when you're thirteen. It's marvellous.'

'What are you saying?'

'You know what I'm saying,' he told her gently.

'Well, I hate it.'

'Nonesuch was all the home I had until I went up to Cambridge. Every weekend, every holiday from Marlborough, she was there, the house was there. They were inseparable, full of light. I loved her for years.'

Anna laughed bitterly. 'She fucked you for years,' she said. 'That's all.'

He tried to take her hand but she pulled it away. He said quietly, 'It's a mistake to rubbish other people's experience, Anna. Whatever it was, it happened to me, just as Max happened to you. It filled up my life, just as Max filled yours, and it took a long time to escape from. That's all I know.' After a moment he went on, 'I haven't escaped her yet. I don't feel I can simply throw her away. She's a manipulator, she's a monster, but I can't deny her any more than you can deny the violinist. I can't walk away and pretend she doesn't exist. Anna, I want a future too. But I can't have it simply by rejecting the past. I need to come to terms with Stella, sort out some kind of friendship. I owe her that. I'm sorry about this.' He indicated the trees, the blanket, the scattered picnic. 'It was wrong of me. It was too soon—'

'*Wrong* of you? Oh, you bastard!'

Anna pushed him away as hard as she could. 'Who the hell do you think you are, to say "it's too soon", "it's too late"? There are two of us here! Or was I just another knick-knack for that sad bloody collection on the *Magpie*? Just another piece in your famous spiritual jigsaw? You're not helpless. If things are this way, it's because in some measure you want them to be. All that crap about "the bric-a-brac of inheritance"? Spare me, John. You aren't Nonesuch's prisoner, or even Stella's – you've just lost the knack of having feelings for anyone but yourself!'

He stared at her. She stood there for a moment wishing, unreasonably, that he would defend himself. Then she turned and ran back down the path.

Twenty-two

THE FOG I ran through that morning as I fled the house made a perfect reflection of my state of mind. Feelings of confusion, abandonment and impending doom tumbled and swirled in my head, and images leapt out at me as out of the dreams I had caught this last week: Liddy's outraged face; Dellifer's eyes as stark as the moon; menacing figures carrying baskets as quiet as the grave; Vita's food bowl, empty and dark as a pit; wild roads that roared and howled like live things tortured: all of it a maze of meaning, and I, the solitary traveller, struggling to make his way through it all.

So it was, forlorn and desperate, that I ran through Ashmore Village. Two cars passed me, at a snail's pace, the drivers' faces pressed anxiously close to the windscreen. Hedges and trees loomed up out of the fog, to be replaced by a telegraph pole, a postbox, the expanse of someone's lawn. I saw the odd pedestrian, a dog walker, a lone shopper, sneezing and coughing, swathed against the weather (even the dog, a small, miserable-looking terrier, wore a buckled tartan coat). I even thought I saw Anna and the man from Liddy's boat: they swam up out of the mist, then were sucked back into it again as if they were ghosts.

Perhaps we are all ghosts, I have thought since then, existing briefly in a fog, unaware of the grand context into which we were born. For what possible autonomy, what force of self-will, can be exerted in such a world?

I ran the length of the main road. There was no sign of my sister.

I sniffed around dustbins and gate-posts and sheds, but the scents were as muffled as the air. I slipped through the lych gate and into the churchyard, sifted through the muted smells of turned earth and tended flowers; the sharp aroma of wet holly and yew; the tang of damp stone; the passage of human feet. Vita had not been here, of that I was sure.

I crossed the fields towards Glory Farm and the iron tracks. Nothing. Turning back towards the village, on the path to the common, though, my nose twitched. One of the rabbit runs, a much-trodden path through bracken and bramble, gave back my first clue to my sister's whereabouts. A faint, sweet scent, slightly fishy; another, muskier. I breathed in deeply. Vita certainly, with another cat, a female, just out of heat. Could it be Liddy? My heart sprang up. I bent my nose close to the ground and followed the scent assiduously. Almost twenty feet further on, there was a scrabbling of feet and a rustle of vegetation; then the fog parted and a rabbit bolted past me, eyes liquid with fear. I stared into the swirl of mist it left behind, then touched my nose to the ground once more. Here, the scent was fainter, less distinct. I lost it for a moment, circled around in panic, and found it again. My heart beating with anticipation (Liddy, oh Lydia), I sniffed along the trail. After a while, it started to twine back upon itself, as if some sort of confusion had occurred, before coming to an abrupt halt. I lifted my head and stared past my nose. It seemed to be the entrance to a small wild road.

Once inside, the compass winds blew furiously, all of a tangle, so that my lion's mane tied itself into knots and whipped me hard across the face. Usually, the highways funnelled their air currents down their length, so that the only squalls of turbulence you encountered were at multiple junctions, where nests of small highways met a major thoroughfare. Such a gale I had not encountered before. And it smelled. It smelled of something acrid and deathly; something fiery with hate. I feared for Lydia, I feared for my sister; I feared for myself. Even so I set my head steadfastly into the blow and plodded along, planting my feet firmly on the highway floor to keep my balance, but though I marched for a hundred yards in all directions, there was no sign of another living being.

With a sinking heart, I exited back on to the common, only to find myself confronted by the trunk of the great oak under which

I had buried the human tooth. This was not where this little highway should normally have debouched; but at the time, foolishly, I thought nothing of it. The wild roads are notoriously convoluted and hard to navigate, and I had already compounded matters by entering them in an overwrought state, rather than with the clarity of mind and purpose required for a productive journey.

Dejected, I gazed across the misty common, and as I did so my eye was snagged by a sudden flash of russet. At first I thought it the flaming leaves of that garden escapee, the Japanese maple; then proper perspectives reasserted themselves and I realised that whatever it was lay closer to the ground than even the shortest tree; and, moreover, it was moving.

I narrowed my eyes. The fog swirled and the object disappeared. Only to be replaced by a more familiar shape. Dark, tattered – a cat!

It was the rightful Dreamcatcher of Ashmore.

For a moment I felt nothing but fury; then as he approached I could see that he was moving with the utmost difficulty, lurching along like a creature in pain, and whatever the red thing was, it appeared to be bearing up his weight.

At once I was running. I called his name—

'Hawkweed! I'm coming—'

At the sound of my voice, I swear the russet object became sharply attentive. I saw, for a split second, a head, finely delineated: a pointed snout, large, triangular ears; then there was a blur of movement and all I was left with was the impression of something long-backed and brush-tailed and as big as a dog, all burnished apple-red, save for one marked grey patch along its flank; something that moved as slickly as a wave, and vanished as silently as it had appeared.

'Grandfather!'

By the time I reached him, my grandfather was decidedly alone.

He was reeling by then, the fight long gone out of him.

'What happened to you?' I cried, all anger dissipated to concern. 'Were you attacked by the great red beast?'

In response, the old cat managed a thin smile. It was more lopsided, even than usual.

'Nay, laddie,' he said simply. 'What you saw was just a friend.

A friend with a long and curious history, but a great and good friend to cats like us. I have a sense it will not be long before you meet him yourself.'

And he would not be drawn any further on the subject.

Instead, I asked him what had happened to reduce him to the terrible condition in which I had found him: there was a gash across one haunch so deep and vicious that the flesh appeared amid the fur as purple-red and pearled with fat as the packaged meat Anna stored in the refrigerator. One eye was hazed with partly dried blood; the other was swollen and shut tight upon itself. He limped heavily. It must have been a terrible fight. I could not imagine another cat inflicting such injury upon my indomitable grandfather.

'It's the highways, laddie,' he said at last, leaning upon me to get his breath. 'There's a Dream out there poisoning them.'

I stared at him, uncomprehending.

He sighed, and his one good eye flickered as if he might pass out where he stood. 'Get me home, Orlando. Get me home.'

We must have made a strange sight, my grandfather and I, as we staggered back to the cottage. We had to take the human way, for my grandfather would not be leaping fences for some considerable time to come. We came up on to the main road through the clearing mist like two lost souls. People turned their crying children away from the sight of Hawkweed's wounds, and watched us solemnly as we passed. I fixed them with a fierce gaze, for I did not want their help, but no one moved towards us anyway. Closer to the cottage, I could hear raised voices. Some altercation appeared to have broken out between the old man who helped Anna sometimes in the garden and an old woman in horn-rimmed glasses, who had chosen this unlikely time to upbraid him for the fact that his old apple tree had some weeks ago dropped a dead branch over the hedge and into her cold frames. Perhaps he was happy for the excuse to avoid her ranting, for as he caught sight of the pair of us limping home, his face furrowed with concern. He came after us slowly, leaning on his stick, and when we came at last to the cottage reached over and fiddled with the latch on the front gate and swung it open so that we might enter.

266

Anna, her face streaked, the skin stretched tight and shiny where tears had fallen and dried, came up the road a moment later, only to see Mr Thompson apparently opening her front gate for no good reason. She quickened her pace.

'He's proper poorly,' was all he said as she approached. 'Poor old beggar.'

Anna, her thoughts already in disarray, stared at him, uncomprehending. 'I beg your pardon? Who do you mean?' Possibilities rattled through her head: John, meeting with an accident as he followed her at a run down Cresset Beacon? Max? (But Mr Thompson would not know him from Adam, her brain corrected immediately.) Orlando—

And there was Orlando on the doorstep, looking a little bedraggled, for sure, but not obviously ill or injured. She bent to inspect him, and found, crouched behind him at the back of the boot-bench, between wellingtons and Goretex and the stiff brush she used for cleaning the porch of leaves and cobwebs, the old cat Hawkweed.

Later, after a bustle of activity, I lay beside my grandfather. Above us, the springs of the spare-room bed brushed our ears. It was hot, very cramped, and not a spot I would have chosen in which to recuperate, but it seemed to suit Hawkweed well enough. Anna had opened the front door, and had run to the cupboard under the stairs, where she kept such horrors as the roaring stick that sucked the carpets. Puzzled, we had limped cautiously inside after her, but when he had heard the tell-tale creak of the willow cat basket, Hawkweed's head had gone up as if at the crack of a shotgun, and gaining a sudden energy and awkward strength that belied his injuries, he had lithely evaded her attempts to catch him, and had instead established himself here, well out of arm's reach, despite Anna's many attempts to encourage him out.

Dellifer had spent some time attending to his wounds.

'Cat spit cures all,' she said at last, quoting that old feline adage. She gave the area around his flank another lick for good measure. By the way Dellifer was fussing around him I could tell that she was more agitated by his demeanour than by the nature of his injuries. I watched her practical ministrations with a certain shame at my earlier outburst, but she said nothing to reproach me.

When my grandfather's face had been cleaned of the caked blood, it looked only as fearsome as it did normally, and I found it much easier to watch him as he slept, debilitated from his exertions. Waiting for him to wake up again, though, I found frustrating in the extreme. Not only did I want to know what had happened to him on the wild roads, and what might have become of my missing sister: I was also desperate for any news of Lydia.

It is well known that a cat has the ability to wake any sleeper by the power of a stare, but if my grandfather felt the weight and imperative of my gaze upon his sleeping face, he gave no sign of it; no doubt being entirely too well versed in repelling such unwanted attentions. And completely exhausted from his experience on the highways, my conscience reminded me sharply.

After what seemed an eternity, he yawned and an eye opened blearily. At once, Dellifer was upon him, asking how he was, whether she should lick his forehead some more; if he wanted something to eat. Eventually, Hawkweed suggested he might manage a small vole, to keep his strength up; and sent her off, knowing it would take her an age to find one at this time of the year.

I could barely wait for her to leave the room before launching into my own inquisition.

'So, Grandfather, tell me now, quickly while she is gone: whatever happened to you? And did you see Vita, and my friend Lydia?'

The old cat's eyelids flickered wearily. Then he fixed me with a pale and one-eyed stare and said in an irritated fashion, 'Can't you leave me be for just a little while, Orlando? There is nothing that can be done for now.'

But I persisted, and in the end Hawkweed hunched himself uncomfortably over his elbows and sighed deeply. 'I will come to Vita in due course, Orlando; but first I must tell you about the Dream. I had hoped I would never have cause to tell you about it, laddie. It's been dormant for so long now, I truly thought it laid to rest. I should have known better . . .' his voice trailed off, husky with despair.

I leaned forward, willing him to continue. After a while he coughed – or rather, retched phlegmily, then after a moment's hesitation, as if he was considering hawking the contents up on to Anna's carpet, he reconsidered and swallowed them down again. He blinked several times as if they tasted particularly vile. 'The Dream,' he said vaguely, as if in a dream himself. 'Ah, the Dream. Human fear is a terrible thing, Orlando. Perhaps the most terrible thing there is.'

I frowned. Why was it he could never speak in a straight-forward manner to me? Why must he always beguile me with riddles?

'When I was a lad,' he began again, and my spirits sank. Here was I, awaiting urgent news, and my grandfather had started reminiscing about his distant youth. I wondered if his recent experiences had finally brought on the senility I had perceived in the oldest cats of the village: cats who sat on doorsteps and windowsills gazing vacantly out at the world, a thin line of spittle drooling from one corner of the mouth; or, like Old Niggle, whose owners would no longer allow him in the house for fear of his incontinence and unstable temper, a cat who lay out in bushes beside the road ready to waylay passers-by with a loud string of obscenities, or to follow them pathetically, reciting tales of his derring-do, back in the good old days when he'd been the alpha male and had a harem of willing females awaiting his thorough attentions . . .

But my grandfather was not to be deterred by my evident lack of interest in his early exploits; nor was his vicious temper in any way softened by his injuries.

'Orlando!' he hissed, a paw snaking out to cuff me soundly about the ear.

Shocked beyond words at the speed of this geriatric invalid, as I had so quickly been categorising him, I stared at him open-mouthed.

'A fool you are and a fool you will remain if you do not pay attention to what I tell you.'

He was not the first to have called me a fool. Someone else had done so recently, though I could not remember then how it had come up. Lydia, most like: Lydia, certainly . . .

'When I was a lad,' my grandfather started again, 'my own

grandfather, that great old dreamcatcher Fidelius the Black, came to me one night. "Hawkweed", he said, "there are many dangerous things in this world, but none so potent as a woman's jealousy and fear". And he explained to me how he had observed from a lifetime or more on the highways, how women's dreams often differed from men's. He had noticed that they sometimes dreamed deeper and darker than their male counterparts, and he believed that while men channel their daily frustrations and energies into work and sport and even war, women have fewer outlets for their wilder sides; moreover, he said to me, some women love more fiercely than any man, sometimes with a powerful and dangerous force. And if something were to come between such a woman and the object of her desire, well, it would engender great peril.

'Now, I have to say to you, Orlando, that human emotions were a mystery to me then, and remain a mystery to me to this day: what I do know, however, is that they can be truly destructive.

'I was barely more than a kitten, not much older than you are now, when he told me this, and perhaps things are different in the world now; but I had seen so little of it then, had not experienced any sort of love for myself—'

I wondered whether my grandfather could see the flush I could feel prickling beneath my fur in the gloom of the bedroom.

'—so I had no idea of what he was telling me. Then, in that maddeningly oblique way that dreamcatchers sometimes have,' he gave me an odd look, which might have involved a wink, since the gleam of his good eye seemed to flicker for a moment, 'he suggested I come on an excursion with him. We walked through Ashmore Village on the human roads and I was already becoming bored and thinking my grandfather was wasting my time, when we arrived at some grand gates. There he stopped; and I began to reassess matters. There is something about the old manor house that has always made me uneasy: even then, I tended to avoid it in my explorations of the village.'

I recalled my own single excursion into the grounds of the big house; how the dream that had caused the rift between me and Liddy had goaded me to the top of the great tree.

'We made our way through the great gates, and as we did so,

the light of the new day shifted through indigo, to the soft grey of a woodpigeon's wing, before emerging at last as a cold and ominous red,' my grandfather went on. He told me how he and Fidelius had run across the dewy grass, quick and nervous, in full and open view; how they had skirted the orchard and taken cover in the lee of the strange little mazy garden that was planted there.

I was holding my breath now, captivated by my own grandfather's narrative. I knew the garden to which he referred – a labyrinth of low shrubs in an intricate design – for I had glimpsed it as I fell from my precarious perch in the cedar tree, clutching on to the dream.

'We sat there, Orlando, and we watched. We watched as a woman came out of the house. A tall, thin, old woman.'

This was less than exciting. I had been waiting for the appearance of a monster; and all he had to offer me was a crone. There were lots of old women in Ashmore, and there was nothing more terrifying about them than the threat of a cup of water being thrown over you if they thought you might be about to do something amongst their peonies.

But then he told me how she had walked around that maze in the oddest fashion. Not as if she were going anywhere, but as if she was bewitched and unable to take more than two steps in any single direction. She was,' he stated again, 'an old woman: a *very* old woman – all folds and wrinkles and swollen joints – but I could not take my eyes off her, and neither could Fidelius, for she had a powerful magnetism, even to the eye of a cat, something strong and . . . animal.

Then he told me how, at the heart of the pattern, she had opened a jar and started rubbing its contents all over herself. As meticulous as a cat she had been in her grooming, and by the time she had finished, and shaken the last few drops on to the ground as if as an offering, a transformation had taken place.

'Where before her skin had been thin and grey, wrinkled and spotted with age, now it glowed as pink as the dawn, as soft and luminous as a rose petal. I do not know if there is such a thing as magic in the world, Orlando; nor whether the word "witch" still has any true meaning. Nor do I know much about the nature of humans' anatomy; but I do, now, know about age, and I am telling you, laddie, that the woman who went back into the house then was a far younger woman than the one who came out.'

And then he told me of the robin, the bird that had landed in the centre of the knot garden and pecked at the ground where those last few drops had fallen: how it had flown away full of vigour, its breast feathers as red as new blood.

'I saw that bird again, Orlando. I saw it only a few days ago.'

I stared at him, my mind working hard. 'But Fidelius has been dead for many years,' I said slowly. 'And everyone knows the little birds live for only a few seasons . . .'

He nodded, his one eye enigmatic.

Was this another of his fairy stories, designed to teach me something of the Great Cat's wisdom?

Hawkweed was silent for a moment, remembering. Then he told me many things about the nature of the world, and about Ashmore village in particular, that I had rather not have known.

He told me about the nine lives of cats: how there was something that humans called reincarnation that could bring you back, when you had lived out your natural span, if not in this life, then in another. 'And it's all tied up with wild roads, you see, Orlando,' he said.

I did not, but for once in my life I kept quiet.

'The highways run, as you know, all over the world, channelling its energies – all the dreams, all the souls of the world – and it is up to us, the dreamcatchers, to keep those highways clear and hale. It is fear, laddie: fear's the thing that does most damage; in life, in dreams. Fear of ageing; fear of death; fear of loss – of power, or love. If you get enough fear running through the wild roads, the consequences are terrible: death and corruption will tear their way out of the highways – and not just in dreams, laddie; but in souls; and that's a fearsome thing indeed. A really frightened soul does not want to die: it will come back again and again, seeking an escape from death itself.

'There are places, Orlando, where the highways also run through times as well as through the geography of the world. Some of these wild roads have hardly any true existence of their own, but are merely echoes of old memories, old cat-lanes from a bygone age remembered fondly by those who once used them, or in stories told by mothers to their kittens. In time, they fade, seal themselves off and die away. But some, laddie, stay open and alive because an especially strong dreamer has entered the system, a dreamer driven by fear. Such a dreamer can drive the highways to double back on themselves, as the dreamer seeks previous, happier times in its evasion of death. Here, in Ashmore, we have such a rare configuration. We have had it all my life, and for as long as any of my forebears can remember, for Ashmore is a very old village. And, since luck is against us, we have here in the village the strongest dreamer I have ever heard tell of.'

Now, this was all very interesting in a rather pointless way, but it was of no practical use at all.

'Look,' I said, more brusquely than I had intended, 'none of this helps us to find Vita. Besides, you still haven't told me why you upped and left me to eat all the dreams of the village for the past few days.'

A spasm of pain crossed Hawkweed's face; then he sighed.

'Orlando and Vita. Vita and Orlando. Silly names, silly cats. Why I have been cursed with two such idiot grandchildren, I will never know; and one of them destined to take over my job.' He shook his head sadly. 'I will, given your insistence, pass over the more theoretical aspects of this matter; but you may soon wish you had known more. Let us, then, get to the meat of recent events, since you have the attention span of a gnat.'

Clearly, he was feeling better.

'I upped and left you to it, as you so eloquently put it, in order to protect you from the Dream, laddie.' He emphasised the word with the rolling 'r' he used when particularly irritated with me. 'It's back, you see, Orlando: the one, the worst of them all. Only ever happens when the three of them come together, and she starts to lose her man again to the younger one, and panics.'

'Which three? What do you mean?' Now I was completely thrown.

Hawkweed stared at me as if were being deliberately obtuse. 'The witch, her cousin and your Anna,' he said succinctly. 'The witch loves him; he loves Anna, and she – well, from her dreams, I'd say she loves him too. And that's what sets it all in motion, yet again: their infernal triangle. Life after life after life they keep on making this pattern—'

'But why,' I interrupted rudely, wanting this to be over with, 'why if they keep making this pattern can't they see what they're doing and stop it?'

The old cat shrugged. 'Twists of time, twists of fate, who knows? The old one knows it all: she remembers each life; but the other two – I watch their dreams and still I'm not sure how much they recall. Little flashes, jolts of memory, but no sense of the pattern they make. The witch, though, she knows it's coming round again, yet no matter what she does, it seems, still she loses the game. And she's older now: her soul's frailer. Her powers are not what they were. So when she feels that loss creeping up on her again, her terror grows, and so does the Dream. Now, it's stronger and more destructive than it's been in any of my lifetimes.

'Yet I thought, in my arrogance, that if I could track it down at last, I might be able to put an end to it once and for all; and if that had been the case I would never have had to burden you with the knowledge of its existence, let alone enrol you in its pursuit. But, unfortunately, here I am,' – he indicated his wounded body – 'and it's still out there, gaining strength. You may have noticed how over the past few days the people of Ashmore have been suffering more nightmares than usual. Nightmares breed nightmares, Orlando, and even with both of us working separately, we have not been able to catch them all; yet the more that are left, the more the Dream gathers its own momentum. Last night was the worst possible time your idiot sister could have picked on which to take her first trip on the wild roads.'

I looked away, feeling absurdly and needlessly guilty.

'Do you know, Orlando, who took her on to the highways last night?'

I shook my head, though I had my suspicions.

'The Dream is loose on the wild roads of Ashmore, laddie; and last night I tried to confront it. Had it not been for the young cat who was with Vita, I might have died.'

I stared at him.

'I was searching up and down the little westway,' he went on. 'All night I'd been coming across disturbances in the air currents, dreams behaving in a strange fashion, tumbling in the wrong direction to the prevailing compass wind as if drawn by something altogether more powerful. Something more powerful than nature is an awesome thing indeed; nevertheless, I decided to follow them. All those convoluted little highways between the canal and the common, they were in turmoil by the time I arrived. Something unnatural was indeed there: I could sense it in my whiskers. By the time I got to the locus at the old holly, where the roads fan out into the village, my fur was standing on end, as if I had blundered into an electrical storm.

'I turned a corner, and there it was: the Dream, flowing like the Great Fire, scorching the wild road around it; and behind it, trapped by a loop of burning highway, were two young cats; both female. I believe one of those cats was your sister Vita. It can be hard to perceive the identity of cats on the wild roads; but something about the eyes—'

He broke off.

'And the other cat?' I asked, too quickly.

'I do not know who she was,' Hawkweed said grimly. 'It was all such . . . confusion. For, as I appeared, the Dream sensed an enemy and came straight for me. Vita's companion leapt at it, knocking it away from me, though not before it had done some damage. Then there was howling and smoke and the highway writhing like a live thing, till it burst open, and I was thrown clear.'

I held my breath and waited.

Hawkweed sighed. 'I believe it had not yet gathered its full power; or we would none of us have stood a chance.'

'But what about Vita and her friend?'

My grandfather looked shamefaced. 'I do not know, Orlando. I was in a bad way; even so, I tried to re-enter that wild road. But I was slow and disorientated, and by the time I had managed to crawl back inside, the Dream had gone, and so had those two cats; though I thought I might have seen just the flick of a striped tail in the distance. Despite my wounds I searched the area for hours, aided by the good friend you later found me with.

'I fear, laddie, that Vita may have fallen prey to the Dream.'

I felt the blood drain from my face, my heart become chill. Surely he couldn't mean—

'Is she dead?' I heard my voice: too loud, disembodied, nothing to do with me at all.

There was a scuffling noise; a faint thud, and a terrible shriek.

'Dead?'

Dellifer had returned at just the wrong moment. The vole lay prone on the carpet between us like an accusation.

The old wet nurse confronted Hawkweed, eyes blazing. I had never seen a more discomfiting sight: it was as if a kitchen mop had suddenly gone feral. 'Where is my foster child, Dreamcatcher Hawkweed? What has happened to my little girl?'

He quailed before her. 'Ah, Delly, Delly,' was all he could say.

I thought she would strike him then; but instead she drew herself up, spat with contemptuous accuracy into his open eye, and declared venomously: 'You have never loved another soul but your own.'

Stumbling over the dead rodent in her urgency, she fled from the room. I heard an exclamation from downstairs as she bolted past Anna. Then she was gone.

'I'm going after her,' I cried.

My grandfather looked pained, but said nothing to stop me.

Dellifer was quick, but not as fast as a determined young tomcat. I caught up with her on the edge of Ashmore Common.

'It's my fault,' she wailed. 'First you; now your sister. I should have stood up to him when he took you for a dreamcatcher. I should have kept a better eye on Vita.' A sob racked her. 'I should never have let him bring me here!'

By 'here' I imagined she must mean Anna's cottage, which she hardly ever left. 'Nonsense,' I said, as soothingly as I was able. 'Dellifer, if you hadn't come to us, we would have died.'

'Perhaps it would have been better,' she said in a strange tone, obviously in no mood to be reasoned with.

She turned from me, ran blindly on to the common, and hurled herself into the first wild road she came to. Dismayed, I flung myself after her. Inside, it was oddly quiet, as if even the highway winds had lost the will to blow. I rounded a corner, and there she was, small and white in the perpetual gloom. It took me more than a moment to register the wrongness of this. Then I stared and stared. Of all the cats I had ever seen on the highways, Dellifer was the only one to remain as she was in the outside world. No lion, no tiger or lynx, she – but Dellifer as she ever was: thin and white as a skein of string.

I came to a halt behind her, shaking. 'You're . . . you,' I pointed out, stupid with shock.

She turned, cocking her head. I had forgotten how deaf she had become. From my great height I looked down at her. One of my paws could have crushed her flat, even by accident: and even as this peculiar thought came to me, I was overcome by her courage. To enter the wild roads at the best of times required fortitude; a strength of spirit made rather easier by the comforting knowledge that in entering, you would at once be transformed into your primal self, your inner great cat. To enter the highways knowing not only that they were in turmoil, but also that you had to do so in your frail domestic form, took a bravery I knew I could never aspire to.

'They did things to me at that place,' she said in a tone I had never heard from her before. She did not look at me as she spoke. 'It was such a long time ago now. Many lives past. I was barely older than a kitten myself, and pregnant with my first brood. I don't even recall now who the father was . . . not that it matters, given their fate. One of the old brutes she kept there, I suppose. Still remember the smell, though: ah yes. Old piss corroding metal cages. That awful stuff she brewed up. No cat should ever be allowed to smell such a thing. And to think the woman had some in our house, had the temerity to open it right in front of me . . .'

I had not idea what she was talking about now. Instead, I asked loudly, 'So what happened to your kittens, then?'

'Never got as far as that, my darling. Never fully born. But I've been producing milk on and off ever since the day she took them from me, in that life and in others since. If it had not been for old Hawkweed and his friend the fox, I'd be there still. I pray you will never be trapped in your own fate as I have been. I regard it as my curse. That, and this body I can never escape.'

The fox . . . A memory flickered at the edge of my thoughts. Foxes were red, weren't they? The red of an autumn leaf, Dellifer had once said to me; the red of Reynard . . . The thought fled, to be replaced by a sudden searing understanding: Hawkweed had fetched Dellifer to us for her milk. It had never been her own choice. I felt stricken, and it must have showed in my face.

'Not your fault, my dear, not at all. The young are never to blame for the sins of the old ones. And that's why we must find

277

Vita, my darling. She is an innocent in all this, and she must stay that way.'

And so we searched, Dellifer and I, up and down the highways of the village for hours and hours. It still being daytime out in the world, the crowd of dreams had yet to emerge, which made our progress easier; even so, our search made two things clear to me. The first was that the wild roads of Ashmore had been disarranged so catastrophically that even I was not entirely sure of where we might next emerge; the second was that there was no sign at all of Vita and Lydia.

I thought about Lydia a lot as we ranged around the highways. Dellifer was never one for idle chatter, and now, determined and despairing, every iota of herself concentrated on peering myopically through the gloom, she had not a word for me. Lydia, with her golden fur and her gleaming eyes: what sort of transformation overtook her as she entered the highways? I wondered. Hawkweed had mentioned her striped tail – a tiger, then, or a . . . surely something grand and gorgeous. What a pair we would make, together on the wild roads! I thought about the immense courage she had shown in saving my grandfather from the Dream and my heart swelled. No wonder she was so contemptuous of me, a sad dreamcatcher who could be distracted by some piddling human fantasy from mating with a creature so fine.

We came back, at last, to the confluence of roads that had used to debouch at the woodland pond on the edge of the old orchard. I could sense their geographical position had changed, but not by much. What did seem to have happened, however, was that more roads had been added: or perhaps some of the wider highways had been split by the violence of the Dream's convulsion. A knot had occurred. We followed one small tributary, then another, and ended up back in the same place. We took a third highway, which crossed and recrossed itself until my head was entirely turned around. As we emerged into the confluence again, from a different direction altogether, we were able to make out a figure, sitting motionless in the dark. 'Vita!' Dellifer called, at the same time as I cried 'Liddy!' But as we approached, I saw at once that it was neither of these cats. Silver and barred, with ears that sprouted tufts of fur as feathery as spring barley, I knew her at once; and my heart sank like a stone.

This was the cat my grandfather had seen with my sister. This was the one who had saved him from the Dream: it was Millefleur, descended from a dreamcatcher herself, who had danced with me on the highways in her beautiful lynx form; Millefleur, whom I had spurned.

'Millie!' I called, and my voice rose into the still air like a howl.

Her head came up and she stared at us wildly, her eyes like lamps. She was crouched over something, guarding it between her front paws as if it was the most precious of objects. At once, Dellifer and I were running.

I suppose I had thought to see my sister lying there, injured, perhaps even dead; so I was mystified to find the lynx protecting what appeared to be a single silver ring, spotted with blood. Dellifer, however, did not appear mystified at all; instead she hurled herself at the lynx, spitting and hissing, claws out to rake and tear. 'You!' she shrieked. 'You . . . harlot, you deceiver!'

I was entirely bewildered.

Millie batted the old cat away with a careful paw; claws sheathed, she held her at arm's length, where Dellifer fizzed and bubbled like a witch's familiar.

'Stop this! I have done nothing to harm Vita—'

But Dellifer was not to be appeased. 'Evil. You are evil. What have you done with her?'

I got between them and spoke loudly and distinctly into Dellifer's better ear. 'She would do nothing to harm Vita, Delly. I know her. She . . . she has a good heart.'

Now Dellifer rounded on me. 'You would say that, wouldn't you? I smelled her on you when you came back that night; just as I smelled her wicked temptress's scent in the kitchen when she gave that . . . thing to Vita.' She indicated the silver ring. I frowned, puzzled.

Finally, Millie lost her temper with the old cat. 'You have a nerve, you old hag,' she said coldly, and her eyes were steely, 'to accuse *me* of smelling evil. Do you think to hide your own stench, by accusing others? I knew as soon as I came into that house where *you* had come from. Once the witch has touched you, you carry her smell always. You have the stink of death upon you, the touch of the Dream itself.'

At this, Dellifer gave an ear-splitting howl and, elbowing her way past Millie and me, fled down the highway and out into the world at a random exit.

I have to admit I could follow none of this exchange at all, but to see poor Dellifer further upset was more than I could bear. With a furious look at Millie, I turned and chased after her, yet again.

What happened next happened so suddenly I was never very sure of the sequence of events; nor even of the time period in which they took place. You will think me mad, I know, and I cannot blame you for it; but if I tell you that I saw Dellifer – long and thin and pale as a streak of light – run out on to the village's misty main road, turn to look back at me as if I had called her name, and be bowled over under the wheels of a great dark vehicle, you might understand some of my confusion. A confusion helped not at all by the sight of a tall woman with long dark hair and a flowing black coat exiting the gleaming car and, reaching without hesitation beneath its gleaming chassis, extracting the limp body of a small white cat, which she smiled upon with great tenderness, before stowing it on the back seat and roaring away into the distance.

And this time when she looked at me and smiled, she appeared to have her full complement of teeth.

Twenty-three

ANNA WAS lying on the sofa hating herself, a cup of tea left to grow a cold skin on the table at her side, when someone knocked on the door. For a moment she thought it might be John, but it was only Alice Meynell. Anna was thankful, in a way. It simplified things. How do you stay angry with a man who spread warmth all through you not three hours ago, then spoiled everything? How do you not? Alice, always a relief, stood on the doorstep with one hand on her hip and the other cradling her motorcycle helmet. She was wearing a new set of leathers, in red and white to match the bike.

'Alice. Good Lord. You look like a parrot.'

'I do, don't I?' said Alice comfortably. 'Max Wishart bought them for me.'

'It's amazing how people's tastes can change. Oh Alice, I'm so glad to see you! Come in and talk to me.' Anna indicated the Kawasaki, which was propped up in the lane outside. Heat rose from its engine and shimmered in the clear winter air. 'Did you know you've left that thing going?' she said.

Alice looked less comfortable. 'Yes,' she said. 'Actually I can't stop. I just wanted to— God, I hate having to do this.'

'Alice, do what?'

'Anna, one of your cats got run over.'

'No,' said Anna.

She wasn't really listening after that. She put her hand to her mouth. 'Was it Orlando?' she said, thinking of the quick, marmalade-coloured shape she had seen darting away through the fog that morning. She felt bemused. She felt her lip begin to tremble.

She said, 'Oh no.'

'I'm really sorry, love,' Alice was saying. 'I think it was the old one, I can't remember what you called her—'

'Dellifer,' said Anna quietly. 'Her name was Dellifer.'

'It was up near the common. There's a dip there that often has standing fog in winter, you've to treat it with a bit of care . . .' She shrugged. 'Anyway, I was there when it happened. Stella Herringe went into it all over the road in that bloody great boat of a Mercedes, talking nineteen to the dozen to the bloke in the front seat—'

'Poor Dellifer,' said Anna. 'Oh, poor old thing.'

Alice looked away. 'I know,' she said. 'I know. But it must have been quick. You know? Because when I got off to help, the old bag just waved me away. She was all, the cat's dead, nothing either of us can do now, why don't you mind your own business.' She ran her hand through her hair. 'What a bitch,' she said. 'So I got back on the bike and left her to it. I don't know what happened after that. I didn't really know what else to do.'

'Her name was Dellifer,' Anna said. 'I don't know where she came from and I don't know what I would have done without her. She meant everything to those kittens.'

She gave an odd little wail and began to sob. Once she had started, she couldn't stop. Everything rolled over her. She was inconsolable. She would never forgive herself. Images of Dellifer – leaking milk on to the best cushions, boxing the young Orlando's ears to teach him manners, past her best as a mother but still determined – now seemed to merge with all the other painful matters of Anna's life. The failure with Max, the death of Barnaby, the retreat from London, all this nightmare with Stella and John – the growing sense she had of herself as someone who couldn't make a life: the old cat became a symbol of it all. Anna put her face in her hands and wept and wept and wept.

'That bloody woman,' Alice said. 'I could kill her.'

'Oh Alice,' said Anna. She sniffed. She tried to laugh. 'I'm cold out here,' she said, 'And I need a tissue. One way or another I haven't had a very good day.'

Alice stared into Anna's raw, wet face and realisation dawned suddenly. 'This isn't just about the cat, is it?'

Dumbly, Anna shook her head.

'Ah,' said Alice. 'Is it him?'

'Oh you don't know, it's not just him, you don't know anything—'

Alice, always quick to detect self-pity, said: 'You'd better tell me what it is then, my girl. Or you'll get no sympathy from me.'

'You sound like your own grandmother,' said Anna.

Alice dropped her helmet on the doorstep. She went over and switched off the Kawasaki. She came back, picked the helmet up again, put her other arm round Anna in a creaky leather-smelling embrace, and ushered her inside. 'Sit down there,' she ordered, indicating the chair by the Aga, and began to make tea in her own inimitable fashion.

'Nothing wrong with my grannie,' she said.

'Let's see then—' she said later.

In addition to tea she had made peanut butter sandwiches, very thick, and after that eaten some marmalade on toast. She had turned the heating up. The kitchen smelled warm and inhabited for a change; the kitchen table was littered with used knives, open jars and bits of local cheese in wrinkled shrink-wrap.

'—the sky's fallen in on you because though you did very well at school and university, you always felt you could have done better. The sky's fallen in on you because, despite the fact that you were one of the most successful women at TransCorp, you suspected the male dealers didn't rate you. Am I right?' Instead of allowing Anna to answer, she began to tick off further points on her fingers, using one of the dirty knives. 'You blame yourself for failing to understand Max Wishart's character (which, though I like him lots, is not necessarily that of Captain Reliable). You blame yourself for the death of your cat Barnaby, and – correct me if I'm wrong here – the deaths of practically every other cat in the world. The sky has fallen in on you because you've had a row with John Dawe, known to be Ashmore's, not to say the universe's, most difficult man. And finally—'

With exaggerated care she replaced the knife on the table-top.

'Finally, the sky has fallen in on you because John Dawe's fifty-year-old cousin once taught him how to shag?'

She shrugged.

'Everyone has to learn,' she said.

'The problem is,' said Anna. 'I don't know if it ever stopped.'

Alice considered this with the matter-of-factness of eighteen years. 'Well, you can see she's nuts about him,' she admitted. 'But I'd say she doesn't get as much of him as she'd like, not by the way she watches him in the pub. It's a greedy look, like watching your dinner getting served by mistake to someone else when you're starving hungry. I feel quite sorry for her, poor old dear.'

'I hate her,' said Anna.

'Well, that's a start,' Alice got up. 'I can see you're feeling better,' – she retrieved her motorcycle jacket from the floor, hauling it across her shoulders in a single fluid movement – 'so I'm off to pick Max up from the station.'

Anna felt contrite. She hadn't given Max a thought. 'How is he?'

Alice grinned. 'He's a man, Anna. One sneeze is pneumonia, closely followed by viral myocardia and death. Pins and needles means life, but in a wheelchair.'

'So what is it, then?'

'Well they don't really know. It's not MS, though. You can get them to say that he might have had a virus. But you can always get them to say that. His osteo always thought it was a trapped nerve, maybe some kind of RSI. It could be down to the way he holds his instrument.' She winked. 'So I'm off to hold his instrument for him now, and we'll see if that will cure what ails him.'

'Best of luck.'

Alice gave Anna a look her mother would have called 'direct'. 'Come and have a drink with us later,' she invited, 'at the Green Man. Oh, and another thing,' – she worked her helmet energetically down over her head, talking at the same time, so that her voice proceeded oddly from its cushioned interior – 'if our Stella's got her claws into John Dawe, you'd better be prepared to fight for him.' With that, she was out of the door. A moment later the Kawasaki burst into life and roared away down the road with its front wheel in the air.

Anna stared out into the garden, and thought about Dellifer. She decided to phone Nonesuch, so see if anything could be done. Then, because her motives were so mixed, she decided not to. She was, she knew, as interested in finding out where John had gone after the argument at Cresset Beacon as she was in discovering the fate of the old cat. The mistress of Nonesuch, always merciless to the morally confused, would take immediate advantage of that. Suddenly the telephone rang. Anna stared at it in a kind of terror, convinced suddenly that Stella would be at the other end if she answered. She let it ring and ring. At last she picked the receiver up and jammed it to her ear. 'Hello?' she said sharply. 'Who's this?'

'No need to shout,' said Ruth Canning.

'Ruth, I'm so glad to hear you, I—'

'Are you all right?'

'I'm fine,' said Anna miserably. What else could she say? It would take ages to tell Ruth everything, and even then, what could she do? It was a long way from Hackney to Ashmore. 'I'm fine,' repeated Anna, who had never felt so isolated in her life.

'You don't sound it,' Ruth said. 'Look, can I do anything?'

'No, no. Don't. Honestly, I really am OK.'

Ruth rang off, puzzled. Anna stood by the phone, thinking miserably, I must do something. I must do something. Ten minutes later she was sitting at her PC. Ruth's voice had reminded her of Engelion Cosmetics. If she was to take John away from his cousin, it was time to understand as much as she could about Stella's activities. The hard disc of the computer buzzed and rattled to itself; the browser flickered into life; search engines were dispatched.

The files started innocuously enough with the official Engelion website's home page, which spread itself enticingly across the screen in the sumptuous pinks and greys and golds of the company livery. These colours were repeated in the main image, which showed a German supermodel from the eighties, known to be past her best. Naked but for some carefully engineered satin, she looked unfeasibly unlined and glowing as she endorsed the remarkable rejuvenating powers of Englion's firming and regenerating serum. 'I've worked hard and played hard; and I've earned the best – Engelion,' she claimed. Above her, left of the company masthead, Stella Herringe gazed serenely out of a smaller image, all cheekbones and sleek black hair and startling green eyes. Stella, who was at least ten years older than the supermodel, somehow looked the younger of the two.

'Beauty is a performance. It is the performance of your life. Push back the damage of the years,' Stella invited. 'Why let age wither you when the power to reverse time lies in your own hands?'

There followed a long list of quasi-technical details, which completed themselves with a further mission statement: 'At Engelion we spend more than half of our resources testing the product to make certain it is safe for you to enjoy.'

Anna clicked irritably out of the site, and found instead an article from an on-line news agency, dated the previous August:

Protesters arrested at research facility.
Fifteen animal rights activists were taken into custody yesterday when they attempted to set fire to an isolated building in farmland in the Oxfordshire countryside. Unconfirmed reports identify the building as Hale Farm, one of several properties owned by Allbright Chemicals Ltd. Demonstrators claimed that the building was being used in the process of animal testing of ingredients for British cosmetics company, Engelion plc. A company spokesman, Oliver Holland, denied that Engelion ever tested any of their products on animals. 'We are completely committed to a beauty without cruelty ethic,' he stated. But a spokesperson for the Anti-Vivisection League remained unconvinced. 'We've been keeping an eye on Allbright and Engelion for some time now, and we've gathered some pretty damning evidence. Even though testing so-called beauty products on animals is now illegal, it seems that all some companies have to do to avoid prosecution is to claim some spurious medical application for their work. But if the courts won't do something about these practices, we'll be taking matters into our own hands.'

Soon the web address for the Anti-Vivisection League site glowed in blue on Anna's monitor. Tentatively, she double-clicked the link.

Guinea pigs with shaved heads and weeping sores stared out of row upon row of wire cages; rabbits with ulcerated eyes were forced to receive more liquid into the affected areas via pipette; a monkey shrieked in silent outrage in the inimical grip of a stereotaxic device; dogs with the tops of their skulls trepanned sat staring patiently into the middle distance, as if imagining a different kind of world; a kitten with every part of its head trapped inside a complex vice comprising so many levers and clamps that it looked like a medieval torture device, writhed as a hand introduced an electrode into the exposed tissue on the crown of its head.

Anna felt her heart contract, her mouth go dry.

A banner ran across the bottom of the screen. 'Join the VN,' it read, 'and do something about it!'

She clicked on the banner. Up came a new site. It was crude in appearance, the lettering and layout basic. Content was more important than form here, and the content was simple. In bold capitals it declared: 'A Call to War! The VN (Vivisectionist's Nightmare): Fighting for Animal Rights'.

Beneath the headline there was a list of places and dates. This had not been updated for some time. In the middle of the list, Anna spotted an entry for Hale Farm. 'Cats bred for testing here. Take action: August 18th,' it read. And then, halfway down a subsidiary list, of those implicated at Hale: 'Herringe, Stella; Holland, Mark; Holland, Oliver'. No explanation for their inclusion was given. She remembered Mark and Oliver in their identical Paul Smith suits, staring around at the countryside as if they had never seen it before. 'Is that a jay?' she remembered one of them asking her. 'We thought it was a jay.'

The last item she found was about the use of foetal material from animals in anti-ageing treatments. Engelion was listed as one of the companies that had, until recent legislation, been pioneering in this area.

'You bastards,' she whispered.

Anna switched off the computer and stared at the dead screen. When she closed her eyes, she saw the laboratories. When she closed her eyes, she saw the patient, trepanned dogs, the tortured kitten with its mouth open on an unending cry of betrayal and despair.

She went to the bathroom and took down the pot of cream Stella had given her earlier that year. She took the lid off it and washed its contents down the sink, careful to make sure none of it touched her hands. Then she opened the back door and threw the pot into the dustbin. She stared out into the darkened garden, remembering how the bright fox had brought her Orlando's mother. She remembered all that pain, all that determination, all that trust. She thought about Dellifer, who couldn't stop herself from being a mother. Sleet was beginning to fall out of a leaden sky. Anna thought she might phone Stella Herringe after all, and tell her some of these things. Instead she wandered about the cottage, switching on all the lights. She switched on the television, only to be rewarded with the wretchedly cheerful theme of *Animal Hospital*. She tried Radio 4, where she found in progress a discussion about the future of the Euro. She read for a while, made soup and toast, and waited for her kittens to come home. By ten o'clock, the cat-flap had not so much as rattled. She switched on the outside light. She called their names. She banged a teaspoon on the food bowl. Nothing. She tried the same at the front door, then crossed the road to the pond and called again. All she got back was a resounding silence. She remembered what John Dawe had said that morning: 'Cats wander. They have their own lives.'

'Be careful with your lives, you two,' she said softly into the night. 'However many you may have.'

She wondered how she would have felt if she had ever used the Engelion cream.

The old tomcat was still in the spare room, crammed under the bed, hard up against the skirting board out of her reach. He smelled as bad as ever, and appeared to be sleeping until she pushed a bowl of moistened Science Diet towards him. His one eye opened. It regarded her with its customary gleaming hostility, then transferred its attention to the bowl. She smiled, 'Still got one life left, then, you old monster?' she said fondly. One of her anxieties thus assuaged, she made her way up to bed.

The nightmares were terrible.

Ashmore Dreams

Winter

All the villagers have been plagued with nightmares in recent nights. No one appears immune. Even Alice has wrapped her Kawasaki around a tree, time after time, in her dreams. The man who sleeps beside her, kicked by her flailing feet, finds himself running through a forest in which all the trees are howling. At Glebe Cottage, all the children can do is scream about monsters; all their parents can do is to scream at each other. Victoria McEwan dreams once more of a single night of infidelity. It starts pleasantly enough: a nice dinner, good wine, an attentive, charming man; but by the time they have retired to an illicitly booked hotel room and she is waiting for him to emerge from the bathroom, it becomes skewed; then awful. Each time she dreams it, something different and more disturbing wakes her in a sweat; this last time when he removed his robe, his body was covered in tiny red crustacea, ravenous for her flesh. She picks up a magazine, tries to stay awake.

The widow Lippincote is visited by her dead husband, and not as she prefers to remember him. Reggie Candleton dreams he is working in a nuclear plant and that the sirens have just gone off.

Even the old Hewett sisters, who as far as anyone knows them is concerned, have never done a bad thing in their lives, are afflicted with broken sleep. In her narrow single bed with its tight, white sheets, Eliza finds herself subjected to a harrowing ordeal involving a hooded man she is sure she knows; while in the room next door Catherine struggles in a terrible cocoon, as a great black spider, with the word 'Mother' spelled out in speckled markings on its forehead, leans over and wraps another thread around her.

Anna, meanwhile, unsurprisingly dreams of damaged creatures. Three-legged dogs, voiceless monkeys and eyeless cats trail her endlessly around a huge, dark house. She is searching, running down corridors, driven by the terrible conviction that unless she finds the right room soon, something will be lost forever. She opens one door and a gale of laughter banshees out; another door gives back a reflection of herself and her motley followers, replicated to infinity through a myriad of reflections. A third door opens and skulls and bones come tumbling out, throwing up great clouds of dust. The creatures that follow her crawl patiently through the charnel heap, sniffing and tasting. Their snuffling disgusts her, and on she runs. Most of the remaining doors are locked, until at last, the corridor comes to a dead end. There are no doors left to open. Beyond the final wall, though, she can hear someone – a man – calling her name. His voice is full of fear. Desperately, she tears at the wall. It is softer than a wall should be: its textures clog her fingernails, it gives to applied pressure. She digs, she bites at it: and the tortured animals rip and tear at it as well.

The wall starts to bleed . . .

Twenty-four

FOR THE rest of that day Millefleur was my rock.

I was filled with fury, a glorious, intoxicating, dangerous fury; a fury that burned in my head like a sun; a fury that coursed through the muscles of my shoulders and jaws, filling me with raw and brilliant power as the two of us ran the length and breadth of Ashmore, running and roaring, as if to do so was to rage against the world.

She was my rock, because she would not let me stop: she understood, I think, that the mindless corporeality I had given myself up to was far preferable to the maudlin stupor I might otherwise sink into, left to myself and the knowledge that my whole world was falling apart before my very eyes. For with my grandfather gravely injured; my sister vanished; my stepmother killed not a dozen yards in front of me, without Millefleur and her wild energy, I think I might simply have cast myself into the nearest wild road and offered myself as a sacrifice to the Dream, in the hope that having taken the only able dreamcatcher in the area it might be propitiated and travel on to terrorise another area.

Ostensibly, we concentrated our efforts on searching for Vita – howling her name like wolves bereft – but secretly, all the while we went bowling down lanes, burrowing through bramble heaps, bursting through hedges, it was Lydia who was at the heart of my quest.

However, we found no sign of either of them; and what we did find was infinitely more disturbing. Scorched trees; burned grass. Mangled highways, trailing the residues of the life they channelled into puddles on the sodden, freezing ground; dead and broken-backed animals flung wantonly here and there as if by a massive hand. A rat, its hind legs trailing uselessly along the ground, made its painstaking, implacable way across the main road, on a beeline for its nest, as if the very action of reaching this familiar territory would heal its fatal wound.

'Not even to a rat,' Millie said below her breath. 'This should not happen even to a rat.'

She took the thing cleanly between her jaws and carefully severed the vertebrae in its neck. Then she carried it, flopping out of either side of her mouth, and laid it in the ditch, where she covered it with moss. I watched all this, astonished, but said not a word. Between us, we despatched two badly injured squirrels and a buck rabbit; a crow and a bleeding badger cub, its head all caved in where it had been dashed against a tree. And then we ran and ran, as much to clear the stench of death from our heads as to cover the ground.

As last, heart pumping and lungs protesting, I found that I had to call a halt. Had I not, I think Millefleur would have run beside me without a word of reproach until her great heart gave out. I fell down on to my side, panting like a dog, and she joined me there, her breath steaming into the dark and freezing air.

'Where are they, Millie?' I managed at last through great heaving gasps. 'Why is there no sign of them?'

She looked at me oddly then. 'They?'

I realised my error and hastily covered my tracks as best I could. 'Vita, I mean. Where can she be? How could any cat vanish so completely?'

The tabby-and-white held my gaze steadily, and I knew then that she could see right through my skull, into the selfish thoughts that lurked there, thoughts of a beautiful, arrogant, golden cat, not my own lost sister. 'The highways have her,' Millie said cryptically. 'They have her now. We can do no more.'

I stared at her, aghast. 'We can't just give up on . . . her.'

Millefleur sighed. 'I think we must, Orlando,' she said quietly. 'They have swallowed her down further than you or I can go: and if you keep on searching with such fervour, you'll wear yourself to nothing, and what use will that be?'

Defeated, exhausted, we trailed back to the cottage. In through the cat-door we crept, into the dark and silent kitchen. And it was then I realised, with a terrible surprise and guilt, that I was ravenous: for there, where Anna always placed them, were the two food bowls on the floor beside the cupboards, and they had recently been refilled. Millie's stomach growled like a bear's. Her eyes gleamed, and then suddenly we were both applying ourselves with rapt attention, choking the dried pellets down as if they were caviar and we, beggars at a feast. We were just chasing the last few flavoursome morsels around the bottom of each bowl when Millie's fur suddenly stood on end and she leapt away in shock. Still chewing, I looked up. I could see immediately why she'd reacted in the way she did, for there in the doorway was an apparition: a hunched, dark shape, moonlight reflecting from its single eye.

It was Hawkweed, my grandfather, Ashmore's dreamcatcher – and a sorrier-looking cat I had never seen.

He faltered into the kitchen and now I could see the extent of the damage. One eye was swollen tight shut. His fur, customarily oily and unkempt, was bedraggled and disordered, streaked with dried blood. He favoured one hind leg; for the deep wound across the haunch on the other side still wept a noxious pale fluid. How he had even managed to get down the stairs, I could not imagine.

'No luck, laddie?'

I shook my head. 'She's gone, Granfer. Vita's gone.'

The old cat licked his teeth thoughtfully. 'Aye,' he said. 'Thought so. Gone through the knot. Gone to ground.' He took a pace towards me, saw Millefleur, and stopped dead.

'Aha,' he said, and his voice was hoarse and rasping, 'my saviour, if I am not mistaken: the beautiful lynx?' The grin he gave her was awful to behold, as if the muscles of his face were warring to express different emotions at once: mad fury; misery; a brave attempt at gallantry.

The sensible, competent Millie became strangely bashful and coy, and I began to perceive something of the sexual power my old grandfather had once wielded. I cannot say it pleased me much.

'My father was a dreamcatcher, sir: it was my pleasure to help in whatever way I could.'

Hawkweed's ears twitched. 'Your father, you say?'

'Fingal Whitethorn, sir.'

'From up past Westley?'

She nodded.

'Old Thorny!' The visible eye went misty. 'Fingal Whitethorn's daughter, well I never. A fine dreamcatcher, your father was, my dear: light on his feet and fast as a viper's tongue, and such a one for the ladies—' here he caught himself in a most uncharacteristically sensitive fashion '—before he met your mother, of course.'

Millie grinned. 'And for a long time afterwards, I fear, but she always knew it about him; he made no secret of his appetites.'

'Saved by the father, and then again by the daughter,' Hawkweed mused. 'Now that must be some kind of record.' He regarded Millie steadily, then brought the weight of that single-eyed stare to bear on me. 'She's a rare baggage, Orlando: she'll do you well. Very well indeed.'

Millie flushed and looked away.

'And there I was,' he guffawed, 'thinking you was some numpty lad mooning around after that little bit of golden fluff down at the canal: that girlie down on the boat where I gets my sardines. She's no better than an alleycat, that one, for all her fine airs and graces. Even had the gall to give me the wink once. Lucky for her, I had other things on my mind.' He licked his mangled lips.

Shocked to the bone at this horrible perspicacity, I opened my mouth to deny all, defend my beloved, challenge my grand-father's lack of chivalry: then thought better of it, for had I risen to his bait I am sure he would happily have turned upon me and demonstrated his vicious temper. In his current condition, that was not wise.

Without missing a beat, the old dreamcatcher went on: 'Now this fair maiden's daddy, he wouldn't have hesitated: he'd have been all over her like a vet's fingers! Had a few scraps in our time, he and I, over the ladies, till he moved over to Westley. Damn good job for me he came back into Ashmore when he did, though, or I'd have been a goner.'

And he went on to tell us of his first, and almost fatal encounter with the Dream, many years before. 'Thought I knew it all, I did. I'd been dreamcatching for the best part of a year, and nary a surprise or a problem. Then the nightmares started: little things at first – funny-looking monsters dreamt up by the kiddies; a few dead relatives and sucking pits. I welcomed the challenge at the time: bit of fun, I thought, at last. Then they began to get a bit stronger, a bit more frequent. Certainly kept me busy for a while. But nothing I couldn't handle: I was pretty fit in those days.' He grimaced at Millie. 'Then this great fiery black thing appeared; led me a proper dance it did – all over Ashmore: aye, and further. Those highways that run from round the manor house to down near the common, they're as tangled as a rat's nest: follow one for any distance and you find yourself in Timbuktu – and not even this Tuesday! Some of 'em'll take you right back to the days of Queen Bess, and beyond: witch-hunts and cat-burnings, not pretty at all . . .'

Now I had no idea what he was talking about. He must have received quite a blow to the head, I thought, from this latest episode, and I glanced anxiously at Millefleur, concerned that she was a witness to my grandfather's obvious senility, but her attention was unwavering. Indeed, she watched my grandfather as if he were some kind of hero.

'Ugly bastard it was, and stinking to high heaven. Finally ran it to ground out to the west of the village, in amongst the roots of that big old ash tree that came down in the last storm. Had the beggar cornered, but then it turned on me, kept multiplying all over the place: just didn't have enough feet or mouths to keep it down, and it growing all the time. That was where your dad came in: he'd felt the vibrations all the way past Westley and knew it was trouble. Leapt on it, he did: a great big leopard with a fearsome jaw on him; but the thing saw him coming . . .'

Memory hazed the dark yellow eye.

'Went straight down his throat, growing and growing. Choked him to death, and not a thing I could do to stop it. Then up it came again, spewing out of his face like streamers of black vomit; it gathered itself, knocked me stupid and hurled itself off down the roads again before I could come to.

'Poor old Fingal. Knew he was dead as soon as I saw him – not a leopard any more, you see: just plain old Finn, that scruffy black and white lad.

'And now it's back. And you and I, laddie, have to go out there and face it.'

I stared at him in disbelief. 'You must be out of your mind.' The words came tumbling out before I could call a halt to them.

Hawkweed drew himself up, his undamaged eye crackling with fury. I thought that he really would strike me then – even in his invalid state – as he had when I was a recalcitrant kitten who crossed his will; and I am sure the same thought had occurred to him, for I saw one forepaw give a twitch of intent. But he just stood there, swaying just a little – the old warrior, survivor of a thousand highway skirmishes, battered and damaged by his latest encounter – and a mad battle-light shone fiery in his eye.

'You coward!' he roared. 'You boneless, weak-kneed, shrinking puppy!' Saliva shot out of his mouth, between the twisted teeth, and spattered on me: a tangible shower of invective. He trembled in his rage.

It took all of my resolution to square my shoulders to him and not cower away as he expected. 'You are injured, Granfer. You are not fit to go out.'

'There is no choice in this, Orlando,' he growled. 'I will go out there to find it, with or without you.' He clenched his ruined jaw, took a staggering pace forward.

'If you go alone, you will die!' I cried, furious at his wilfulness.

He laughed. 'With Delly gone, what's left to me?'

I was horrified. 'You knew?' This latest piece of tragedy I had been hoping to keep from him until he was stronger.

'You must think me stupid, laddie!' He gave me a look of deepest contempt. 'I felt her pass: yet you could not, standing barely ten feet away! I wonder, Orlando, will you ever really make a dreamcatcher? I think you do not have it in you.'

Then he pushed me firmly to one side and shambled past, his hind leg dragging, his tail kinked like a broken pennant. A few seconds later, the cat-flap clattered and he was gone.

Millie and I looked at one another helplessly.

'I can't let him do this alone.'

Millie nodded slowly. 'If you go, I will come with you.' It sounded almost like a threat.

'No!' This came out more forcefully than I had meant, but I was full of anger. I amended my tone. 'Millie, you cannot even see the dreams – you will only be a hindrance to us—'

Now it was her turn to be angry. 'A hindrance? Had it not been for me, that old reprobate would be dead by now!'

'I know that, I do. But, Millie, if my grandfather and I pursue the Dream, who will look for Vita?'

She bowed her head, then her chin came up and she gave me a direct look that made me squirm. 'That's a cruel shot, Orlando. I feel responsible for your sister, and you know it. But you heard your granfer: *Gone through the knot. Gone to ground.* Vita's gone. And with any luck so has that stuck-up tart from the canal you're so worried about. And since you clearly don't want me around, you *lads* – you *dreamcatchers* – may as well go and pursue your death or glory without me.' And with that, she turned her back on me and marched outside, her tail defiantly high.

Out there, I found my grandfather clawing pathetically at the beech hedge. He had pushed one shoulder into the sparse branches and was now stuck, his strength failing. I crammed in behind him and flattened a way through until we were out into the next garden, our breath steaming like rivers into the freezing air.

A small orange cat, alarmed at the noise of our bulldozing efforts, watched our progress from the top of a shed. It was Ginge. Our eyes met, and I saw in his a shock of recognition, then his gaze slid away and he sloped off the roof and out of sight.

And so it was a few minutes later, that my grandfather and I were once more out on the roads of Ashmore Village, the dreamcatcher with his reluctant apprentice in tow. On the green in front of the pond, a long-legged tabby-and-white cat sat stony-faced and watched us go without a word. I knew from her slope-shouldered, ear-flattened demeanour that Millie did not expect to see either one of us again.

It was the coldest night I can ever recall. The moon sailed negligent and aloof behind high cloud, beaming her white light down upon the glacial chill of the ground, which pressed freezing upon our feet. Frost-blasted plants lay limp and blackened where we passed; and the night hours had made an arctic waste of the Ashmore pond, which had frozen over from shore to shore, all save one small pool where the scarlet tips of willow branches brushed a still-liquid surface. This area had been colonised by a sparse population of ducks and moorhens who clustered there in sullen silence, as if offended at having to share their own meagre body-heat with barely tolerated neighbours.

We walked for some time, on the surface of Ashmore: or rather, my grandfather hobbled and shuffled painfully along, spurning all my attempts to aid him, while I trudged unenthusiastically behind him with the cold setting deep into the bones of my face and legs.

It was, strangely enough, a relief to get into the wild roads. From hobbling invalid to great cat, I watched him transform as the energy of the highway entered him, coaxing out the jaguar within. The broken face filled out: the jaw grew long and heavy; the damaged eye sprung open to gleam as bright as any car's headlamp. The only clue to his true injuries showed in a slight stiffness of the hind legs as he ran.

In addition, it appeared to be just a little warmer inside the highways than it was outside. It was usually bitingly cold on the wild roads, the winds bearing a bitter edge that would penetrate even the thickest of coats, but on this occasion, I remember noting that the temperature seemed less savage than normal, especially around those roads that bisected the common. However, I imputed no more sinister reason to this observation than to think it must mean my body was calibrating itself to the change between the outside world and the highways. Perhaps if I had paid more attention to what my senses were trying to tell me, we might have avoided disaster.

But disaster was pressed from my mind by the sheer difficulty of keeping up with my grandfather. Restored in body and spirit to his rightful quest, Hawkweed roared and leapt down the spiralling vistas of the village's highways with all the awful vigour I remembered from those first days. We ran so fast, I could hardly believe he had time to take notice of any clue to the whereabouts of our quarry, but he galloped along, impervious to my existence, his paws thundering, muscles bunching and stretching, and hesitated not once as we reached confused junctions and confluences of roads. Even in their new configurations, where the Dream had tossed them about, or they had twisted to avoid it, he appeared to have no doubts, though by now I was entirely lost.

This disorientation was compounded by the fact that the highway winds, usually so consistent in their force and bearing, were blowing in all directions at once so that at one moment my mane flew into my eyes, then was blasted flat against my skull. It was an exhausting experience, this persistent battering of the senses; and made all the more frustrating by the complete absence of our quarry.

By now, it was dead of night, the worst time for nightmares, they say: the time, I shuddered to myself, when the Dream would be gathering more power to itself from the dreams attracted on to the highways from the sleeping village. It was unnerving, to say the least; but my grandfather, charging headlong down gloomy tunnels and tenebrous passages, seemed not one whit concerned for his own safety. Or mine.

At last, of all places, in the highway behind the church, he stopped.

He sniffed the air. Even I could tell, with my less tutored senses, that it had a faintly sulphurous taint; but Hawkweed was the master in such matters. He curled his black lip and gathered the odour high into the roof of his mouth where lies in cats a powerful olfactory organ. There, he trapped it with his great tongue, pressing it hard, as if to squeeze from it every iota of information. I saw him *taste* the air, if such a thing can be accomplished.

His pupils flared darkly, as if with sudden passion.

'I knew it!' he declared triumphantly. 'It is her Dream again: it is the one. Ah,' – he inhaled deeply – 'the bitterness, the jealousy: oh, the anguish of it all!'

And then he was off again, with me at his heels, running now like a hound, his nose to the floor of the highway, tracking his prey, and all around us, the air grew warmer.

Then, suddenly, it was before us. At first, I could tell only by the way Hawkweed's fur ruffled and then stood in spikes down his backbone; by the set of his head and the line of drool that fell slowly from his eager mouth. Then a deep rumble began in his chest, and before I knew it, my fur had also crested in its own primeval display of fear and challenge. I paced forward to stand beside my grandfather, and saw, for the first time, the Dream.

For now, it lay, pacific enough, curled into a twist in the

highways as if resting. It was like no other dream I had seen: for it was black, and a dark red glowed at its heart like an ember in the middle of a sleeping fire. Where other dreams were gold and smooth as lozenges, this one was a tatterdemalion thing: a jagged, unruly mass of excrescences and tentacles. Even resting, it radiated a powerful heat, and at last I realised our error. This Dream was too terrible for any cat to defy: it had permeated the highways in a five-mile radius with its uncanny heat; it had broken many wild roads apart and diverted the course of others; it had smashed aside anything in its way with random violence, and now it lay before us.

'Grandfather,' I said softly, but if he heard me he did not acknowledge it.

Instead, he advanced upon the thing as if he thought to catch it sleeping and make an easier dispatch of it. His jaws opened wide and he angled his head for the best line of attack.

The Dream stirred.

Tattered black arms floated out from it to wave gently in the highway winds, like fronds of weed in a pool. The dreamcatcher threw back his head and roared, then with a mighty leap – a leap designed to culminate in a killing blow – Hawkweed fell like a hammer into the centre of the Dream. It shuddered and sighed under the impact. More tentacles unwrapped themselves from its mass and drifted outward as if in surrender. It gaped, as if it were yawning at the disturbance of its sleep.

The tatters rose lazily; and now, rather than weed, it was an anemone: a great flower of black with a beating red heart, a heart upon which my grandfather stood, biting down ferociously.

There was a sudden upheaval. The Dream rose up. It was enormous.

'Granfer!' I cried, for suddenly I could not see him: black upon black, the Dream had him in its embrace.

I hurled myself into the fray. My jaws closed on it and I was rewarded by a mouthful of foul juice, as caustic as bile. My tongue and gums smarted; my eyes stung. Still I bit down.

Terrible images assailed me then: cages of cats, howling like banshees; a woman with burning eyes butchering a kitten. A towering house: a cold, white room; the stench of death; the sweetness of decay. Maggots, blowflies, great knots of twining worms all poured out of it, to be followed by more abstract horrors – a chaos of limbs and eyes and teeth and hair, bound into abominable combinations, which unleashed themselves and shot apart. Clawed hands came snaking out to clutch and rend; and great shags of black hair whipped around our feet and wrapped our throats. The heat was appalling: it was as if what drove the demon was a fire at its heart. It vomited atrocity after atrocity at us, which hung in the air twitching and shrieking before drifting off into the highway winds like scraps of ash.

'Keep fighting, Orlando!' my grandfather cried from the depths of the monster. 'Each wound saps its strength.'

As if to prove his point he raked the Dream viciously with a razored paw. Black fluid bubbled out until it writhed and wailed. We fought on, and on, and all the while, the moon dipped lower in the sky beyond the wild road, heralding the possibility of an early dawn; but I feared that if we did not defeat it soon, we would never see it.

There came a moment when I thought we had our enemy beaten: lion and jaguar, our heads met, jaws clashing, as if the Dream had somehow emptied itself out into the air and left us biting on a hollow sac. I raised my head in anticipation of a victory, and even as I did so, I realised my mistake: for all the Dream had done was to withdraw itself into one corner of its membrane as if gathering its strength for a final onslaught. Black streamers came hurtling out of it, wrapped themselves around my grandfather and began to tighten their hold. His eyes went wide with shock.

'Grandfather!' I yelled, and gathered my hind legs to spring into the melee.

I got no further. Something was holding me by the tail. I whipped around, expecting to find myself entwined by hellish tentacles, but there, behind me, its sharp teeth meeting in my flesh, its feet planted foursquare against my leverage, was the burnished creature I had seen the previous day, aiding my grandfather as he limped across the common.

I roared at it, but it did not let go. A mad light burned in its tawny eyes. I whipped around in fury, swiping at it with huge forepaws, but it danced neatly sideways.

'Get off me!' I yowled in frustration, for my grandfather was now in the throes of the Dream, but all the fox did was to grin and constrict those inimical jaws a further notch.

What happened next will haunt me forever. I remember it only in a series of flickering images: the Dream rearing up so that the highway was forced to arch above it: my grandfather thrashing in its grasp; the highway beginning to tear itself apart under the force of their struggle, silently, like the teeth in a zipper unravelling one by one; a sudden roar of hot wind which scorched the whiskers off my face; then being whirled into the air as the highway convulsed, and falling at immense speed. The fox fell past me and vanished from view; but other images came. I do not know whether they were real or in my head alone, for they were very strange. I saw the world outside the highway, spiralling around and around; at one moment full of black light and white frost, then bright with August sunshine; the cottages by the pond crouching in the darkness were replaced by haycarts in an open field and people sweating as they worked in breeches and long dresses; empty trees stood stark against a moonlit sky, but crows rose cawing into blue air out of a giant, green-faced oak . . .

And then the ground – hard, frozen, cold as stone – came up and hit me.

I lay there, breathing hard, disorientated and confused.

Everything was deathly quiet: for a second. Then all hell broke loose. The gentle little highway that ran behind the church, past the pond and out to Ashmore Common was being ripped apart. It arched, maybe twenty feet above the frozen pond, almost translucent in the night air, and great rends showed in its sides through which spilled gouts of black and violent jets of steam. Inside it, two figures were locked in struggle, one holding the other with many arms, worrying at it as a terrier will worry at a rat.

One more shake and a single black shape came plummeting out of the broken highway. It was Hawkweed, free of the Dream at last. Twenty feet up and on his back, I saw him twist expertly, with the age-old skill and instinct of the falling cat. His tail whipped the air; his legs swivelled and splayed. Feet first, he hit the frozen pond.

For a moment he stood there, incongruously magnificent: a huge black jaguar, limned with silver light, roaring his defiance at his retreating enemy. Then a zigzag of cracks snapped their way across the ice, and down he went.

Without a thought for my own safety, I ran straight out over the crust towards him, my paws skidding uncontrollably on the pond's slippery skin. It took the momentum out of my charge, and though I was more fortunate than my grandfather (for even thin ice will bear the weight of a small domestic cat) by the time I reached the jagged hole where he had gone down, all I could see, far below in the murky depths, was the amber light dying out of one outraged eye.

I do not know how long I sat there, staring into the dark, weed-tangled water, calling my grandfather's name; but by the time I finally gave up all hope, the moon had gone and there were icicles in my fur.

The rage that had consumed me earlier that day deserted me when I needed it most. In place of the burning sun of fury I had felt at Dellifer's needless death, all I had left at the thought of Hawkweed's dramatic end was a cold pit of dread, hanging heavy inside me. I had failed my own grandfather. We had had the old enemy in our jaws, and I had let it go at the crucial moment. If I could have offered myself to the Great Cat then in place of the old dreamcatcher, I would happily have done so, for I was indeed the useless, snivelling, weak-kneed puppy; the fool of fools; the coward of cowards; all those things of which he had so often accused me.

As the cold deepened, my sense of horrible anticipation grew heavier. Slow and exhausted, it took me a long time to under-stand the irrevocable reason for my dread. It was not just that I had failed Hawkweed; it was that now he was finally gone, I was alone. Alone, to bear the burden he had been grooming me for all this while.

I was now the sole dreamcatcher of Ashmore, and as such I was facing a terrible challenge. It was now my fate, and mine alone, to hunt down and eat the Dream that had killed my grandfather, as it had killed so many dreamcatchers before him.

Weary in body and soul, I dragged myself to my feet. My legs and rear were numb with cold as I slipped and slid my way awkwardly across the pond to the rushes at its edge, but by the time I had reached the churchyard, hot aches had begun to flare up inside my skin. Strangely enough, the pain from this return to feeling proved to be all I needed to ignite my resolve.

Even in the grim light before dawn, the Dream was not hard to track.

I did not even have to use the highways to follow its destructive progress. Scorched trees, sere grass, flattened bushes: the Dream had torn through the village like a whirlwind. A large white dish dangled uselessly off one of the cottages on the old terrace; Christmas wreaths had been whipped off doors; small branches lay scattered in the road. I found the blond twins' pet guinea pigs with blood oozing out of their eyes and nose, their sturdy cage a mess of chicken wire and splintered wood, their bedding straw strewn all over the garden. A chimney had collapsed through the roof at one of the alms cottages, and at the corner the lane that led to the manor house a small wire-haired terrier stood barking madly, its lead wrapped around a broken lamp-post, its owner, who had presumably suffered a disturbed night and had risen in the early hours to take its restless dog for a walk, lying insensible beside it.

This last act of destruction seemed to have taken some of the sting out of its havoc: from here its path became hard to track. But I knew now where I was going: I knew where it had come from, and where it was returning, and I started to run.

There were lights on in the old manor house, but the Dream was not inside. As I crept through the towering stone gateway, I could see how a baleful glow dully illuminated its trail across the gardens. Skirting the open ground, I ran quickly towards the cedar where I had caught the dream I had followed from Lydia's home, trying to keep as much under cover as I could manage. To the far east, a corner of sky was showing a glimmer of red light, a tremulous promise of dawn.

The Dream drifted languidly around the corner of the manor house and disappeared from view.

I seized my opportunity and galloped up the garden until I reached the herbaceous borders. From inside the house, I could hear raised voices, but I was past the stage of caring what people said or did to one another when they were conscious. Moving cautiously, I skirted the corner just in time to see the Dream float over the old orchard wall. I watched while it sailed aimlessly over the naked branches of the fruit trees, casting a morbid light, the unnatural antithesis to a shadow, as it passed, and then, brushing the wall on the other side, fell out of sight once more.

Cautious to the end, I walked around three sides of the orchard before catching up with my quarry, where it hovered over a collection of low-lying hedges, cut close and neat to form a complicated pattern. Over the centre of this convolution it bobbed gently, its streamers hanging from it like some particularly virulent jellyfish.

Then it floated to the ground, as if it had finally reached its destination.

With my tail low, walking down on my hocks, I crept around the edges of the knot garden. It took a little while to find an entrance, and when I did, I found I had to weave a path dictated by the complex planting, if I was to stay out of sight. Who knew what senses the Dream might possess? I did not intend to test the numerous eyes I had seen jumbled in its midst.

Approaching the middle of the pattern, I risked a glimpse over the hedges, and there was my enemy, a pool of black, pulsing quietly in the centre of the maze, as if recharging its energies.

I wasted no time. Had I stopped to think for even a moment, I might just have taken to my heels, and not stopped running till I was past Ashmore, into Westley and far, far beyond. Had I stopped to think, it might have occurred to me that out here beyond the wild roads I was no more than a small domestic cat, singularly lacking in the armoury with which I had failed to stop the Dream before. But I had the heart of the lion, if not its weight and size, and I launched myself upon the monstrosity with all twenty claws extended and my jaws open wide.

It was like falling upon a creature that should have been long dead, for all it smelled and gave beneath me, but even so, it squealed like a rabbit when an owl breaks its back and twisted in panic beneath my grip. I felt its panic, and it fuelled my efforts, so that I bit and ripped and swallowed and tried to ignore the burning liquids that shot from the thing, and the shreds of horror that peeled away from its bulk, biting back at me with discorporate mouths. I gulped down its bitter guts, blanking my mind against the images with which it tried to break me; all but one. It was failing, and I could sense my victory, when it threw up an effigy that set my heart racing: a small golden cat, held in a mechanical vice, rolling her beautiful eyes in pain and despair.

It was Lydia.

I blinked and stared, my teeth still embedded in the Dream's membrane, but the image burrowed away from me and out of sight. Frenzied, I went after it, burying my head in that noxious sac so that vile fluids burst open, soaking into my fur, my ears, my nose. I felt myself choking. I felt the Dream's glee.

It began to constrict, as if every remaining part of itself was a muscle. The world started to darken around me. I struggled to breathe. So this is the end of it all, I thought dully: first Dellifer, then Hawkweed, and now the hopeless apprentice dream-catcher . . .

Then there was a cry and something thumped hard into one side of me, and a second later, something else slammed into the other flank. My head shot back out into the air and I rolled, gasping, to the ground. Black stars filled my eyes. A terrible caterwauling split the night: a high-pitched yipping; a bubbling yowl, and the moaning wails of the Dream under assault. I staggered to my feet, only to find the fox who had prevented me from saving my grandfather now, inexplicably, savaging my enemy. And beside him, up to her elbows in black bile, was my friend Millefleur.

My heart welled up inside me and I set to again with renewed will. Between the three of us we drove the thing around that maze. It tried to flee, but found itself hemmed in, the fox blocking its exit in one direction, while Millie and I attacked it from another.

The Dream did not go quietly. It thrashed and shrieked, and lashed out with its ragged tentacles, but at last we got it cornered.

'Orlando,' the fox said, addressing me for the first time. 'This unnatural thing must be yours to despatch. It is your task: it was what you were born and raised to do. You are the seventh Dreamcatcher: it is the Seventh Dream. I know this better than most: it has been my task, and that of your grandfather, to ensure you were brought safely to this point in fate and time. Only you can kill it, Orlando; and only here.'

I stared at him, still muddled from the lack of oxygen and the poisons I had inhaled. The image of Lydia, bound in her world of pain, tormented me, and in the end it was that which drove me forward, a feral grin stretched across my face. I leapt upon my enemy for the last time, bit it to the core and felt it burst its viscera over me with a savage satisfaction. I think now that I had somehow decided that Liddy was trapped inside it, and that by rending it in such a manner I would somehow release her from its toils; but all that emerged from the Dream, at last, was a sigh of anguish, even of relief.

I lay, stunned and exhausted, in a stinking pool, the bile drying to tacky peaks in my fur in that freezing dawn, glueing my eyelids shut. Millie sat beside me, and with much spitting and many frank expressions of disgust, started to groom my spattered face. The fox gazed down at me over her shoulder.

'You did well, Orlando,' he said, his voice husky. 'Hawkweed would be very proud.'

But I could not think straight. I barely knew who or where I was. I opened my mouth, but all that came out was, 'Lydia—'

Millefleur's head shot back as if I had bitten her and her eyes became unnaturally bright. She emitted a small, strangled cry, then turned and ran.

The fox gave me a disappointed look. 'Alas, a hero; but still a fool.'

I struggled upright and stared after Millie's disappearing form, her tabby fur eloquent with the new sun's red light as she fled across the lawns, and a terrible, inexplicable sadness flooded into me.

'But, why?'

The fox shook its head. 'Females are complex, jealous creatures, my friend. And males are stupid and blundering. It's a rather unfortunate combination. One of Nature's rare mistakes.'

'Like the Dream?'

The fox looked at me curiously. 'You really are the fool your grandfather said you were. I thought he exaggerated. I said, "Give the lad a chance, he'll learn: it's his destiny to learn." However, I must say that you're slower even than I expected, which is most alarming.'

This pleased me not at all. I was just about to ask him who the hell he thought he was, to appear and disappear at will and issue such ungenerous pronouncements, when I heard a door creak open behind me.

'Run!' the fox cried urgently, and took to his heels.

But as if to set the final seal of logic on his judgement, I was, inevitably, too slow. A naked crone had emerged from the house and when she saw me, she smiled. I quailed before her and my paws made pathetic little mimes of running as she bent to examine me. I closed my eyes as if to banish her presence, but a pair of hands caught me firmly around the ribs, taking the last of my precious breath, and though I struggled feebly I was hauled up and away and borne into the house my grandfather called the Nonesuch.

The last observation I could make before unconsciousness took me was this: I recognised that crone's mouth; that hair, those eyes. I had swallowed them down, in all their vile, myriad forms, a dozen times in the past hour alone.

Twenty-five

ANNA WOKE. Her heart thumped painfully against her ribs. There was cold sweat on her neck and shoulders, and the duvet had hobbled her legs. She lay curled and panting in the dark, fighting off the heavy pull of sleep. Bits of her nightmares kept replaying themselves in meaningless juxtaposition. One moment she was in some deserted house, opening a door; the next she was trying to make progress through a crowd of refugees. The house, she could have sworn, was one she knew. She recognised those corridors, those uneven walls. The war zone, though, was unrecognisable. A man cried out in a distant street. There were klaxons blaring, megaphones commanding everyone to keep moving. Anna struggled on against the tide, getting an elbow in her chest, a hand in her face, a dragging at her feet. Dismal concrete structures towered above her, mortar-scarred, their windows shattered by bullets. Someone she loved was held against his will in that town. The war was barely a prelude to the disaster that would ensue if she did not reach him.

Sleep was impossible in the face of this. She sighed and flung the covers off. The air was freezing. Why hadn't the central heating come on? Tilting her watch to catch what little light there was in the room, Anna saw that it was only ten to four. She groaned, then, draping the duvet round her shoulders, knelt on the windowseat to gaze out on the dismal morning. Ashmore was in the grip of a heavy frost. There were feathers of it around the edges of the window. The herringbone brick in her front garden was crazed with it: rosemary and lavender stood stark and rimy against the bitter earth. Across the road, the pond was a skating rink, except for a dark hole in the centre where it looked to Anna as if something like a small log had broken the surface.

'You might as well get up,' she told herself.

She rubbed her hand over her face and stumbled into the bathroom. In the middle of her shower, her heart began to pound again and she thought: It's John! John is in danger! Then she thought: it was only a dream.

She remembered his hands on her and lifted her face to the showerhead and let the water fall unchecked.

Half an hour later, she had combed her wet hair back from her face and put on a fleece jumper, a pair of warm moleskin jeans and some bulky woollen socks. She sat at the table downstairs, her hands cupped round a mug of tea, and leafed through the printouts she had made from the internet the previous night. In the glum morning light, the abused animals looked even more forlorn. They looked wrenched, and tired out and scared. This is no good, she said to herself. People would do this to each other if we let them, they would find the best of reasons. I can't just sit here feeling like this. I have to do something, I have to go and tell Stella what I think of her.

On the way, she would go and apologise to John. It wasn't fair to blame him: the bars of his cage were emotional, but he was as trapped by them as any research animal.

Before she left, she took the empty mug out into the kitchen. Orlando and Vita had been back in the night. Their bowls were empty. You greedy pair, she thought with relief. Then she thought: what on earth do they find to do out there in weather like this?

Cats. Cats and their strange little lives. She smiled.

Outside, it was so cold that each breath she took felt like a separate block of frigid air forcing its way into her lungs. She tucked her scarf firmly into the neck of her Barbour jacket and set off, with her hands deep in her pockets. The lanes were full of broken sticks, and even quite large branches, as if high winds had swooped over the edge of the downs during the night, then vanished like the turmoil in her dreams.

Down at the Brindley cut, the narrowboats huddled on the motionless brown water, their upperwork lumbered with bicycles, leaky water-cans and tubs of doomed geraniums.

John Dawe's boat looked a little more alive than the rest, its fresh paint and recently polished brasswork bright in the developing light of day. A line of frozen washing – towels the consistency of crispbread, jeans with sculpted wrinkles – stretched from a hook on the cabin roof to the raised mooring post on the towpath. Boat life, bohemian life: it was a cheerful scene. Her spirits raised, Anna addressed the washing. When it resisted, she ducked smartly under it, and peered into the *Magpie*'s shadowy interior.

She could see some furniture. The foldaway bed was down, blankets trailing off it. His laptop, open but switched off, remained connected to the cellphone following some recent transaction. There was unwashed crockery stacked in the sink. Otherwise, it was dust and objects: she made out the skull of a crow; the long yellowed spine of some foreign snake; a leather backgammon set; dyed feathers, tied to a stick. She had grown used to these things. There were days when she even missed them. This is no good, she thought, and jumped up on deck. Everything there was shut down, put away, tidied up. There was no smoke from the chimney, which meant that the stove had gone out. She rattled the door against its little brass padlock. She looked hopefully across at the other boats, but they were silent. Everyone was asleep, or had fled wherever canal people flee in winter from the muddy towpaths and grim lines of willows. She banged the cabin roof with the flat of her hand.

'John?' she called. 'John!'

But she knew he wasn't there.

She got down off the upperwork and tried to see in through the windows again. She had more luck this time, and it was all bad. On the Formica-topped table, by the bread board and milk jug stood a bottle of Calvados and a jar of instant coffee with the lid off – the things he had used to fill his flask for the 'picnic' the day before. He hadn't been home since. After she left him at Cresset Beacon he had headed straight for Nonesuch, and whatever solace he was used to finding there. Anna stood on the towpath, banging her hands together in the cold. If that was what he wanted, then let him. They so richly deserved one another. She could walk away from them both now, leave them to the emotional prison they had constructed for themselves up at Nonesuch all those years ago. Damn, she thought. Oh, damn, damn, damn. Because she knew in her heart that he didn't want the prison, and only she could free him. He was manacled to the thirteen-year-old boy he had once been, and she would have to go and separate them and prise him out of that place. It was time to break his dependence on Stella forever. Gritting her teeth, she retraced her steps to the lane and started up the long hill back into the village.

The sun cleared the trees in the birchwood as she came up towards the common. It was a wintry sun, pale and brassy, and it was doing little to help burn off the frost, which had cemented the tangles of couch grass in the verge and shellacked every dip in the road. Past the postbox, amid a litter of broken branches, she came upon a dead squirrel. It didn't seem to have been run over. Perhaps, she thought, it had misjudged a leap during last night's gale, come down with all these shattered limbs of birch. Were squirrels active at night? She had no idea. She bent to retrieve the stiff little carcass. It lay as light as a paper carton in her hands, its lips curled back over curved orange teeth, its black eyes bulging in astonishment.

'Sorry, old chap,' she whispered, dropping it gently into the brambled hedge. 'No time to give you a decent burial.'

She squinted into the sunshine that spilled between the birches. There really were a lot of branches down. Something made her quicken her pace, and by the time she reached the corner of Allbright Lane, she had broken into a jog. A light breeze rose, and brought the hoarfrost off the trees and telephone wires in hard little flurries like dry snow.

It was a strange morning.

Some way along Allbright Lane she came upon an elderly man kneeling in the road. He was dressed in a neat, old-fashioned camel overcoat and a tweed hat. She knew him by sight – he and his small wire-haired terrier were fixtures at the Green Man – but couldn't remember what he was called. The dog had wrapped its lead around the base of a broken lamp-post, and he was trying to disengage it. Excited by the novelty of this situation, the dog ran round and round in tight little circles, barking and snapping and winding the lead tighter.

'Can I help?' said Anna.

At that moment the dog seemed to get free of its own accord. The man regarded her with a kind of flaccid irritability. When he stood up, she saw that he was grey in the face. Melted frost had left dark patches on the knees of his trousers, a dark bruise discoloured his left cheek. 'Mind your own business,' he said. He yanked the dog smartly away and pushed past her without another word, as if she had made him some shameful offer.

Anna watched him go.

Suddenly she remembered his name.

'Mr Cunningham!' she called. 'Are you all right?'

No reply. With a mental shrug she passed on, beneath the towering yew hedges, until she reached the gates of Nonesuch House.

In 1482, Joshua Hering, determined on the New Build but fearing the effect of Ashmore's winter easterlies on his susceptible second wife Elizabeth Marchmount, had been as cunning in his choice of location as in any other enterprise. The site was sheltered by the landforms themselves. As a result, Nonesuch had done well in last night's gale. The terraces were tidy, the great plantings untouched. But still air encourages frost (as Joshua himself had soon discovered), and as Anna made her way up the long drive, it seemed to her that every twig, every needle, every blade of grass was sheathed in transparent ice. The air was laden, hard to breathe. Her fingers and toes grew numb. It was a bitter place for a human being, let alone a small animal; yet halfway to the house, she heard a mewing sound quite close.

From the shelter of some rhododendrons emerged a tabby-and-white cat, long in the leg but sturdy in the body, with a bizarre little crest of fur on its head and an odd look in its eyes, companionable and cautious at the same time. It stood, shifting its weight from one paw to another on the cold ground, and purred. Anna knelt down. She made soft clicking noises. 'Puss,' she said. 'Puss?' The tabby had a look around, then approached her. 'You see?' she said. 'I'm all right. I'm OK.' It sniffed at her fingers, its nose cold against her skin. It butted her hand. She stroked its cool, smooth fur for a few moments, running her hand firmly down its spine and off its long tail.

'Who are you then?' Anna asked, rubbing it under the chin. There was no collar. 'One of Stella's strays?'

Even as the words left her mouth she realised, given what she now knew, how frightening and paradoxical an idea that had become. But the cat left her no time to meditate on this. Instead it wove itself twice more round her legs then set off at a brisk trot, tail up, through a gap in the rhododendrons and on to one of the great lawns at the front of the house. About ten yards off, as if it had realised Anna was not following, it stopped and looked back enquiringly over one shoulder.

Anna smiled. 'Goodbye then,' she said, and she carried on up the drive. The tabby ran in front of her, and wound itself so tightly round her legs again she had to stop or tread on it. It mewed insistently. It made very direct eye contact with her.

'What do you want?'

Not to be stroked, clearly: as soon as she bent down, it ran off again.

'Look,' she said. 'This is ridiculous.'

Nevertheless, she followed. The tabby set off into the middle of the bleak, icy expanse of the lawn, stopping from time to time to make sure Anna was still there. It was nervous in the open, she could see. Whenever it looked up and noticed the walls of Nonesuch, it crouched suddenly, and seemed likely to change its mind; finally it put back its ears and took off at a run, leaving behind a faint curve of footprints in the frozen turf. Reaching the corner of the house, it looked back once and disappeared. 'Damn!' said Anna, who had become involved despite herself. She followed the footprints, and was soon confronted by an old wall of soft orange brick, beyond which could be seen the tops of a number of gnarled and leafless trees. The Nonesuch orchard: Stella's famous medlars from sixteenth-century stock, with their soft and rotten-tasting fruit. The cat waited for a moment, then it was off again, running more confidently along the base of the wall, through an open gate, down a leafless walk—

—and into the knot garden.

Paths of coloured gravel separated the carefully clipped lines of box and germander which crossed and recrossed the open space in great whorls and spirals, hidden in the geometrical complexities of which you might never suspect the Herringe initials, the Herringe ego – waiting like a spider, trapped like a bird, since 1482. Anna came to a halt. She stared. While the little cat sat and watched, she put one foot carefully in front of another and walked three sides of the design. She admired the accuracy of it, the precision. It was a clock which told Herringe time, a site of mystery and arrogance. Anyone watching from the house would have seen her frown, as if she had half-solved some puzzle. Should she walk on? This way, or that? The whole thing was somewhat spoiled, she noted, by a mass of broken and flattened stems at the centre of the maze, where the coloured gravels had been scuffed away to reveal the soil beneath, sticky with some dark residue.

When I came to, I had no idea where I was. The surface I lay on was dark and cold. It stank, of urine and faeces, and something sweet and cloying to which I could put no name.

I struggled up, feeling dizzy, every muscle aching from my ordeals, to find myself in a kind of narrow concrete run hemmed in on both sides by metal cages, a hundred of them or more, piled up higgledy-piggledy and glinting in the red light of dawn. At one end of the run was a closed door; at the other a blank wall. Inside each cage was a cat or kitten, each one of which regarded me with deep curiosity.

'Who are you?'

A skinny female Siamese, her blue eyes crossed in concentration.

'He's a boy—'

A tiny black-and-white.

'He's just another stud—'

A big old tabby, past her best.

'Let me see!'

Many of the cages contained more than one animal. They crowded to the bars to get a look at me, and now I could see that they were all queens, some mated, some not. If I tuned out the rank smell of the place itself, their common scent washed over me, resolving into a hundred signatures impressed on the air like graffiti on a wall, musky, distinctive, strange.

'I'm Orlando.' I croaked.

My throat was still clogged with scraps of the Dream.

'Orlando? Is it you?'

I was only half conscious until then. The sound of that voice turned me round so fast my head spun.

'Liddy!'

There she was, her perfect face pressed up to the wire of a cage near the bottom of the stack! I made a few unsteady steps across the concrete and stared up at her.

'Oh, Liddy!'

'It's Lydia,' she reminded me.

At once there was a chorus of, 'Hark at Lady Muck—', 'Ooh, Queenie's off again' and 'Little Ms High and Mighty—'

'Oh, leave her alone,' said a bored voice.

My heart swelled. 'Lidd— oh, Lydia. I've found you at last.'

This brought some cackling from the tiered cages.

'Found her at last, has he?' 'Oh he has. He's found her all right.' Then: 'You've arrived a bit late to be the gallant champion, Sonny Jim. Someone got to her before you. 'E was quite forceful.'

'Pardon?'

'I said: 'e was quite forceful.'

More cackles, and a certain amount of rough mimicry.

'Lydia,' I said, 'what's wrong?'

She turned away. 'I'm pregnant,' she said dully.

It was the cruellest of disappointments.

'I'm sorry,' I whispered, as much to myself as her.

'No need to be sorry,' said Lydia. 'Although if you'd come earlier, of course—' She sighed.

At this I looked so glum even the chorus of queens could think of nothing to add. Then one of them, a brindled matron little more than a vast slack belly topped by the tiny, wedged-shaped face and slanting yellow eyes that spoke of early good looks, said, 'Hey, don't take it personally. We're all up the spout here; or will be soon.' Some private thought occupied her for a moment. 'I always wanted a lot of kits,' she said. 'This'll be my third litter in eighteen months.' She gave a bitter laugh. 'Not that I've ever seen a one of them.'

'Who has?' said a voice I couldn't locate.

'Count your blessings, honey,' someone else advised. 'I see mine all the time. In my dreams.'

With this, a fierce inturned silence descended on them all.

I stared from face to face, bemused. 'Who are you? Why are you here?'

Their spirits were restored. A gale of amusement swept the cages.

'He in't the stud, darlin', that's for sure.'

'He surely ain't.'

'Pretty, though.'

'Oh he's surely pretty.'

And then, to me:

'Something's happening here, sweetheart, and you don't know what it is. None of you cats outside know what it is.'

'How could we?' I said.

'You don't care to know.'

'That's not fair,' said Lydia suddenly, from the back of her cage. 'He can't help the things humans do.'

'What things?' I said. 'What things?'

One of the older queens took pity on me. 'Some get brought in like your friend,' she said. 'Most are born here. Our lines go so far back we can't remember them. We've lost the thread.' She looked at me with a kind of shy regard. 'We were never outdoor cats like you.'

Other cats took up the story, and passed it from cage to cage.

'We're bred here and it's what we know as home,' said one.

Another said: 'She mates us until we die. You quicken, you're ready to drop, but she lays you open with a knife, and takes the kittens every time—'

'We never see the kittens.'

'She takes the kittens every time—'

'—and what she does with 'em then is anyone's guess, since we never see 'em again.'

'—never see them again.'

Silence.

'This woman,' I said. 'Who is she?'

'Oh, we're in hell,' said the bored voice from the back. 'And she's the devil.'

Dreamcatching, I thought, was nothing compared to this. All

that running and fighting, it was hard work, yes: but how simple and clear-cut compared to this slow, deadly penance, worked out without reward in the stink and grey light of the cages. I felt humbled. The cats before me might have taken refuge in madness and depression. Instead, they bore the misery of their lives, the futility of their dearest impulses, with humour and companionship. I looked from face to face. Every one of them seemed as beautiful as Lydia.

'And you've never tried to escape,' I said.

'Look around you, sonny,' said the voice from the back. 'How would you do it?'

I stared at the bars, the seeping concrete, and felt foolish. 'No,' I said. 'I see. No one could get out of here.'

'Except when you're finished with,' someone said, 'and you go out in a plastic bag.' Lydia made a noise of suppressed terror and began to fling herself against the bars. There was some attempt to calm her. Then the voice from the back said:

'I only asked how you would do it. I didn't say that no one had ever escaped.'

'But—'

'Don't listen to her dear,' I was advised. 'She's mad.'

Several voices hastened to agree.

'I'm not mad,' said the voice from the back. 'I often wish I was. I had a life before I turned up in this hell. It was a good life. If I was mad I might be able to forget it.' There was a pause, and in the silence I could almost feel the invisible cat shrug. 'Still, I'm not mad yet, and there it is. Unless it's mad to be awake while this lot sleep, and see something they all missed. If *that's* mad, of course, then I am.'

'There's no need for sarcasm, dear,' the fat queen reminded her gently.

'No, no, I suppose not. We're all in this together. Well, this is the story: it wasn't that long ago, the end of last winter, I'd guess, though it's hard to keep track of the changing seasons in here. It was night, deep night, and dark, that kind of dark in which you can still see but you're never sure *what* you can see. Do you know what I mean?'

'I know,' I said. 'It's the most exciting darkness there is.'

The voice received this with amusement. 'You'll grow out of

that, sonny,' it assured me. 'You'll grow bored, because the dark promises so much and delivers so little. Or you'll grow to fear it precisely because of what it delivers.' Another pause. 'So. Silence, but for the breath of sleeping cats. Darkness, but not perfect. The concrete floor seemed to shimmer faintly. I could see the bars of the cages, the indistinct outlines of the rooftops against the sky. Suddenly, I smelt last year's leaves, and there, in the middle of the floor, dancing round in a little eddy, dim sparks and motes of light! The air felt damp and charged, the way it feels before a storm. A silent lightning-flash blanched the faces of the sleeping queens. I turned my head away; when I looked again, a great red *fox* stood in the middle of the floor. His reek filled the place. He looked around him and I swear he laughed.'

'Laughed?' I said. I knew that fox. I knew that laugh. But what had he been doing *here*?

'He laughed, that animal, and said, "Well here's a go. Got it first time." Then he saw where he was, and that gave him something to think about, and he was silent after that.'

'What happened then?' I said.

'Do you think I know? I have no idea to this day what *happened*. I can tell you what I *saw*, though. The fox – he had a grey patch on one flank, I remember that, where it looked as if some old injury had healed – counted his way along the tiers of cages. When he reached a certain point, he looked up. There was that extraordinary flash of light again, and he was *inside* the third cage up, with the astonished tabby who lived there. She hardly had time to wake up. Even as I watched, he was picking her up in his cunning great mouth. There was another flash, and they were both back on the floor. That fox could open a highway wherever he wanted. I've never seen a talent like it.'

'I don't understand!' I cried. 'Lydia! I know this fox!' But Lydia was shivering to herself at the back of her pen and gave no sign that she had heard. 'Did he say why he was here?' I asked the cages at large. 'Some of you must have woken? Some of you must know something?'

'They know nothing,' said the voice of the unseen cat. 'And neither do I. He walked to the centre of the floor, put the tabby down for a moment, and stared around him. Then he looked straight at me, as if he'd known all along I was awake, and said,

319

"I can't help now, but I'll send someone when I can. Tell them to endure a little longer." Then he picked up the tabby and ran full tilt at that wall over there. They were both gone long before he reached it.'

Silence.

'I'll never know what he meant. How can we do anything else but "endure"? We're in hell.' There was a dry laugh. 'Goodness knows what he wanted that tabby for. She was a poorly little thing. And she was so pregnant she probably had her kits in his mouth.'

While I was trying to make something of all this, Lydia threw herself against her bars again. 'Please help me!' she called. 'Orlando!'

I had no idea what to say. The fox had promised they would be saved. Circumstances had conspired to bring me here, but what could I do? I was as trapped as them. I ran up and down between the cages. They watched me silently. I stared helplessly at the blank wall towards which the fox had run before he disappeared. At that very moment, I heard a faint scraping noise from the other side. Then, rather louder, a thud. Dust trickled down. I felt the fur rise on the back of my neck.

☯

The cat Millefleur watched Anna Prescott tread the little maze, then stand stock-still as if she had been switched off. That was the problem with human beings: you never had the slightest idea why they did the things they did. And it was so hard to get their attention. Right, she thought. That's enough. This won't save Orlando. She opened her mouth and produced the most penetrating noise in her vocabulary. It was impressive, and had worked for her, she recalled, even when she was a kitten.

☯

A piercing yowl. Anna roused herself. Visions, dreams, inchoate images of times she didn't remember. The little box hedges at the edge of the knot garden had been planted and trimmed, she thought, to make the words '*Tempus Fugit*'. It was difficult to get a decent perspective so close up, and some of the letters had perhaps become fused together over the years. What did it mean?

If she tried, she felt, it would come back to her: but the tabby-and-white cat – now stalking about on the doorstep of a French window Anna recognised from her last visit to the house – wouldn't let her concentrate.

'What?' said Anna.

The cat stared at her. It closed its mouth deliberately, then, as if performing a charade for the benefit of a half-wit, began scratching at the closed door. 'Why don't I help you with that?' enquired Anna sarcastically. The handle gave beneath her hand. The cat slipped inside so easily, and vanished so completely, it was like a conjuring trick. Anna put her head round the door.

'Stella?' she called. 'John?'

Silence.

With a quick intake of breath, she stepped out of the light and into Nonesuch. At once, she was overcome by a sharp chill – but whether this was merely physical or caused by the guilt of entering Stella Herringe's house uninvited, it was hard to know. To judge by the hardwood floors and white walls, she was somewhere in Stella's apartment. But where the rest of the flat maintained a pristine chic, here was all the evidence of life lived day-to-day.

Items of clothing had been strewn over the furniture and on the floor, including a frayed and unglamorous old candlewick dressing gown. (It was pink, Anna remarked, and rather grubby, and it had been dropped just inside the French window, as if someone had let it fall at their feet before stepping into their bathroom, rather than their garden, dropped as if shedding an old skin.) Antique mirrors hung like paintings on every wall, arranged so that you couldn't move without catching a glimpse of yourself from some unnerving – not to say unflattering – angle: no wonder Stella found it so hard to relax. Cosmetics lay scattered on every surface – lipsticks without their tops; bronzing pearls and tinctures; eyeshadows in every imaginable shade; brushes and pencils and eyelash curlers. An open pot spilled pale, translucent powder across a black marble mantelpiece. Firming creams, wrinkle creams, creams to feed the skin. Many of them bore the Engelion label. Others, however, had been put together in a distinctly amateurish fashion, bearing cheap stationers' sticky labels applied untidily over the original packaging. The labels offered no clue to the contents of the pots other than a hand-written scattering of numbers that appeared at second glance to be a collection of dates. Lids off, they spilled their thick, disturbing perfume into the morning air.

Anna stared at herself in a mirror. She raised her hand to her face, lowered it again. All around the walls, the same shadowy woman raised and lowered her hand.

On a Louis Quinze desk to the left of the door she found a collection of photographs in antique silver frames. Stella in the sixties, all Twiggy hair and false eyelashes. Stella more recently, holding an elegant Russian Blue in her arms (a caption along the bottom read 'Ms Stella Herringe and Grand Champion Circassian Gogol III'). The classy head-and-shoulders print used on the Engelion website. Here was John Dawe, sitting cross-legged on the deck of the *Magpie*, glowering into the camera with a tiny golden kitten cupped in his hands. And here were both the cousins, caught by some official photographer at a fancy dress party long ago. Stella had chosen a beaded gown which showed off her shoulders. The print was sepia-tinged, distressed with some cleverly applied brown mottle designed to look like mildew.

Anna picked it up and stared. John was dressed in a high-collared suit and remarkable fake mutton-chop sideburns. Despite that, he didn't look more than fifteen.

All over the room, on chairs and coffee tables, on the floor with the discarded underwear and empty coffee cups, books were scattered. Many of them had been put aside carelessly, open and page-down, as if by a reader who couldn't settle to one thing at a time. Some looked brand-new, others like original editions of very old works indeed. There were recent issues of *Harpers & Queen* and *Vogue*. There was an academic paper from an American university headed 'Teratogenicity in feline fetuses'. Anna leafed through a battered volume of poetry by Robert Mannyng, inscribed *Handlyng Synne: The Cursed Daunsers*; a leatherbound tome bearing the legend *Cosmetick Preparations* (this, she put down quickly); and a pamphlet by one William Herringe, dated 1562 and entitled 'The Diminutive Tyger'. A copy of Webster's *The White Devil* lay among the make-up on the mantelpiece, its flyleaf inscribed to Stella in John's distinctive hand:

'For Stella,' Anna read, 'Your beauty, O, ten thousand curses on't!/How long have I beheld the devil in crystal!/Thou hast led me, like an heathen sacrifice/With music and with fatal yokes of flowers/To my eternal ruin. Woman to man/Is either a God or a wolf . . .'

'A God or a wolf,' Anna mused softly.

She shivered. Putting down the book, she stared around. The room was like a locked diary, its pages encoded in the obsessional languages of clutter, narcissism and waste. But the lock was also its own key. It was a visible show of character, of personal history. It was the key to Nonesuch. It was the key to Stella Herringe – who and what she really was. Before Anna had time to turn it in the lock, there was a noise behind her.

Anna, expecting John or his cousin, whirled round. Her hand flew guiltily to her mouth. 'I didn't—' she began to say.

But it was only the tabby-and-white cat, which had leapt up from nowhere on to the gilt and ormolu dressing table and begun knocking down every small item it could find. After each outrage, it looked up at Anna deliberately as if to say, 'There! What are you going to do about that?' The tubes and tubs of make-up, the little white pots with their pink and gold labels, rolled and bounced across the floor.

'Hey!' cried Anna.

She tried to scoop the cat into her arms, but it evaded her deftly and fled into the next room. She chased it through the rest of Stella's apartment, and then out into Nonesuch itself, where she quickly lost her bearings. Corridors multiplied, smelling of damp plaster and ancient floor polish. The cat scampered up one staircase, down another. 'Wait!' appealed Anna. The cat ignored her. 'What am I doing?' she asked herself. 'What am I *doing*?' Through the open doors of rooms she had never seen, she caught glimpses of broken furniture, fallen mouldings, nests of broken lath and horsehair stuffing. At one point there were noises, faint and distant, somewhere ahead of her: but when she stopped to listen, all she could hear was her own breath scraping in her throat; and if they had been human cries, they were not repeated. Then, without any warning, she was in the Long Corridor. Clara de Montfort stared down at her contemptuously from the wall. The cat took one look back to make sure Anna was still there, gathered speed as if for a last effort, and disappeared into the Painted Room.

Stella's dinner party might never have taken place. The table and chairs had been spirited away, leaving for furniture a couple of long Jacobean benches scarred and blackened by use which, isolated in the middle of the room, somehow made it look emptier than it was. Brassy light spilled through the casements, to fall in long diagonal bars across the age-blackened boards. It gilded the dust-motes. It picked out the details of the trompe l'oeil painting on the opposite wall. It discovered the tabby-and-white cat, sitting complacently in the middle of the floor, one leg stuck in the air while it thoughtfully washed its behind. When Anna entered the room, it stopped washing and looked up at her expectantly.

'What?' said Anna.

She shrugged. 'I hate that painting,' she said. She went over to examine it nonetheless. The fake courtyard lay under its fake illumination, less like life than ever. 'Why would anyone do this?'

Her voice echoed in the amplified silence of the empty room.

She heard a faint cry.

The cat shot to its feet, darted between her legs, and began to claw frantically at the painting.

'Stop that!' said Anna.

The tabby only clawed harder. Little flakes of paint and decaying plaster fluttered to the ground. Everything's rotten in this house, Anna thought suddenly. 'You mustn't do this!' she warned the tabby, thinking how angry Stella would be. When the cat ignored her, she tried to drag it away. It writhed in her hands like a single coiled muscle: bit her wrist. 'Ow!' Fragments of last night's dreams turned and shifted in Anna's head. There was another faint cry from behind the painting.

'There's something there!' said Anna. 'Isn't there?'

The tabby ignored her, but continued to claw and bite at the wall. Plaster fell away in lumps. Faint cold airs seeped into the Painted Room, bringing with them a sharp, ammoniacal smell. All at once there was a commotion, a barrage of yowling and mewling from the other side of the painting, and rising above that a demanding wail she recognised only too well. The tabby backed away and sat down suddenly, looking exhausted.

Anna got down on her knees and – all thoughts of Stella's anger dispelled – began to try and enlarge the hole. She found that the tabby had given up for a good reason: the rotten plaster, which had been like damp icing sugar to the touch, had given way to firmer stuff. There were battens behind it, supporting the tough old lath. Anna got up and kicked at it awkwardly. This achieved nothing, though it caused the cats behind the wall to redouble their cries.

'Damn,' she said. 'Damn!'

A familiar pink nose appeared in the hole. Anna stared puzzledly.

'Orlando?' she said. 'Is that you?' Then, with a growing sense of horror and disorientation: 'Orlando? How did you get behind there?'

She renewed her efforts with the wall. A few minutes later, she was slumped at the base of it, panting. Her fingers were bruised and cut. She had broken most of her fingernails.

'Orlando,' she said. 'How could you be so silly?'

She said: 'I don't know what to *do*!'

Then her eye was taken by the Jacobean benches in the centre of the room. They looked heavy, but manageable. Picking the nearest one up, she ran at the wall with it. There was a muffled booming noise, a shock ran up her arms, the bench clattered to the floor. She studied the wall. Once more, she thought, struggling to pick the bench up again. A minute or two later, bruised and exhausted, she was looking through the painting at the secret of Nonesuch. Beyond the fake courtyard, she now realised, the real one had always lain in wait for her.

Joshua Hering would not have recognised it. His tranquil out-door space, not much larger than the Great Hall and designed, perhaps, to protect the ailing Elizabeth Marchmount from draughts as she took the air in the spring and early summer of her last haunted year, had been floored with concrete and roofed over with chicken wire. It was walled on three sides with cage upon cage of cats. On the fourth side – where the trompe l'oeil painting had depicted the glassed-in arcade with the open door – was some kind of workroom housed in a modern lean-to construction resembling a Portakabin.

Anna stared at the rows of cages.

Stella's rescue cats, was her first thought.

Her second was: But why hide them?

Orlando ended this speculation by pushing his face into the hole and purring loudly. He tried to rub his cheek against hers.

'Now wait a minute,' she said. 'Just wait a minute!'

Too excited to move away while she kicked down the rest of the painting, Orlando got covered in plaster and stood there, blinking and sneezing and shaking himself vigorously, until she had finished. Then the tabby-and-white jumped through eagerly, and the two cats greeted one another with obvious delight.

'Well!' said Anna, a little jealous. 'You *are* good friends!'

She gave them a moment or two, then swept Orlando up and squeezed him against her until he complained.

'Oh, Orlando!'

The walk between the cages subdued her; but she never forgot the contents of the workroom.

Bright lights, even temperatures, the little hums and clicks of electricity busy about its work. Stainless-steel sinks with hospital taps. White walls racked at eye-level with what could only be surgical instruments. Shelves lined with jars of clear fluid. Once she had seen what was in the jars it was hard to look away from them. Hard not to. Beside one of the sinks was something she took to be a huge casserole dish – when she lifted the lid an inch, the smell was so thick it could have choked a cat. It was a thousand times more powerful than the smell of Engelion firming products – rawer, less dilute, less *polite* – but it was the same smell. It poured out all over her like the contents of a fat-rendering factory, until she shuddered and slammed down the lid.

At the back of the room stood a floor-to-ceiling industrial freezer, old-fashioned but powerful, cased in bare metal. A gust of vapour engulfed her as she pulled it open. Vacuum-sealed plastic packages, hundreds of them, were stacked on the shelves. She picked one up at random and turned it over. Whatever it was looked like a piece of pink meat. It was hard to tell what animal it might have come from when its original shape was so distorted

326

by the sealing process. It was labelled with a cheerful-looking sticker featuring a design of hand-drawn flowers. Anna had seen the same labels on the produce of the Ashmore WI – mincemeat, jams, fruit preserves. She had even bought a bundle of them herself, against the far-off and unlikely day when she bottled the fruit from the espaliered quince in her garden. On the sticker was written in a spiky, old-fashioned hand: '7/9/00: (m) s: CG III: d: 13834'. The handwriting was identical to the handwriting on the pots in Stella's room.

She replaced the package, picked another. The label on this one offered a date from the previous winter and the following cryptic description: 'f: 1 day old. d: 9378, remvd gdn Pond Cott'. Anna stared at it, a horrible suspicion forming in her head. She turned the package over, to find herself confronted by a bulbous, rather deformed blue eye. It was Orlando and Vita's sister: the poor, dead kitten she had buried, now shrinkwrapped, naked and skinned. Anna shrieked and ran out into the courtyard. She began running from cage to cage, undoing the doors and banging them open.

'Get out!' she cried. 'Get out, get out!' The cats stared at her. Some had leg muscles so withered they were unable to stand; they hunkered down and stared at her, paralysed, perhaps, by the idea of freedom. Other jumped down happily enough, only to mill puzzledly around the ankles, looking up for guidance. All the cages were numbered. When she found 13834, its occupant turned out to be a black cat with a huge, debased body and tiny, wedge-shaped head. It looked at her nervously. 'Get out!' she cried. Tears were pouring down her face. 'Oh please get out!' She reached in and lifted it down. Once it had the idea, it ran off quickly enough, heading for the hole in the wall. Anna stared wildly about. She was at the heart of Nonesuch. The cages reeked. The whole courtyard reeked. Everything she had found was a betrayal, and it made her numb with anger and misery. I should have left the poor things locked up, she thought, until I could get the RSPCA in here. Then she thought: But I'll never be able to lock an animal up again.

She was trying to decide what to do next when a human cry rang out from somewhere in the house. It was cut off suddenly, and not repeated.

The cats shifted uncomfortably, ears flat to their skulls.

'John!' called Anna. '*John!*'

Silence, heavy and forbidding.

Full of dread and last night's dreams, she rushed back into the Painted Room. She had to wade through cats. They milled about indecisively for a moment, then followed her. One moment the courtyard was full of them: the next they were gone like smoke.

Anna poked her head out into the Long Corridor. Nothing. She looked right and left; then, under the sardonic gaze of Clara de Montfort, moved deeper into the house. An open hallway, known for some reasons as the Courseway, led her to a servants' staircase with steep, narrow risers and walls polished at shoulder-height by generations of maids. Up went Anna, and the rescue cats flowed after her, maintaining a cautious distance: when she looked back all she could see was eyes, flat, reflectant, neutral, in the brown-stained light of the old stairwell. Orlando and his friend were among them somewhere. She wasn't sure how comfortable that made her.

Deep Nonesuch, where time hung in the air like a smell: sounds were muffled or curiously amplified here, swallowed by passageways, sucked out of the thick old leaded lights and into the open air. You couldn't trust a sound in Nonesuch. It was hard to track down. The house was like a maze, as if it had deliberately replicated itself and overlaid room upon room, doubling and redoubling its passageways. Up on the top floor, all the bedrooms had names – the Rose Room, the Chinese Room, the De Montfort Chamber. They were all old. They were all empty. They all smelled of mildew and decay. At the door of Lady Germain's Solar, Anna thought she heard a noise. She pushed the heavy door tentatively, and it swung open without a sound, as if to welcome her in. She stuck her head through the opening. The Solar did not live up to its name: inside it was dim and brooding, the coved and ribbed ceiling looming over monumental Jacobean furniture. Voluminous swathes of jacquard-framed diamond-paned windows which allowed through only the feeblest glimmers of winter light. The sound came again, muffled, indistinct, as if someone were trying to suppress it. Compelled now, she stepped inside. The room, however, revealed itself to be entirely uninhabited: it had been, she sensed, from the heavy, thick air, for years and years. Even so, she found herself seized by an unaccountable dread, to the extent that the hairs on the back of her neck began to lift, one by one, as if in warning. But warning of what? There was no question that the room was empty, but still she turned wildly around and around, assailed suddenly, irrationally, by thoughts of haunted houses, slamming doors, bulging walls; by fears that she might find herself immured, swallowed up by the house and its history, as had the maker of the muffled cry.

'Don't be silly,' she told herself sternly. 'It's only an old house. Old houses make strange noises all the time.'

At last, she took a deep breath, steadied herself, and turned to leave.

She had just reached the doorjamb, her fingers closing on the rough, lacquered old wood, when she heard a moan: low, anguished, male. She froze where she stood, heart hammering, cold waves of reaction rippling through her stomach and spine. The sound had come from somewhere so close at hand that she felt it almost as a physical presence, and she was overwhelmed at once by the need to run away and save herself and the conviction that the source of the noise had been John.

The next door down the corridor was identified as Jonathan Herringe's original Great Chamber. Its door – all dark oak in bossed squares – stood open two inches. Anna peered in with considerable reluctance.

Heavy felt curtains had been drawn against the day. The room stank of wax from the candles that burned in the old cressets and wall-sconces. Replaced again and again as they consumed themselves, they had made contorted, dripping sculptures. For all this effort, their light seemed undependable, and the bedroom furniture – ebony cabinets, a tallboy, a massive walnut chest inlaid with marquetry and ivory panels – seemed to emerge from a smoky brownish haze. In the middle of the room stood the monstrous four-poster bed imported from Esting House in Leicestershire by Anne Barnes early in the seventeenth century, its drapes of muslin and brocade swagged back to reveal two figures.

Some time in the night, Stella Herringe had cut off her hair. During this process, completed with the help of a Sabatier knife, she had also cut herself, in several places. There was still some hair on her head, and some on the floor around the bed. She was wearing a long old-fashioned nightdress, and the stiff linen folds of that were also full of hair. How she had found enough to tie her cousin's wrists and ankles to the pillars of the bed was unclear: but there he lay, looking exhausted. Had she tried to cut his hair off first? If so, the knife had laid open his scalp in one or two places, and blood had run into the stubble along the line of his jaw. Had she cut his clothes off him before or after he was tied down? That was unclear, too, but there they were, in a heap at the side of the bed. She was kneeling astride him, with the nightdress hitched up.

She still had hold of the knife.

'Don't you remember?' she was saying, in the dull, patient tones of a woman who has been arguing all night and still sees no hope of regaining what she knows she has lost – who suspects, indeed, that the point of the argument had already been lost when the argument began. She sighed and got up, walked stiffly across the room to relight a candle which had guttered out. She trailed her fingers across the walnut chest.

'Look,' she said. 'You *must* remember this.' She laughed. 'A kiss is just a kiss,' she sang. 'As time goes by.'

Something had happened to Stella. When she moved into the light, Anna could see that the lace at the throat of the nightdress was not lace at all, but the papery white folds of her skin, where it hung from her neck and chin. Pale blue veins marbled its surface. Her cheeks had sagged and withered, her bottom lip dragged away from her mouth at one side, her blue eyes stared out vague and watery. She sat on the end of the bed and began to pick at her yellowed feet. 'Surely you remember how we used to meet after evensong, run at barleybreak with the children, dance in the ring while old man Worsley and young Jack Corbett played pipe and tabor for us?'

She laughed like a girl.

'Do you remember when I was Clara de Montfort and you were John Mountjoy? Oh John, surely you remember *that*!'

This brought no response from the bed.

'At Knole?' she said suddenly. 'With that little bitch when she was Anne Clifford? I knew you two had only been reading Chaucer together!' A laugh. 'She hoped I would be jealous, but

I'm not stupid, John, I was never stupid. I knew you'd be there in the formal garden, Midsummer's Eve, to dance with me. Why don't you dance with me any more? You never do.' She brooded for some seconds on the unfairness of this. 'I never wanted the bolts of silk, John, even if they were the colour of my eyes. I only wanted you to be looking at me. You knew that.'

Silence.

'You used to know that.' She looked at the knife in her hand. 'You knew everything. All those ancient languages, John! It was you who taught me them. Why, it was you who started it all!' She got up and hammered angrily on the walnut chest with the heel of her hand. 'And, also, you know, I had you on this, the night the Great War finished. You brought me in here and fucked me until I could barely breathe, while your mousy wife snored in the room next door. Have you still got the mark where I bit you? I suppose not. And what did she call herself in those days. Was it Olivia, John? Was that what the little whore called herself?'

She sat down and took his head gently in her hands.

'I *want* you to remember, John,' she urged him. 'Four hundred years together, dying and returning, dying and returning, always in love. Why can I remember when you can't? Is that fair?' She stroked his forehead, then touched it with the tip of the knife. 'It must be so damned convenient to just die and forget. Because really, John, you're a coward, aren't you?' She put the knife down and pulled his head towards her. His face disappeared into the loose skin of her throat. 'Shush, shush, there. *Such* a coward! There aren't many like us. We should take care of each other, you and me, but you run away every time. First you run to her, and then you run to death.'

She let his head drop.

'Well this time,' she said, 'I'm going to keep you.'

The man on the bed cleared his throat. It made a thick, painful sound in the room. 'I think you're mad,' he said. 'Can I have a drink?'

'No. Not if I'm mad.'

He swallowed. 'I'm really thirsty,' he said.

She shook her head.

He said: 'If any of this is true— Well, how desperate you must be to hang on to it all. Desperate and frightened.' He lifted his head to peer at her. 'There's something wrong with you, Stella, something I don't understand. Whatever it is, though, I think you're as mortal as me. We all have to die.'

'Wrong,' she said. 'Wrong.'

She looked down at him thoughtfully. 'Come on,' she said, 'you're going to try some of my special elixir.' She poked around vaguely among the clutter on the floor by the bed. There was a click as the lid came off a little pot. A faint but unmistakable smell in the smoky air. 'Look,' and Stella. She straddled him. 'Here. No, don't move your head like that!' She bent and kissed his mouth, then straightened up again.

'All right then,' she said.

She picked up the kitchen knife and drew it lightly down his chest. After a moment, a line of blood appeared.

'I'll just rub some in,' she said. 'This stuff can really get under your skin. It's the formula I make only for myself: my own secret recipe, but for you, my darling, I will make an exception. Once you've had it you won't be able to get enough. I use it every day. What Mark and Oliver sell for Engelion is very diluted mix by comparison, yet sales are going through the roof!'

Anna, who had been watching all this with a kind of stupefied horror, felt something brush against her leg. She looked down.

'Oh!' she whispered. 'But you mustn't!'

'Who's that?' called Stella Herringe. 'Who's there?'

A hundred cats pooled around Anna's legs – cats large and small, young and old, fat and thin, sick and well, cats tawny and orange, tabby and black, cats patched and striped and spotted – they flooded into the Great Chamber, where they ebbed and flowed like a sea, jumping on and off the furniture as they pleased. They singed themselves in the candles. They sniffed and blinked in the waxy smoke. They coughed up hairballs. They had brought with them a rank and honest smell. Their eyes glittered. They no longer had the air of victims. Stella Herringe stared. She made feeble pushing motions, as if trying to shoo them back into their cages. They had the energy of long imprisonment and the consistency of smoke.

'But my work,' she said. 'All my work.'

She looked from the cats to Anna.

'You!' she said. 'You again! Who are you this time? Olivia

Herley, Phyllida Howard, Lady Anne Clifford? No, this time you're just some jumped-up little trader from the City. Well you can't have him.' She looked down at the knife in her hand. Anna, who had come further into the room, took a couple of steps back. Stella said, 'You always have him.' She seemed bewildered. 'Do you see?' she said. 'We're two halves of the same thing. We complete one another. What would you know about that? Look, Anna dear,' she said, as if she was offering milk and sugar in some Drychester tea-room, 'there's a symmetry to this, and all you ever do is break it—'

Her rheumy old eyes brimmed with tears.

'Can't you just leave us alone?'

'You don't love him,' said Anna, who was keeping her eye on the knife and trying very hard not to think about the implications of what Stella had just said. 'You don't love anyone. I found out your dirty secret: I found your victims, your vile little *beauty parlour*. You made a monster of yourself, and now you're trying to make monsters of the rest of us.'

Stella looked around at the cats. 'All that work,' she whispered. 'All those careful breeding-plans. Some of those lines went back unbroken four hundred years.'

She threw the knife away. She smiled into Anna's face. 'Who would ever want to look like this?' she said reasonably, pinching at the loose skin of her jowls. 'Would you? Wait until it starts happening to you, we'll see what you have to say then! No woman should have to age: our youth, our beauty is the only power we have over the world. And now we don't have to lose it! Who can deny us the right to keep it? Who can deny us?'

Anna pushed her aside. 'There isn't any "us" here,' she said. 'There's only you. And look what you've done.'

Stella tottered backwards. The cats, seizing their chance, swept across the room and engulfed her. She clutched at them as if to save herself, then stumbled heavily into the big oak tallboy. Candles toppled and fell. There was a moment of calm. Anna stared at Stella, Stella stared at the cats: hot candlewax sizzled where it lay. Then, with a soft whoosh of displaced air, the draperies round the bed caught light and the whole room seemed to fill with fire.

'Christ,' said John Dawe.

Stella got up and put her hands over her face. She ran about aimlessly. She did a kind of jig at the foot of the bed. 'John, look,' she said. 'I'm on fire.'

'I'm sorry I can't help.'

She dragged herself towards him, then caught sight of the discarded pot of Engelion cream and reached for that instead. The linen nightgown smoked off her back. She got some of the cream on her fingers, and from there on to one cheek, where it sizzled like fat in a pan and gave off such an appalling stench that it overpowered the reek of burning cloth and wood. 'Help!' she called. She struggled towards the door, one arm outstretched in front of her. The cats, maddened with fear, falling over each other to escape the flames, knocked her down again and fled, pell-mell, from the room.

Anna, meanwhile, worked at John Dawe's bonds. Fear made it hard for him to keep still. Her eyes streamed, the smoke was already in her lungs. She kept giving up in despair and holding his face in her hands to kiss him, then scrabbling furiously again at the knots in Stella's hair. Who would have thought it would be so strong?

'I'm sorry, John—'

'The knife,' he said. 'Anna, the knife!'

Anna stared at him, struggling to make sense of the words. Knife, she thought dully.

'Stella's knife. It went on the floor.'

'Oh, the *knife*!' she said.

The smoke was so thick she couldn't see. Eyes streaming, she dropped to her knees and swept her hands across the floorboards. Nothing. She crawled a little further away, made another pass with her hands. Something gripped her by the ankle, and she was pulled under the bed. She screamed. There was something under there, rolling about, hissing and panting to itself, clutching at Anna's ankle, her thigh, her arm. Stella Herringe, face blackened, teeth white as a toothpaste advertisement. 'I'll outlive you, Anna,' she said. Then her agony rolled her off somewhere else. Anna dragged herself out into the smoke again.

'I can't see you!' John called.

'I'm still here.'

'Anna, I can't see you. Get out while you can!'

'I won't go without you,' she said. She tried to get up, but her legs wouldn't obey her. It got harder and harder to concentrate. The heat had shrivelled her tear ducts, and she thought the back of her coat might be on fire. This is how it happens, she told herself. You're bemused and you can't do anything and you die. She located the edge of the bed and used it to drag herself upright. Come on, she encouraged herself fiercely: Come on! John was calling out all the time, his voice frightened and alone, 'I can't see you! I can't see you!' She couldn't bear it. Then the blade of the knife made a grating noise beneath her foot. She bent down dizzily and there it was, gleaming silver through the smoke. She had it in her fingers when the windows blew in. Glass sprayed about. The fire rumbled and sucked air. There was a kind of blink, a shift in the light, as if the laws of physics were suspended for a moment, subsumed under a more flexible description of things. Long splinters of glass seemed to turn over and over in the air in slow motion. Then the flashover roared across the room two or three feet below the ceiling, vaporising everything in its path. The associated blast picked Anna up like a doll and threw her across the bed. She lay there for a moment with her mouth open.

'Are you there?' said John Dawe. He made a choking noise.

She sawed and sawed at the binding hair. It was hopeless. His legs came free, then his arms. But his eyes were closed and he didn't seem to be breathing any more. She shook him. 'I was here,' she said. 'I didn't go away.' She said: 'Don't you dare give up. Don't you dare!' His eyes flickered open for a moment, then closed again. She was pummelling helplessly at his chest when she heard a fresh commotion in the room behind her. Voices. Hands grasped her firmly by the shoulders and tried to pull her away. 'No,' she said, 'not without him! Don't you dare!' She held on to him for dear life. Her tear ducts burned but she couldn't cry. 'Not without him.'

Outside on the lawn, waiting for the ambulance to arrive, she lay wrapped in a damp blanket looking up at the sky. It was the most extraordinary fragile blue – one of those winter skies that shades away to a green so tentative you aren't entirely sure it's there at all – and across it moved a single pure white vapour trail the shape of a cat's whisker. Anna didn't think she would ever see anything so perfect. She wasn't aware of pain, in fact she felt rather drowsy much of the time. Seconds stretched out to minutes as her thoughts drifted by. Occasionally she got cold. Occasionally, she became aware of Alice and Max as they swam in and out of her field of view. Max would lean over her and smile and say, 'How do you feel?' and she would answer, 'Not as good as you,' or just: 'Safe.' Then Alice would say:

'The ambulance won't be long now.'

Alice held her hand. Sometimes they talked together, too quietly for Anna to hear. She wondered what she looked like. She was too dazed to be frightened.

'Are you discussing me?' she said.

'Only your awful taste in country houses,' said Max.

She smiled up at him. 'Are the fire brigade here?' she asked. And: 'Have you told me that before? I keep forgetting.'

'We called them first,' Max said.

'From the bike, it didn't look too bad,' said Alice. 'Of course, we were going quite fast,' she admitted. 'We didn't think of an ambulance. Then, when we got here, there were all these cats milling about on the front steps. I remembered what you'd said about Stella running a refuge, so we went charging inside in case some of them hadn't managed to get out, and that's when I saw Orlando. He was in one of those bloody awful old passageways, miaowing his head off in the smoke. When I tried to pick him up he ran off. I thought the fire had panicked him.' She spread her hands. 'That's how we found you, by trying to catch Orlando.'

'Orlando,' Anna said.

She drifted off.

Time echoed around her like a huge and complex old house. 'Cross a threshold here,' she remembered Stella Herringe saying, 'and you've moved two hundred years before you know it.' That was true, Anna now saw, as much for life as it was for Nonesuch. If you were lucky – or perhaps unlucky – you would cross the threshold of all your other lives, remember who you had been. Perhaps in dreams like these, you would approach the edge, look out over the mists of time, fall into . . .

*

She shook herself awake, full of panic, with oddly familiar names – Anna Clifford, Olivia Herley, John Mountjoy – tumbling through her mind. 'Lift me up!' she said. 'Lift me up, Max. I want to see him again. I want to make sure he's all right.'

'Steady on now.'

'Lift me, Max.'

Max helped her to sit up. The scene that met her eyes was a curious mixture. Two bright red fire engines were parked on the drive. Firemen ran purposefully about, shouting orders, lugging hoses. Smoke was still pouring up out of the roof of the house; there was even some seeping out from between the great front doors. But only a little way away from all this activity, the lawns of Nonesuch spread themselves tranquilly in the winter sun. And there, beneath the grandest of the cedars, only a little way away from where Anna sat, a large marmalade cat sprawled on his side, licking the smell of fire out of his coat. One of his ears was a little charred, and every so often he twitched it and looked thoughtful; but he shone in the sun like a bowl of oranges. A short way away from him, John Dawe's cat Lydia was sitting up as elegant as a drawing in gold ink, to have her neck groomed by the tabby-and-white, which seemed to have lost to the fire its odd little crest of fur. Suddenly Anna thought: *I am one who becomes two; I am two who become four; I am four who become eight; I am one more after that.*

'I'm so glad they're all right,' she said firmly. 'But that's not what I want to see. Help me, Max.'

'He's OK, Anna,' said Alice. 'He'll be fine.'

'John? John?'

'He should rest, Anna.'

'I want to know he's all right. John?'

John Dawe coughed. 'What?' he said.

'You look beautiful, even with no hair.'

He chuckled.

'Just look over there,' she said after a moment, 'at that cat. Atum-Ra, to the life.' She thought about this. 'Lord of Life,' she amended. 'They're so much more resilient than people. Do you think they have any idea of the things that go on around them?'

John Dawe, her beautiful, beautiful man, looked up at her, his eyes bright in the smoke-blackened mask of his face, and took her hand. His fingers closed tightly on hers for a moment, then he started to cough again. After a moment, the cough turned into a laugh.

'I doubt Lydia does,' he said. 'She sleeps too well.'

Later that day, the bodies of two of Ashmore's oldest inhabitants came to light. The first was discovered by Mrs Anscombe when she came, as she did every afternoon, to feed the ducks. The surface ice had receded on the edge of the pond, where it was melting into a kind of slurry at the base of the reeds. Something dark had come to rest there, half-submerged in the slush. When Mrs Anscombe bent to examine it, her hands flew up to her face. 'Oh my word, you poor old chap,' she said. 'You poor old beggar.'

Unwrapping the strands of weed from the old cat's legs, she lifted the body of Ashmore's dreamcatcher free of the ice.

The firemen found Stella Herringe.

She had, by some miracle or force of will, made it through the house and out of the French windows. There her luck and her life had run out, and she had finished up near the centre of the knot garden, bent into a foetal curve like something dug out of volcanic ash. With the exception of a single patch of pink skin – curiously, it was on her right check, which had been as exposed to the fire as any other part of her – she was charred from head to toe. Her knees had curled rigidly up to her chin as if she were protecting something precious, but this position is found all too often in victims of fire; and all the pathologist could say later was that he had found an unrecognisable twist of plastic fused into her fingers.

Epilogue

ANNA POURED the last cup of tea from the big pot and handed
it to Ruth Canning. Ruth accepted it and settled back into
her deckchair with a sigh. 'Now this, I could get used to,' she said,
shading her eyes against the late September sunshine the better to
watch Sam and the children playing French cricket on the lawn
with Max and Alice. Max, pretending to a greater com-
petitiveness than was actually called for, had started to bowl
overarm, much to the delight of Fin and Dylan. They squealed
and ducked and squealed again. They thought it exceptionally
funny that Alice had to run all the way to the great cedar to
retrieve the ball.

'Look at them,' said Ruth. 'What a shower. Stop laughing like
that, Fin, and pull your trousers up. Pull his trousers up, Sam.'

'What's that tea like?' asked Anna. 'Are you sure you wouldn't
prefer Pimm's?'

Ruth gave her a look. 'Oh, very *Country Life*,' she said. 'Very
lady of the manor.'

Anna smiled. She *was* the lady of the manor, she supposed; but
it was still hard to think of herself like that. Especially since she
still found the house rather sinister, even without its former
occupant, and preferred to spend her time out here, in the garden.
Quite a lot of Nonesuch had burned down in the end – though the
structure was sound there had been great damage to the interior.
But Stella, controlling to the last, had left a fire-proof safe in her
apartment, and inside it a copy of a will which deeded the house,
along with her personal bank accounts, to her only living relative,
John Dawe. That sum, by itself, had made it possible to begin the
repairs; that and the sale of Anna's cottage, snapped up after a

339

day on the market by a couple called Tony and Fiona (who had made some money designing restaurants in London and were looking, as Fiona put it, for 'somewhere quiet to think about things further'). The insurance was only now starting to come through, and restoration would be a long haul, but Anna was trying very hard to look upon Nonesuch as her home. John had seemed so determined to reclaim it, to save it from its ghosts, and was now pursuing the restoration with an energy and commitment that almost frightened her.

She shook the Pimms around in its jug. 'I'm not sure I fancy it either,' she said. 'It was Max's idea.'

'Given Alice's influence, I'm surprised he didn't suggest something a bit more robust.'

They watched the cricket for a minute or two, then Ruth said: 'How are your hands today?'

Anna looked own. Her scars were almost invisible now, but they would always show a little against a tan. She flexed her fingers. The sun glinted off the white gold of her wedding ring.

'Oh, they're not so bad,' she said softly. 'Not so bad now.'

They sat sipping their tea, enjoying the sun. A white pigeon fluttered down from one of Nonesuch's gables and began to peck about on the grass in front of them. There was a sudden squawk, a considerable flapping of wings, and a small, aggrieved wail.

'That damned kitten!' said Anna.

☯

'Look at that kitten!'

Orlando the cat lay with his elbows tucked under him, eyes half-closed against the sun. 'Lydia, you should teach her better: she'll never catch anything if she chatters at it first like that.'

'Criticise other people's kittens when you've had some of your own,' Lydia replied. 'She was only playing anyway. Weren't you, my darling?'

The kitten regarded its mother with scorn, then ran full tilt at Orlando, paws out for a fight. They rolled around growling at one another, and were soon joined by the rest of the litter. All three kittens were boxy and short-coupled, with dense blue-grey fur. Lydia didn't seem to have passed on much of her heritage. And maybe that was as it should be, Orlando thought, perhaps unfairly. He regarded Lydia askance and felt strangely empty. There had been a time when to lie beside her on the grass like this; to share a house with her, to share a life with her, would have been his wildest dream. Now he was less sure of what he wanted.

Lydia, meanwhile, had turned her head to the other cat present. 'Millefleur, whatever am I going to do with them? They're too old to rough and tumble like this. And he keeps encouraging them.'

But Millie wasn't listening. With a faraway look in her eye, she had watched the pigeon fly up into the shadow of Nonesuch: a flash of white disappearing into the dark, and remembered a small tabby cat whose white socks had flashed just so, before she disappeared for ever into the maw of the highways.

'When I have kittens, I shall call my daughter Vita,' she said.

Orlando, upside-down with three little ruffians on top of him, looked sad.

'*If* you have kittens,' said Lydia.

☯

'If I had a boy,' said Anna, 'I think I'd call him Barnaby.'

Ruth wasn't going to have this. 'Anna, Barnaby is the name of a cat. You can't call your offspring after a cat. Besides, it shortens to Barney. Do you want that for you child? You aren't pregnant again, are you?'

'No, no I'm not.'

'Because you only just had Eleanor.'

'I know that, Ruth.'

As if summoned by this conversation, Eleanor herself arrived, pushed by her father in a buggy of sturdy off-road design. Neither the fall of Nonesuch nor the death of his cousin had changed John Dawe much. He still had the rangy, energetic walk. He still wore black Levis and cotton sweaters with the sleeves pushed up. He still wore the most ridiculous boots. And yet he looks so much more himself, Anna thought, watching him exchange a few words with Sam. What she meant by this she couldn't quite say. Being a father had grown him up: perhaps that was it. She thought: I'm his wife. I never expected to be a wife. Or a mother. As for the darker side of it all, they rarely discussed it. You cannot be an ordinary couple if you admit that you have lived other lives, or that much of the behaviour that brought you together has somehow been programmed by a past with which you have no familiarity. Stella Herringe had known herself – or something in her had. Stella Herringe had been aware of her past lives. She had remembered them in detail – or believed she had. Past and future had all been one to her. But John had nothing but a few odd dreams – fading, now that he was a father, like his obsession with dreams themselves – like echoes of something heard at a distance: a sense, as he sometimes said, that there was more to him than met the eye. As for Anna, she remembered nothing at all of the past. She was Anna Dawe, née Prescott, no more, no less. And her dreams, she preferred to believe, were only dreams.

'Do you think she was right? Do you think we really have lived all this out before?' she had asked him, the day they moved into Nonesuch. 'Some awful triangle, repeating and repeating itself?'

But they both knew there was no answer to that.

John Dawe laughed at something Sam had said, then pushed the buggy over to Anna and Ruth. 'Your turn now.'

'Is she asleep?'

He made a face. 'At last. I wish I was.'

'Dylan was the same,' said Ruth. 'He didn't want to miss out on life for a minute.' She stood up to get a better view. 'Anna, every time I see her she's more beautiful!'

Anna admitted this, with some complacency. 'I suppose she is. That black hair! I thought it was all supposed to fall off after the birth.'

Eleanor opened her eyes suddenly. 'What an unusual shade of green,' said Ruth. 'She doesn't get that from either of you, does she? Look at me – no, *both* of you. I thought so. Hazel and brown.'

She laughed up at John. 'Anyone in your family have eyes like that?' she asked him.